STONES

— OF —

FIRE

STONES

— OF —

FIRE

A NOVEL

ALAN
JOSEPH

Cover design by Victor Mingovits

Manufactured in the United States of America

ISBN: 978-0-615-83364-4

Library of Congress Catalog Card No: 2012909269

0   9   8   7   6   5   4   3   2   1

To Alexander—my grandson, friend and dive buddy. You were taken from us before you could truly experience the prime of your life, but in the short time you were with us you brought a smile to everyone's face and brightened the world around you. May the light you left us never dim. I love you and miss you.

PROLOGUE

Pierre Bonfils awoke in a sweat. He had tossed and turned all night long, unable to fall into a restful sleep. His small band of men had met secretly three days earlier, planning and making the necessary arrangements after ten long and harrowing years of anticipation. The decade had passed slowly and they longed to return to their homeland, but knew the journey could not be attempted until the time was ripe. Their patience had finally been rewarded and it was now time to make the final preparations for the task they had trained and readied themselves for most of their adult lives.

The large contingent of knights had long since dwindled to but a few in number. Pierre and his compatriots had risen in the ranks and were now trustworthy and respected in the leadership's eyes. They would only get one chance to succeed and there was no better time than the present to make their attempt. Pierre constantly wondered what would happen if they should fail. Would anyone realize what they had attempted to accomplish? Would their brethren ever know the fate that had befallen Pierre and his brave comrades? Would their sacred possessions be lost for all ages, never to be recovered for posterity?

. . .

"IT IS TIME, Pierre. We must move quickly now," Laurent uttered softly.

"Wh-what did you say, Uncle?" Pierre stammered, as he was shaken from his own deep thoughts by his uncle's whispered interruption.

"We must ready ourselves now. There is no time to lose. Get your men together quickly and quietly. The others are nearly aboard readying the ship as we speak."

Pierre shook the cobwebs from his mind and realized the importance of his uncle's words. He rose from his bed fully dressed, strapping his sword on as he got up to leave the room. He took one last look around at the self-inflicted prison that had been his home for the last decade. There was nothing remaining for him in this room, or this god-forsaken land, for that matter. Before leaving, he reached deep inside the secret crevice he had constructed behind his bed. He took out a ring and medallion, placing the ring on his finger and medallion on his belt. He was now ready to fulfill his fate and the destiny that awaited him.

"Let's go!" Pierre whispered to his uncle as they silently left the room, quickly joining the others who were quietly gathering outside. They had worked late through the night for the last two days, moving as many of the items as possible from their hiding places deep in the tunnels onto the two ships anchored in the harbor below. One last trip into the tunnels and they would have retrieved the possessions which were rightfully theirs. As they lined up in groups of two, they looked at one another and then, as if in unison, up to the sky in prayer.

Quickly and quietly they made their way deep into the tunnels below, emerging with chests and satchels containing their remaining possessions. Their plan was going exactly as devised until a cry rang through the stale night air.

"Traitors! Where are you going with our treasure? Stop immediately!"

"Hurry!" Laurent yelled to his men. "Pierre, take your group to the ships. The rest of you, stay with me. We will attempt to delay them for as long as we can. You must get away. It is your birthright. It has always been your destiny."

"No, Uncle!" Pierre cried out. "It is suicide! If we hurry, we can safely make it to the ships and set sail."

"No. There is not enough time. We must prevent them from manning the cannons or the ships will never leave the harbor safely. Quickly! Go now! There is no more time to waste. Sons of Zadok, we must not fail!"

Pierre nodded with reserved acquiescence and discreetly wiped a tear from his eye as he turned to his men and ordered them to collect the remaining treasure and make for the two ships waiting in the harbor.

"We will not fail you, Uncle."

"Nay. It is not I who you must not fail. It is our God and our people. Their faith and trust have been placed with you. Go quickly now, before it is too late."

As Pierre and his men reached their ships, they saw their comrades valiantly buying them precious time with the last breaths of their lives. With sadness and apprehension, Pierre gave the order to hoist the sails and navigate the ships out of the harbor into the open seas.

Cannon fire erupted around them, but they were quickly out of range, thanks in large part to the valiant efforts of their fallen brethren.

Pierre stood aboard the deck of *La Lumiere*, taking one last look back at the dot that had been their home. After saying a silent prayer for his uncle and fallen friends, he focused his efforts on plotting a course safely away from this harsh land back to his homeland. The land of his forefathers. The Promised Land he had longed to go to since his birth.

PART
ONE

1

Jack donned his dive equipment as he gazed out at the calm waters. The sky was clear and sunny. The warmth of the Floridian climate felt good on his aging body. The excitement of the find and the questions it was already posing raced through his mind, but he tried concentrating on putting on his wet suit and dive gear, doing the pre-dive checks along with his dive buddy, and coordinating the dive plan prior to his descent. Even so, his mind kept thinking back to Sam's recitation of the days leading up to the strange find on the ocean floor.

The hurricanes that year had been especially vicious and unyielding, sparing little in their paths, both above and below the ocean floor. The turmoil below the sea from the hurricanes' wrath had been especially chaotic, unearthing new finds and burying old standards, secreting old mysteries and revealing new ones. One wreck that visitors and locals alike had dove for years was broken up into hundreds of pieces and dispersed throughout the ocean floor for miles, dislodging all the marine life which had made it their home for years. Coral and algae were distributed in ways previously thought impossible. Even the fish seemed lost in the aftermath of the storms, traveling in schools and areas previously unheard of.

One of Sam's divers had been out with a dive crew on a live-aboard a few months earlier over the long President's Day weekend. The seas had just begun to calm from the effects of the many hurricanes and Sean was filling in for a sick relative on the dive crew. Sean Knight had worked for Sam for about three years and was a valued member of his team, but when he got the call from his cousin, Armand, he had little choice when asked to fill in for him on the live-aboard. Armand had saved his life during a dive off Australia's Great Barrier Reef years earlier when he was filming a shark dive, and Sean owed him. Besides, Armand's wife, Michele, was pregnant and they needed Armand's income to carry them through the winter. So Sean asked Sam for a short leave of absence and Sam reluctantly agreed. Sam had wanted to have a full crew scouring the ocean for treasures unveiled by the violent storms. Little could Sam know that Sean's brief respite would parlay into one of the strangest and most historic finds of all time.

Sean had been with the live-aboard crew for about four days when it happened. Near the end of the dive trip one of the divers, Gary, had been photographing interesting coral arrangements and searching for the colorful fish he had heard about when he accidentally brushed against some fire coral. He had been warned about it by the crew and told to wear dive gloves for protection. But, being the "experienced" novice from New Jersey with all of thirty dives under his belt, he naturally ignored the pre-dive instructions regarding the stinging fire coral as well as the emergency medical procedures one follows in the event of accidental contact. As Gary felt the pain from the sting course through his hand, he panicked and began writhing around 60 feet below sea level. The more he twisted, the more he came into contact with the coral and the more pain he had to endure. It became a vicious cycle with no end until Sean caught a glimpse of the diver's problems. Sean quickly left the group and went to Gary's rescue. However, before he could reach him, Gary had managed to cut the straps from his expensive $2,500 underwater camera gear, and both divers watched as it slowly sank to the bottom. Sean managed to get Gary to the surface, sans camera, where the dive master administered first aid. Gary, having been rescued from the fire coral fiasco, began threatening all sorts of legal action if his beloved camera gear was not recovered. Since he pretty much knew the coordinates of the fire coral encounter, Sean volunteered to try to recover the equipment. As Sean descended, he could only think about Gary's stupidity and selfishness, wondering how he had gotten himself into such a predicament. Soon he would be thankful.

Sean descended below the fire coral and had soon reached the ocean bottom, about 120 feet deep. As his eyes scoured the ocean floor, he was surprised at the strange geography he saw. The ocean floor was not normally a level terrain, but there were many anomalies that he found difficult to explain. Some of the coral appeared to have settled upside down, and there were more dips and crevices in the floor than normal. He tried to shake the questions racing through his mind and to focus on the task at hand.

"Find the stupid camera gear and get home," he muttered to himself.

He was tired of the live-aboard and the novice divers who thought they knew everything. It was a wonder there had not been more problems on this trip.

As he swam along the ocean floor observing the anomalies, he finally caught a glimpse of Gary's camera. But something was strange about the way it was floating in the water, almost as if it were perched upon a pedestal. As he swam closer, he began to notice part of a mast. He had never known of any ships in this area before, and he had not heard of any wrecks in this area caused by the storms. As he closed the gap and swam closer to the camera, he was sure it was part of a ship's mast. He untangled the camera and, after securing it to his Buoyancy Compensator, he began to explore his find. Sure enough, it was a ship, but whose ship, from where, and how had it gotten there? He had worked for Sam for several years, but he was a diver, not a historian or archaeologist. He began searching for clues and brushed the ocean sand away from what appeared to be the deck of the ship. He could only get a partial glimpse since most of the vessel was buried beneath the sand.

The ship appeared to be a sail ship, similar to the old galleons he had dived with Sam's crew. He could not be sure, but it was definitely not from the twentieth century, or even nineteenth century. More than that, he could not tell. As he swam around the area of the find, he thought he spied part of a cannon. He tried to move the sand and silt away, but it was too thick and he had no equipment. He realized that he would not be able to spend too much more time below. He was running low on air and quickly reaching his no-decompression limit. If he did not begin his ascent to the surface immediately, he would be in danger of contracting the bends. He hoped Gary's camera had not been damaged in the coral encounter as he tried to take some photos of his "find." The power had been left on and the battery was low, but he thought he could probably get off a few quick shots. He took a shot of the mast, the deck area and the cannon. As he was about to begin his ascent, he saw a glimmer as the sunlight broke through the water. At first he thought it was a fish, but, as he swam closer, the colors gleamed from exposure to his dive light. It appeared to be an amulet of some sort, but one like he had never seen before. It was round, encircling a six-pointed star with a hand in the center. In the triangles of the star were stones which appeared to be eyes. Sean dug the amulet out of the silt and ascended to the surface after concealing it in his dive vest for safe keeping.

After Sean boarded the dive boat he told Gary he would check out his camera and make sure there was no damage. Gary was relieved that the camera had been recovered and was more concerned about convalescing, so he allowed Sean to retain possession of the camera for a short period of time. Sean quickly went below to his cabin and began to disassemble Gary's camera. The first thing he removed was the memory card, replacing it with a blank one of his own. While he did not know what he had found on the ocean floor, he knew it was not something he wanted anyone on the dive boat to be aware of. He stashed the memory card and the amulet in his gear and finished the trip without incident. As soon as the boat docked, he went directly to the *Scavenger* with his find.

The *Scavenger* was a majestic-looking ship, more closely resembling a medium-sized yacht than a dive vessel. It had state-of-the-art equipment, dual blowers (mailboxes) and twin diesel engines. It was capable of supplying air to the divers from above, and also contained ample storage for scuba tanks. It could hold a crew of eight and had space for a small lab. To Sam Katz it was his baby...his pride and joy, a salvage vessel with no equal.

Sam was his usual jovial self and welcomed Sean back with a grin and big bear hug. He began joking with Sean about his trip, making fun of the live-aboard ship and divers.

"How many upchucked?" Sam asked, chuckling. "Anybody lose a fin or other equipment?"

"Nope," said Sean, "but one guy lost his brand new camera."

"Was it one of those Kodak waterproof throwaways?" Sam asked.

"No, a top of the line Nikon with an Ikelite housing. Quite expensive and pretty heavy too."

"Don't tell me you went after it for him?" Sam incredulously asked. "I hope he gave you a good tip."

"Nah, better than that. I got this piece of jewelry for my troubles."

Sean was grinning from ear to ear as he removed the amulet from his gear and showed it to Sam. Sam had never before seen an amulet quite as decorative, although he had seen similar-looking jewelry before. Any jewelry shop along the strip or in the local malls carried a "Star of David." Most of the religious shops, or any shop that carried Judaic items, carried the "Hamsa" or "Hand of Miriam." In fact, he had one hanging on the wall of his home for good luck and to keep the "evil spirits" away. He had never seen one before which had incorporated the star, the hand and the eye, but he thought little about the shape until Sean explained further.

"I dove to the ocean floor to retrieve this guy's camera. Thinking what a dope this guy was, I tried pulling the strap but it was caught on something. As I kept pulling, the amulet became exposed. I had little time to explore because I was getting low on air and approaching my no-decomp limit, but I did get to snap a few pix with the guy's camera. Here's the memory stick. How about breaking out the equipment so we can get a look?" he asked.

Since Sean seemed so excited and Sam had nothing else to do, he played along and started up the computer equipment to see the photos Sean had taken. After the card was loaded in and the pictures began to materialize, Sam was almost speechless.

"Wh...whh...where did you find that?" Sam stuttered. "It looks like some kind of ship, maybe a galleon or some other multi-masted ship. Did you get any better pictures? Is that the barrel of a cannon? Sean, what the hell did you find down there?"

Sean was basking in the glory of his find. He had never seen Sam so excited. He wanted to prolong this moment, but he also wanted to get back to his discovery and find out what was really lying deep below.

"These were the best pictures I could take under the circumstances. The best I can gather is that the hurricanes dislodged the sand below and uncovered the ship. I couldn't get a good idea of its size. There was too much sand and silt covering it. I wouldn't have even given it a second thought if I hadn't glimpsed the amulet. Do you think it's worth anything?"

Sam could not be sure. It looked ordinary enough, made of gold and some stones. He would need to get it cleaned up to determine what the stones were and attempt to get an age approximation on the piece. But his interest was definitely piqued by the prospect of a new, undiscovered find.

"I hope you can lead us back to the ship's location," Sam said, giving Sean a nudge. "Otherwise, you just wasted the last hour of my time."

Sean assured him that he had entered the coordinates in his dive computer and felt certain he could retrieve the location.

"When do we go check out the ship?" he exclaimed, barely containing his enthusiasm.

"Hold on there. We don't even know what it is we're looking for. We need to do a little more research and figure out what type of salvage equipment we're going to need."

Sam tried to blow up the photos to get a closer look at the find. They discussed their options for about an hour or two and finally decided that a short excursion to attempt to locate the ship would be in order. They would bring two or three days' worth of oxygen with a crew of four of their most trusted divers to investigate what was on the ocean floor. If the find was worthy, they would put together an expedition to begin the monumental task of salvaging the ship and its contents.

Sean left exhilarated. Hopefully this would pan out and he

would make his mark in Sam's organization. He knew he was trusted and respected, but he wanted more. He wanted to be the old man's second-in-command, but he knew it would take a lot to replace Geoff, Sam's crew leader and closest friend. Geoffrey Hunter had been with Sam from the beginning of his excursion into the depths of ocean salvaging and treasure hunting. Geoff's father had been with Mel Fisher's crew when they uncovered the Antocha, and Geoff had heard all the stories of the wonders beneath the sea waiting for someone to uncover them. Geoff was a valued member himself of Mike Maguire's team when he uncovered the 1715 Fleet lying in the Florida ocean's bottom, off Vero Beach. But when Sam launched his own salvage operation, Geoff hooked up with him. Apparently Geoff's wife was somehow related to a third cousin of Sam's who convinced Sam to lure Geoff away from Maguire's operation. It would take a huge find and a lot of luck to replace Geoff in the hierarchy.

Three days later the boat had been prepared and loaded and the crew chosen. Sam would be along for the ride, Capt. Tom Reed would handle the boat, and the divers, Geoff, Sean, Jim Wood and Billy Owen, would have the chance of a lifetime to search the ocean floor. In order to ensure they had proper backup, Sam's "adopted daughter," Carly Edwards, would also tag along.

Carly was a marine archaeologist whom Sam had met several years earlier. She was a slim brunette, about five feet six inches tall, with olive skin and a muscular build. She had been in a huge fight with her current boyfriend when Sam had happened along. Apparently her current beau had wandering eyes and decided to move a new plaything in, much to Carly's dislike. She had given her paramour the ultimatum, "It's either her or me!" Unfortunately, he had chosen the new plaything and Carly found herself out on the street with her clothes, books and a few memorable possessions when Sam happened to be passing by. He immediately befriended her and gave her a place to stay. Since that fateful day, she had quickly become a respected member of Sam's treasure hunting team.

The word on the dock was that Sam and his people were going out to explore the seas and check out some new equipment Sam had recently purchased. Since no one knew what they would find and they didn't want anyone else horning in on their excursion, they kept a tight lid on the true purpose of their aquatic journey.

The weather was sunny and warm, not unusual for this time of year in Florida. The water was a little choppy but manageable. Jim and Billy were kidding Carly about her new hair color while Sam, Geoff and Sean kept close watch on the instrument bearings as they headed out into the ocean. After three or four hours of cruising they arrived at the designated coordinates. They dropped anchor and began preparations for their first dive. The diver down flag was raised as the divers geared up and prepared to enter the water. Geoff and Sean went first, followed by Jim and Billy. Armed with their dive lights, the foursome dropped to the bottom, about 120 feet from the surface. They began looking for clues or any evidence of the ship Sean had seen, but they could find nothing but sand and coral. A few fish swam by ogling at the divers. After 20 minutes of searching they were slowly coming to the conclusion that Sean's coordinates were off.

They decided to return to the original coordinate and fan out in a circular grid pattern. They knew they could only remain at that depth for another 10 minutes without jeopardizing their no-decompression time and their remaining air. After a few more circles covering a geometric area of approximately 50 feet, Geoff spied the anomaly on the ocean floor. He signaled to the others and they quickly swam for a closer look. It definitely looked like something was buried, but they could not be sure. They were out of time and low on air. They made a better coordinate marking and slowly ascended to the surface, downcast, but hopeful that their next dive would be more rewarding.

As they boarded the boat, Sam anxiously questioned them about their progress. When he saw the look on Sean's face, he knew they had not found anything. After they got out of their dive skins, they assembled in the cabin and discussed their next move. They had wasted precious time searching for the proper coordinates and could not afford to waste as much on the next dive. The plan was for Geoff and Sean to return to the dive site after the appropriate surface interval had elapsed and explore the anomaly further. If they were able to uncover anything, they would mark the coordinates with a buoy, which would float to the surface, and the other divers would then take over the exploration. While Sean was glad to be part of the original descent team, he was concerned that he might not get the glory of the find, but there was nothing he could do about it now.

After four hours had passed, Sean and Geoff geared up again and hit the water hoping for better results. They descended directly to the programmed coordinates and began digging around the anomaly. Sean's dive knife entered the soft sand and hit...nothing. He knew he had seen something here the other day. Where was it? What had happened to the ship he saw? As he frantically dug around in the ocean sand he lost sight of Geoff, who had swum about 75 feet to the east of where Sean had been digging. Geoff had been following an eel which had seemed to appear and disappear in the sand. The eel's movements were odd, different from anything he had witnessed before. It almost seemed as if the eel was searching for an entrance. Then he saw it. It looked like the barrel of a cannon. Could this be what Sean had seen when he rescued the camera? Geoff took out his knife and banged on the barrel to get Sean's attention. As he did, he turned and saw the stonefish, but it was too late! Naturally capable of camouflage, its gray and mottled color had made it appear more like a stone than a fish. Sensing Geoff as a potential threat, it had raised its needle-like dorsal fin spine in defense. Unable to react quickly enough to avoid contact, the dorsal spine pierced Geoff's forearm and the fish released potent venom from the glands located at the base of the spines. Geoff was in excruciating pain from the surprise encounter. Sean saw the attack and quickly swam to Geoff's assistance. As he did, he also noticed the cannon. Thinking quickly, he tied the buoy line to the cannon, inflated the buoy and let it float to the surface. He wanted to explore the site further, but knew he had to get Geoff back to the boat for emergency medical attention. Geoff was blacking out and needed Sean's assistance to reach the surface.

When they got to the boat the crew saw Geoff's condition and quickly became alarmed. Sam was beside himself. Capt. Tom quickly got the medical kit out and began applying first aid to Geoff's wound. He removed the pieces of spine and tried to force the blood out. As he did, some of the venom was released with the blood flow. He soaked Geoff's arm in hot water, cleaned and bandaged the wound, then told Geoff to make sure the arm was kept elevated. As he began to chart the return course back home, Sean exclaimed, "What do you think you are doing? We can't just leave without seeing what's down there."

As Tom and Sean began to argue, Geoff interrupted.

"He's right," Geoff said. "I'll be fine. We'll only be here for another day or two anyway. I think I can handle the forced R & R."

Sam was reluctant to accede in Geoff's request. Geoff looked pretty pale and his forearm had swollen considerably, but Geoff insisted he would be fine. So, begrudgingly, Sam waived Tom off and told him they would remain another day.

But that was it, if they could not uncover what lay below, or if Geoff appeared to get any worse, they would haul anchor and return to shore immediately.

That night the crew was restless. They had started this trip upbeat, expecting to find something of importance. Instead, their leader was injured and they were no closer to their goal. Time was running out, and perhaps this whole expedition was cursed. They had been so quick to agree to search for their glorious day in the sun that they had ignored any possibility of defeat. Perhaps the eye in the amulet was cursing them instead of bringing them good luck. Or, perhaps the evil that the amulet had been created to protect against was stronger than the amulet itself. Divers are a superstitious lot, and these and many other thoughts went racing through their minds as they drifted off to sleep.

The next morning Sean was the first to arise. As he made the coffee, Carly awoke to the aroma and quickly dressed. She had originally thought Sean was rude and abrupt when they had first met. But as she had gotten to know him, she began to see his caring side. Yes, he was impetuous, but he was also funny and quick-witted. He had volunteered to fill in for his cousin on the live-aboard, even though he disliked that type of work. On previous excursions, he had helped her carry her equipment when she tarried behind. And those blue eyes of his...they were enough to make a woman weak in the knees as they gazed back at you.

Carly quickly dressed and went topside. She slowly approached Sean just as he began to pour himself a cup of coffee. "Did you make enough for two?" she asked.

"No, only enough for one giant cup. What do you think?" he dryly replied.

"Well, don't be so snippy! What did you do, get up on the wrong side of the bed this morning? I was only trying to make conversation," she said as she began to turn away.

"Wait! I'm sorry. I didn't mean to be so rude. Can we start over?" he asked her.

"Well, all right," she said.

"Good morning, starfish. How would you like a cup of fresh coffee made just for you?" he asked with a sarcastic tone.

"Oh, you're insufferable. Just pour me a damn cup, and try not to burn yourself," she spit back at him.

This sure wasn't going as she had planned. She had wanted to be nice and strike up a witty conversation, hoping they could get closer. Instead, they seemed to be polarizing each other. Just then, Sam and the others came topside.

"What are you two early birds up to?" Sam asked.

"Just trying to get a good cup of coffee out in the middle of nowhere," Carly replied. Sean handed Carly her cup of coffee and asked Sam and the others if they wanted any.

After breakfast, the group checked on Geoff before considering their next course of action. Color had returned to his cheeks, but his arm was still quite swollen. He assured them that he would be fine and they retired to formulate a new dive plan. Since they were one diver short, Carly volunteered to make the next dive with Sean. This would give her a chance to examine the cannon firsthand and determine whether there was any sense continuing on their quest. It would also give her some time with him, even though it wasn't quite what she had in mind.

As they entered the water together a strange sensation began to come over her. She sensed she was embarking on a journey from which she could not return. It was a premonition, and she began to think she should have stayed ashore. She shook off the feeling and focused on her descent, following the buoy line to where Sean had tied it. Both she and Sean kept a close eye out for the stonefish or any other danger in the deep.

She began to examine the cannon more closely while Sean explored the surrounding area. The cannon appeared to resemble those she had seen on galleons used by Blackbeard and the like, with one distinct difference. There was a strange marking on the base, unlike any she had seen before. It was definitely a marking, but of what? The elements had not been kind to the cannon. It was pitted throughout and corrosion had begun to set in. If it had not been covered by the sand for as long as it had, there would have been nothing left to examine. But the markings puzzled her. The cannons she had previously examined had never exhibited any kind of markings before. They were always fairly plain, made of simple cast iron and formed for one purpose: to fire deadly shells. But this one appeared to have been made to stand out as a standard or sign of the ship. Why? She decided to try to get a picture for a closer examination topside. As she held her dive light in one hand, she focused her camera with its high-intensity flash with the other. Suddenly her eyes began to glow. Underneath the cannon was a box. It was small, about the size of a small jewelry chest. Sean saw it as well.

He swam down to try to retrieve it, but the cannon was too heavy. He tried to dislodge the box, but it was wedged in too tight. Carly swam alongside Sean for a closer look at the box. It, too, had strange markings on it. They looked like letters, but not any kind that she could read. She took a few more pictures and then tried to help Sean loosen the box from the clutches of the cannon, to no avail. Their time was running out, so they reluctantly returned to the surface to report their find.

After surfacing, Carly rushed to the computer to load the camera card and examine the photos. Sam and the others followed while Sean exclaimed, "There's a box down there wedged underneath the cannon. It looks like it might contain something precious, but we couldn't get it loose. It had stones on it, similar to the amulet. We've got to go back down with a cable and try to raise the cannon so we can get the box out!"

"Hold on one minute, young man," Sam said, trying to slow Sean down. "Tell me real slow like. What exactly did you see?"

Sean repeated what he and Carly had observed in the cannon area.

"I knew something looked strange," Carly called out. "Look at this," she said as she pointed to the photo of the cannon. The marking appeared to be a Star of David in a circle, just like the amulet, only this one had an eye in the center, without the hand. "What does it mean?" she asked. No one seemed to know. Not one member of the crew had seen anything like it before.

"Those look like Hebrew or ancient Aramaic letters," Sam exclaimed as he looked at the picture of the box. Carly was beginning to feel a little ashamed. Even though she was born Jewish, she had not been raised in an observant household and knew little of her religion. Sam would try to get her involved, but she always had excuses. She had always tried to ignore her heritage and bury it from her mind. She would disassociate herself from any connection to Judaism, intentionally shying away from anything relating to it during her college days. She had avoided any archaeology courses containing Jewish content at all costs. Now she wished she had been more attentive to her heritage, or at least studied a little more during her college days.

The letters were barely discernible from the photos, and the crew knew they would have to make an attempt to retrieve the box. Jim and Billy grabbed the necessary gear while Tom hooked a cable to the winch. The two divers dove to the wreck area, descending as quickly as was safely possible. When they reached the bottom with the cable, they carefully examined the area surrounding the cannon and box. It appeared the cannon had broken loose from its mountings and was wedged against the box. The mere weight of the cannon was all that kept the box from their grasp. Both the cannon and box appeared to be resting on some kind of platform, perhaps the ship's deck, but it was hard to tell. They needed to be careful lifting the cannon without disturbing the surrounding area. They used the radio in their dive masks to describe the situation to Tom and Sam above. They did not feel that the winch could hold the full weight of the cannon, so they decided to try to lift enough of the cannon in order to release the box from its grip. Retrieval of the cannon would have to wait for another day.

"Raise the cable slowwwly," Jim radioed to Tom. "I'll tell you when to stop."

Tom started up the winch and slowly tightened the cable. It soon became taut and refused to budge.

"Hold it!" Jim yelled. "I think we're going to have to hook it in a different place."

Tom lowered the cable again and Jim and Billy refastened the cable closer to the base of the cannon.

"Raise away," Jim yelled, and the cable became taut again. This time the cannon began to move, but not enough to move the box.

"Can you get any more power from the winch?" Billy asked.

"No," Tom replied. "That's all I've got."

Billy suggested they keep the pressure on the cannon with the winch while he tried to wedge a pry bar under the cannon. It was a dangerous maneuver, but it was their last resort. They had nothing more powerful on the boat and were running short on time themselves. Billy pried away while Jim tried to pull the box loose. After several tries, the box began to move.

"It's budging!" they cried out. "Keep the line taut. I think we're making progress," they both radioed to Tom.

Finally, they were able to wrestle the box loose, and Tom lowered the winch. Billy and Jim brought the box to the surface to the jubilant cries from the crew above.

2

Carly and the others rushed to get a look at what the two divers had retrieved from the ocean floor. It appeared to be a stone chest, white in coloration, but not marble. It seemed to have some kind of limestone base. The top contained inlaid stones, with a mixture of turquoise and silver in a pattern similar to the amulet Sean had discovered earlier. The box was rectangular in shape, approximately two feet wide by three feet long. But it was the inscription that caught everyone's attention. It appeared to be written in an ancient language, but each word (if that was what they were) was separated by a period or dot. Carly immediately realized that it was similar to some of the Phoenician writings she had studied in grad school, but it also seemed somehow connected to Hebrew letters she had seen years ago. Whatever it was, they would need more experienced help to decipher its meaning.

They set the box down on the table to get a closer examination. Jim and Billy went below to get out of their dive skins and into dry clothes. Sam told Sean to get the camera and document their observations. As they approached to get a closer look, an eerie feeling overcame the group. It was an unexplainable sensation, but they all seemed to feel it at the same time. They each looked at one another, but no one made a sound. Then Sam exclaimed, "How the heck do you open this thing?" It looked like a box, but there was no apparent way to open it. There was no lock or clasp. No hinges. No locking mechanism. It appeared as if the top was fused tight against the bottom. There was clearly a top and a bottom, but no access point.

"Let's pry it apart," cried Sean, unconcerned about the integrity of the find or the possible historic significance.

"No!" yelled Sam. "We have no idea what it is, or if it contains anything of interest. But I am not going to sacrifice the archeological or historic significance out of an impetuous desire to get a look inside."

They paused to consider their options. They had no sophisticated equipment on board to x-ray or internally examine the box without destroying its integrity. No one on board had the knowledge to decipher the inscription. Without some idea of what they were looking at or where it may have come from, they would have no idea of the significance of their find, or whether there was any economic future in further examination. One thing was certain: they could not leave the area without getting some answers.

"Carly!" barked Sam. "I want you to get on the computer and try to figure out what this could be. Start with the inscription. Figure out what language this is. Search all known archives to determine what ships and cargo may have been lost in this area. Get me some kind of answer so I have some idea of what we've got laying beneath us."

Sam was not an experienced diver, but he loved the water and was used to being in command of those around him.

Although he had previously managed the family farm in upstate New York, he was no small-town hick. He was a Yale graduate, having graduated magna cum laude, and had obtained a masters degree in Business Administration before returning home to manage his father's dairy farm. He had expanded the 30-acre family farm into a small dynasty before tragedy had befallen his family. By the time he sold the farm, he had become the owner and director of a nationwide string of dairy farms employing more than 300 people. After selling off the corporate assets he bought a yacht and sailed down the coast to Florida, where he eventually settled.

Sam had always been an avid boater, having sailed frequently while in college. In fact, if he had not felt obliged to take over the reins on the family farm when his father became ill, he probably would have sailed around as many islands as possible until he settled on an occupation which interested him. But fate was not so kind, and he put his nautical interests on the back burner while he thrust all his energy full-time into salvaging the family farm. Sam always longed for the sea, but settled instead for weekend jaunts along the Hudson River and sailing on some of the local lakes in the tri-state region. After tragedy struck, he cast aside all his fears and returned to the dreams of his youth.

Although he was in his sixties, he had always been an active man. Only five foot seven inches tall, with short cropped hair to hide his graying features, he still commanded respect when in the presence of others. His rotund facial features and paunchy midsection deceived many, friends and foes alike. He was quick-witted with his old-world Yiddish humor and sharp tongue, but was also more agile than most imagined, probably due to his farming days and extensive sailing experience.

Sam was not leaving until he had sufficient time to assess the situation. If this was truly a find of a lifetime, he was not going to pass it up. It had been years since he had felt this intense about something, and he was not going to let this feeling slip away so easily. Geoff was feeling better and was now up and around, so there was no immediate reason to hoist anchor and return to land.

"Get the box into the salt water tank now and be careful with it," he said. He did not want to take any chances that the oceanic air or human interaction would cause any clues to be lost while they searched for the answer.

Geoff still felt slightly woozy from his earlier experience, but was now deeply involved in the quest to solve the mystery of the box. He brought it below to the salvage tank and tried to conduct a closer examination without the sophisticated equipment he had not thought of bringing on this excursion. The markings were extraordinary, unusual in the lines and dots present in the design. But there also appeared to be something else faintly present on the exterior corner of the box. It was a symbol or some design, but he just could not make it out.

Geoff stood there trying to figure out a way to enhance the markings. He knew the solution would hopefully do the job, but that would take time, and time was not a luxury they had at the present. Scraping could potentially destroy anything of value, so he had to find another way to expedite the process.

Meanwhile, Carly was desperately searching the Web for answers to the mystery of the box. What did the symbol mean? What was the significance of the amulet, and what was the strange language on the box? It had been a long time since she had had this many questions with no answers. Everything had always come easy to her, during her education in school, as well as throughout her occupational endeavors. She was a quick study and thought well on her feet. She seemed to retain the information she processed, storing it for future reference. But she had never come across anything as puzzling as this. Yes, she thought, things in her life had always seemed to come easy to her, except where her personal life was concerned.

She began to drift off in thought. All her life, her choice in men had always been poor. She had always thought herself a good judge of character. She was obviously intelligent and had always made the right choices throughout her professional career. She was well respected by her peers and had even been published in several professional journals. But her choice in men...well, that was definitely a different story.

First there was James. Boy was he handsome, and a smooth talker, too. She fell for him immediately with his blond hair, blue eyes and boyish grin. Unfortunately, she had fallen along with a dozen other women, as she later learned. It took her two years, but when she finally came to the realization that he had been using her for her connections and money, her heart had shattered and it took a long time for her to recover. She turned to liquor and drugs to numb the pain. She became known as the "ice woman," untouchable by all. She would choose her partner, party with him or her until she had her fill, then leave her most recent lover for another, as the mood struck her.

Then there was Patrick, the Irish guitar player. He had picked her up during one of her karaoke flings. She was drunk and stoned and so vulnerable. She had quickly become bored with her partner at the time, and Patrick had walked up on stage with his guitar and just started strumming to the song she was trying to sing. He had actually made her sound good, if that were possible. It did not take him long to get her alone and have sex with her, rough and exhilarating sex in a semi-public area, while her poor partner waited patiently for her to reappear. The poor fool was clueless, and he might still be at the table waiting for her, as far as she knew. She left with Patrick that night and stayed with him for about two months. The sex was phenomenal, but he was as shallow as a Neanderthal, and about as smart. Yes, she sure could pick them.

That had been about five years earlier, before Sam saw

something in her that not even her parents had believed existed. Her parents had written her off as worthless long before she ever went to college. Even though she had been a virgin throughout high school, her parents had never believed her and kicked her out of the house as soon as she graduated. If not for her determination and the availability of student loans, she would never have gotten into college, much less grad school. It had been at least fifteen years since she last had any contact with them. Sam had tried to get her to reach out to them, but she could never forgive them for turning their backs on her, for not believing in her, and most of all, for not loving and accepting her as parents do of their children. Sure, she had faults, but she never deserved their enmity or distrust, and as far as she was concerned, they could rot in hell with the devil.

Sean's image popped into her mind. He sure was an enigma with his dark brown hair, bronze skin, stocky but muscular build, and those blue eyes of his. Yes, that must be it. Those blue eyes piercing through her, mesmerizing her, paralyzing her. It took all her willpower to act naturally around him. If only this morning had gone more smoothly. If only she had been more amiable, more pleasant, more seductive. If only....

"Any luck yet?"

Carly jumped. Sam was peering over her shoulder, trying to see what was on the computer screen.

"Find any clues to the markings or the writing on the box?"

"No," she said as she tried to collect her composure. "You startled me. I didn't hear you come in."

"Sorry, but I was just checking to see if you came up with anything. Geoff's getting nowhere. There's too much oxidation, too much encrustation to get a quick answer. He has no idea when he'll be able to clean that box up. So it's up to you. What have you got so far?"

Carly felt awkward and ashamed. Instead of concentrating

on the box, she had been reminiscing about the past and dreaming of the untouchable future. She tried to hide her embarrassment and replied, "I just can't seem to get any leads on this thing. I've tried all the alphabets I've ever come across, with no luck."

"Let me take a closer look at the photo, maybe I can figure something out. I thought I saw something familiar when I first looked at it."

Relieved that she had concealed her earlier thoughts, she quickly handed Sam the photos of the box.

"It looks familiar, but I just can't seem to place it," he kept saying. "I'm just an old Jewish dairy farmer, what could I have been thinking?"

Then it hit him. "Doesn't some of this look like Hebrew?"

Carly took a closer look. "Well, there are some similarities, but not enough to really tell for sure. If it is Hebrew, it sure is ancient, and this ship was from the sixteen or seventeen hundreds."

"Maybe you're right," Sam said. "This amateur archaeologist will leave the expert to her work. Good luck. I'm turning in. It's been a long day." Sam turned, kissed her on the cheek and slowly walked out of the cabin, leaving Carly to her thoughts and the pictures of the box.

"Maybe I can find a connection through the amulet," she thought. So she took a closer look at the amulet. It appeared to be made of silver, but she could not ascertain its age. It could have been lost by some snorkeler or diver, or it could be hundreds of years old. There just did not seem to be a way to tell. The stones looked ordinary enough, but the combination of stones and that hand, what did it mean? She Googled "star" and found over 500,000,000 hits. She then Googled "hand" and discovered more than 3,000,000 sites. She kept thinking and tried "Jewish star," but again came up with almost 7,000,000 possibilities. She thought to herself that this was definitely going to be a long night as she reached into the cupboard and pulled out the bottle of Dewars. She slowly poured herself a glass as she nestled in for a long, lonely night. She always felt better with scotch. It helped her think clearly, or so she thought. It had helped her through those long nights studying for her finals in college. She had relied on it to get her through grad school and her thesis, too. And it sure helped her get over her romantic dysfunction over the years. Yes, Dewars was her friend and crutch, and she turned to it again; if nothing else, she was at least guaranteed a good night's sleep.

She took a swig. It sure felt good going down. She took a few more, then returned to the amulet. As she studied it closer, it became clearer. How had she missed it earlier? Was she that blind, that ignorant? The hand. It clearly was a hand. Where had she seen it before? She thought long and hard, and, after another glass, it finally hit her. Venice! The old Jewish quarter, the ghetto. It had been years since she was there, but what did she remember about it? During the 16th century many Jews had migrated to Venice and had become a major financial force. They were the bankers and merchants who had the international connections and the assets to control the trade. They were the professionals, such as doctors and lawyers. While much of Europe, such as Spain, persecuted them, Venice protected them. Many Jews had migrated to Venice after the Spanish Inquisition of 1492. But by the mid-1500s, even in Venice they were not spared from persecution. The Doge recognized the practical need for the presence of the Jews; after all, the financial stability of the state was at stake. So instead of expelling them, laws were enacted creating a secure place for them, the ghetto, a place where they were segregated from the rest of the population at night in order to placate the Catholic Church, but where they were able to continue their daily occupations in order to keep the Venetian state the international power it had become. The term came from the iron foundries located in the area. The Jews were forced to reside in that area and even pay for the guards who watched over the few gates allowing egress over the canals. In the Ghetto Vecchio, there was a shop specializing in Jewish artifacts. Among other things, it sold hands. The hand was an old symbol of luck or protection, but what was it called? If she could only remember.

Carly plugged in the words, Googling "Jewish hand." Almost 6,000,000 hits. "Hamesh." "Hamsa." She checked the first few and confirmed her hunch. Hamsa in Arabic, Hamesh in Hebrew: an old amulet for magical protection from the evil eye. It was also known as the Hand of Miriam by the Jews and the Hand of Fatima by the Arabs. It may have even predated both societies. Some sites described the symbol as referring to an ancient Middle Eastern goddess whose hand or vulva warded off the evil eye.

Okay, so this thing, this amulet, could be old. But what about this star? Carly kept digging and finally found a picture of a pendant, the Jewish Hand of Miriam, found inside a Jewish star, the Star of David, surrounded by six apotropaic all-seeing eyes. It appeared to be an ancient Jewish symbol to ward off evil spirits. Carly took a breather and poured herself another scotch. She was making headway and felt congratulations were in order. After a few more swallows, she returned to her laptop and continued her search.

She quickly typed "Ancient Hebrew." Damn, another multi-million hits. Doesn't anything come easy anymore? She muttered to herself and began clicking on the various options. After a half an hour of dead ends, she hit pay dirt. Apparently the Hebrew alphabet, similar to the Aramaic alphabet, derived from the Phoenician alphabet. Before the current Hebrew alphabet came into existence, there existed the Paleo-Hebrew alphabet, which was used until the creation of the modern Hebrew alphabet in the centuries before Christ. Damn, Carly thought, Sam was right all along. Maybe there is a Jewish connection. But what was a Jewish relic never before recorded doing on a 17th-century galleon in the middle of the ocean off the coast of Florida? Carly's head was beginning to spin. Were the questions and puzzling pieces that seemed to have no logical connection to each other getting to her, or was the booze finally beginning to hit? It really didn't matter to her. It was getting late and she was tiring quickly. While she apparently had some answers, she was no closer to the solution. The world around her was beginning to spin and the day, which had started with such promise, had developed into such a failure: her desire for Sean was still unrealized and she was no closer to attaining the significance of the amulet. She slowly, dejectedly moved away from the computer and laid on her bed dreaming of Sean, his two-day old beard, sinewy chest, and those blue eyes that would cause her to freeze at a moment's glance.

3

Geoff kept staring at the box encased in the liquid solution he had concocted to restore the writing to a more legible form. He had to make the process move more quickly, more expeditiously, but how? He kept staring at the box and then it hit him. *Fool!* he thought to himself. All this time he had been focused on the writing, but why not focus on the box?

He began to examine it more closely. He grabbed the magnifying glass and scrutinized every aspect of the box. He wrote down its measurements and dimensions, checking every angle for any flaws or clues that may evolve. He tried to determine its metallic makeup, but was uncertain whether it was silver, stone or some other substance. Time and the elements had concealed the answers well. But Geoff was determined. Something inside him was driving him towards the inevitable conclusion. He knew he was part of something big and he was not going to let up. Sam was depending on him and, in his heart, he knew this was important. It was earth-shattering, revolutionizing, a discovery that could change the world, and he was part of it.

Geoff took a gamble and removed the box from its tank. He again slowly examined every facet of it, beginning with the bottom. It seemed plain enough. A solid shape, rectangular in design. Nothing out of the ordinary. He moved towards the sides. Even with the encrustation, they appeared smooth and straight. The top symmetrically mirrored the bottom, but it had that damn marking, that lettering or whatever it was. If only he could clean some of the scum off. Then it hit him. He recalled reading about a method some Frenchman had been experimenting with, using an alcohol-based solution mixed with other chemicals. He began to mix his own compounds and gently brushed it on the box. He left it for a couple of hours and then returned to observe the results. Some of the lettering was becoming more visible, but, more importantly, the solution was beginning to clean the outer portions of the box. It was becoming clearer that the construction of the box was more complex than he originally thought. While he could not discern the boundaries between the top and bottom of the box, he could tell that the designer had taken great pains to disguise its appearance, making the two sides seem to merge.

He carefully examined the sides and came to the conclusion that there was a top and bottom. There had to be a locking mechanism, and he was sure he could find it. He just needed more time. He then submerged the box in the new solution and let time work its magic. He turned to his laptop and searched for answers on the internet, Googling "magic boxes," "sacred boxes," and any other description he could think of. The answer had to be out there somewhere and Geoffrey knew he was bound to find it.

As the sun began to break over the horizon, Carly awoke feverishly from her bunk. Sweat was pouring from her body.

She was cold and clammy and her sheets had been drenched from her perspiration. She tossed and turned, trying to get her bearings, finally realizing that daybreak was arriving as the remnants of the scotch that she had devoured earlier was discharging from her pores. She saw visions of the hand, the Star, and the amulet being offered to her, held in the outstretched hand of...was it an angel, a man, or perhaps the hand of God?

Carly had never been religious. She had always doubted God's existence. Just a con made up by men to control those around them, to give them power over the weak and timid. How many wars had been fought in the name of God, Allah, Jupiter and Shiva? Every major civilization throughout time had invoked the name of their god to justify their imperialistic desires. Even the Church used God's wrath and desires to instigate the Crusades, to create an all-powerful clergy holding property and wealth beyond compare; to create a state...no, a country, which at one time was more powerful than any other in the world...the Vatican. Yes, the concept of God was used through the ages to justify man's avarice, man's violence, and man's brutality. It was used to keep women in their place, to try to contain the strengths of the female gender. And the Church was not the only offender. Every religion has the same faults. Islam has its jihad, claiming that a Palestinian state had been divinely ordained; and the Jews claim that the creation of the state of Israel had divine biblical origin. No, she had never been one of the faithful, but after last night, after her research on the amulet and the ancient Hebraic text, she was no longer such a staunch agnostic. Perhaps she was wrong. Perhaps there is more to this divine entity which has driven mankind since the beginning of time. She was no longer so sure of herself.

Carly shook the cobwebs of sleep from her mind, dashed her face with some cold water to clean off the sweat and the booze, and to also awaken her senses. She quickly threw on some shorts and a shirt and scampered topside to report her findings to Sam, not realizing it was only six a.m. As she climbed the stairs to the deck she noticed the sun slowly floating above the waves, a bright red ball rising from the water's edge, turning the blackness into a palate of orange, yellow and blue. Dawn was breaking and a new day was beginning. Would this day turn out better than the last? Only time would tell.

Carly made some coffee and waited for the rest of the crew to rise. She kept thinking about the amulet with the different colored stones set within the circular portion of the all-seeing eye. Her brain ached from the liquor of the night before, but the caffeine was easing the pain and she kept thinking about the Star and its history. What had she read? Was the star a mystical symbol, used in magic prior to its acceptance as a Jewish symbol? Some scholars seemed to think so. But she recalled the article she read about the "Seal of Solomon," the ring King Solomon supposedly wore throughout his reign, part of the legacy that would become Solomon's treasures. There was something about the legend that kept drawing her back to it, but what?

"A penny."

"Huh?" Carly stammered, almost dropping her coffee cup in her lap.

"A penny for your thoughts. You looked so entrenched in thought," Sean said. Carly had been so deep in thought that she had not heard Sean stir from his bunk below, navigate the ladder to the upper deck, or even enter the kitchen area. She was startled by his appearance, but glad to see the animosity from last night was gone.

"Have you been up long?" he asked her.

"About an hour, I guess. I spent most of the night researching leads. I'm not sure if any of this means anything, but the amulet appears to be of an ancient design, perhaps dating back to the early Israelites. It's made up of the Star or

Shield of David with what appear to be six precious stones inside six all-seeing eyes. The eyes are symbolic of the evil eye, to curse all those who oppose the owner. The hand was known as the "Hand of Miriam" by the Jews and the "Hand of Fatima" by the Arabs. Its purpose was to ward off evil spirits like the evil eye. The writing on the box appears to be some sort of ancient text, possibly a precursor to Hebrew. I found some articles on the old Phoenician alphabet and its similarities or development into an alphabet known as Paleo-Hebraic, which is believed to be the alphabet used by the early Hebrews, and later developed into the Hebrew alphabet used for thousands of years by Jewish scribes and scholars."

"But what does all this have to do with a 17th-century sailing vessel armed with cannons sunk in the waters off Florida?" It was Sam speaking. Carly had been so wound up in her explanation and those blue eyes of Sean's that she failed to notice the emergence of Sam and the rest of the crew.

"I haven't figured that out yet. I need to know more detail about the box and the inscription, if those markings are, in fact, an inscription. We need to clean up that box."

"I agree, but I need more time and more sophisticated technology than we have with us on this damn boat," Geoff said, bringing the clear weight of reality back into focus. The crew slowly began to realize that they were going to have to return to shore in order to unravel the next phase of this mystery.

"Looks like a storm's beginning to brew off the horizon anyway!" Billy yelled. "We better mark our final bearings quickly, tie down our gear and get the hell out of here now. Looks like we've only got an hour before that thing's going to hit us, and from the weather reports, it ain't gonna be pretty."

The entire crew nodded in agreement and began to make the necessary plans to return to shore. Dejected and sullen, they began to store their dive equipment and haul anchor, making sure they had correctly logged their present coordinates and location for when they would return to continue their exploration in the waters below. As the boat's engine screamed to life and the vessel turned towards home, Carly sat staring at the empty ocean, looking at the foreboding sky. She could not keep herself from thinking that, perhaps, they had begun to unleash something from the past, an old curse, or maybe even worse, the wrath of...dare she even think it...God.

After returning to the dock, the crew quickly unloaded their gear along with the amulet and box, which was still soaking in the desalinization tank. They had beat the storm by at least a half hour and they wanted to quickly return to the task at hand before any interference from nosy onlookers, other potential treasure hunters, or any other obstacle might come their way. As they entered Sam's complex, they breathed sighs of relief. No one had seen them carry their treasure from the boat, and the rain had just begun to engulf the surrounding area. Safely within Sam's "Treasure Trove," they began to unpack. Billy and Jim took care of the dive equipment, rinsing out the BCs, wet suits and other gear, then refilling the tanks in preparation of the return voyage to the treasure site. Tom began scouring the many maps and historical records he had accumulated over the years searching for some sort of clue to the mysterious vessel's origins or intended destination. Geoff, Sean and Carly went to work on the treasure. They tried to blow up and enhance the photos, hoping to get a closer look at the shipwreck, the surrounding ocean floor, cannon and box. With a little luck, perhaps a clue might be developed from the enhancements.

Unfortunately, no new information was obtained, and they then turned their attention to the amulet and box.

Meanwhile, Sam was on the phone with Jack detailing the last few days' events. He knew Jack had planned his excursion to Florida earlier in the year and Alexandra, Jack's wife, was already at the condo waiting for his arrival. It had only been a few days earlier that he and Alexandra had met for lunch and had discussed Jack's ongoing trial and his impending arrival. Excitedly, Sam described Sean's experience and find, as well as Geoff's encounter with the stonefish. By the time he got to the box, Jack's curiosity had been well aroused, and there was no doubt that Jack would be part of the crew when Sam resumed his search the following week. Sam was sure that would give Geoff and Carly enough time to learn more about the mysterious box and amulet.

The week had gone by without too much success. The photos were leading nowhere and the box was still in the tank releasing no new clues. The cleaning process was taking far longer than anyone had anticipated. Tom had developed no leads regarding the shipwreck and Carly could find no information regarding the strange markings from the medallion, cannon or box.

Jack arrived right on schedule and anxiously examined the amulet. He had seen jewelry with the Star of David before. New York, as well as South Florida, had shops selling the Hamsa as "good luck" door or wall ornaments, as well as in jewelry. The eye was a whole different matter, and he had never seen the three together in one design. He looked more closely at the pendant and asked Sam about the stones.

"Any idea what's with the different colored stones? And why six?"

"We haven't been able to figure that out yet," Sam replied in a puzzled tone. "We even thought of contacting a jeweler to examine the piece, but didn't know if we could find one we could trust."

"Where's this box of yours I've been hearing about?"

"It's still in the tank. Come on, I'll show you." Sam grabbed Jack's arm and led him to the adjacent room where Geoff was muttering about how slow the process was removing the encrustation from the box. Geoff exchanged salutations with Jack and then showed him the box.

"How does it open?" Jack asked.

"If only we knew," Sam and Geoff replied almost simultaneously.

"Can I take it out to get a closer look?"

"Just be careful," Geoff cautioned.

Jack carefully removed the box from the tank and laid it on a clean towel. He examined the markings and symbol on top.

"What kind of language is this?"

"Carly thinks it may be Phoenician or ancient Hebrew or Arabic," Sam said. "She's leaning toward ancient Hebrew, since we have the Star and Hand, but she can't be sure. We need to raise some of the markings to figure out if they are letters and if they mean anything, but this damn process is just taking too long."

"Can I see that amulet again?" Jack asked.

"Sure, it's in the other room. Come on," Sam said as he started heading towards the door.

"No, I meant can I see it next to the box."

Sam looked at Geoff and Geoff nodded affirmatively. "It's not going to mess up the process any. I'll get it for him, Sam."

Geoff retrieved the amulet and handed it to Jack. As he took it from Geoff, Jack noticed a striking resemblance to the symbol on the box. He laid it next to the box and called the two over.

"Look at this! Am I hallucinating or is the amulet the same size as the sign on the box?"

They took a closer look and definitely saw the resemblance.

"But there's no eye on the box, only a star inside the circle," Geoff observed.

"Yeah, and where's the Hand?" Sam questioned.

"Look, you said the amulet was found by the site. There was a cannon with a similar design covering the box, right?"

Geoff and Sam both nodded in agreement.

"Then the symbols must match. Can't we get this box cleaned up any more? Or what about getting an x-ray or some other imaging device to examine it more closely?"

Sam and Geoff both looked at each other and grinned. "Why didn't we think of that before? But where can we get the necessary equipment?" Sam wondered aloud.

Geoff had friends in a local science research facility and suggested they try to enlist their aid. Sam was not thrilled at the prospect of letting anyone else in on their discovery until they had more information about what they were holding, what they might be looking for and where they stood as far as owning the claim. But they had no other choice. All their leads were exhausted and they needed more information before they went back out and made fools of themselves. Reluctantly, Sam agreed to let Geoff take the box for a more intricate examination.

5

Carly was busy researching at the archaeological library looking for any leads. She tried to find out all she could on the Star, but could discover nothing definitive. The Hand was used as a good luck charm by many Semitic civilizations, including the Hebrews, but she had previously discovered all that during her scotch-assisted research binge on the boat. Her mouth was watering and she kept thinking she could sure use some Dewars about now, but she knew she had to keep focused on her research. Besides, she would get kicked out if she were caught with anything stronger than water.

She had brought copies of the pictures with her and kept returning to the enlargement of the medallion. It must have been a beautiful piece of jewelry when it was first made, she thought to herself. She was entranced by the stones, but could not identify them. And what puzzled her the most was the purpose behind the different stones, all of a different color. Who designs a piece like that, unless they were birthstones for six different children? Carly was stumped. She kept staring at the stones, until she started to make out some of their colors. Red to reddish-orange, blue, green, purple...nice colors, pretty colors, but what type of stones? Some of the colors seemed to be similar, but the stones appeared different. She needed to find out more, but did not have the background. Perhaps a jeweler or gemologist could help, but she knew Sam would never go for it. Did the amulet contain precious stones, or were they just everyday, common decorative stones used in costume jewelry? Well, she had no time to ponder such nonsense. It really didn't matter, nor was it getting her any closer to answering the questions at hand...what was the symbol or marking, what language was on the box, where did it come from, what was the vessel it was on and what else had been transported with it? After hours of dead ends, she was getting frustrated and decided to leave. Besides, she needed a drink and some male companionship. Maybe Sean was available.

Meanwhile, back at the boat, Sean had enough of being left out of the loop. After all, he had been the one to find the amulet in the first place. He had recovered the box. If not for him, Sam would never have known about the treasure, or whatever else may be down in the wreck. And all he was getting for it was a pat on the back while everyone else went their own way looking for answers. He felt helpless and used, cast aside like a worn utensil. He had just about had it and did not care if he was around when they went back to the wreck site. He was sure he could find it on his own, maybe even beat them to it and scarf up the treasure himself. That would really put them in their place.

He needed to get out and think, maybe get some fresh air and loosen up. As these thoughts raced through his mind, he decided to clean up and go out on the town. He washed up quickly and threw some money into his pocket. He was walking out the cabin door, putting his watch on with one hand while cradling his shirt in the crook of his other elbow, when Carly came barreling down the corridor right into him.

"Hey, why don't you watch where you're walking, you idiot!" Carly screamed.

"For a girl, you're sure not very graceful," he retorted with a sarcastic tone.

That was it! She had just about had enough of his sarcastic humor and boorish attitude. Whatever she thought she had seen in him earlier vanished. Instead, all she saw was a dim-witted, idiotic, poor excuse for white trash, and she didn't hesitate to tell him so, after which she proceeded to slap his face with all her might. She swung to hit him again when she slipped, spinning around 180 degrees and falling towards him. Sean caught her, spun her around, then looked her right in her green eyes and said, "I've had enough of your arrogant, self-righteous nonsense. Who are you calling white trash? Everybody knows where you came from, where you were before you wormed your way into Sam's good graces. And don't think I don't know about your attraction to booze and drugs. Who the hell do you think you're kidding anyway? It's about time you got taught a lesson, girl!"

Sean grabbed her by the cheek with each hand, looked her glaringly in the eyes, tilted her head slightly towards the left and towards him, and then he kissed her...HARD...right on the lips, shoving his tongue deep inside her mouth. He kept her like that for what seemed like minutes. Carly began to lose her breath as well as her balance. When Sean finally released her, she stared at him, her face flushed and red, her heart pounding, gasping for air. As Sean began to turn away she grabbed his head and pulled him back towards her, kissing him back voraciously, returning all that she had just received from him. Sean's shirt dropped to the floor, forgotten in the moment. He left it there, cradled her in his arms, and carried her with one arm under her back, the other under her legs, as he furiously kicked open his cabin door. He had desired her from afar for some time; little did he realize that Carly had felt the same way.

Hours later they lay in his bed, satisfied and exhausted. Sean wanted to know where Carly was heading in such a hurry. Sheepishly, she told him how she had longed for some male companionship, preferably his, and had come to see if he wanted to go into town for some drinks and relaxation. He laughed and explained that he had fostered similar thoughts, although Carly was not included in the scene he had pictured.

"Man, you sure know how to boost a gal's ego," she sourly complained.

"Aw, don't be mad. I just meant that I had no idea you would have even given me a second thought, especially after the way you were treating me out at sea. I figured I'd go out and have a few drinks and try to loosen up, but this was a much better alternative."

"Why does this have to be an alternative? It's not that late, and I still need a drink. Besides, who knows what might happen later? Maybe you'll get lucky twice in the same night," Carly whispered seductively into Sean's ear.

They looked at each other and laughed.

"Why not! Let's get dressed and hit the town. Where the hell did I put that shirt, anyway?"

Sean and Carly quickly dressed and headed off the boat and into town, unaware that they were about to embark on a dark journey into a world that would make Pandora's experience seem as harmless as a Mother Goose nursery rhyme.

Geoff had taken the box to the local science research facility. When he arrived, he immediately sought out his old friend, Adam. They had been schoolmates and eventually continued on to marine occupations, with Geoff becoming a commercial diver and Adam a marine biologist. When Adam got the job at CMRC (the Caribbean Marine Research Center) in Palm Beach, the two reestablished their friendship and would meet on frequent occasions to reminisce about old times and discuss new finds and theories. Geoff felt confident he could trust Adam with their discovery.

"Hey, Adam!" Geoff yelled. "How's it going?"

"I'm fine, but what brings you down here so late? And what the hell happened to your hand?" Adam asked.

"Diving accident. Nothing to worry about. But that's not why I came. Can we go someplace private? I've got something I need to show you."

Adam led them into a private office and questioned Geoff about the secrecy.

"One of our crew found this while diving. We're not sure what it is, but it appears to be a box with no way inside. What do you think?"

Adam examined the box more closely, asking about the markings. Geoff filled him in on the theories as he took a closer look, and then suggested using an x-ray machine. After ensuring that such a procedure would not destroy the integrity of the box, the two retired to the x-ray room for a closer examination. To their surprise, the x-ray revealed no useful information. They tried various other tests with similar results. They were able to faintly make out the outline of interlocking pieces within the box, but could not distinguish any significant edges to assist in opening it.

"What in the world did you guys find?" Adam exclaimed. "I've never seen anything like this. You sure this didn't come from outer space or something?"

"No, just from the distant past, I think," Geoff sullenly replied. "Isn't there anything else we can do? Any other technology we can use to try to open this sucker?"

"What's with this marking?" asked Adam. "Can't you get this portion cleaned up any better?"

The two spent the next six hours working on cleaning the marking on the box. After numerous attempts, they were finally able to restore the marking to a legible level. When Geoff observed the finished result, he was in awe. It appeared to be an exact replica of the amulet, but with the stones missing. That's when it finally hit him.

"The amulet!" he exclaimed.

"The what?"

Geoff related how Sean had found the amulet, describing it in detail to Adam, down to the colored stones, eyes, hand and star. Perhaps there was a connection between the two. Didn't

Jack say the amulet and the marking on the box were the same size? What if they pieced together? What if the amulet was a key? Geoff was ecstatic and told Adam he had to return to Sam with the box. After swearing Adam to secrecy and promising to update him with any new information, Geoff left with the box, but not before Hector Silas had silently entered the room and overheard the latter part of the conversation.

Hector Silas was a research assistant, having been associated with CMRC for a little over one year. No one knew much about him since he usually kept to himself. He was always short of money and seemed to appear at the most inopportune times, like now.

"Whatcha got there?" he quickly asked.

"It's of no concern to you," Adam replied. "And just what are you doing here anyhow?"

"I saw the light on and thought everyone had already gone, so I figured I'd better check. I only came to turn out the lights."

Unsure of how long he had been there and what he had overheard, Geoff had no choice and had to take him at his word. Geoff told him they were working on a secret project and asked him to forget about anything he may have witnessed. All too quickly, Hector acquiesced to his request and exited the room.

"Can he be trusted?" Geoff asked Adam.

"I don't know much about him, but he couldn't have heard or seen anything of great import. Besides, what could he know? That you found something that looks like a box on the ocean floor? So what?"

"I guess you're right. Since we don't know anything, what could he possibly know?" Geoff said as he scooped up the box, returning it to his knapsack as he left the complex.

7

"I got no idea what it was, but it looked old! Must've been worth a mint since they were all nervous and fidgety when I walked in. I played dumb, but I caught a sneak peek at it. It looked like a box with jewels or some markings on it. They'd been in there for hours, so somethin' must be up," Hector rapidly reported on the telephone. He needed money, a lot of it and quickly, and figured that reporting his observations would accomplish his immediate goal. After all, it had worked before.

The Cartel had approached him shortly after he had first started at CMRC. He always seemed to need money and they knew it. They told him to keep his eyes open about any finds and other significant information. CMRC was always in the loop about any important marine discoveries, whether they were new species, shipwrecks, plane wrecks, Coast Guard drug interceptions, or lost items found in the sea. The Cartel's tentacles were far-reaching and information about any of these items could often prove useful. This time was no exception. The man on the other end of the phone listened intently to Hector, taking copious notes, and then thanking him for his loyalty before promising to see him rewarded for his efforts and hanging up.

Geoff strode quickly to the boat, unaware of the Cartel's knowledge and interest in the box. Without thinking any more about Hector's intrusion, he returned to report his findings and theories to Sam and Jack. Upon his arrival, he described the efforts he and Adam had made to discover the box's secret. Even though they had been unsuccessful, he showed his employer the box, which had been cleaned up and partially restored to its former opulence.

"Where's the amulet, Sam? I think I may have figured this thing out after all."

"It's in the other room, but I thought you couldn't get the box open or even figure out if there was anything inside."

"Remember when we first showed you the box, Jack? You looked at the amulet and said the size and shape on the top of the box appeared to be the same as the amulet, only the stones were missing," Geoff hurriedly explained.

"Yeah, but what of it?" Jack asked.

"Suppose the box had a lock. There would need to be a key, right?" Geoff grinned.

"We don't even know if this is a box. And even if it were, where's the lock and where's the keyhole?" Sam was getting frustrated with Geoff and tiring quickly of this game. He had been up way too long and needed to get some sleep.

Geoff led the two over to the amulet and, after trying several different positions, finally placed the amulet against the stone box. On the third try he finally got the star on the amulet to match up to the box. After getting the amulet to set inside the design on the box, he slowly twisted the amulet to the right.

"Be careful!" Sam cried out. "What are you trying to do, destroy what we've uncovered so far?"

"Shhh!" Geoff replied. "Of course not, but I think we may have found our key."

"What are you talking about?" Sam was now getting aggravated with Geoff's impetuousness, and was about to tell him so, when something inside the box clicked.

"What the hell was that?"

The three men looked at each other, then back at the box. Geoff had stopped twisting the amulet, but the top refused to come off. Instead, after exerting slight pressure on the amulet, the inside quadrant of the box, amulet and all, separated from the box, revealing a hidden chamber within the central portion of the box below the amulet's imprint.

"What the...it's got a scroll of some sort inside!" Sam cried out. "Geoff, you're a genius!"

Jack moved closer and began to examine the scroll carefully. He put on some gloves and meticulously unrolled the parchment with a pair of forceps handed to him by Geoff. After unrolling the parchment, the three observed strange markings, similar to those outside of the box. Was it a message? A warning? Was it a lost ancient language, or merely a crude hoax? Jumbled thoughts raced through their minds as they pondered what was before them. Jack grabbed the camera and quickly photographed the new discovery.

"Where's Carly?" Sam wondered aloud. "She should be here. Maybe she can decipher this."

8

Carly was in no condition to decipher anything. She had gone to town with Sean and was enjoying herself for the first time in many months. She was dancing, laughing and downing Dewars with beer chasers. She hadn't a care in the world, and Sean was keeping up with her drink for drink. After several hours they had become boisterous and been told to quiet down or leave. Indignantly, Carly jumped up from her seat, arms flailing.

"You don't know who you're talking to!" she exclaimed. "We're the next 'Indiana Jones!' We're gonna be so rich, we could buy this place and blow it up, sending it to the ocean floor."

"Stop it, Carly." Sean tried to quiet her down. "You don't know what you're saying. Nobody needs to know anything. Sam will kill us if this gets out."

"Screw him! What does he know?! He never cared about your feelings. This was your find, not his. But what kind of credit are you getting? What's your share going to be? Daily wages and a pat on the back?"

She was right. Sean began to wonder whether he would get any of the glory. But now was not the time or place to discuss it. If this conversation went any further, neither he nor Sam would have anything to show for their troubles.

"Knock it off, Carly," Sean whispered in her ear. "We don't even know what we've uncovered, but until we do, we've got to keep this to ourselves. If this gets out, we'll all end up with nothing."

Suddenly Carly realized he was right. Sheepishly, she began to sit down. Had she said too much? Had she jeopardized their discovery? Would Sean ever forgive her if she did?

"I'm sorry," she said as she began to cry. "It's just that the amulet is so beautiful with all those stones, and so mysterious with that star and hand. And…it's your discovery, not his. You deserve some recognition. You dove for it. You risked your life for it! You recovered it from the ocean floor!"

Sean realized Carly had totally lost it. She was beyond control, an emotional wreck. Whether it was the booze or her own despondency, it was time to get her out of there before she said something they would all regret. He gently took her by the arm and raised her up from her chair. Cradling her in one arm he gently, but persuasively, directed her towards the door.

"Come on, it's time to go home."

As they walked out the door, he took one quick look around, but failed to spot the stranger standing in the shadows by the bar eyeing them as they left, making mental notes of what he had overheard them say. As they slowly walked back to the boat, Carly's head rested on Sean's shoulder. He softly caressed her neck and hair, oblivious to the stranger following in the distance.

As they approached the docks, Carly began to stumble, the

exhaustion of the evening, her emotions and alcohol finally taking their collective toll. Sean could barely keep her on her feet as they walked towards the *Scavenger.* Sam and Jack had left the lab and climbed to the deck for some fresh air and to collect their thoughts. They had decided to search for Carly when they heard sounds coming from the docks. As they struggled to see clearly in the dimly lit area, they saw Sean trying to drag Carly along. Carly had become dead weight, and her legs no longer cooperated. Sean was on his own, trying to drag her along. After realizing that she had just about passed out, Sean draped her over his shoulder and began to carry her towards the boat.

"What the hell is going on out there?" Sam and Jack both asked.

"She had a little too much at the bar and kind of died on me along the way. One of you want to give me a hand here?" Sean pleaded. "She's heavier than she looks."

Jack slowly walked down the boat ramp and assisted Sean in bringing Carly aboard. Meanwhile, the stranger watched silently from the shadows, making mental notes of the three men and one woman boarding the *Scavenger.* After Carly was safely on board, Sam glimpsed back at the docks. He thought he saw a shadow move, but, as he tried to take a closer look, Jack called out for him to help hold the cabin door while they carried Carly inside.

9

The next morning, Carly awoke with a splitting headache. It was nearly 11 a.m., and her normally steady balance had been substantially altered by her evening of partying. Instead of the veteran boater, she felt more like a novice cabin boy, seasick on his first ocean-bound excursion. The room was spinning, her stomach was queasy and her mouth was dry. As she sat up and tried to take a step, she almost stumbled out of the bunk and onto the floor. She managed to make her way to the sink by clinging to the cabin walls and splashed cold water on her face. The coldness stung, awakening her senses, and bringing some life back to her aching body. The room was still spinning but she slowly began to bring herself back to the present, recognizing her surroundings and hoping that she wasn't going to regret too many of her actions from the evening before.

What the hell had she been thinking? Sean must think her a fool. Had she embarrassed him? Would he ever look at her again with anything other than disdain and contempt? Had she embarrassed *herself?* What stupid things had she said or done?

The crashing in her head got louder and sharper as she tried to remember the events from the night before. She needed to clear the cobwebs from her head. She needed coffee, or a drink. No, coffee. Drinking had gotten her into this mess and she didn't think it was going to get her out of it this time. She groped her way up to the mess hall and poured herself a mug of hot, black coffee. As it slowly trickled down her throat, she heard a noise coming from behind her.

"Morning, sunshine. We thought you'd be sleeping the day away. You don't look so hot."

It was Sean, with his irritating, condescending mannerisms and tone. It always seemed like he tried to pick a fight or rile her up at her weakest moments. What happened to the sensitivity and understanding he had shown her last night, or had it all been a dream?

"I'm not in the mood, Sean. I don't know what you put in my drink last night and I don't appreciate your tone this morning."

"Drink? Hell, girl, you downed three-quarters of a bottle of scotch with twice as many beer chasers, and you think I spiked your drinks? I couldn't even keep up with you last night."

Carly's worst fears had been realized. She had truly made a fool of herself in front of Sean. Not only would she never be able to get close to him like she had hoped, but he would never let her live last night down, or so she thought.

"Hey, don't get all wound up," he said. "I was just having a little fun. Are you all right?"

"No, I'm not. What the hell did I say last night? What did I do? What did *we* do?"

"Before or after we left the boat?"

Carly could take no more. She began to shake and started to cry. A feeling of worthlessness came over her and made

Sean step back, puzzled. He had never expected to see brash and bold Carly relegated to a weeping female. He also never expected that he would care about how she felt or how she looked at him, but he did. Even more surprisingly and out of character for him, he took a step forward, reached out and took her in his arms, slowly stroked her hair and pulled her close to his chest. He kissed her lightly on the forehead and whispered that everything would be all right. The pain in her head began to subside, the feeling of hopelessness faded away and calm began to take over. Maybe she had misjudged Sean. Maybe she had misjudged herself.

Sean consoled Carly and finally got her to calm down and return to some semblance of reality. After learning that she had only gotten very drunk and was then brought back to the ship, she seemed to be more relaxed and at ease. Sean did not discuss her intimations regarding losing out on the glory of the find, nor was her brash exclamation of their discovery mentioned. As far as Sean was concerned, her comments from the evening before were strictly their secret. It was at that moment that Sam entered and approached the two of them.

"I don't know what the hell's going on between the two of you, but we need you both down below. We got the box opened, but we don't have the faintest idea what we've got!"

Carly and Sean turned towards each other with a look of relief. Maybe things were starting to turn around, both for them personally and professionally. Sam's comments implied that Sean was a necessary part of this team, wanted and needed, along with her own expertise. As they headed below, arm in arm, to view the latest discovery, smiles slowly crept onto their faces. Out of the corner of his eye, Sam noticed the bond developing between the two and warily accepted the relationship beginning to blossom. He knew it was pointless to comment since Carly had always been headstrong and did not readily accept advice. Hopefully, whatever relationship was developing between the two would not interfere with their discovery and the mystery left to solve.

Once below, Carly's smile turned to a look of amazement. "Who would have thought the amulet would act as the key to the box. Was this scroll the only thing inside?"

Geoff nodded. "That's all I saw when the thing popped open."

They all wondered aloud at the engineering of the box.

"How could the box remain watertight all these years?" Sam asked.

.   .   .

NO ONE SEEMED to have an answer, but the answer did not matter at that time. The more important question was what was on the scroll.

"Can you decipher it?" Jack asked as he turned to Carly, pointing at the scroll. The photos they had taken earlier were laying alongside the scroll. Some of the photos had been blown up to better illustrate the markings.

Carly moved closer and began to examine the scroll. It appeared to be of ordinary parchment, similar to those she had seen in the museum when she was studying for her degree. The bigger question was, how long could they expose the parchment to air before it would start to disintegrate? She was glad Geoff had taken photos of the parchment and, after examining the markings on the scroll, as well as the texture of the parchment, she decided the safest thing was to roll the parchment up and store it in a proper container to preserve it in its original form.

After ensuring the integrity of the scroll was protected, she moved on to examine Geoff's photos more closely. The markings did not appear to be random, but rather seemed to consist of an alphabet, set down on the parchment with a purpose, as if they were words speaking from the past. But what were they trying to say, and who was sending the message? Carly felt helpless and ignorant, feelings she had experienced in her personal life, but never professionally.

Carly had graduated at the top of her class in high school and undergraduate college before obtaining her graduate degree in marine archaeology from East Carolina University. Again graduating near the top of her class, she went on to work and study her craft globally. While she was still in undergrad, she had earned the nickname "Ice Queen." She had no time for most of her classmates and no time for relationships, whether male or female, since her goal was to become financially independent as soon as possible. Unfortunately for her, such tunnel vision would leave her emotionally scarred and ultimately dependant on the wrong people for most of her life.

As far as academically, she easily outshone her peers and rarely had difficulty analyzing any of the projects her professors thrust upon her. As she graduated and entered the real world, her skills quickly progressed and she became well-recognized in her field for her eye for detail and her ability to solve the mysteries hidden in the ocean depths. If her emotional psyche had been half as secure as her professional prowess, she would have easily been in the forefront of her field, receiving high fives and adulation from scientists worldwide. But Carly was always fighting her demons from within. She found solace and peace, at least momentarily, in booze and drugs, not realizing until far too late that such reliance would always restrain her in her professional goals and keep her from realizing the independence and recognition she constantly desired. After bouncing from man to man and job to job, Sam had found her one night laying drunk and beaten in that alleyway where her latest "true love" had cast her, along with her few meager belongings.

Sam had nursed her back to health and attempted to heal her emotional wounds along with her physical ones. He had given her a secure home without asking any questions in return and provided her with free rein on any treasure hunting excursions. Outwardly, Carly appeared fully healed, confident and secure in her surroundings. She had even kicked her drug use and cut back on her drinking, for the most part. While still bearing the "Ice Queen" moniker, she had learned to accept her faults and concentrate on the treasures hidden under the sea.

As she examined the photos more closely, she experienced for the first time in her life the uncertainty and ignorance of the human civilization. Man has been on this earth for thousands of years, developing from one civilization to another, conquering and destroying one civilization after another, destroying artifacts and unique advances which would prevent future generations from progressing as rapidly. Had their recent find been just another example of the callousness and selfishness of some ancient civilization, destroying any mention of the amulet, leaving no clues to its purpose or its reason for being on the sunken ship? The uniqueness of the markings on the cannon and box left no doubt in her mind that the artifacts belonged to some civilization or ancient organization and were only a smaller portion of a larger treasure awaiting their discovery.

She needed the assistance of a linguist, someone who knew ancient languages long forgotten.

"We need help!" Carly finally said, looking up from the photos. "I don't have the linguistic background to interpret these markings. The best I can tell is that these may be ancient Hebrew, but we already knew that from the markings on the cannon. But I can't figure out what they mean. We need someone more familiar with ancient languages and concepts. Any suggestions?"

The four of them looked at her dejectedly. None of them wanted to share the glory of the find or the possible treasure that awaited them. But without help, they all knew they would probably not get beyond the amulet and box. The dilemma they faced led to only one real answer.

"I guess we need an expert, but where can we go and who can we trust?" Sam questioned. The three of them looked at Carly.

"Didn't you go to school with anyone or meet anybody in your travels who might help?" Geoff asked.

"Semitic cultures and ancient history were not my forte, or my interest. Maybe I can look online and try to get a lead or two. We could post an ad on the Web or copy the photos."

"NO!" Sam shouted hurriedly. "No advertisement. Let's find someone we can trust, then decide what we divulge."

Having had the ground rules set, Carly went online searching for an expert to lend the much-needed aid. Geoff returned to examine the box again, with Sean and Jack close behind.

Sam retired to his cabin to get some rest and ponder the day's events. As he entered the cabin he spied the morning's paper and thought he would catch up on the latest news.

Sam grabbed the paper and sat in his favorite chair in the cabin. He had brought the chair from his upstate farmhouse, bringing all the memories of the good times with his wife and daughter with it. His daughter would jump from the chair to the floor as a little girl, while his wife would yell from the kitchen for her to be careful not to break her neck. Sam would always intervene and allow his daughter to continue, even after she had ripped the chair's arm. He had gotten it reupholstered three times since those days that seemed so long ago. The last time had been two weeks before that tragic Sunday, when he lost the two anchors in his life. He had almost left the chair, but could not bear to relinquish the sweet memories that stuck to it, the laughter and smell of the closeness, love and good times. He could always hear their tender voices when he sat in the chair. He could smell his wife's perfume and his daughter's hair when he closed his eyes. The chair was his bastion, his fortress from the outer world, the only place where he could relax and let himself go, releasing all anxiety and despair. It was the one place he could escape the loneliness he felt every day of his life.

As Sam relaxed in his chair, he opened the paper, reading the sports section first, as always. The Super Bowl was over and spring training camps for his baseball teams were beginning to kick into high gear. He loved to read about the latest gossip: who was missing camp, who was worrying about being traded, and who was seen around town, either receiving a DWI or arm in arm with some actress or model.

Seeing nothing of interest in the sports section, he then turned to the headline news. The war was still ongoing with casualties and car bombings as usual. The public polls continued to fluctuate between approval for the war against terrorism and the desire to bring our children and loved ones home. The stock market was riding the latest high and the politicians were delivering their latest double-talk, gearing up for the local and national elections which were still more than a year away. Then his mouth dropped. He couldn't believe his eyes! Right there on page 5 was the announcement he had never considered:

"WORLD-RENOWNED ARCHAEOLOGIST HERMANN STOMPMEYER ANNOUNCES LAST MINUTE PLANS TO ATTEND MUSEUM FUNDRAISER."

Hermann Stompmeyer was an expert in Semitic cultures. Apparently he had rescheduled his itinerary to allow him to attend next week's fundraiser at the museum. He planned to arrive on Wednesday and spend the rest of the week in seclusion at some socialite's mansion on the water. Had the "Hand of Fate" blessed them with this turn of events? Did he possess the knowledge they sorely lacked and needed? More importantly, would he help them, and could he be trusted?

Sam leaped from his chair and ran out of his cabin in search of the others. Breathlessly, he proceeded along the outer deck and ran down the steps to the lower area, where the others were attempting to uncover the mysteries of the box. Carly was working feverishly at the computer, searching for a name she might recognize.

"How about this guy? Ever hear of a Hermann Stompmeyer?" yelled Sam, waving the news article around while almost tripping as he entered the lower cabin area.

"Who?" asked Carly.

"This guy! Look at this article. Does this guy have the qualifications we're looking for?"

Carly looked at the paper and scanned the article. He certainly had the qualifications and expertise, at least from the propaganda spewing forth from the newspaper. Carly quickly googled his name and reviewed some of the articles listed about him. Professor of Antiquities, renowned expert on Semitic languages and cultures, extensive travels throughout the Mideast and the ancient lands once comprising Palestine. He certainly fit the bill, but what was he doing here?

"This guy sounds like the answer to our prayers, but how do we get in touch with him, and will he help us?" asked Geoff.

"Looks like we have an angel smiling down on us. I guess the medallion may be bringing us the luck we need. It certainly was a coincidence to have this guy change his plans to come to our neck of the woods," Sean chuckled. "Which one of us should try to contact him?"

As the group bantered about their options and tried to make plans on how to contact the professor, Jack watched silently, remembering back to his days as a Navy SEAL. "There is no such thing as coincidence or luck. Fate is a frame of mind and luck is the wish of desperate men. Coincidences are only precursors to disappointment. Be wary and alert." The words of his instructors haunted him, but why?

10

Hermann Stompmeyer was a short, stocky man of 63 with small eyes, a bald head and a rotund face which sported a short, grey goatee. He spoke with a German accent, but was fluent in many languages, both modern and ancient. He walked hunched over with the support of a cane that he always carried. In fact, he had quite a collection of canes and walking sticks that had been accumulated throughout his many travels.

Over the years, he had publicly and secretly attended and supervised digs throughout the Mideast. He had attempted to examine the area surrounding the old Temple in Jerusalem, but both the Israelis, as well as the Arabs before them, had prevented him from making any real headway at that location. He had been able to secretly unearth various ancient finds in Turkey and Iraq before those governments discovered him there and relieved him of his discoveries, all supposedly in the name of "national security."

While he was a well-known archaeologist, well-respected in his field, he was also known to cut corners and shy away from the red tape necessary to conduct an authorized dig in many sacred places. As a result, many of his discoveries either ended up on the black market or were confiscated by the local government's Division of Antiquities. His ethics were questioned by many, but his knowledge of the ancient world, especially from the early Greeks through the Spanish Inquisition, was unrivaled. His many finds through the years, as well as the numerous donations of the artifacts he had uncovered over time, had placed him near the top of his field in both demand in speaking engagements, as well as public recognition. While there were some in his field who would question his respectability and morality, there were none who questioned his knowledge of the ancient world.

Through the years, Hermann had collected many artifacts, selling some on the black market unbeknownst to most of his colleagues. At times he had to bribe some of the government officials in order to obtain safe exit with his discoveries from his various digs. He seemed to have an endless supply of financing from his anonymous benefactors and never spoke of the source of his funds. He lived in a restored medieval castle in Germany overlooking the Rhine River and traveled a majority of the year, speaking at various archaeological functions and guest lecturing at many universities. He demanded quite a price for the honor of his presence at one of these lectures and had the ego to match the cost of his appearance.

On this particular occasion, he had been asked by one of his benefactors to appear at the Florida Museum of Natural History's annual fundraiser. Actually, the word "request" was a kinder description of the demand placed on him by his benefactors. He had been visited in the middle of the night by two eerie-looking characters and provided an airplane ticket with flight information for travel to Miami. He was told that he would be appearing at the fundraiser and would be provided with further instructions upon his arrival. When he had attempted to protest, the taller one of the two had backhanded him across the face and glared at him with piercing black eyes. The shorter one told him not to anger them, since they had treated him well over the years and had saved his hide more than once. If pushed, they promised that his entire world as he knew it would come to an end, and he would have to pay dearly for his many indiscretions over the years. So, of course, he magnanimously accepted their gracious invitation to attend the fundraiser, without having any inkling about what he would be getting himself into. Within one week's time he reluctantly left his castle in Germany high above the Teutoburg Forest, and boarded his first-class flight to Miami.

Hermann had grown accustomed to luxury and found it hard to live without it. Even on his archaeological digs, he would often require special accommodations be in place before he would appear at the site. He had gotten used to money and was unwilling to give up his epicurean lifestyle. As a result, he had quickly found himself in the grips of his two benefactors. He owed his freedom and his wealth to them and, as he had found out all too often, also his soul. So Hermann dejectedly packed his bags and boarded his Lufthansa flight from Frankfurt to Miami. As he settled into his first-class seat, he tried to imagine what was awaiting him in the USA.

11

Sam decided that he and Carly would attend the museum benefit together and attempt to make contact with Hermann Stompmeyer. It was Sam's hope that they could engage him in a private conversation away from the crowd and obtain some background information from him. If the information was enticing enough, they would reveal the true purpose of their meeting to him and possibly bring him back to the boat to examine the relic.

While Sam was getting busy selecting his attire for the evening, Carly had quietly slipped into Sean's cabin, hoping he was there waiting for her. To her delight, he had just emerged from a shower as she entered the cabin.

"Well, well, princess. To what do I owe this surprise?"

"I wanted to see you before I left with Sam."

"Sure, you're going out to a party, having a good time, and you get the glory to meet and discuss my find with this guy. What do you expect me to do while you're catering to them?"

"Don't be that way, Sean. Please don't sulk. You know I would rather be with you. And don't worry, I won't let Sam take all the credit. I'll make sure your name is included in the conversation and you get full credit for the find, you should know that by now. Besides, let's not bicker. That's not why I came."

"No, well exactly why did you come? Sure it wasn't to gloat?"

"No, silly, I wanted...needed to see you. I just had this itch to see you before I left with Sam."

Carly slowly moved towards Sean's still-naked body dripping from his shower.

"Here, give me that towel and let me show you the proper way to dry yourself."

"Proper way? I didn't know there was a right or wrong way to dry myself."

"Well, the wrong way is alone. The right way is with my help. Let me show you."

Carly grabbed the towel from Sean and slowly caressed his body with it. A smile crept onto his face and the anger slowly began to leave his body. An uncontrollable fire began to replace the anger. He could no longer help himself. Carly was right. This was a much better way. He reached out and grabbed her and the two of them fell to the bed, mingled together. Carly and Sean spent the next twenty minutes in commingled bliss. She slowly drew away from Sean realizing that Sam would be waiting for her.

"Gotta go, and I still need to take a shower myself. I can't go like this, especially now."

Carly withdrew and quickly threw her clothes on. She threw Sean a quick kiss, ran out the cabin door and headed towards her cabin to quickly get ready for her land excursion with Sam.

Jack watched Carly as she brushed past him with an unusual glow about her and a bounce in her step that he hadn't noticed before.

With a knowing smile he said, "Running a little late, aren't we?"

Carly blushed and mumbled something under her breath that Jack was not quite able to make out. Besides, Jack had other things on his mind. He intended on heading back to his condo but, as he disembarked, he spied the tall gangly stranger lurking in the shadows. Something did not seem quite right. The stranger appeared to be hiding from view. In fact, had Jack not seen the glow from the stranger's cigarette, he would never have noticed the man. There was no one else on the docks, and none of the other boats nearby appeared to have any crew aboard. Jack decided to play his hunch and walked towards the man's hiding spot while appearing to fumble with his cell phone. As Jack approached, the man moved back deeper in the shadows. Jack did not give the man or his hiding place a second look. He wanted to know more about this man, but dared not acknowledge his existence. He would need to be careful not to spook the man. So Jack continued on his way, contemplating his next move.

Jack decided to walk to the end of the dock and took his own hiding spot out of the stranger's view. What an odd chain of events had recently unfolded. This archaeologist appearing at just the right moment, and now this stranger watching the ship's movement. It all seemed too coincidental, too pat and too suspicious for Jack's liking. Instead of returning to his condo, Jack settled in and dialed his cell phone.

"Hello, Brian. It's Jack. I need you to check something out for me."

Brian Laird was a friend of Jack's from his Navy SEAL days. Actually, they had briefly attended college together and found themselves standing next to each other on the recruitment line when enlisting. After completing their training, they had performed countless successful missions, each saving the other's hide on more than one occasion. After the war, they parted ways, Jack to law school and Brian to the police academy. During Jack's tenure in the District Attorney's office, they had crossed paths on many occasions. Years after Jack left the office and entered private practice, Brian had retired from the force and opened a small private investigation firm. Jack utilized Brian's services on many occasions, and Brian still had innumerable contacts in both law enforcement and high-level security government agencies.

"Listen, I need you to get me some background on someone."

"Can't it wait till the morning, Jack? I'm watching the game and the Knicks are actually winning this one."

"Sorry to interrupt on such a momentous occasion, but this is urgent."

Something in Jack's tone disturbed Brian. It had been a long time since he had heard such urgency in his friend's voice.

"Okay, what is it you need from me?"

"I need everything you can dig up on an archaeologist by the name of Hermann Stompmeyer, all the usual stuff as well as anything classified on him."

"A scientist? You're pulling me away from my game for a 'Bowtie'? What gives?"

"I'll fill you in later. How long will it take you?"

"I'll get on it right away. If I can shake some people up at this late hour, I may be able to get you something by early a.m."

Jack was restless and impatient but realized he would have no choice in the matter. Beggars can't be choosers and he was definitely begging for some information. He would have to wait and could only hope that his friend could shake some pertinent information out quickly.

"I guess I have no choice in the matter, but call me as soon as you find out anything of interest."

Brian told Jack he would call him as soon as he learned

something. Of course, he had no idea what he was looking for or what would be of interest to Jack, since Jack ended the call without explaining anything further to him. He guessed Jack had faith in his psychic abilities. Brian chuckled at the thought then reached for his phone book. It would be a long night and he would be calling in a lot of favors before the sun rose.

12

Carly showered and dressed quickly, realizing that Sam would be impatiently wondering what was keeping her. She was in no mood to answer any of his questions, so she made every effort to ready herself as expeditiously as possible. She even amazed herself at the short time it took her. She left her cabin and soon entered Sam's.

"I'm all ready to go. Should I bring anything? What's your game plan as far as this evening goes?" She hoped that by keeping the conversation focused on their excursion Sam would not realize how late she was nor ask any questions that would draw embarrassing answers from her. Then she blushed, irritated at herself for even thinking that any of her answers would be embarrassing. After all, what did she have to be embarrassed about? She was a grown adult, capable of making her own decisions and living her own life. She needn't answer to or explain herself to Sam, or anyone else for that matter.

"Something wrong, Carly?" Sam had planned on answering

Carly's inquiry but noticed the redness in her face and the faraway look in her eyes.

"Wh-What?" she stammered. "No, nothing's wrong, I was just thinking of something I forgot in my cabin. Sorry. But really, how are we going to handle this guy tonight?"

"We'll just have to play it by ear, but if we don't get moving, we'll never get a chance to meet this guy. We're late enough as it is. And by the way, where have you been all this time? I was getting ready to send out a search party for you."

Carly's ruse had backfired and she knew it. Not much got by Sam and he was not going to let her tardiness go unquestioned. Reluctantly, she told him that she was with Sean and had lost track of time.

"Be careful with him. I don't think you should get too close to him. He's a good boy and a pretty good diver, but he can get kind of high strung and I'm not sure he's the one for you."

Carly's face reddened again, only this time it was from anger, not embarrassment. "I don't live your life and I don't expect you to live mine. I can handle myself. You don't think I can judge a man's character?" Carly almost choked on the words as they came out, realizing that Sam knew her better than most and had usually been on the mark about her prior beaus. But Carly was not going to give Sam the satisfaction of acknowledging his point, so she pressed onward.

"I'm old enough to make my own decisions without consulting you first! Besides, I'm an educated girl who's been around long enough to learn from her mistakes."

Sam realized he was fighting a losing battle and did not want to argue with Carly, especially on the way to the benefit. He knew they would both have to be on the same team, allied together, if they were going to make their anticipated meeting with Stompmeyer work to their advantage. So instead of pursuing the conversation, he put his arm around her and walked her out of the cabin.

"Let's drop it. I'm sorry. We need to concentrate on the amulet and box. I'm not sure how to approach Stompmeyer, but I think we should get to the benefit and see if we can't facilitate a chance encounter with the professor."

Carly forced a smile and agreed, relieved to drop the subject of Sean and her past love life and mistakes. They were demons she did not want to face at this time. Together they left the boat and walked towards Sam's Lincoln, which was parked in its normal spot around the corner. Sam opened the passenger door for Carly and she slipped into the seat. As Sam closed the door and walked around towards the driver's side, the stranger slowly made his way towards a Volvo parked in the shadows. Jack wanted to warn his friends of the intruder, but thought better of it. He would need to follow this guy and find out what he was doing spying on them, but now was not the time to expose himself. He knew he could not leave his hiding place without showing himself, but thankfully he knew where Sam was headed. If the stranger was following Sam, Jack knew where to find them. Both Jack and the stranger waited until Sam pulled away from the curb. Jack watched the stranger slowly follow in the Volvo and made a mental note of the color, make, model and plate number. When Brian called back, he would have him run the information, but he did not want to interrupt Brian while he was delving into Stompmeyer's background.

Jack started to leave his hiding place but quickly froze. Was his mind playing tricks on him or did he hear the hum of a motor? He glanced around, but saw nothing. He waited and, after a few seconds, a black Mercedes slowly pulled out of the adjacent alleyway. Jack tried to get a better look at the car, but it was too dark and the car's windows were all tinted. Was he beginning to get too jumpy, he thought to himself? Then he realized that the Mercedes was pulling away without any headlights on. The occupant obviously did not want to be seen. No, Jack was not being jumpy. He knew his suspicions were accurate. Something was going on and he did not like it. If he didn't find out who these people were and what they wanted, he was afraid his friends would be in danger. As soon as it was safe, Jack ran to his car and headed towards the benefit. Although he didn't want to disturb Brian again, he knew he had to, so he called his friend and this time filled him in on what had occurred from the discovery of the amulet and box up to the two strangers. Brian was concerned for Jack's safety, but Jack brushed his friend's concerns aside. Brian wrote down the information on the two strange vehicles and promised to get back to Jack with information as quickly as possible. After they hung up, Jack began to wish he had Brian in Florida with him.

13

Sam slowly made his way through the Florida traffic and entered the interstate. It was not an extremely long ride to Hollywood, but it was long enough to give both him and Carly time to simmer down and make peace with each other. It was a cool night but the sky was clear and the stars shone brightly in the evening sky. Once on the interstate, the traffic seemed to dissipate and they had clear sailing most of the way.

It had been years since he had been at the Westin Diplomat. It was a luxurious hotel on the Atlantic with huge towers jutting up from the land and a magnificent view of the ocean and the surrounding coastline. The golf course was first class and many celebrities would attend the numerous events and gala charity affairs that were often held in one of the grandiose hotel ballrooms. As Sam wound the Lincoln through the manicured grounds of the hotel, he wondered how to approach Stompmeyer without arousing suspicion and without allowing the wrong people to overhear. He slowly pulled up to the entranceway as the valet approached to take his car.

"Checking in or attending the gala, sir?"

"We're attending the gala. Don't know how long we'll be."

"Very well sir. We'll take good care of your car for you," the valet responded as he took the keys from Sam.

Sam gave the valet a five dollar bill and he and Carly headed into the hotel as the valet pulled away with his car.

"Wow, this is some place," she exclaimed.

"It is Hollywood," Sam responded. "Let's see if we can find this Stompmeyer character and bend his ear before the crowd arrives."

The two of them headed towards the ballroom designated for the charity event. As they walked together, they did not notice the Volvo pull up, nor did they notice the tall, gangly stranger exit and furtively glance their way. If they had, they would have noticed that he did not quite fit in with the hotel's regular clientele, nor did he appear to be a patron of the arts attending a $500 per plate gala. The stranger slunk into the lobby, checking the exits and the guests milling around. He knew he could not attend the gala, as he had no ticket, but had to figure a way to follow his quarry without being noticed. He casually walked towards the ballroom area and eventually spied his means of entrance. There was his ticket in, quietly leaving for a quick smoke: the waiter fit his general description and his attire would allow him entry without suspicion. The stranger followed the unsuspecting waiter towards the exit and, as they left the ballroom area, the stranger glanced around, making sure no one saw him leave. When he felt it safe, he pulled the switchblade from his pocket, quietly came upon the waiter from behind and deftly slit the waiter's throat in a singular motion, slicing the carotid arteries of his victim. As he did so, he grabbed the waiter, gently guiding him to the ground, being careful not to get blood on the waiter's outfit, knowing he would need it to complete his plan of surveillance.

After stashing the waiter's corpse in a storeroom closet, the stranger quickly donned the waiter's uniform and reentered the ballroom to observe his quarry. Sam and Carly had already entered and were searching for the professor themselves when the stranger grabbed a tray of champagne and approached them.

"Champagne, madam? Sir?" he asked.

He needed to be within earshot of them to make sure the plan was going as anticipated. He also needed to make sure Stompmeyer played his part as directed. If anything went wrong, he would use the alternate plan they had devised. He would kidnap one or both of them in order to obtain the items retrieved from the ocean depths and find out where the rest of the treasure was located.

Carly took a glass of champagne from the waiter, but Sam brushed him off.

"No thanks. Not tonight."

"Very well, sir."

The stranger left and headed towards the closest group of people, still keeping a wary eye on Sam and Carly. They were there for about 45 minutes before they saw Stompmeyer arrive. The man was elegantly attired and played the part of the honored guest well. He barked out commands to the various waiters, parading around with his black cane glittering with silver and diamonds. He was, or at least appeared to be, in all aspects the proud German aristocrat, honored to be chosen as the guest of the museum benefit. Of course, nothing could be further from the truth. In reality, he detested those who attended such affairs. They knew nothing of the arts, nothing of history, nothing of the value, cultural and financial, of the various relics and artifacts uncovered over time. No, they only were interested in the public perception obtained by being "patrons of the arts." They were interested in the money and prestige that went with the title. By donating to such causes, the public would believe that they were charitable and reputable, and would thus spend their own money on the many corporate and commercial efforts of these patrons.

As he looked around, he spied those familiar banners with the red pyramids. What did the public care about Venezuelan oil? CITGO, one of the top ten oil companies in America, is controlled by a dictator who loathes the United States, calls for its demise, and demeans the country and its politicians, especially its president. Chavez, an outspoken critic of the United States, causes unrest throughout the world and pulls the strings of this "American" corporation, a wholly owned subsidiary of the national oil company of Venezuela. Chavez is the same man who nationalized the Venezuelan oil fields and threatened to do the same to the banks full of American corporate monies. But instead of rejecting this foreign intervention by this dictator, corporate America and a multitude of Americans choose to fund his excesses by purchasing fuel from him. While some have tried to boycott, the company unleashed their PR people to concoct a "charitable scheme" of donating oil to the needy. It's a valiant effort, but is no different from the Robber Barons of old, devouring all the wealth of the people, lining their pockets with gold and riches, then doling back some of the wealth to the general populace, a minute portion in comparison to what's taken. Yes, these "do-gooders" are detestable, only in it for their own interests. Of course, Stompmeyer had little room for criticism, having fallen victim to the excesses of humanity himself.

Stompmeyer entered the ballroom and a swarm of people immediately surrounded him trying to curry his favor, hoping to ingratiate themselves with him. He enjoyed every minute of their kowtowing and toyed with each for all it was worth, until the stranger approached with a tray of champagne.

"Would you like a glass, sir?"

Startled, Stompmeyer slowly broke away from the crowd and headed towards an obscure corner of the room while the stranger gleefully followed.

"Wh-what are you doing here?" Stompmeyer stammered.

"Just making sure you do as you were told and don't mess things up. They were worried about your initial reluctance to come and get involved."

"Who was worried?"

"Never mind! You just do as you're told and you won't need to worry about anything. See those two standing over by the balcony?"

"The old gentleman and young lady?"

"Yes, those two. They're the ones you are supposed to meet. Make sure you're not too anxious. We don't want to arouse any suspicion. The old man is the owner of the salvage ship. The girl is a marine archaeologist and something like a daughter to him. See what you can find out and report back to me as soon as you know anything. If I'm not here, I will see you in your room later tonight."

And with that the stranger handed the professor a glass of champagne, gave a slight bow, and headed back towards the crowd, furtively glancing from side to side to ensure that no one had observed his encounter with the professor.

14

As the Mercedes pulled up to the entranceway a valet rushed over towards the driver's door. The man inside handed the boy a crisp fifty dollar bill and told him to keep the Mercedes nearby.

"I've got some important business with a guest and then I must catch a plane at the airport so I don't have time to waste. This was a last minute meeting and it's cutting into my tight schedule. Keep the car ready for me, understand?"

The valet nodded in assent and held the door as the driver exited. The man was of normal height and appearance, in his forties, with a boyish face and captivating smile. He had indistinguishable features and looked like a stockbroker dressed in his two-button, taupe sharkskin suit. He spoke with a slight Eastern European accent, which the valet was unable to place. He walked with an arrogant strut and headed towards the lobby of the Westin. The man did not look back, assured that the valet would heed his request without hesitation. After a quick glance inside the lobby, he spied the stranger following Sam and Carly towards the elevator leading to the ballroom. He quickly deduced where they were heading and waited until they were all well on their way before entering an adjacent elevator. He pushed the button and headed up towards the ballroom, pondering why the stranger had followed his prey to the hotel. In his arrogance, he neglected to observe Jack watching with interest as the entire scene unfolded.

Jack had followed the stranger in the Volvo, as well as the sharkskin-suited pursuer, and had no idea what was going on. Why were they following Sam and Carly? At first Jack thought the stranger might have been someone associated with Carly's somewhat tawdry past. After all, he did have the appearance of someone she might have associated with in those earlier days, or at least a member of the crowd she hung out with. But the other guy was another story. He was not her type at all, and why would both take such pains to secretly follow her? Something more was going on.

Jack was tired and wanted to return to his wife, but he knew he had to get to the bottom of this. As his thoughts drifted to the tall, athletic brunette who was waiting patiently for him at his condo, he opened his cell phone and dialed.

"Honey, it looks like I'm going to be a little late. Something's come up and I need to deal with it before I come home."

She knew from Jack's tone that it was serious. They had been together for nearly thirty years and could read each other like a book.

"What's wrong?"

"Nothing, I hope, but I'm not sure. I need to check out some things and then I'll know for sure."

Alexandra knew better than to argue with him. "Where are you?" she asked him apprehensively.

"I'm at the Westin."

"What are you doing there? Are you there with Sam and

Carly? I thought they were going together."

"Not exactly," Jack quietly replied. "I can't get into it right now, but someone followed them here and I'm trying to figure out why. They don't know I'm here and I don't intend on letting them know yet."

Alexandra was beginning to worry. "Why don't you call the police?"

"And tell them what? That two guys followed my friends to a museum fundraiser? No, the police would not do anything and both these guys would know that someone was on to them, although on to what, I don't know. No, I think I'm going to sit back and study this thing a while. Besides, I'm waiting for Brian to call me. I've got him digging up some info for me."

Now Alexandra was really worried. Jack never called Brian while on vacation or during the night unless it was an emergency. Jack's bravado had won him many tight cases, but sometimes he thought himself a "James Bond" kind of guy, and that would often land him in trouble.

"Jack, you promised! No more hair-raising expeditions. No more cloak and dagger stuff. You haven't been a SEAL for years. You're a lawyer...and a husband and grandfather. You swore to me after that excursion in Venice that you would never put yourself in danger like that again! I want you home NOW!"

Alexandra was almost in tears and Jack was beginning to feel guilty, but he knew his friends were in danger and he had to discover what was going on before it was too late.

"Honey, this isn't Venice. I'm sure there's a simple explanation for all of this and it will be cleared up in no time."

But Jack wasn't so sure. Venice was another excursion that had turned into an adventure. He had been shot in the arm and barely escaped without more serious injuries, thanks to Brian and a few other friends. He had sworn to Alexandra then that he would not get involved in any more dangerous adventures. He hoped he would not be breaking his promise this time.

Jack was undeterred and Alexandra knew she was not going to win this discussion. "Be careful and call me soon. You've really got me worried now. Oh, and by the way, your granddaughter is scheduled to arrive on Friday. Apparently she put up such a fuss that *your* son finally relented and agreed to fly her down here while she recuperates. So you better wrap up this foolish business quickly."

Jack paused for a moment. "Paige is coming down here, now?"

"Why, is that a problem?"

"N-no, not at all," stammered Jack. "I should be able to wrap this up quickly. Oh, and don't worry, I'll be fine. I'll call you when I'm ready to leave."

Jack ended the call and made sure the phone was set on silent. He did not want his presence made known to the two strangers he had followed to the hotel. Jack arrived at the upper level where the Great Hall was located. He knew the fundraiser was taking place inside the Great Hall and slowly made his way around the hallway area searching for either stranger. It was then that he spied the first stranger exit the closet area dressed as a waiter.

"Now what the hell's going on?" Jack thought to himself.

Jack waited until the stranger entered the Great Hall, then quietly made his way towards the area that the stranger had just come from. He opened the door carefully and saw nothing but a storeroom with supplies. He was about to close the door when he saw the pool of red in the corner. He took a quick glance around, making sure no one was watching. As he entered the storeroom and slowly made his way to the corner, he knelt down for a closer inspection and his stomach suddenly became queasy. A sickening feeling overcame him. He had seen death before: in the war, as a prosecutor, and even as a defense attorney. Seeing death had never become easy for Jack. The eerie, unsettled feelings in the pit of his stomach he got when confronted with death only seemed to get worse with time. He constantly had to fight the nausea and dizziness he experienced at the sight of a dead body. Regardless of how he felt and the physical symptoms he exhibited, Jack knew he had to get a hold of himself and rationally evaluate the situation. True to form, he was able to block out the confusion in his mind, the desire to panic, and he calmly began to appraise the situation. Harkening back to his days prosecuting homicides, he realized he had to be careful not to disrupt the crime scene. Jack carefully peered into the corner and observed the dead waiter with his throat slit in what appeared to be one smooth line. He did not observe any other readily apparent injuries on the poor man, no other bruises or wounds. He knew that he had to get out of there quickly, without being seen.

Jack slowly backed away from the dead body and inched his way towards the exit, being careful not to disturb anything and making sure he did not touch the walls or any objects in the storeroom. Jack did not want to contaminate the scene any more than he may already have, and he definitely did not want to leave his own fingerprints for the detectives to find. He carefully opened the storeroom door and peered out, making sure the coast was clear. Seeing no one in the immediate vicinity, he quickly left the storeroom mausoleum and made his way back towards the Great Hall. He needed to make sure Sam and Carly were safe.

As Jack rounded the corner of the hall he jostled against the man in the taupe suit.

"Excuse me! I'm sorry, I did not see you there!" Jack exclaimed with sweat dripping from his brow.

"Are you all right?" the man asked with that European accent that Jack could not place.

"I'm fine, just a little queasy. I think I'm getting a bug or something," Jack lied, trying to cover up for his inattentiveness. "Are you attending the fundraiser?" he asked with an innocent smile.

"No, I was just looking for a friend of mine. I thought I saw him come up the elevator, but I seem to have lost sight of him," the man replied as he gazed around as if he were searching for someone. "How about you? Are you one of those museum benefactors I keep hearing about?"

"No, just a lawyer on a short vacation, hoping to get away from the stress of the courtroom for a little while." Jack was regaining his composure as the words continued to roll off his tongue, distorting the truth to cover up his reason for being in the hotel. The man appeared to be buying Jack's story and Jack felt relieved, but wanted to distance himself from the man as quickly as possible. He knew this man had nothing to do with the waiter's murder, or at least it did not appear so, but he needed to ensure his friends were safe and figure out a way to unravel this mystery without tipping either stranger off.

The man was beginning to act bored with the whole conversation and wanted to depart as well. After exchanging apologies one more time, both men left each other's presence. Jack took one final glance back as the man wandered into the Great Hall, seemingly greeting one of the guests as if they were long lost friends. But Jack knew better, having followed the man from the docks.

As Jack turned, he spied Sam and Carly and was careful to hide himself from them. He needed to make sure they did not see him. While the Great Hall was large, and several hundred guests were meandering through the ballroom conversing with the various museum staff and honored museum guests, Jack knew it was only a matter of time before Sam or Carly spied him, or before the stranger possibly recognized him from the dock. He needed a safe place where he could conceal himself, but still be able to maintain his surveillance of both strangers until he was able to uncover the purpose both men were trying to accomplish.

Jack found a large clump of decorative palm trees and decided that this was the best hiding spot. After finding an inconspicuous space nestled between the palms, he quietly observed the events unravel. Many movers and shakers of the local economy and political arenas had attended and were apparently trying to cement their places in society. He had not been situated for an extremely long time before he spied the gangly stranger and the professor, together in an unobtrusive corner of the ballroom. He could not hear what was being said, but it was obvious that each knew the other well.

"Coincidence, my foot!" Jack thought to himself. His suspicions had been confirmed. Luck had nothing to do with the arrival of the good professor. There was apparently a more sinister motive behind his appearance in Florida. It was clear to Jack that the amulet was the most obvious reason. But the pieces still were not falling into place. Why would an amulet found on a sunken ship bring together a German professor in archaeology, a killer, and third stranger, the man in the taupe suit? What was the connection? At least it appeared that the professor and the killer were both working for the same employer, whoever that may be. But what about the other stranger? What was his role? He also appeared to be tracking Sam and Carly, or was it the gangly stranger the man was after? Jack needed answers and he needed them quickly. He was uncomfortable in continuing this charade much longer, but he also did not want to interrupt Sam until he knew more. Hopefully he could contain the situation with the knowledge he had up to this point.

Jack continued to survey the gala and the attendees. He observed Sam and Carly, who both appeared to be enjoying themselves despite their initial reluctance to attend. The killer and the professor had separated and both were now mingling through the crowd. Absent from this scene was the third stranger, the man in the taupe suit. He had seemingly disappeared, vanishing in the Florida heat. Jack could not believe that the man would simply leave after taking such pains to follow his quarry to this location. Jack was sure the man was still around, but where?

Damn it, where the hell is Brian with his report. It shouldn't take this long to run down some information, Jack thought impatiently to himself. It seemed like days since he had last spoken to Brian requesting the background on the good professor, although it had only been less than two hours. But Jack knew that the sooner he had the information from Brian, the sooner he would be in a better position to formulate a plan of action. It was clear to Jack that he had to leave his hiding place before his presence was discovered by Sam or Carly, or even worse, by the gangly stranger.

Jack decided that it was time to up the ante and make something happen. He nonchalantly removed himself from between the palms and casually left the ballroom area hoping that no one had noticed his departure. As he left, he quickly glanced around. He saw the gangly stranger heading towards Carly as Sam approached the professor. Jack knew he had to make a move now before it was too late. Quietly, he made his way to the nearest house phone and dialed.

"Quick!" he cried. "Call the police! A man's been murdered! In the storeroom closet by the Great Hall! It's terrible!"

Just as quickly, Jack replaced the receiver and left the area. Jack hoped this would force the killer to vacate the area and at least give him some breathing room to deal with the professor.

15

"Professor Stompmeyer?" Sam held out his hand and offered it to the man with a smile. "I've long been an admirer of you and your expeditions. I've got a fleet of salvage boats and a keen interest in subjects of your expertise," Sam explained while chomping on his cigar and vigorously shaking the professor's hand.

"Really?" the professor replied, feigning surprise. "I'm proud to make your acquaintance, sir."

"Please, don't call me sir. It's Sam."

"Very well then, Sam. Have you discovered anything of interest as of late?" the professor shrewdly inquired, hoping not to be too conspicuous in his questioning.

"As a matter of fact, there was an item we discovered that we thought might be of interest to you."

"Really? What might that be?" the professor continued, still feigning ignorance.

Sam was a little uneasy jumping into the subject so early in the conversation, so instead he decided to change the tenor of the discussion. "I understand you are well versed in antiquities and ancient cultures?"

"Yes. I believe I am."

"Have you ever come across any ancient medallions?"

"Oh yes, many. Were you interested in any one in particular?"

"We found one which looks a lot like the Hand of Fate."

"It's been my experience that they were fairly common, both in the ancient world as well as today's society. What makes you think this one is ancient?"

"Well, it's encased within the Star of David, with eyes attached between the points with different colored stones." Sam was eagerly watching the professor, trying to gauge his reaction.

"Interesting." The professor was stroking his beard while glancing around through the crowd. In the corner the gangly stranger, although appearing to serve hors d'oeuvres to the guests, smiled approvingly at the two men conversing. The professor began to sweat, feeling the piercing sting of the stranger's smile and glare. "I'm not sure if I have ever seen such an item. Do you have it with you?" he asked Sam with a slight smile on his face.

"No, I'm sorry, I don't. Anyway, can you tell me about your most exciting discovery? I'm really quite interested in your work. I understand you have traveled and explored an extensive portion of the Middle East." Sam was trying to be careful and not divulge too much information without feeling the fellow out first.

The professor was not deceived by Sam's obvious attempt to change the subject. He knew the man was trying to feel him out, so he led him on, giving him what he hoped he wanted to hear. "There have been so many exciting discoveries, I'm not sure I can choose one which stands out as the *most* exciting. I have enjoyed excavating many ruins throughout Israel and ancient Palestine. I recall once unearthing an ancient Jewish town from King Solomon's time beneath an old Arab village north of Nazareth in the Galilee. We even found remnants of a settlement in the same area dating back to the last Jewish revolt during Roman times, around the time of the destruction of the Second Temple, replete with underground tunnels. Some of the pottery and other utensils dated between 60 A.D. to 70 A.D."

Sam's jaw fell and his face could not hide the astonishment he felt. This man had certainly experienced many things foreign to yet, in a bizarre way, also close to Sam's heart. He was about to trust this man with his soul when the sound of alarms and sirens interrupted their conversation along with the music and laughter heard within the ballroom walls.

"What the devil is that?" the professor asked.

"Sounds like sirens. Police or ambulance, I think," Sam replied, looking a little shaken.

Just then Carly came running over to Sam. "Did you hear? There's been a murder!" Carly exclaimed with a combination of shock and terror in her voice. "Some waiter had his throat slit right here under our noses. This is awful." Carly was nearly in tears and beside herself.

Sam cradled his arms around the girl and tried to calm her. "Slow down, girl. What's that you say? A murder? How do you know it's not some prank?" Sam asked incredulously.

"The police commissioner was in the group I was talking to when a cop came up and whispered something about it in his ear, only it was loud enough for me to hear. I saw the commissioner's face turn white and he quickly ran out of the room with the cop. I followed and got a glimpse of the body before the cops cordoned the place off and made me return to the ballroom. It was awful!" Carly broke into tears again and gave an uncontrollable wail.

"Easy now." Sam gently patted her back. "I'm sure it will all be fine. The police should discover the culprit and sort this thing out quickly. It was probably some jealous husband or enforcer for some gambling debt. Let's get you a drink and settle you down.

"You'll excuse me, professor. We'll have to continue our conversation some other time. I'm sorry, but I must attend to my niece." Sam politely turned and gently walked Carly towards one of the nearby tables.

The professor nodded sympathetically as he watched the two walk away. He then turned and glared at the gangly stranger. This was not the first time the man's impetuousness had interrupted one of the professor's missions. The man was dangerous and clearly a liability. Why was he the only one who saw it? He would have to report back to his employers and explain the danger in persisting with this maniac tagging along. The man's foolish actions may well have jeopardized the entire evening. The stranger merely glared back at the professor, seeming to read the man's thoughts. Goose bumps ran down the professor's spine and he glanced away, afraid to reveal the trepidation which had come over him. As he glanced back, he saw his compatriot disappear into the crowd. The professor knew that the man would be back in the shadows of his life soon, and the momentary failure of the killer's actions would not dissuade him as easily as the professor had been. With a faint sigh, the professor turned to retire to his room when he spied Sam and Carly. He began to approach them when he was intercepted by a police officer.

"Excuse me, sir, may I have a word with you? We're trying to speak to everyone in the hotel. Have you seen anything or anyone unusual tonight?"

"No, I don't think so. Why, what's wrong? Did something happen or did someone get hurt?" the professor said, feigning surprise.

"It appears that one of the hotel employees has been murdered. Are you sure you didn't hear or see anything unusual or out of the ordinary? It's really important. Please take a moment to think."

Stompmeyer stood pensively for a few moments before replying, "No, I'm sorry. I only arrived from the airport shortly before entering the fundraiser. I barely had time to change and ready myself for the event. I saw no one in the halls, having arrived late, and immediately began mingling with the others. Since I am unfamiliar with the hotel, as well as the area, I would not know what would be out of the ordinary or suspicious. I'm sorry I can't be of more help, but I do wish you luck. May I retire to my room now? This whole experience has made me extremely anxious and I would really like to lie down."

"Of course," the detective responded. "Sorry to inconvenience you. If you think of anything which might be helpful or hear anyone talking about it, please give me a ring. Here's my card."

The professor took the card from the man, gave a slight bow, then turned away and headed towards the exit, making sure not to appear to be moving too hastily or casting any suspicion upon himself.

16

"You fool. What were you thinking! You not only brought unneeded attention to this event, but may have caused irreparable damage to my efforts to gain the salvage man's trust." The "salvage man" comment was referring to Sam. "You'd better be sure you were not seen by anyone, and I don't want anyone seeing you leave this room. You had best stay away from me until I have assayed the situation and hopefully convinced Mr. Katz that he needs my help. I know how to reach you if and when I need you. Now get out of here!"

Hermann Stompmeyer was normally a calm man, not prone to violent outbursts. While he was used to being in command on one of his digs, he was normally not so aggressive when dealing with the Cartel's enforcer. But this time the man had pushed him too far and had jeopardized the task he had been entrusted with. The professor's superiors would not be pleased with what had occurred and Stompmeyer drew his strength from such knowledge. Dmitry Petrov, the gangly stranger, had now become dispensable and a liability in Stompmeyer's eyes, and the professor saw an opportunity to rid himself of this barbarian. As soon as he could get the man out of his hotel room, he intended on contacting his superiors to have the man recalled. It was enough of an affront to have been shadowed by this murderer, but to have been ordered around and threatened by him was well beneath a man of his station, an aristocrat such as himself.

Dmitry Petrov was not a man to trifle with. He looked much younger than his sixty-two years. He had survived several communist regimes during the various stages of the decline of the Soviet Union. Although born of peasant parents in a small village outside Kiev, he rose quickly through the ranks of the Soviet Army and was soon recruited by the KGB and taught the various art of interrogation, self-defense and espionage. His enemies often underestimated Dmitry's cunning and skill. All they saw before them was the tall, gangly man who looked liked an emaciated version of a string bean; a man who had an awkward appearance, always looking disheveled, with thin, greasy, stringy black hair partially covering his eyes. He was an expert marksman, well versed in all forms of weaponry. He had killed many men while in the service of his country and thoroughly enjoyed fulfilling what he saw was his duty. Perhaps it was his enjoyment of the act of killing that eventually led to his departure from the KGB. While he was an expert at the spy game, he grew bolder, more arrogant as the years progressed. He became quick-tempered and would indiscriminately view friends and foes, superiors and subordinates in the same light. One day he was unceremoniously handed his walking papers and escorted out the door, told never to return to Lubyanka.

It was shortly after that fateful day that the Soviet Union disbanded and chaos reigned in the new Russia. Soon the Russian Mafia began to thrive, and men like Dmitry were needed. He did not remain unemployed for long and his many skills ensured his quick rise through the hierarchy. It was at that point that the Cartel approached him, and soon he became, or so he thought, an indispensable member of the inner circle.

Just who did this poor excuse for a German aristocrat think he was talking to? Dmitry had paid his dues and had proved his worth ten times over. What had this man done for the Cartel? The blood began to boil in Dmitry's veins and he became exasperated. With clenched fists he turned and began to speak, "You do not order me around! I do not answer to you! I watch you to make sure you do your job as you were ordered, without interference from others. Those are *my* orders!"

The professor was unshaken. Instead of backing away from Dmitry, he took a step forward. He picked up his cane and pointed towards the door. "Leave immediately! This is the last time I will tell you. My next act will be to call our employers."

Dmitry unclenched his fists. In one catlike move he had grabbed the professor's throat, pushing him back against the wall. "Do not ever threaten me again. I am not your servant and you are surely not my superior. I could snuff you out like a flame in less than one second if I so desired."

Stompmeyer saw the blackness in the man's eyes, one hazel and one grey. An odd combination, he thought. "And what do you intend to do, slit my throat like you did the waiter's?" he asked his attacker. "I'm sure you can easily explain my absence to our mutual friends abroad."

The point hit home. Dmitry released his grasp and let the man go.

"I will leave now, but I will be waiting for your call. Do not disappoint me or keep me waiting too long. Remember, I know how to find you."

Without another word, he turned and slid out the door. Stompmeyer was relieved the man had left and was pleased at the strength he had shown in standing up to the killer. After taking a moment to regain his composure, he picked up his cell phone and dialed the international number he had programmed into its memory years ago. "It's me. We have a situation that needs to be addressed immediately if you expect me to succeed in my task." Stompmeyer recounted the evening's events before retiring, pleased at how he had handled himself and the situation thrust upon him by that maniac Dmitry.

17

Jack watched as the professor left the ballroom after being interviewed by the detective. Although no one else noticed, he observed the professor look back in apparent trepidation several times. *Good,* he thought to himself. *At least the professor isn't so sure he's in the clear yet. Hopefully he won't be too anxious to continue his conversation with Sam. At least not until I've had a chance to find out more about him and warn Sam.*

. . .

JACK SILENTLY EXITED the hotel after ensuring that the professor and the killer were no longer a threat to Sam or Carly. As he headed towards his car, he noticed that the Mercedes was no longer in sight. Clearly the man in the taupe suit had decided not to stick around while the police were investigating the waiter's murder. Jack was unable to locate the killer's Volvo, but assumed he had fled the area rather than answer questions from any inquisitive policeman. What Jack didn't realize was that the killer had not left the hotel, but instead was having a confrontation with the professor in Stompmeyer's room.

As Jack slid behind the wheel of his car his cell phone rang. He looked at the caller ID and saw it was Brian. "It's about time you called. I thought I would never hear from you."

"Cool your jets, man," Brian responded. "These things take time. I had to pull in huge favors to get the answers you were looking for."

"Okay! Sorry I'm so impatient, but the stakes have gone up. Stompmeyer's associate, or at least I think he is, just murdered someone."

"Are you okay?" Brian asked worriedly. "I'm catching the next plane down there. These guys are for real and you don't need to be playing with them."

"What do you mean?" Jack asked.

"Stompmeyer's a well-recognized expert in archaeology, but he comes with a lot of baggage and shady connections. No one has ever been able to pin anything on him, but it's believed he's involved with an organized crime Cartel of international proportion. Interpol has been watching this guy for years with no concrete results. It seems that he has led a charmed life and been able to slip out of any sticky situation. He's made millions through his 'discoveries' and has adapted to an aristocratic lifestyle. He even lives in a castle, moat and all!"

"What about his public appearances? Anything on his scheduled itinerary?" Jack asked.

"That's just it. He's got no public itinerary. He seems to show up when there's something for the Cartel to gain," Brian explained.

"Any idea when he agreed to appear at the museum's benefit?" Jack knew he was on to something and was almost afraid to hear Brian's answer.

"Yeah. It appears one of the sponsors received a call from

this guy's supposed representative three days ago advising that
Stompmeyer was scheduled to meet some socialite in the area,
had heard about the fundraiser, and offered his services. The
museum apparently jumped at the chance, thinking they could
cash in on someone of Stompmeyer's celebrity character and
maybe even use the guy's connection with this socialite to pick
up additional bucks."

Jack was more convinced than ever that the professor was
a threat to their discovery. "Brian, I think I'll take you up on
your offer. You still willing to fly down here?"

"Hell yeah. I was getting bored laying around in the 'Apple'
anyway. Let me make some arrangements and I should be able
to leave tomorrow."

"Thanks," replied a relieved Jack. "I'll tell Alexandra you're
coming. You can stay at the condo with us. We've got lots of
room."

Jack's mind was reeling. Their little treasure hunting
excursion had gotten them involved with organized crime and
a murder investigation. He knew he could never convince Sam
to back away from his discovery, but they needed to develop a
plan before the professor realized they were on to him.

Jack decided he had better head home to Alexandra before
returning to the boat. On his way to the condo he called the
boat. "Tom? It's Jack. Has Sam returned?"

"Not yet. It's too early. They should still be at the fundraiser."

"I doubt that. There's been a little trouble and they should
be on their way back. Listen carefully. Don't let anyone else
on the boat and don't let anyone leave once Sam and Carly
return. Oh, and whatever you do, don't let them talk to that
Stompmeyer guy until I get there."

"What are you talking about? Are they all right?" Tom asked
with a cracking voice.

"They should be fine, but Stompmeyer's not what he
appears to be and I don't want him near the boat until I can

fill you all in. But be careful, don't spook him. He runs with a dangerous crowd."

"Yeah, right. Mummies and other spooks," Tom responded in a sarcastic tone.

"I'm serious. There's already been one murder!"

"What are you talking about?"

"A waiter at the fundraiser was murdered by Stompmeyer's associate. I can explain more later, but just do as I say until I get there, understand?" Jack was in no mood to get into a long explanation and was not about to discuss the matter any further.

Tom realized that Jack was serious and he agreed to follow his instructions.

Relieved, Jack pulled into the condo complex, waving at the guard at the gate as he drove by. A few minutes later he opened the door to his condo and was met by Alexandra.

"What in the world is going on? Where have you been all this time and why is Brian involved?" Alexandra was rambling on, her green eyes blazing with anger and worry.

"Hold on a minute and I'll explain. Don't I even get a kiss or hug hello first, hon?" Jack reached out for her, but was instantly pushed away.

"Don't you 'hon' me, Jack Matthew Talbot!" she roared back.

Jack was beginning to get nervous. He knew she was in no mood to hear explanations judging from her demeanor, and once she pushed him away and used his full name, he knew there would be no talking to her.

"Honey, calm down a minute and listen. I'm trying to explain if you'll just give me a chance." Jack's tone was more serious now, without the levity from earlier. Alexandra just glared at him, but she did not move or speak, which Jack took as a good sign, a sign that she was beginning to melt and he was starting to get through.

Jack tried to calmly describe the evening's events to her.

He filled her in on the discovery of the amulet and the strange box with the ancient writing hidden inside. After explaining the purpose of Sam's excursion to meet the professor, he recounted his discovery of the two strangers and the strange occurrences of the evening. As he described his discovery of the murdered waiter, Alexandra gasped and began to tremble.

"What in God's name have you gotten yourself into, Jack Matthew Talbot?"

This is not good, he thought to himself. *She's resumed using my full name.*

"I didn't get myself into anything. Sam's on the verge of an important discovery and he needs my help." Jack was hoping he could play on Alexandra's feelings and her relationship with Sam to quell her fears and trepidation.

"Sam can take care of himself. What are the police doing about all this?"

"They're investigating the murder, as far as I know." Jack could feel his progress slowly slipping. He could tell that this discussion was not going to end the way he had hoped.

"What do you mean, 'as far as you know'?" She was talking slower now, which was never a good sign. "Don't tell me you never spoke to the police! Are you insane?" Alexandra was beside herself by this time.

"Honey, listen. I didn't see the guy commit the murder and I can't say for sure that it was related to Sam's discovery. It's all conjecture on my part. If I went to the police with what I know so far, a lot of innocent people could be hurt. Even this Stompmeyer's reputation could be ruined if I'm wrong."

Alexandra's eyes were beginning to well up. Her look began to soften and Jack knew he was beginning to get through to her.

"Look, you're not Rambo, you know. You're just a semi-retired lawyer on a short vacation expecting to do a little diving. You're not Indiana Jones or James Bond, so what are you trying to prove?" Alexandra spoke not out of anger now, but out of real concern.

"I'm not trying to be a superhero. I'm just trying to help my friend and protect him. If I had gone to the police and told them what I know and what I suspect, even if they believed me, it would only have made matters worse. If either of the strangers had been located, I doubt they would have divulged anything and the police would ultimately have had to release them. The same goes for Stompmeyer. And then those guys would have realized that we were aware of who they were and they would probably disappear and someone else would take their places. We would have no idea who had taken their places, and the crew would be in even more danger. As long as we know who the enemy is, we can be wary of them and control what they know."

Jack was trying to convince Alexandra of the practicality of his actions just as he was trying to convince himself. But he was also beginning to develop a plan of action. *Yeah,* Jack thought to himself. *Keep your friends close by and your enemies even closer. It might just work.*

"Besides," Jack continued, "Brian should be here tomorrow and you know how good he is at gathering intelligence. He told me he had some friends in the area who could keep a watch on the crew. So you see, there's really nothing to worry about."

Jack moved closer to his wife and put his arms around her. He could feel the tension slip away from her body and the two embraced fervently. Jack knew he had to get back to the boat soon, but he could not leave his wife just yet.

"It's just that I love you so much and worry so about you," Alexandra dotingly said.

Jack realized Alexandra was concerned, but he felt obligated to warn Sam and the others and help them see this thing through. After explaining this to his wife and assuring her that there was no need to worry, Jack left the condo and headed for the docks, praying that his assurances and promises were correct.

18

As Jack headed towards the *Scavenger* he gazed up at the night sky. There were no stars out, but a sliver of moon floated in the twilight like a fluorescent pencil stroke held high. The ocean waves crested on the beach as a cool breeze blew in from the water. Palm trees swayed gently from side to side and Jack thought to himself that this would have been a beautiful evening any other time, had the chaos and violence earlier not occurred.

Jack slowed as he approached the dock and parked. He looked around, hoping not to see either of the two strangers from earlier in the evening. Seeing no intruders, he left the safety of his car and slowly walked down the dock. As he neared the *Scavenger* he spied Billy standing watch. *Good,* he thought to himself, *at least Tom took my warning seriously and Sam didn't give him a hard time.*

"Hey Billy, everything quiet so far?"

"Not a peep. Tom said we would be seeing you tonight. What's up with all the security?"

"I'll fill you all in later. I've got to speak to Sam first. Where is he?"

"Up here!" Sam bellowed from the bridge. "What's all this fuss?"

Jack boarded the ship and met Sam on the bridge. After filling him in on his observations from earlier in the evening, he asked Sam about his meeting with the professor. Relieved that the meeting had not progressed too far before the police arrived as a result of Jack's anonymous call, the two retired inside to the main cabin, where Tom and the others were anxiously waiting.

"You were at the hotel this evening?" Sam asked Jack.

"How come we didn't see you?" Carly questioned.

Jack described to the crew how he had seen the gangly stranger watching the ship and, becoming suspicious, had waited until Sam and Carly had left with the two strangers following at a distance. As he continued to relate the events of the evening, Carly glanced towards Sean with fear in her eyes. Sean moved closer to Carly and assured her everything would be all right. The rest of the crew looked on as they began to understand the relationship beginning to develop between Sean and Carly.

"I don't want to break up anything between you two lovebirds, but we've got a real problem here and we need to concentrate on how we're going to deal with it." Tom was obviously annoyed and did not intend to hold anything back.

"If this professor was sent to find out more about our medallion and box, how did he learn about it?" Tom continued to take the lead and expressed the concern that Jack and Sam had both felt.

"Are you sure your buddies at the science lab didn't talk to anyone?" Tom grilled Geoff.

Geoff assured Tom and the others that his friends at CMRC often dealt with highly classified information and would not have divulged their find to anyone on the outside.

"Well, how else could an outsider have found out?" Tom continued. "Did any of you talk to anyone outside of this room about the box or the amulet?" Tom looked around at each member of the crew.

"Billy and I haven't left the boat since we docked," Jim assured Tom, "and no one called in or out."

All eyes turned to Sean and Carly.

"The two of you went out the first night we docked, didn't you?" Billy exclaimed, jumping up.

"Yeah, and you guys really tied one on that night. I saw you carrying Carly in all tanked up," Jim joined in.

Sam stood up and faced the two of them. "Is that so? Did either of you say anything to anyone that night? And just how drunk were you?" Sam was obviously upset, but was it at the possible leak or was there something else?

"Calm down, old man." Sean was obviously not going to allow anyone to place the blame on him. "I found that amulet and led you to the wreck. I've got just as much a stake in this as any of you, maybe even more. Do you think I would be foolish enough to blow it by bragging about it to everyone before we even loaded up any treasure?"

Carly looked hesitantly at Sean, her mind racing, trying to remember what they had said and done that evening at the bar. Something was eating at her from deep in the recesses of her alcohol-clouded mind, but she just could not recall what, and Sean's argument made sense to her, so she moved closer to him, grabbing him by the arm; then she roared out, "I can't believe you would even insinuate such a thing!"

"Hold on everyone," Jack interrupted. "Let's try not to cast blame on anyone. We need to keep calm and try to rationally figure out how this leak came out so we can deal with it appropriately. Until we figure it out, we can't know how to deal with the professor and our two strangers."

They all looked at each other and nodded in agreement.

"Let's backtrack," Sam began. "If Billy and Jim never left the ship or spoke to anyone, it would appear that rules them out. Tom, what about you? Have you seen or spoken to anyone else?"

Tom thought hard and replied that he had barely left the boat. He had not mentioned the find to anyone.

"Well, other than Jack, I haven't spoken to anyone about the box or medallion," Sam volunteered. "In fact, when I spoke to Jack, I don't think I even told him about the treasure until he boarded the ship, did I?" Sam looked at Jack with questioning eyes.

"No, Sam. I knew nothing about the substance of the find until I boarded the boat. You told me you had something to show me, but told me nothing more."

Sam let out a deep sigh of relief, satisfied that he was not the source of the leak, which also meant he was not the cause of the poor waiter's murder.

"Was there anyone else with you when you showed the box at the lab?" Sam turned toward Geoff.

Geoff thought for a few moments then replied, "I'm not sure. I really can't remember, but I don't think so." He had forgotten about the incident with Hector.

After the entire crew had questioned each other one more time, Sam looked at Jack and asked, "What are we going to do now?"

Jack began to fill them in on his plan. All were admonished not to divulge any information to any outsider. They then developed their strategy in dealing with the professor. It was decided that his expertise was needed, and they attempted to devise a way to use his knowledge without letting him learn too much about the shipwreck. Sam elected to contact the professor at his hotel and convince him to board the *Scavenger* to view his find. They hoped that once he was aboard the boat, they could head out to sea without providing the professor the opportunity to contact any of his cohorts.

19

The crew began to ready the *Scavenger* for the next expedition. Oxygen tanks were loaded and filled, and the booms and motors were checked and rechecked for any defects. No one was going to take any chances of failure on this voyage out. There was too much at stake, and time would definitely not be on their side, not if there were others out there also seeking the treasure.

Extra copies of the photos of the box and the parchment were made, and the originals were secured by Sam in the ship's safe. They had decided to try to keep the original from the professor as long as possible.

Sam had contacted the professor at his hotel and scheduled an appointment to meet with him later that afternoon. Apparently the professor had changed his plans about staying with the wealthy Palm Beach socialite after the hotel murder was discovered. He did not want to bring any undue attention upon the socialite, knowing that she might be needed later on as a vital contact with his superiors if his rendezvous with Sam and his crew proved rewarding.

Brian arrived right on schedule and was settling in at Jack's condo. Alexandra was still giving Jack the cold shoulder, but seemed glad that Brian was going to be staying with her. Brian filled Jack in on the rest of the intelligence he and his contacts had gathered.

"Apparently the guy you tailed to the hotel was driving a Volvo registered to the Romanian embassy. Those plates were diplomatic plates. My friends at Interpol have been extremely interested in an underground enclave of stolen antiquities collectors. They've suspected our good professor for being associated with this group for quite some time, but they've never been able to get any solid proof. In fact, other than rumors, there is no real proof of the group's existence."

Alexandra was now listening intently as Brian continued to divulge the results of his inquiries to Jack. "So now you guys are going out looking for ghosts along with sunken treasures?" she sarcastically commented.

Brian was undeterred. "There have been a number of unexplained deaths throughout Europe over the last two decades that Interpol has kept open in their own 'Cold Case' files. Apparently, after the fall of the Soviet Union, all kinds of gangsters and other unsavory types began appearing throughout Eastern Europe. The Iron Curtain was secretive enough, and us westerners knew little about the USSR, other than what our government or theirs wanted us to know. Hungary, Slovakia, Romania, Poland, Yugoslavia and all those other Cold War countries were basically off limits to most of us. There's a lot of dark, secret stuff hidden in those old countrysides. Spooky castles and caves and who knows what. Dracula's castle in Romania, Slovakia's haunted castle of

Cachtice, and countless others. Many of those places became excellent hiding spots for the old communists, who were no better than red gangsters."

"So what are you trying to tell us?" Alexandra was confused. "How does all this relate to some shipwreck off the coast of Florida?"

"I don't know," Brian said with a sigh, "but at least one of the cars that followed Sam to the Westin was registered to the Romanian embassy and has no business being in southern Florida."

"What about the Mercedes I saw?" Jack asked. "Were you able to find out anything about it?"

"Unfortunately, no. For some reason the plates don't seem to be registered to anyone. But I've still got one of my guys looking into it further."

"So what connects a Romanian diplomat and a German archaeologist?" Jack asked aloud.

"What if the guy's not a Romanian diplomat?" Alexandra was now intrigued by the mystery and began to offer her insight. "Suppose your murderer stole the diplomatic plates and used them to ease his travel throughout the U.S.?"

"I thought of that, but there have not been any reports of stolen diplomatic plates or vehicles," Brian replied.

"Suppose the theft has not been uncovered yet," Alexandra continued.

"It's a possibility, but there's no way we can get the Romanian government to look into the matter without tipping off our murderer."

"Brian's right, honey. But thanks for the insight." Jack was grateful that Alexandra was beginning to get interested in their search.

"This doesn't mean that anything's changed. I'm just trying to understand what kind of foolishness you're getting yourself into," replied Alexandra with a cold, icy stare.

Jack quickly turned back to Brian and asked him if he had gathered any other intelligence that could prove useful. After hearing that Brian had no other useful information to offer, Jack got his stuff together and readied himself for the voyage out to the shipwreck.

20

Carly was seething in her cabin. Sam had left her on the ship, refusing to bring her along to his meeting with Stompmeyer, claiming it would be too dangerous. Although she realized that his fears were warranted if Jack's concerns about the professor were accurate, she had a hard time believing a scientist with Stompmeyer's credentials could be connected to such a nefarious act. She decided to learn as much as she could about the professor and Googled his name on her laptop. While she surfed the internet, Sam was on his way to the Westin to meet with the professor. Tom insisted that Sam not go alone, so he sent Geoff with Sam.

Upon arriving at the Westin, Sam and Geoff entered the lobby and proceeded toward the elevators leading to the club-level suites. As they waited for the elevator to arrive, Geoff sensed they were being watched. He glanced around. Since it was midday, the lobby was fairly crowded. Guests were checking out and there were some early arrivals attempting to register.

Others were milling about, waiting for their spouses, or for the remainder of their party to meet them so they could begin the day's activities. A few lone stragglers were looking at maps or other brochures, or biding their time on the sofas or chairs reading the morning's newspaper. As he looked around, he thought to himself that most of the occupants looked strange, but none of them appeared to be spying on Sam or himself. Eventually the elevator arrived and the door slid open. A young couple exited, smiling and holding hands, while a tall, thin and gangly man brushed by the two men pushing Geoff into Sam. The man spoke with an accent, apologizing for his awkwardness. Geoff nodded back at the man, who seemed to give a strange smile, even though he never looked Geoff straight in the eye. Sam and Geoff entered the elevator and Sam pushed the button for the club-level floor. As the door closed, Geoff turned towards Sam.

"Is it me or was that guy weird?"

"Which guy are you talking about?"

"The one that pushed me into you."

"I really didn't notice. Let's keep focused on our meeting." Sam was in no mood for any distractions.

Dmitry settled into one of the lobby chairs and smiled. To any onlooker, it appeared that he was wearing headphones listening to an iPod or some similar apparatus. As he nestled into the chair, he remotely activated Geoff's cell phone and began recording the entire conversation. He was glad he had the foresight to implant the Trojan in Geoff's cell phone. It was a stroke of luck that Sam had brought Geoff along. Dmitry had originally planned on returning to his car and activating the bug implanted in Stompmeyer's room, but Geoff's appearance provided an opportunity he did not want to waste. Once he had obtained a list of Sam's crew, it was a simple matter to acquire the crew's cell phone numbers. By choosing the crew leader, Dmitry was sure he would be kept abreast of all the important information. It was then a simple task for him to send a text message to Geoff's phone, ostensibly from Geoff's cell phone provider offering updates. Once Geoff called the number for the updates, the Trojan was uploaded and installed. It appeared to be working well, and Dmitry was able to overhear the entire conversation between the two. Hopefully he would also be able to overhear their meeting with Stompmeyer. He was taking no chances with the old fool and would make sure he was nearby if and when the treasure was found.

21

Stompmeyer was anxiously awaiting Sam and Geoff's arrival. When they knocked on his door, he could barely contain his excitement. He knew they would be coming to him for assistance regarding some treasure, but had to conceal his knowledge of the purpose of their meeting in order to gain their trust.

"Ah, Mr. Katz. You arrived here quickly since our telephone conversation. Please do come in." Stompmeyer held out his hand to greet the two men cordially.

Sam and Geoff entered the suite and looked around at the luxurious accommodations. It was a rather large room, decorated in a modern style, with a large seating area consisting of two sofas and several chairs. There was a small dining table in the corner adjacent to the wall. Most of the walls consisted of windows stretching from one foot above the floor to approximately two feet below the ceiling. Gazing out from the windows, the men were greeted with an extraordinary view of the ocean and Intracoastal Waterway. It was midday and the sun was a giant orange ball reflecting off the water. Both men were amazed at the view from the room and simultaneously turned towards their host.

"This is an amazing view you have here. I'm glad you agreed to meet us. Professor Stompmeyer, this is Geoffrey Tanner, one of the men from my ship. I believe that when we met at the museum fundraiser, I told you I was involved in shipwreck recovery."

"I do recall some of our brief conversation before the police barged in and disrupted everything," the professor replied, playing coy.

"That was a terrible revelation hearing about a murder in this hotel," the professor continued. "I considered returning to Europe or, at the very least, checking out of this place into safer environs. The hotel staff insisted I stay and convinced me that the property was really quite safe. After careful consideration and many assurances from the hotel, including this kind upgrade to one of these beautiful suites, I decided to stay. Please, Mr. Katz, would you and your associate kindly be seated while I order some refreshments?"

"Thank you, professor," Sam responded courteously. "As I understand it, you are quite an expert in antiquities."

"I believe you exaggerate my expertise, but thank you, sir."

Sam continued to speak in generalities while he felt the professor out. The professor deftly dodged most of Sam's questions regarding his means of employment and elegant lifestyle. The professor tried to convince Sam that he had descended from an aristocratic family and, through his lineage, he had made the acquaintance of many wealthy benefactors who were always interested in collecting antiquities and assisting the arts in locating lost treasures for the many museums to put on display.

Sam and Geoff watched as the professor pontificated,

buying none of his propaganda. They both thought to themselves that it was a good thing Jack had discovered the professor's association with the man who had followed Sam and Carly to the hotel the other evening. If they had not been armed with that knowledge, they probably would have been captivated by the professor's distortions and would have naively divulged all they knew about the medallion, the box and the shipwreck.

"Professor," Sam interrupted, "have you ever seen a medallion similar to this in your studies?"

Sam held out one of the photos of the medallion and closely watched the reaction on the man's face.

"It is quite difficult to tell without examining the actual item. Do you have it here with you?"

"Unfortunately we do not. But this photo has been enlarged to provide as much detail as possible. Can you tell us anything about it?" Sam was playing it close to the vest and was not prepared to divulge any more without some affirmative response from the man.

The professor reached out and examined the photograph more closely. He reached for a magnifying glass laying on the desk and looked closely at the stones. "These stones all appear to be of the same caliber, but they each appear to be of a different variety. Have you had the stones examined for authenticity and type?"

"Unfortunately, we have not yet been able to do that. We were afraid any examination would cause the medallion to deteriorate," Geoff explained to the professor, being partially truthful in his explanation to the man.

"What about the design? Does that tell you anything?" Sam was beginning to push, hoping for an answer before showing the contents of the box.

"I'm afraid that I cannot tell you much more without examining the medallion or learning more about the dating of the piece or types of stones which make up this piece. I'm sorry." Stompmeyer had been playing coy throughout the discussion but at this moment was being entirely truthful.

"Many different peoples have crafted medallions such as this through the ages, some with the evil eye, some without. The hand has been used to ward off evil spirits through the ages. Mideastern cultures have identified with the hand over the centuries. The Arabs called the hand 'Hamsa,' or 'Hand of Fatima,' referring to the daughter of Mohammed. The Jews would call it a 'Hamesh,' or 'Hand of Miriam,' in reference to the sister of Moses and Aaron. There have even been some discoveries pointing to its existence prior to both Judaism and Islam. There have been some archaeological discoveries which indicate the hand referred to an ancient Mideastern goddess, whose hand would ward off the evil eye."

The professor was certainly knowledgeable about such artifacts, but had revealed nothing to them that Carly had not uncovered during her internet search on the ship.

"But have you ever seen the hand, the eye, and the Star of David in one amulet such as this?" Sam was growing impatient and was hoping to get more of an answer than a Google search would uncover.

"Unfortunately, no. Perhaps the design is a modern replica lost by some guest on a cruise ship. I understand you get many cruise ships in the area."

Sam realized that the professor either would not or could not provide any more information on the amulet. He reached into his pocket and produced the photo of the parchment retrieved from the box.

"What do you make of this? We found it near the amulet and thought it might be of some guidance." Sam handed the photo to the professor.

Stompmeyer could not contain his surprise upon viewing the photo. "Where did you get this?" he exclaimed. "Do you have the original parchment? I will need to examine it more closely."

"Exactly what is it?" Sam asked.

"It looks like ancient Hebrew, but I can't be sure unless I examine the original."

Both Sam and Geoff looked at each other and thought the same thing. *He knows exactly what it is, but obviously doesn't want to explain it.*

"Can you translate any of it from the picture?" Geoff asked the professor.

"It's hard. The lettering is not so clear. There appears to be a reference to stones. I will really need to examine the original parchment. Can you bring it here to me?"

"That's not possible," Geoff quickly answered. "The parchment appeared to be very old and brittle. We did not want to risk its destruction so we kept it on the boat and have tried to protect it from the elements." Geoff was now taking a chance in divulging too much but he continued on. "If you get your things together now, we can bring you to it."

Sam took the photo from Stompmeyer and nodded in agreement. "We've got a sort of mini-lab on the boat. I'm sure it will be more than adequate for you."

Dmitry was sure Stompmeyer would stall for time and contact their superiors with the news. Astonishingly, as Dmitry began to head out of the lobby towards his car, he heard Stompmeyer agree to immediately accompany Sam and Geoff. Infuriated, Dmitry quickly headed for the door, neglecting to notice the sandy-haired gentleman silently observing his every movement.

22

"Get the men and the boat ready now!" Dmitry barked into his own cell phone. Something seemed odd about the visit and conversation with Stompmeyer. If Sam and Geoff were interested in information from the professor, why were they so evasive with the information they provided? Dmitry was savvy enough to recognize a ploy to entice a quarry to enter your lair. He had often used the same technique himself. He knew the professor was being lured to the boat, which also meant that they had somehow become suspicious. If he intercepted them now, he might never get to learn the secrets on the boat. Instead, he felt confident that he could keep within range of Stompmeyer and the Trojan implanted in Geoff's cell phone. He would then be in a position to surprise them on their boat when the time was ripe.

Stompmeyer was too excited about the parchment to realize the predicament he was putting himself into. In his haste he had forgotten to notify his superiors or leave word with his contacts about what he had learned or where he was heading.

Sam and Geoff soon arrived at the dock. They looked around, making sure they had not been followed. This had been easier than they had imagined. Confidently, they strutted down the dock with Stompmeyer eagerly following.

"There's my ship, the *Scavenger.*" Sam pointed proudly. "Watch your step as you board."

The rest of the crew were waiting anxiously for Sam's arrival. They half expected Stompmeyer to be following, since they were sure Sam would not disclose the full contents of their discovery.

Carly watched closely as Stompmeyer boarded. She had dug as much dirt as she could on the good professor and knew enough to be careful around the man. She only hoped that the others would take care as well. She knew he was much more dangerous than he appeared.

"Observing your competition?" Jack playfully said as he approached her from behind and put his arm around her shoulder.

"That man can't be trusted. I've been spending the last two hours researching him. You should see all the dirt he's been involved with."

"I know, but he's our best shot at interpreting the parchment. Once we're seaborne we should be able to contain him and keep him under control. Just make sure he has no access to any communication equipment."

Once aboard the *Scavenger,* Stompmeyer was taken to the library and given a closer look at the medallion.

"It's exquisite," he said as he examined its workmanship and construction. "These gems appear to be flawless. We must do some testing on them to determine what they are."

"Not yet," Geoff objected. "Testing could ruin the medallion or cause it to decay."

"Very well," Stompmeyer replied reluctantly. "Can you show me the parchment?"

Sam motioned for him to sit down as Geoff carefully produced the parchment. As soon as the parchment was set on the table, the ship's engines roared to life.

Stompmeyer looked up from the table with a startled look. "What was that?"

"Just the ship's engines, professor," Sam responded. "No need for alarm. We fire them up regularly to run the generators and recharge all the equipment. It keeps the electric costs down and enables us to make sure all the mechanical stuff on the ship is in working order, for when we actually go out to sea." Sam hoped his explanation would placate the professor until he had examined the parchment and been able to translate its meaning.

If Stompmeyer had not been so enamored by the parchment, he would have easily seen through Sam's ruse. But he could barely believe his eyes when Geoff produced the writing. He had only seen such writings when he had examined the Dead Sea Scrolls years ago.

"Did you find this at a shipwreck here in the Atlantic?"

"What if we did?" Carly had just entered the cabin and questioned Stompmeyer.

"There is no scholarly explanation for such a writing to be present in this region," Stompmeyer continued. "This is ancient Hebrew. It predates any of the writings you may be familiar with from the Hebrew texts of the Middle Ages. It may even predate the Dead Sea Scrolls. This is a phenomenal find. We must examine the shipwreck site further."

"We couldn't agree more, professor," Sam replied as he gave the signal to Tom to head out to sea. The engines roared and the boat slowly maneuvered away from the dock.

"What's going on?" Stompmeyer asked in a panic.

"We're heading out to the shipwreck site just like you said."

"But I didn't mean right this minute. There are arrangements I need to make, and—"

"And what, professor?" Sam asked. "You've confirmed what we expected. This is obviously an important find. We certainly don't want anyone else moving in on our wreck before we've had time to fully examine it, right?"

"But of course," Stompmeyer hesitantly agreed. "I only meant that we need to carefully consider and prepare for this expedition. I will need some work tools and equipment if I'm to be of any assistance."

"Don't worry, professor, I have most of what you need aboard the ship," Carly interjected. "We also have access to most internet search sites, including any online journal archive you may require."

Stompmeyer resigned himself to taking this spontaneous journey to sea and returned to his examination of the text. "I will need a computer and something to write on, if I'm to translate this. It may take some time since some of the text has worn away."

Outside, Dmitry was watching the *Scavenger* disembark.

"Quickly, you fools!" he hissed to the men on his own boat. "I told you to be ready when I arrived. We don't have much time. If we lose them, I'll have your hides."

Dmitry had overheard Stompmeyer's discussion with the crew of the *Scavenger* and realized that the ship was heading out to sea, back to the shipwreck site. He now knew from the crew's actions that Stompmeyer's cover had been blown. He also realized that Stompmeyer was unaware that the crew had caught on to him. "The fool is helping them unravel the mystery without knowing his own mystery's been solved," Dmitry said to himself.

As the boat took off in chase of the *Scavenger*, Dmitry went below to check in with his superiors.

"He went *where?*" the voice on the other end yelled as Dmitry smirked. Dmitry continued to relay the conversations he had overheard in the hotel and aboard the *Scavenger*.

"I want you to follow them to the shipwreck site and then dispose of them once the site has been located. Is that clear?" the voice on the other end continued.

"What about Stompmeyer?" Dmitry inquired.

"I leave that up to you."

"Very well. I will contact you once we have located the wreck." Dmitry smiled as he cradled the receiver. He looked forward to seeing the good professor get what was coming to him.

23

After hours of toil, Stompmeyer finally translated the parchment:

"With these stones of fire, judgment, retribution and vengeance shall be thine."

"What does that mean," Jack asked Stompmeyer.

"What's a stone of fire?" Carly asked.

"I'm not quite sure. There's a passage in the Old Testament attributed to the prophet Ezekiel which some scholars claim refers to Satan. Could you please get me a Bible?" Stompmeyer turned to Geoff and motioned. A short time later Geoff returned with a Bible and Stompmeyer furiously searched through the pages for the correct verse.

"Here it is, Chapter 28. Look here." Stompmeyer showed them the passage referring to the son of man, the King of Tyre and the cherub walking on the holy mountain of God up and down amidst the stones of fire.

"I don't understand," Carly said. "What does an old Hebrew proverb have to do with this?"

. . .

"I'M NOT SURE, but it's the only reference I'm aware of to 'stones of fire.'"

They read the Ezekiel verses over and over without obtaining any further understanding. Carly reread the verse again, then began from the beginning of Chapter 28. The words ran over and over in her mind. She kept looking at the references to stones, precious stones: sardius, topaz, carbuncle, sapphire, onyx.

"What exactly were the stones of fire?" she asked Stompmeyer.

"No one really knows for sure. Some scholars believe they were the adornments worn by Satan or Lucifer, the devil, before he was cast out of heaven by the Lord."

"I get that, but were they actual stones, gems, or something else?"

"That's what we don't know. Why do you ask?"

"Well, look at these references to the various gems such as sardius, topaz, carbuncle. Do we know what they looked like?"

"Of course. At least, we know what most of them were."

Carly searched for the pictures of the amulet. After locating the clearest enlargement, she showed it to Stompmeyer. "Look at the stones in the amulet. Could any of them be the gems in the verses?"

Stompmeyer looked closely at the photo. He grabbed a magnifying glass and then studied the picture of the amulet.

"Hmm. Where is the amulet? Can I examine it, please? You may be on to something."

Carly told him that Sam had the amulet in safekeeping. She promised to discuss the matter with Sam and left the cabin in search of her uncle. Stompmeyer remained in the cabin, continuing his examination of the pictures. After allowing sufficient time to ensure that there would be no interruption or eavesdropping from Carly, he searched for a means to contact his superiors.

The cabin contained no telephone or shore-to-shore radio. It was sparsely decorated, apparently being used to examine recently retrieved treasures and other items recovered from shipwrecks. There was an intercom system, which he assumed was used to contact the bridge. Stompmeyer wished there had been time to bring his own satellite phone, but Sam and Geoff had rushed him out of his room without giving him the opportunity to grab anything beyond his cane. He had not even had time to leave word with anyone concerning his whereabouts or destination. Their actions in isolating him with such speed seemed odd to him, but he did not dwell on the thought. If he had, he would have been aware of their suspicions of him.

He looked around the room a second time and realized there was no means of contacting the outside world within the four walls of the cabin. Then he saw the laptop they had been using for their research and it dawned on him. He carefully approached the computer and entered his email address. As he began typing, he glanced around several times to make certain that no one had entered to observe his communication with his superiors.

Carly felt she was on to something so she hurried across the deck in search of Sam. As she was rushing through the ship, Sean exited his cabin, jostling her.

"Hey, darling. What's the rush? Have you been ignoring me?" Sean reached out and pulled her close to him, gazing into her green eyes longingly.

"Not now, Sean!" she exclaimed. "I need to find Sam. We need to examine the amulet again."

"Calm down, precious. We have lots of time. We're still hours away from the wreck site."

Sean slowly stroked her neck and hair, silently pleading his cause with those devilish blue eyes of his. Carly felt herself relaxing in his embrace. It had been too long since she had felt his body close to hers. Somehow, Sean seemed to be able to make the stress and problems of the world dissipate and evaporate away. This time was no different. She felt herself slowly floating into the fantasy that he always led her to. As if in a trance, she was led by him back into his cabin, slowly, methodically approaching his mattressed cloud of paradise. As Sean led her into his bed, Carly was engulfed in the passion of the moment, forgetting completely about Stompmeyer and the medallion.

It had only been ten or fifteen minutes, but to Carly it had seemed like hours.

"I've got to get up and find Sam. I left the professor in the library and we need to examine the amulet. We think the parchment is a clue to the medallion."

Carly was slowly returning to reality and the task at hand. She quickly dressed and ran out of Sean's cabin after giving him a quick peck on the forehead. He lay there, smiling at her, admiring her slenderness and grace as she bolted out the door.

While Carly resumed her search for Sam, Sean's curiosity forced him to reluctantly extricate himself from the warmth of his bed and his recent tryst with Carly. After dressing, he wandered toward the library to investigate this new breakthrough for himself. As he opened the cabin door, Stompmeyer was frantically hitting the keys on the laptop.

"What are you doing there?" he asked the German.

Startled, Stompmeyer hastily ended his communication and exited from the screen before Sean could observe what he had been attempting.

"I-I'm trying to find out more information on these verses

from Ezekiel," Stompmeyer stammered, trying to disguise his actions with a lie.

"Let me see," Sean replied as he approached the table.

Stompmeyer was able to retrieve Ezekiel's verses before Sean could catch a glimpse of the emailed message being sent over the web. Stompmeyer showed him the verses and the references to the stones, comparing the pictures with the words.

"Your friend Carly went to obtain the amulet for closer examination. She is quite a remarkable woman."

"Yes, she is," Sean replied, grinning back at the man, "much more remarkable than you could ever imagine."

Stompmeyer caught something in Sean's tone which he recognized as more than mere comradery, more than mere admiration. Stompmeyer had survived these many years by being an astute judge of character and by reading the body language of those around him. Not many could fool him. He could tell Sean was an ambitious man, always aching to escape from the world he felt trapped in. He could also tell that the man was deeply enamored of Carly, possibly even in love with the woman. He took note in his mind, realizing that this insight could be useful in the future. He was aware that Sean had been the original locator of the amulet, so he began to pump him for more information regarding the wreck. At the same time, he subtly intertwined inquiries about the makeup of the rest of the crew.

Meanwhile, Carly had reached Sam.

"What are you doing out here? Where's the professor?" he asked her.

Sam was clearly irritated by Carly's appearance topside.

"It's all right," she said. "He's below examining the parchment and photos of the amulet. We think we may be on to something. We need to inspect the stones on the amulet. Where is it?"

"Whoa. Slow down a minute, girl. Just what are you talking about? And why did you leave the professor alone? You know we can't trust him." Sam's annoyance was obvious. Carly realized she had made a mistake. She quickly explained to Sam the results of the past several hours, leaving out her brief tryst with Sean.

"How long have you been gone?" Jack asked her. Jack had been standing alongside Sam, admiring the brilliance of the sea, how it reflected the warm glow of the sun as the white caps of the waves danced against the ship's bow.

"Only long enough to search below and topside for Sam. It couldn't have been more than a few minutes," she lied.

"You get back to the professor, now!" Sam barked. "We'll go get the amulet and meet you below. And don't leave him alone again! You know we can't trust the man. The last time we saw him, someone was murdered by his associate. Do you want the murderer to find us?"

Carly retreated below, realizing that Sam had a point, although she thought he was being overly cautious. While she acknowledged to herself that she may have been careless, she was also angry at Sam for treating her like a child. He never seemed to accept her for who she was and always appeared to prod her, to push her forward. For some reason, she felt, she never seemed to meet his expectations. She was quickly becoming tired of this treatment and longed for the recognition and respect she felt was due her. Perhaps Sean had been right days earlier. Maybe it was time for her to spread her wings and leave this nest.

Since their initial romantic interlude the other day, Sean had been treating her differently, more gently (for the most part), and definitely with more respect and admiration. She had begun to feel different. She felt differently about herself: more sure, more bold, more confident. She was also beginning to feel differently about Sean.

True, he was crass at times, and not as well educated as herself. Yes, he could be arrogant and stubborn, but there was definitely something more to him. He had the looks of a Greek Adonis, with two-day-old stubble. His dirty blonde hair and azure blue eyes were mesmerizing. His arms and biceps felt like a Rodin sculpture enveloping her in his embrace. He always seemed so sure of himself, so confident in his stride and his decisions. Yes, her feelings for the man were becoming more intense with every contact, both on a physical level as well as on an emotional one.

24

Carly entered the cabin just as Sean was finishing up his description of the shipwreck. The professor seemed fixated on how the amulet's symbol was also embedded in the cannon.

"I've never seen a symbol take on such meaning before," Stompmeyer said pensively. "Oh, Miss Edwards. I'm sorry. I did not hear you enter. Have you located the amulet?"

"Wh-what are you doing here?" Carly asked Sean.

"I just thought I'd see what progress you guys have been making. The professor here has been explaining this Satan stone thing to me."

"It seems more like you were telling the tales. But it doesn't matter. Sam is on his way down with the amulet. Have you discovered anything else since I've been gone, professor?"

"Unfortunately, no. But your friend has been describing the ship and some of its features to me. It is very interesting. What is a carrack doing in these waters?"

"Carrack? What are you talking about?"

"The ship you found. It appears to be a carrack, based upon Mr. Knight's description, as well as the photographs you've shown me. It was a Mediterranean ship used primarily for exploration during the 15th and 16th centuries. One of Columbus's ships was a carrack, and Magellan had a carrack fleet. No one has ever discovered such a shipwreck in North America. Most of the discoveries have been along the European coast or the Malaysian coast, where many Portuguese carracks have been located."

Sean and Carly turned in unison, facing Stompmeyer with puzzled looks. Simultaneously they responded, "We thought we had found a Spanish galleon."

"There are some similarities in appearance, but the galleon came into existence much later in history. You might say the galleon was the next step in 'ship evolution' after the carrack. By the mid 16th century, shipbuilders began to change the hull design of the carrack in order to improve efficiency and make the ship more maneuverable and seaworthy. No, this wreck was most definitely a carrack. Look at the round stern. The galleon's stern was narrower and flat, not rounded."

As the discussion continued, Sam and Jack entered with the amulet.

"What's going on?" Sam cast a distrusting look at Stompmeyer.

"It appears our wreck is older than a galleon," Carly giddily exclaimed.

"What do you mean?" Jack was as confused as Sam at this point.

Stompmeyer repeated his history lesson on ships of the middle ages for the two newcomers. After explaining the differences between the two types of ships, he turned toward Sam with an outstretched arm. "Is that the amulet? May I examine it closer, please?"

Sam handed the medallion to the man, still puzzled by the history lesson on the shipwreck. As Stompmeyer took a closer look at the medallion, Jack moved towards the computer and began typing: C A R R A C K. As the computer discharged responses from the web, Jack accidentally clicked the back browser. An email site suddenly appeared on the screen. Jack took a quick look at Stompmeyer, then returned to his Web search. After a few minutes of surfing, he confirmed Stompmeyer's history lesson. The drawings on the computer screen appeared similar to the photos of the wreck he had been shown. As Jack searched further, he discovered that there was another type of ship used during the 15th to 16th century, the caravel. Apparently, Columbus's flag ship, the *Santa Maria*, was a carrack, but his two other ships, the *Pinta* and *Nina*, were both caravels. As Jack looked more closely at the various depictions, a thought occurred to him. The carrack and caravel were similar in shape and design, the only difference being size. Could the wreck be the smaller caravel, rather than the cumbersome carrack described by the professor? As he pondered this query, his concentration was broken by Stompmeyer's bellowing voice.

"Unbelievable! These stones set within the amulet are exquisite. I've never seen anything quite like them before. Look! This one appears to be a carbuncle...and this one topaz. This one is an emerald. I'm sure of it. This one is definitely sapphire, and...yes! Yes! Look here! Sardius or carnelian. The stones of fire! Just like in the prophesy! Unbelievable!"

Stompmeyer was beside himself. He could feel himself on the brink of a discovery never before encountered by science: the ability to finally provide proof of a prophesy from the Old Testament. And for once, he would not have to pay any bribes for the privilege of being in the forefront of such a discovery.

"This is truly unbelievable!" he continued. "We will need to carbon date this piece for its authenticity. This could be the work of a prankster utilizing Old Testament prophesy, but it does appear to be genuine. Is there a more concrete connection to the ancient parchment?"

"Slow down, Dr. Stompmeyer. Before we go any further, I need to understand what you have been so excitedly trying to say."

Sam was taking no chances until he first understood what the man had uncovered thus far.

"Mr. Katz, the parchment you showed me earlier is written in ancient Hebrew, also known as Paleo-Hebrew, a language long ago forgotten. The Jews ceased using the language in the early part of the second century, around 100-135 AD. It is believed the alphabet evolved from the Phoenecian alphabet. Some examples of this ancient Hebrew alphabet can be found in the Dead Sea Scrolls. The parchment you were kind enough to allow me to examine made reference to the 'Stones of Fire.' The only reference I can recall about 'Stones of Fire' can be found in an old prophesy by the Hebrew prophet Ezekiel. Some believe that prophesy refers to the fall of Satan and God's displeasure in his fallen angel. As such, God removed from Satan's possession the sacred 'Stones of Fire.' The passage describes the stones in detail, six of which are represented in this medallion. But we need to date the medallion scientifically, in order to verify its authenticity and connection with the parchment."

"The box." Carly felt the words slip out before her mind could control her tongue.

"What box?" Stompmeyer turned towards the girl with a bewildered look on his face.

"The parchment was found in a container, a box, containing a secret compartment. The medallion appeared to be the key that opened the box." Sam glared at Carly as he reluctantly apprised the man of the efforts undertaken to discover the secrets of the box.

"May I see it?"

"We'll have to go to the lab. We have it soaking in an attempt to better preserve it and to try to examine it more closely. Sean, would you please show the professor the way?"

As Sean got up to lead the way out of the library to the lab, Carly began to follow.

"Not you, Carly. I need to discuss something with you before we accompany them."

Sam's voice was calm but strained. Carly knew she was in for it. Without showing much emotion, she remained behind while Stompmeyer followed Sean to the library. After the two left, Sam faced Carly.

"Close the door, please."

She knew what was coming next. She quickly got up and shut the cabin's door. As she turned to face Sam, she began to cry.

"I'm sorry, but I got so wound up in what the professor was saying I couldn't help myself."

"It's a good thing we're out at sea and there's no one for miles around. I told you I don't trust that man. Now he knows almost as much about the wreck as we do, maybe even more. We can't let another slip like this happen again. I'm very disappointed in you, Carly."

Jack had never seen Sam so upset. He slowly approached his friend and put his arm around him.

"Calm down, Sam. You know we would have had to show Stompmeyer the box sooner or later. At least he's answered some of our questions about the wreck, although I'm still not sure what an ancient parchment's doing on a Mediterranean shipwreck 100 miles off the Floridian shore."

"I guess you're right," Sam acknowledged. "But I still don't trust the man. At least we've been able to contain him and prevent him from divulging any information about our discovery to the outside world."

"I'm not so sure about that."

"What do you mean?" Apprehension slowly reappeared on Sam's face.

"Carly, was Sean here with the professor when you left to find Sam?" Jack looked directly into her eyes and sensed the answer he feared.

Carly sheepishly replied, "No. But the professor was busy studying the parchment and the medallion. Besides, he couldn't leave the ship. We're miles out to sea."

"Did you use the computer for any research while you were with the professor?" Jack continued.

"Of course I did. Why?"

"You didn't, by any chance, log on to any email account while you were with him?"

Concern was now overtaking every inch of Carly's body. She dropped to her knees and buried her face in her hands, tears streaming down her cheeks.

"Oh no! What have I done?"

Sam looked helplessly at Jack and then turned to Carly. He sank to his knees alongside her, put his arms around her and pulled her towards him, trying desperately to console her.

"It's not your fault, dear. I shouldn't have left you alone with him in the first place. We will just need to be more careful from here on in. He couldn't have divulged too much to his people. After all, they already knew we had found something, and he didn't uncover the connection between the amulet and the parchment until after we returned. We'll just need to keep more than one person with the good professor at all times."

Sam gently patted the back of Carly's head, trying to reassure her, and himself, that all was well. With a worried look, he glanced towards Jack.

"What do you think?"

"I think we need to get to the wreck as quickly as possible and find out what else is on that boat. We also need to keep a close watch out for any other ships in the vicinity and make sure the professor is kept from contacting anyone else until we know what we've uncovered. I think someone should be manning the radar and sonar at all times."

"You're right. I'll tell Tom immediately and then meet you in the library. Carly, go with Jack and make sure the professor's not leading us on a wild goose chase. Do you feel up to it?"

Carly nodded and began to wipe the tears from her eyes.

"I'm sorry I let you down, Sam. It won't happen again. You know I love you."

Carly tried to force a smile to her face and gave the old man a quick peck on the cheek. Jack followed Carly out as Sam went to locate Tom. As they walked towards the library, Jack stopped Carly and turned to look at her.

"Are you all right?"

"I think so."

"Good. Do you know anything about ancient ships?"

"Not much. Why?"

"Because I'm not sure if the professor was being totally honest with us or if he was just mistaken, but I think our wreck may not be a carrack. I think it may be a smaller ship such as a caravel, although I don't know if it makes much difference. Do you know anything about the two types?"

"Not really, but I can try to do some research later, if you like."

Carly was beginning to feel better about herself and the two of them continued on, entering the lab just as Stompmeyer began to examine the box.

25

"Hurry up and cast off. We need to leave NOW!"

Dmitry was growing impatient with his makeshift crew. It had been nearly six hours since the *Scavenger* left the dock with Stompmeyer. Even though he had the GPS activated in the unwitting fool's cane, the Russian preferred to leave nothing to chance. He would have preferred to be in closer proximity to the ship and follow it from a safe distance while still remaining within quick striking distance.

Through his contacts, Dmitry was able to charter the services of an 80-foot-long dive vessel, large enough to accommodate the men he had chosen for this task, as well as their equipment. The vessel could accommodate a crew of 50 and included a sufficient number of cabins to ensure he had whatever privacy he required, as well as a large galley and storage area. Due to time constraints, Dmitry was only able to locate three of the agents he had hoped to use on this task. All three were well-seasoned, ex-KGB agents who had been members of the elite Soviet Naval Spetsnaz, the Russian Naval Special Forces. Two of them were highly trained veterans of the reconnaissance and sabotage arm of Spetsnaz known as Delfin. The remaining five men were either friends of the ex-KGB agents or local hoodlums referred by Cartel connections in Florida. Anxious to get under way, Dmitry had his men load and store the equipment in the staterooms on the boat. Once that task had been accomplished, Dmitry ordered the captain and his crew of five to head out to sea in pursuit of the *Scavenger*.

As the ship slowly accelerated to a cruising speed of ten knots, Dmitry settled into the cabin he had chosen as his command center. As his men began to unpack the equipment, he turned briskly and yelled out to the tall Russian entering the cabin.

"Borya! Quickly! Unpack that GPS tracker and place it here on the desk. We must immediately begin our tracking of the German before they get too far ahead of us."

Borya was 6'6" and more closely resembled a football linebacker than a Russian Navy diver. He had served with Dmitry and had been one of his most trusted agents during the Cold War. When the Soviet Union began to dissolve, he had left the Navy, demoralized by the weakness of the country's leaders and the direction in which they were leading the country. With democracy making a slow progression, he followed Dmitry in his nefarious activities with the Cartel. He had proven himself indispensable on more than one occasion. Although tall and bulky, he could move extremely quickly and was usually underestimated by his opponent, both as to his speed and intelligence.

After several minutes, Borya had the tracking equipment fully assembled and operational.

"Look, Dmitry! It would appear our target is approximately 60 miles northeast of our current position. How fast did the captain inform you our vessel could travel?

"He said our maximum speed was 14 knots. Why?"

"Because it would appear that our target is cruising at almost 15 knots. If they keep up this speed we will never catch up to them."

"We do not need to catch them this early, but we must be in closer striking distance. I will speak to our captain and try to get him to increase our speed. Once our target anchors, we can continue to close in on them. Hopefully, by that time, we will be closer than four hours away from them."

"We should make sure our men have their equipment assembled and everything else is in place."

Borya was a born leader and had been in charge of one of the most elite reconnaissance and sabotage units in the Russian Spetsnaz. His men were always ready for action at a moment's notice.

"You are correct. But someone must monitor the tracking device and relay the proper coordinates to the captain."

"I will send Makar to do that. I'm sure he has already assembled his gear and has prepared himself to complete any mission ordered."

"Good work, Borya. We will meet back here in one hour to discuss our progress and make our preparations."

Makar was a Russian Navy diver of Ukrainian descent. He had completed many missions under Borya and was well-trained in electronics and munitions. It was quite by accident that Borya had found him for this mission. After Borya had separated from the navy, he had lost track of most of his comrades. Makar had spent four more years in the navy without seeing any real action. After several mishaps with his commanding officers, he decided to return to civilian life. He spent a few more years as a soldier of fortune, hiring out his services to the highest bidder. Unfortunately, he often seemed to choose the losing side and spent much of his time lingering in one prison or another. It was during Makar's last escape from incarceration that fate intervened and steered him to Borya. The two had quickly recognized each other and he was instantly recruited.

Borya left Dmitry's cabin and proceeded to direct the rest of the group.

"Good. I see you have assembled your gear, Makar. Listen, I need you to perform a task for me while the others ready themselves."

Makar approached Borya and listened carefully while Borya relayed instructions to him.

"I understand. It will be done as you asked."

Makar withdrew to Dmitry's cabin and received further instructions from Dmitry regarding the tracking device. In the meantime, Borya began barking orders at the remainder of the group.

"Quickly, unpack your gear and assemble your weapons and dive equipment! You must be ready to engage at a moment's notice. And be careful! I don't want any of the ship's crew to be aware of what we are doing. Understood?"

The remainder of the band all nodded in the affirmative as they rapidly commenced their preparations.

26

"Do you know who they are?"

Jack appeared worried and concerned. Brian had just called him and reported information that a group of ex-Russian spies or mercenaries had just left the dock in a dive boat. It appeared that they were heading out on the same coordinates as the *Scavenger*.

"No, I'm sorry. The group moved too quickly to get a reading on who they were. My contacts reported that a thin, dark-haired Russian quickly assembled a gang of eight to ten men and hired one of the less-reputable captains to take them out to sea."

"Do you think the leader is our waiter?"

"It's a possibility. Homeland Security was trying to monitor some of the men. They believe they were ex-Russian Special Forces. Do you want me to alert the Coast Guard with your position?"

"No. We need to investigate the wreck first. The government's involvement will only delay and complicate matters."

"I don't like it. It's too dangerous. If this guy is your waiter, he's already killed once. And even if he's not, if these guys are Russian Black Ops, you're biting off more than you can chew if they're coming after you."

"I doubt they'll try anything in these waters so close to U.S. soil. But don't worry, I'll be careful. I need you to keep me informed of any news on this group, but I really need you to get me a full background on Stompmeyer. I need that info yesterday. If he's connected with this group of mercenaries, I need to know now."

"Okay, I've been working on it, but I still don't like it. That professor of yours is a slippery character. This hasn't been as easy as we'd hoped. You be careful."

Brian knew there was no use arguing with Jack. He was too stubborn and pigheaded. Instead, he decided to contact a few friends in south Florida and organize his own little band of Special Ops forces.

Jack briefed Sam and Tom on the possible danger and told them to keep the information from Stompmeyer and the rest of the crew for the time being. The *Scavenger* slowed its course and gradually came to a stop at the coordinates slightly northeast of the wreck. The crew began preparations for the dive as Geoff directed the placement of the video monitor.

"Before any of the team enters the wreck, I want a full video scan of the exterior of the ship. Go slow, because I want the professor to be able to analyze the ship from above. Once you have completed a full 360, slowly enter the wreck and video the interior. Be careful. We don't know how stable the boat is and I don't want anyone hurt. After a full video scan, wait until I give the next order. Understood?"

Geoff was taking no chances. He wanted to give Carly and Stompmeyer time to analyze the video before a full dive was commenced. Perhaps, between the two of them, they could shed some light on the origin of the wreck and possibly its contents.

Sean grabbed the video lead and began his descent down to the wreck with Billy following behind. The visibility was unusually clear for that time of year. As he approached his destination, Sean slowly looked around. The ocean floor consisted of a vast network of rainbow-colored coral emerging from the sandy bottom with scores of fish, sea fans, anemones and other forms of sea life. Every dive made Sean more aware of the vastness of the ocean, the unexplored depths holding secrets mankind might never unravel. The beauty and majesty of the ocean and its inhabitants always seemed to bring Sean in awe of God's majesty. After his customary praise to God, giving thanks for being granted the privilege of being allowed to witness such grandeur, Sean returned to the task at hand. Billy swam behind him and, slowly, the two divers began to circle the wreck, sending the video feed to the surface.

"Fantastic! Just as I suspected. It appears to be a carrack, built in the late 14th or early 15th century. Look at the detailed workmanship. I've never seen anything quite like it before. At least not so well preserved."

Stompmeyer was elated. This would be a first. He could see the publicity and accolades now.

"What was such a ship doing in these waters? All the wrecks I've ever heard about were found off Europe and in the Mediterranean."

Carly interrupted Stompmeyer's premature congratulatory vision. Irritated at her insolence, he knew she was correct. What was this ship doing here?

"Perhaps that is why we have sent the divers down to search its cargo, my dear," Stompmeyer replied with a belittling smirk.

Carly ignored his sarcastic tone and replied, "I understand that, but can you offer your best 'educated' guess at what this ship with its strange insignia was doing in our waters?"

Stompmeyer had greatly misjudged the girl and was now paying the price. In an attempt to pacify her, he moved closer and pointed out the strange insignia on the cannons.

"Those are the same markings as on the medallion, correct?"

"That's what I was referring to. Have you ever heard of a coat of arms consisting of markings such as those?"

"Not in all my years of exploration. I assume you tried to research those markings before you contacted me?"

"Of course we did. We couldn't find any record even closely resembling them. What do you make of it?"

"I'm not sure," replied the professor. "Let's see what else the video discloses."

Geoff listened to the two of them and continued to bark orders into the headset to the divers below.

"Do you see what might have caused the wreck?" he asked.

Sean moved the video feed closer to the ship's hull as he continued to proceed around the wreck.

"There does not appear to be any damage caused by a battle at sea," said Sean. "Since we are too far out for it to have struck a reef or other obstruction, my best guess would be damage from a storm."

Topside, the crew examined the video screen and concurred with Sean's conclusions. Other than wreckage from rolling on the sea bed, there did not appear to be any substantial damage which could be attributed to a battle, a cannonball, or other obstruction. But if it sank due to weather, what was it doing out here during such a storm and what kind of cargo was it carrying?

"Okay. That's enough of the hull. Can you get us a closer look at the upper deck? Let's see the steering mechanism and defenses."

Sean and Billy ascended to the upper deck and began a sweep with the video of the upper deck's contents. The steering wheel and rudder appeared no different from ships of centuries ago.

"There doesn't appear to be anything out of the ordinary here. The wheel and rudder are overgrown with algae and coral. The cannons look similar to the one we saw on our last trip here. I think we should enter the hold and see what's inside. What do you say, Geoff?"

Sean was beginning to get impatient and wanted to continue with his exploration. He had enough of documenting the site.

"No. I want to get a closer look at the cannons. Do they all have the same markings as the medallion?" asked the professor.

Stompmeyer's curiosity had been aroused and he wanted to fully explore the outer portions of the ship before the divers entered the interior.

"It's definitely a carrack, but I've never seen one built quite like this. It's of an earlier vintage than those used by Columbus and the other explorers. It's two-masted with a single rudder. It also appears larger. Astonishing! Simply astonishing. And the medallion's markings appear on all the cannons, don't they?"

The crew stared at the video from below. Anxious to continue their exploration, they urged Geoff to order the divers to enter the interior.

"Sean, hook your line mid-deck and continue below, but be careful!"

"Aye-aye, sir!" Sean mocked his first mate. He motioned for Billy to hook the tether line reel and turn on the dive light. Carefully, they began to slowly descend into the bowels of the wreck. As they dropped, startled fish stirred from their rest and instantly came to life around them. Schools of hogfish and jacks swam in front of the divers. Sean watched as the fish seemed oblivious to the two of them. Then he felt a tap on his shoulder and followed Billy's hand as it pointed out to his left side. Three barracudas floated motionlessly as the divers carefully entered the main cabin area. Oddly, most of the furnishings were missing. Perhaps the age of the wreck and the currents over the many centuries had relieved the living quarters of its contents. Sean was concerned that the ship's cargo would be empty as well.

After videoing the cabin area the two divers proceeded below into the cargo hold. Hoping to find a clue to the ship and its contents, Sean slowly traversed the entire area. Remains of flasks and utensils were strewn throughout the bottom. Pieces of crates and chests were scattered amongst the skeletal remains of what appeared to be the ship's crew. As he slowly maneuvered around the wreckage, a sharp voice bellowed through his headpiece.

"There! To the right, at two o'clock. Do you see it?"

Billy heard the voice as well and turned his light in the general direction. The two divers saw the symbol again, the shape and design of the medallion, only this time much larger. It had been burned or carved into a wall of the ship, near the upper portion of the wall.

"What the hell?" Sean was clearly confused. Were they aboard the vessel of some secret sect?

.   .   .

"HEY, PROFESSOR. SOME direction here. What's going on? Just what the hell does this symbol mean and what should I be looking for?"

Stompmeyer was just as confused as the rest of the crew.

"I don't know. Can you move the debris from the flooring around the wall?"

"We'll try," Sean replied.

After several minutes, the floor area had been cleared.

"Look. There appear to be slots in the flooring, evenly spaced in a rectangular shape."

Sean motioned to Billy to shine the light in the area he had just described as he grabbed the video feed and panned the floor for the crew on the surface to view.

"It looks like something rectangular, but moveable, was set along this wall. Any idea what it could have been, professor?"

Stompmeyer was stymied. "No, I'm afraid not. Do you see anything else on the wall or floor?"

Upon closer inspection, Sean noticed something on the floor.

"Look at this! There appears to be another compartment below. I can't quite make out what's down there, but it looks like there is some kind of lock or catch on the floor. Can you see it?"

"Yes, we do. Can you get it opened?"

. . .

"WE'RE TRYING, BUT we can't pry it up with our knives. We're going to have to come back with better equipment."

"Have you covered the entire area of the wreck yet?" Geoff asked. He wanted to make sure all the preliminary examinations had been completed before recalling the team and beginning preparations for any recovery efforts.

"I think so." Sean wanted to get topside as soon as possible. He knew the longer he stayed down at this depth, the longer it would be before he could safely make another dive. As he turned to begin his ascent, Billy stopped him.

"Look over there."

Billy shined his light in the corner and began to swim towards the object laying on the floor.

"It's just a goblet, Billy. Don't get so excited."

Billy ignored Sean's taunts and reached for the object. As he did, he saw what appeared to be another storage area below, only this time the floor planking had been broken from the shifting of the ship.

"Look! Another storage vault! Bring the video here."

Sean joined Billy and pointed the video below. Shields and

ancient weapons lay strewn in the vault below. They tried to reach down, but were unable to touch the cache.

"Okay. We've seen enough," said Geoff. "Get back up here so we can prepare a team for entry and recovery. We need you to get a sufficient surface interval in so you can dive again. I want to recover as much as possible before it gets dark."

Sean and Billy acknowledged Geoff's command and retraced their entry path by rewinding the tether line. As they ascended towards the *Scavenger,* Billy placed his find, the goblet, in his sack for a closer inspection during his surface interval.

27

"The target is stationary."

"What are its current coordinates?"

Dmitry had wondered how long the *Scavenger* would travel before casting anchor. It was imperative that he obtain its current location so an assault plan could be formulated. Makar relayed the coordinates to Dmitry as the leader consulted with the captain.

"That would put them about six hours from our current location," the captain advised Dmitry. "We can no longer travel at top speed and must slow our approach in order to conserve fuel and engine efficiency. Unfortunately, our craft is quite old and cannot be used as a speed racer."

Disappointed at the captain's response, Dmitry reluctantly retired below to discuss assault and boarding options with his team. In order to approach the *Scavenger* undetected, his ship would need to maintain a safe distance out of radar and sonar range. He was taking no chances that this mission would fail.

"Borya, how close can we get to the target without being detected?"

"It depends on the sophistication of their radar and sonar. I would assume their sonar has an outside range of two miles, although it is possible to obtain up to a five-mile range with a sophisticated government-authorized system. I highly doubt our target would be equipped with such a system. Their radar, however, could easily have a range of over 100 miles."

"How long can your divers remain underwater?"

"That depends on the dive depth, nitrox mixture, and distance they travel."

"If we sent teams out to board the vessel and also secure the wreck, how close could we anchor our ship?"

"Using the underwater scooters would maximize our bottom time, preserve air, and add increased speed. A diver could travel up to three miles per hour with as much as two hours of battery time. If we equipped the diver with dual nitrox tanks, I would suggest anchoring a little more than three miles from the target area. That would allow our teams ample time to secure both the wreck site and target vessel. It would also put our ship within ten to twenty minutes of striking distance. We will just have to hope that the radar operator believes we are a fishing vessel. We will have to slow our approach to the target area if we want them to believe our fishing vessel cover story."

Dmitry was somewhat satisfied with the plan. He was not happy about slowing his approach towards the *Scavenger*. The ship had already gained too much time on him. But there was no other choice. Instead of a six-hour approach time, it was agreed that they would slow their cruise speed and anchor 3.2 miles from the *Scavenger's* current location. It would take them roughly six and one-half hours at their reduced speed to reach their anchor point. After allowing another hour and one-half for the dive teams to complete their missions, it would be at least eight hours before his crew seized control of the operation.

After analyzing the plan further and discussing the objectives, Dmitry left the details in the hands of his good friend, Borya. Dmitry retired to his private cabin area and reported his progress to his superiors. They still had received no word from Stompmeyer and gave him carte blanche to handle the situation and all dealings with the German.

28

Jack gathered his gear and readied himself for the dive to the wreck. He had eagerly been awaiting this moment ever since Sam had involved him. Geoff, Jim and Billy were already suited up and ready to enter the water. Jack checked his gear one last time and gave the "okay" signal. The four men left the boat, leaping from the platform, and entered the water. They signaled to the ship that they were okay and began their gradual descent to the bottom.

Carly was attempting to console Sean, who was distraught at being left behind. At the last minute he had developed severe leg cramps and Sam made him wait this dive out. Carly put her arm around Sean, drew him close to her and gave him a quick kiss on the lips.

"Let's see what Billy brought us from the wreck. You can walk off your cramp and maybe we can learn something more about our mysterious ship."

Billy's goblet had been soaking in the tank for the last

two hours while the crew analyzed the video and readied the equipment for the next dive. Sean was clearly agitated. There had been more than a sufficient surface interval to allow him to reenter the water on this second dive. He was sure this leg cramp was only momentary. Sam was, in Sean's mind, being overly cautious.

"All right. I guess I have nothing better to do."

Sean reluctantly followed a jubilant Carly below to the soak tank. Once below, they carefully removed the goblet from the tank and began to wipe its exterior.

"What do you make of this?" Sean pointed to what appeared to be a symbol on the side of the goblet. "Doesn't it resemble my amulet?"

Carly looked closer.

"You're right. It does! But something's different about this one. There's no Hand of Fate."

"You're right. And look! Doesn't that appear to be writing on the side?"

As they tried to examine the goblet more closely, they heard a sound behind them. They turned as Stompmeyer entered the cabin.

"I see you have already begun to examine the specimen. Have you uncovered anything interesting?"

As they pointed out the engravings on the side of the cup, Stompmeyer let out a gasp.

"How could I have been so ignorant? It's been in front of me all this time. What an idiot!"

"What are you talking about?" Carly was confused.

"I believe we've uncovered part of King Solomon's lost treasure!"

"Whaaaaat!" Carly and Sean incredulously exclaimed at the same time.

Carly leaned towards Stompmeyer. "What are you talking about?"

"Look closely at the etching on the side of the goblet. See how it is similar to your amulet, yet lacks the Hand? This is the great seal of King Solomon, son of King David, third king of the Jews and builder of the original Great Temple. Look at the inscription on the cup. I know it's hard to make out, but it's Hebrew. Translated, it means, 'May his wisdom and righteousness endure forever.'"

Suddenly it hit Sean.

"Solomon. Wasn't that the guy who split the baby? He's the one with all the great treasure of the Jews that somehow was lost to the ages?"

Stompmeyer laughed. "You are partially correct. The legends claim that King Solomon was the wisest man in the world. One day, when he was holding court, as was his custom, two women came to him to air a grievance regarding a young child. Each claimed that the baby was hers. When neither would relent in her claim, King Solomon proclaimed that since it was unclear who the newborn's mother was, the child should be split in two, and half given to each woman. One of the women looked at the king in horror and, with tears in her eyes, pleaded that the child be spared and given to the other woman. The king knew this act of mercy was from the child's own mother's heart, and declared her to be the true mother. But that has little to do with our wrecked ship. More important for *our* concerns, King Solomon was believed to have possessed great wealth. Tons of gold and other precious metals were quarried yearly from his mines in Ophir. After he built the Great Temple in Jerusalem, many precious religious artifacts were said to be stored there, including the Ark of the Covenant, a menorah made of pure gold, silver trumpets and the Table of Solomon, sometimes called the Table of the Divine Presence. The Bible tells us that he had huge shields of gold made from his mines."

"The shields in the ship's vault?" asked Carly.

"Perhaps," replied Stompmeyer.

"But what's it doing here, in the Atlantic Ocean, a lot closer to the good old U.S.A. than Israel?" Sean asked incredulously.

"When Rome destroyed the Second Temple after the Jewish revolt, historians know that the Romans took many of these items back to Rome. Ten years after the destruction of the Second Temple, the Romans built the Arch of Titus. The Arch was erected to commemorate the subjugation of the Jews and the capture and sack of Jerusalem. Roman soldiers are depicted bearing sacks of loot on their backs, along with the golden candelabra from the Temple, silver trumpets and the Table of the Shewbread, Solomon's divine table. The Romans displayed this treasure for all the public to see, in the Temple of Peace in the Forum, for over three hundred years."

"Do you mean to tell us that they didn't melt the spoils down and recycle the gold and silver for their own use?" Sean was having difficulty accepting Stompmeyer's history lesson.

"Some historians claim that much of the treasure may have been melted down and reused by the Romans to finance one or more of their numerous campaigns. However, ancient historical accounts, including those by Josephus in the first century and Procopius, the Roman Emperor Justinian's court historian in the sixth century, confirmed the sacking of Jerusalem and the public display of the treasures in Rome for centuries. Additional accounts suggest that the treasure was looted by the Vandals during the sack of Rome around 455 AD. There are sporadic accounts thereafter claiming asportation by the Moors, the Byzantines and even the Knights Templar."

"So what does this all have to do with the amulet and our wreck?"

Carly had also begun to question Stompmeyer's theory.

"Listen closely. The markings on the goblet are clearly Solomon's Seal. The inscription, as well, indisputably points to

King Solomon. Undeniably, this goblet is one of the surviving pieces of Solomon's treasure. The markings on the amulet and ship's wall have enough similarity to suggest a connection to Solomon's treasure, or perhaps the Temple's treasure. Without any further evidence about the ship's cargo, and unless your friends can enter and retrieve the remaining items in the ship's vault, we can only hypothesize. Your mysterious amulet and box containing the ancient Hebrew parchment definitely suggest a connection to the Jewish Temple. If the golden candelabra and Divine Table were among the Temple spoils, it is possible other ancient Biblical artifacts were looted by the Romans as well."

"Like what? This isn't Indiana Jones or Allan Quartermain. Do you expect us to believe we're searching for the Ark of the Covenant or some other old Jewish legend?"

Sean was getting impatient with the German's explanations. Feeling he was no closer to understanding what they were after, and still upset about having to remain topside, he was beginning to vent his anger and frustration out on Stompmeyer.

"Wait, Sean," said Carly. "Let's hear the man out. We brought him into this because of his knowledge. If we don't at least give him an opportunity to explain his theories, we might as well have flown solo."

"Miss Edwards is correct, sir. I'm not claiming that we are on the trail of the Lost Ark or any such relic. But do you recall the translation of the ancient parchment?"

As they tried to recall the translation, Stompmeyer provided it to them again,

"With these Stones of Fire, judgment, retribution and vengeance shall be thine."

"I can't be positive, but I believe there may be a Biblical reference to 'Stones of Fire.' If I recall correctly, the High Priest of the Temple wore a breastplate consisting of twelve jewels made from specific minerals, the same stones referred to by the prophet Ezekiel as the 'Stones of Fire.' Do you believe this is all just a coincidence?"

Carly and Sean each thought silently for a moment before turning towards each other and slowly nodding in awe.

"What do you think, Carly? You're the scientist. Do you think the professor may be on to something?"

"I'm not sure, but it does make sense and seems awful coincidental. Maybe we should let Sam in on this and try to get a closer look at the wreck."

All three agreed and quickly went in search of Sam to apprise him of the professor's newest theory.

29

As Jack gazed around at the coral and reef below, he watched the sun's rays piercing the blue water, streaking towards the vast emptiness of the ocean around him. The feelings he experienced when diving were strangely similar to those felt by Sean. The true wonders and majesty of God as the Creator of this world were all laid out before him to absorb and experience. Even the wreck below took on a new life as ocean organisms clung to it, beginning to metamorphose this manmade object into a living city of coral formations, renewing its purpose on the ocean floor.

As they reached the wreck, Geoff tethered the line and entered first. Billy and Jim followed after with the equipment and tools they had gathered for exploration of the hold and vault areas. Jack stayed back and examined the exterior portion of the wreck, trying to imagine the life of a sailor in the early middle ages on such a vessel. As he swam closer to one of the cannons for closer examination, a moray eel slithered from its nesting place in the cannon's barrel. Surprised at this unexpected encounter, Jack decided to join the others inside the wreck. As he followed the tether line through the bowels of the wreck, he took note of the starkness of the interior living quarters. He had encountered numerous wrecks since he had first begun to dive. While some had been cleaned out before sinking, many had contained a multitude of artifacts, whether intact or in pieces. While he assumed they were among the first to explore the wreck, there appeared to be very few artifacts or other items of a personal nature remaining on board.

By the time Jack entered the hold, Geoff and the rest of the crew had already set up the video and begun to examine one of the vault areas. Jack saw the etching on the wall and swam to examine it more closely. As he reached out and traced the markings on the wall, he realized they were identical to those on the amulet. He looked down at the floor and observed the four rectangular slots in the planking. He tried to imagine the object that would have been placed in the floor, but was drawing a blank. As he stared across the room, he saw what appeared to be hooks on the opposite wall. He swam over for closer inspection and followed the wall down to the floor.

"Hey guys. Look over here. Slots, just like on the other side. Looks like the same size and spacings."

Billy swam over with the video and panned it across the area before returning to Geoff and the vault.

Slowly, meticulously, the men began to dismantle the flooring above the vault area. Once they were able to create a large enough opening, Jim volunteered to descend for closer examination.

"These shields are awful large. I'd hate to be the soldier carrying one into battle. Looks like we've got our star and eye symbol again. What did we do, stumble on some medieval Jewish warship?"

"Enough of the wisecracks. What else do you see down there?"

Geoff was not amused and prodded Jim along.

"I can't really tell. There's lots of these shields, though. Do you think we should try to bring one of these suckers up?"

"Not yet. I think we should examine the hold more thoroughly first. Are there any other openings in that vault area?"

"Not from what I can tell. Send me down the video and I'll try to shoot the area for topside inspection."

Billy carefully threaded the video feed to Jim and tried to shine his light around the area to assist Jim in his photography. After several minutes of inspection, Geoff had Jim return to the hold. They then went to work on the second vault, which was made more difficult because the wood planking was completely intact.

"Can't we just work on the locking mechanism?"

"We could if we knew exactly where it started and what kind of mechanism it was. We'll just have to try to remove more of the flooring until we can get a peek inside."

Twenty minutes later, the men had successfully removed enough of the planking to tell that the vault area was empty.

"All that time for nothing. This wreck is beginning to give me the creeps. Let's bring the shields out and call it a day. I'm starting to get a bad feeling about all this."

Billy had seen enough and wanted to get back to examine his goblet. After a few more minutes of complaining, he finally convinced Geoff to begin recovery operations on removing the shields from the hold to the *Scavenger*. Jack decided to explore the outer portions of the wreck and the sea bed area further while the crew gathered their equipment together and began retrieval of the shields from the vault.

Jack followed the tether line to the upper deck of the wreck and took a closer look at the broken ship masts. Lobsters and other sea creatures darted between the remains of the netting and splintered pieces of the poles. A huge manta ray swam by and Jack decided to follow it. As he did, the ray began to dart between the kelp and sea bed, almost as if it were playing a game of tag with the diver. Suddenly, Tom's voice bellowed through his receiver.

"I think you guys are going to have company. Sonar's picking up six objects moving at about three miles per hour in your direction. I can't tell what they are, but I don't think they're fish. Radar picked up some kind of boat anchored three and one-half miles due east of us. I thought it was a fishing or pleasure craft."

Jack began to think. "How long ago did you pick up the boat on radar?"

"About an hour or so ago."

Jack's mind was spinning as he made mental calculations trying to recall assault techniques he had used commanding his SEAL team. As he completed his calculations, his suspicions were being confirmed. Four fully equipped divers being pulled by marine scooters were approaching the wreck. Before he could yell out to warn the crew, one of the divers shot a spear at Billy as he tried to swim towards the *Scavenger*, puncturing his wetsuit and piercing the young man's chest.

Enraged, Jack remained in the cover of the coral and kelp while slowly swimming to his friend's aid. Hidden by the thick seascape, Jack was able to reach Billy, who lay motionless at the ocean floor. Blood was streaming from Billy's wound, shooting out in a circular pattern following the flow of the current. Jack looked into Billy's mask and saw the shock on his face as the life ebbed from his body. As Jack looked upward, he saw three of the attackers surround Geoff and Jim as they exited the wreck, immobilizing them before they knew what was happening and before they could warn the crew of the *Scavenger*.

Jack moved away from Billy's corpse and secreted himself behind a thick mass of coral while he tried to warn the crew of the *Scavenger*. Unfortunately, two more teams of frogmen had already boarded the vessel and had surprised the remainder of the crew just as Jack was trying to radio a warning. Realizing he was now alone, he saw Billy's attacker swimming closer, apparently to confirm his kill. Jack knew he would have only one chance at surprising the man. He carefully withdrew his dive knife from its sheath and waited until the man was over by his friend, inspecting the damage he had done. In one quick movement, Jack positioned himself behind the man and yanked off his dive mask with one hand while severing the carotid artery with his knife. As the man gasped for air, desperately trying to block the blood flow, Jack struck again, slicing the carotid artery on the other side. In seconds, the man ceased struggling and slowly floated alongside Billy's still body.

Jack quickly examined the dead diver. Jack noticed a pistol strapped to the man's leg. As he took a closer look, images from his past entered his mind. He hadn't seen one of these in years. It was an SPP-1, a double action, special underwater pistol, developed in the late 60s for Soviet combat divers. Was this guy a former Spetsnaz, a former Russian Navy SEAL? If so, what was he doing here, and what did he want with the *Scavenger* and its crew?

Jack knew he had little time to figure out this puzzle. It wouldn't be long before the rest of the man's team realized he was missing and came looking for him. Jack continued to search the dead man and located the man's radio receiver. He decided to take it with him, as well as the man's pistol, and began searching for a place to hide until he knew it was safe to surface. He unhooked Billy's air tanks and pulled them alongside as he frantically searched for a hiding spot. As he passed the bow of the wreck, he saw a rope or cable buried in the ocean floor. Jack decided to investigate and stored Billy's tanks under one of the wreck's cannons laying in the sand. After checking his air supply, he let the current pull him in the same direction as the buried rope. Suddenly, the ocean floor opened underneath him. As he swam into the hole, he spied an opening in the wall. He looked back at the wreck and saw two teams of divers entering the water from the *Scavenger's* platform and diving towards the wreck in search of their lost comrade. Without hesitating any longer, Jack dropped into the hole and swam towards the opening in the wall. As he entered, he saw a school of lionfish overhead.

Jack entered the orifice and began descending into the darkness. Before he could turn his light on, he felt the cavity widen. Jack quickly turned on his light and looked around in amazement. He was actually able to break the surface of the water. He looked at his dive watch and confirmed he was one hundred feet below sea level, yet there appeared to be air inside the cavern he had just entered. Carefully, Jack removed his regulator, not quite sure what to expect. To his amazement, there was breathable air! How could that be?

As Jack continued to explore the cavern, he noticed that the space kept expanding the deeper he went. Eventually he reached a landmass within the pool of water. He decided to take a rest and pulled himself out of the water. As he rested, he examined the transmitter he had retrieved from Billy's attacker. He was able to activate the receiver and heard the divers frantically searching for their fallen accomplice. One of them was speaking with an Eastern European accent.

"There, at twelve o'clock. Do you see it? I think it's Makar. The other body must be the American who exited the wreck as we came upon it."

Jack could not be sure, but the accent sounded Russian, and he was sure Makar was a Russian or Ukrainian name. As Jack continued to listen, he was convinced these guys were ex-Russian Navy SEALS. That would explain the pistol and the military precision used by the attackers.

"He's dead! Both his carotids have been slit and his SPP-1 is missing."

"Is the other diver dead? Do you think they both died in the struggle?"

"Highly unlikely. This other one has one of Makar's harpoon's impaled in his chest. There must be another diver around."

Jack began to look around the cavern for a safer hiding spot. It was clear to him that he did not dare to leave the cave and reenter the ocean waters. There was no safe place out there to hide or surface. They were in the middle of the ocean and his boat had been commandeered by some Russian pirates. The cavern was clearly the safest place for him if he could hide himself from his pursuers, but where?

"Fan out, but keep in sight of each other. I don't want to lose any other men."

The leader was not pleased that he had lost one of his men so easily. These were treasure hunters, not trained combat divers like his men. How had something like this happened? He would catch this stranger and make his life miserable...for the short time the man would be allowed to live, that is.

The four divers spread out and began swimming in Jack's direction. As they reached the hole, one of them yelled out, "He could not have come this way. Look, schools of lionfish with nurse sharks circling above. And look, scores of jellyfish hovering. There's no way he swam this way."

The leader agreed and ordered his men to search in the other direction. As Jack continued to monitor the pursuit, he let out a sigh of relief. It appeared that the ocean's predators had saved him from his own predators from the surface. After twenty minutes of futile searching, Borya ordered his men to retrieve their fallen comrade and bring him to the surface.

"What about the other one?"

"Leave him for the sharks.

30

Jack looked around his surroundings. It was dark and damp, yet the cavern appeared large and strangely hospitable. It was almost as if someone had hung out a welcome mat, inviting him in. He had successfully eluded his attackers and appeared to be safe for the present. But where was he, and safe from what, from whom? What was this strange cavern doing in the middle of the ocean ninety feet below sea level? Who were those men who attacked his friends, killing one of his group? Emotion was running rampant throughout him. Anger seethed from within at the death of his friend. Fear coursed through him, causing anxiety and paranoia from the unsuspecting attack he had experienced. The high adrenaline rush was the by-product of his narrow escape coupled with his own aggressive behavior and the evasive maneuvers which had eventually led him to discover this strange place.

After thinking about the events of the last two weeks and realizing that he needed to gain control of the situation and his own emotions, Jack felt he could finally relax and explore his new hideaway. He obviously couldn't leave the cavern, even though the divers had finally left. Lionfish and other dangers awaited him at the mouth of the entrance. Even if he did get out, he had nowhere to go and only a limited supply of air left in his tanks. He had no choice other than to explore his new habitat.

Jack removed his mask and air tanks and began to look around. As he advanced deeper inside, he began to feel he was not the first to explore this cavity. Traces of human habitation surfaced sporadically as he trekked deeper inside. Finally Jack gasped in awe as he shone his light ahead of him. Were his eyes deceiving him? No, he was entering a makeshift room deep within the bowels of the cavern.

He looked around in amazement. The cavern seemed to be immense. It was nearly twenty feet in height and indentations had been hollowed out of the walls, leaving space for lanterns or other methods of lighting. He continued to look within and was mesmerized as his mind processed what his eyes were transmitting to his brain. No wonder the wreck was devoid of furnishings. Somehow, they had all been transported here! There were tables and chairs, desks and even eating utensils, as well as storage barrels methodically placed throughout. What in the world was going on? It looked liked someone had been living here. But who? Why? When? And for how long?

Jack kept prodding forward until, finally, he was nearing the answer. Up ahead, in the shadows, was a figure seated at a desk. But as Jack approached, he realized it was not a living figure, but rather a skeleton. A man had been here before him, but was no more. Had he been trapped here, too, just like Jack?

Surrounding the skeleton were lanterns and torches. Jack lit them to conserve the batteries on his own flashlight. As his eyes adjusted to the torchlit darkness, Jack began to make out the makeshift living quarters of this skeleton. Just beyond, something seemed to glitter as the torch flames danced against the dark shadows of the rock. Slowly, Jack crept closer, holding his arm extended with a lit torch guiding the way.

Gold! Diamonds! Emeralds! And...silver trumpets? What was going on? There were chests upon chests of treasures. Where had they come from and why were they there? Jack was not equipped with the archaeological or historical knowledge needed to unravel this mystery. How he wished Carly or even the professor were with him now!

Jack took a cursory look at the treasure and returned to the skeleton in the adjacent room. Perhaps he could learn more about who the man had been if he could get some clues from his surroundings. On the desk, Jack spied a quill pen and a diary.

Could it be? Had this man left some record for posterity? Jack moved closer and carefully removed the writings from beneath the bony hand. As the book slid out, the right pinky separated from the skeleton's socket.

"Sorry about that, my friend," Jack muttered silently. "I didn't mean to disturb you. I just needed to get a closer look at what you were writing."

Jack slowly eased the pages open, taking care not to rip the paper and destroy the markings. To Jack's amazement, it was not in English. Jack looked closer at the first few words and realized the man had written in French. Thankfully, Jack was fluent in French, and began to translate the text.

My name is Pierre Bonfils. I was born in Marseille on March 25, 1370. My great-uncle was an esteemed member of the Poor Fellow-Soldiers of Christ and of the Temple of Solomon.

Jack read the text twice, making sure his translation was accurate. Could this document be authentic? Was the writer being truthful, or was this some kind of a hoax? How could a Frenchman from more than six hundred years ago wind up here, miles off the coast of Florida, in a cave nearly one hundred feet below sea level? And if his translation, as well as his memory, was accurate, the "Poor Fellow-Soldiers of Christ and of the Temple of Solomon" was the original and complete name of the Knights Templar.

31

Tom was cursing at himself for his sloppiness. He knew he should have been more prepared for a boarding, especially after Jack's warning and picking up the blips on the sonar. Then again, who would have expected a military-style underwater amphibious assault team surreptitiously boarding the *Scavenger* while his divers were in the water? At the same time he had been warning his divers of possible danger, two amphibious assault teams sent by Dmitry boarded the *Scavenger* and immediately took the remaining crew members captive. Even Stompmeyer appeared surprised.

Borya and his three associates had quickly neutralized the men aboard the *Scavenger* and locked them in the main cabin below. After securing control of the boat, Borya made himself comfortable in the radio room and reported in to Dmitry.

"The ship is secure and the prisoners have been contained without incident. I am waiting for the rest of our team to report from the wreck."

"Good. What have you done with Herr Stompmeyer?"

"He is below along with the rest of the crew. He seems quite nervous."

"Keep him that way until I arrive. I will have our captain lift anchor and proceed directly to your location. Don't let anyone touch anything until I get there, understand?"

"Completely....What do you mean by interrupting me? I left orders that I was not to be disturbed!"

Borya was yelling at the diver who had interrupted his report to Dmitry.

"Sorry sir, but I thought you would want to know immediately," said the diver.

"Know what?"

"Our team has returned with the divers from the wreck. Unfortunately, there has been an incident."

"What do you mean, incident?" Borya was getting more irritated by the moment and was in no mood to start playing twenty questions.

"Makar has been killed. Makar shot one of the wreck divers as we approached the site. After we had neutralized the divers inside the wreck, we noticed Makar was missing, so we swept the area and discovered his body near the dead wreck diver's."

"And?"

"Both of his carotid arteries had been sliced, but we don't think it could have been done by the dead wreck diver."

"What do you mean?"

"The dead man had Makar's spear impaled in his chest. We expect he would have expired nearly instantaneously, before Makar would have reached him."

"Are you saying you let one of the divers get away?"

"We don't know. When we approached the wreck, we saw the diver exit and Makar instantly shot him before he could register a warning to the others. None of the other divers inside the wreck could have exited before we captured them.

We saw no one else outside the wreck either upon our arrival or after discovering Makar's body."

"Incompetents! This is totally unacceptable. Where is Makar's body now?"

"One of the men is taking care of bringing his body on board."

"Where are the captured wreck divers?"

"They are ascending the dive platform presently."

"Keep them there. I will be there shortly."

As the man turned to leave, Borya returned to his conversation with Dmitry.

"There has been an incident. It appears that one of these treasure hunters has murdered Makar. I must go now to investigate further."

"Are you trying to tell me that one of the divers escaped?"

"I do not know at this time. I will investigate and contact you further once I know more."

"Very well, but I expected better of your men."

"As did I."

32

Geoff and Jim were on the dive platform, hands tied together, when Borya arrived.

"How many men did you have down there with you?"

Jim looked anxiously at Geoff.

"You, don't look at him. Answer the question!"

Borya kicked Geoff in the side as he spoke to Jim.

"There — there was Billy. He left right before us. Where is he anyway?" Jim looked frantically around in search of his missing comrade.

"Don't worry about him. He won't be joining you. Was there anyone else down there with you?"

"What do you mean he won't be joining us? What have you done with him?" Geoff could barely get the words out as he was writhing in pain from the kick he had received from his Russian captor.

"Don't worry, I'm not talking to you. Keep your mouth shut or you'll soon be joining your friend overboard!"

Geoff caught the man's meaning and tried to signal Jim to remain silent, but he was too late.

"There was Sam's friend, Jack, the New York lawyer. Where's he? You guys get him along with Billy?"

Borya glared at his dive leader, then turned his attention back on Jim.

"Tell me about this Jack."

"I don't understand. What is there to tell?"

"When did you last see him?"

"I don't know. It was shortly after Billy found the goblet. We kept looking through the ship and I think Jack went out to explore the reef area."

"Fool!" Borya turned to his dive leader and backhanded him across his face. "Do I have to do everything myself? If we were back home you would be shot for such incompetence. You are a disgrace to the Spetsnaz! If you weren't already out of the service, you would have been forced out for your ineptitude. Bring these two below with the others, and try not to bungle this assignment."

Borya was visibly outraged by his man's failure. He knew he would have to advise Dmitry of the problem and was unsure how he would react. Geoff took note of the exchange between his two captors as he was yanked from the platform and shoved along the deck towards the stairs leading below. His chest still hurt from the kick he had received, but he tried to study each of his two captors before Borya left to make his report to Dmitry.

"Boss has you in hot water, huh?" Geoff asked the dive leader.

"Shut up," the man replied. "I don't need any lip from you. Just keep walking and maybe you'll get to stay alive a little longer. Keep talking and I'll make sure you wind up as fish bait like your friend."

Geoff knew enough to keep quiet. Besides, his suspicions

had just been confirmed. Billy was the first to leave and must have been attacked by one of these men. Since he was not on deck when they were brought up, he must have been killed. Judging by the tension and demeanor of his two captors, Geoff could only assume that Jack must have eluded them.

One of the guards opened the cabin door and Geoff and Jim were roughly pushed inside, the door clanging shut behind them.

"What happened to you two? And where's Billy?" asked Tom.

He approached the men and began to untie Geoff's hands.

"I think he was murdered by those scum!" said Geoff. "Who are they anyhow, and what do they want?"

"We're not sure," said Sam. "Probably has something to do with our shipwreck. Hey, where's Jack?"

Sam looked frantically for his friend with questioning eyes.

"I'm not positive," said Geoff, "but I think he might have gotten away. There was some kind of argument up top between the head guy and one of his lackeys and I think it had to do with Jack. They kept asking who else was down there with us and told us we didn't have to worry about Billy anymore. These clowns are playing for keeps. We'd better be careful."

Sean and Carly turned towards Stompmeyer. "It's *you*," said Sean. "You're the one who called these creeps in on us. I never trusted you from the start. Who are they and what do they want? Cough it up or you're dead meat!"

Sean suddenly lunged at Stompmeyer. But before he could reach him, Tom got between them and held Sean away.

"Calm down! Losing your head isn't going to solve anything."

"What do you know about these men?" Sam asked Stompmeyer, approaching him.

"I know nothing! You see, *I* am a prisoner just as *you* are."

The reality of the man's statement lingered in everyone's

thoughts. The professor was right. He was also being held captive. Maybe he was not involved, and perhaps these other men were true modern-day pirates at sea.

"We need to figure a way out of here. If only we could contact the Coast Guard or send an SOS," Tom stoically said. "If we don't come up with a plan to get rescued, or rescue ourselves, we're probably gonna be goners just like Billy."

Carly looked at Sean with pleading eyes. "I don't want to die! Isn't there anything we can do?"

Sean put his arms around the frightened girl and led her to a seat near the port window.

"Look! A boat heading this way. Maybe we can get its attention and flag it down." Carly's spirits were rising as she jumped out of Sean's arms and tried to get the window open.

"Don't bother."

It was Jim as he pointed in the direction of the oncoming vessel. "That crew's waving at our 'friends' topside. I think they're rendezvousing with those murderous scum from the sea."

Sam's crew felt the two boats bump as they were anchored together and Dmitry boarded the *Scavenger*. As Dmitry entered the main cabin, he turned towards Borya and instructed him to bring Stompmeyer to him. Obediently, Borya went to retrieve the professor.

"And bring him straight here. No detours! I want to know what these treasure hunters were looking for."

Within minutes, Stompmeyer was being shoved through the cabin door by the burly Russian.

"So, it's you!" cried the professor. "I should have known. Tell your oaf we both work for the same employer."

"Shut up, you fool," Dmitry said. "Our people are not very happy with you at this moment."

"What do you mean?"

. . .

"YOU WERE SUPPOSED to keep in contact. You've been off communication for the past twenty hours. What has been going on and why haven't you kept in touch? I hope, for your sake, that you are not thinking of crossing us."

"Of course not!" Stompmeyer indignantly responded. "Those treasure hunters must have suspected something. Perhaps it was your little incident at the hotel that made them suspicious. In any event, they came to my room and nearly kidnapped me. They refused to allow me to make any calls or arrangements and brought me to this ship. When I arrived, they took off and headed out here. I had no way to communicate with anyone."

"You seemed to accompany them very willingly. I didn't hear you express any opposition when they came to get you."

"You were there? You heard us? How?"

"It is of no concern of yours. I have my methods. Just remember that the next time you try to double-cross me."

Dmitry glared at Stompmeyer as he moved closer to the man and put his arm around his shoulder.

"Now, tell me what you have learned so far. It is nearly time for me to report our progress. What are we doing out here and what is it that we are searching for?"

Stompmeyer stared into Dmitry's eyes, trying to determine if he could trust the man. After looking around the room and seeing the collection of hooligans Dmitry had amassed on the deck outside, he realized that he had no choice. Cautiously, he began to inform Dmitry of a portion of what he had learned so far, knowing that in order to survive he would need to make himself indispensable for as long as possible.

Incredulously, Dmitry listened as Stompmeyer explained about the amulet and the box containing the ancient parchment. He intentionally left out the full translation, as well as his theory about the Stones of Fire and the High Priest's Breastplate, calculating that he would need all the bargaining chips he could gather to protect himself from this loose cannon.

"We think that the shipwreck was carrying some kind of treasure when it sank. The divers were making an initial examination of the wreck when your thugs interrupted. Unfortunately, the divers were unable to relay a report of their findings, so I have no idea if anything of interest was located in the wreck."

"Perhaps we should invite the two divers to discuss with us their observations."

"I don't think you will find them very cooperative after murdering one of their friends. What were your men thinking anyway? Do any of your goons know anything about salvage work? I sincerely doubt it. They don't look the type. If there truly is treasure below, we will need the help of these men, not their disdain and contempt."

Dmitry was unfazed by Stompmeyer's scolding.

"Mind your place!" he snapped back. "Just remember who is in charge here!"

"It certainly is *not* you!" said Stompmeyer. "We both have superiors to report to. I'm sure they would be less than pleased with your methods thus far. Perhaps we should contact them now to discuss the matter?"

Stompmeyer could see that his words were having the desired effect on Dmitry. He was no longer as arrogant or sure of himself. Stompmeyer knew he had to keep the man off-guard in order to ensure his own survival.

"Perhaps you have a better plan, then?" asked Dmitry.

"Let me return to our captives and attempt to convince them to cooperate. They do not know of our connection yet. Perhaps I can uncover additional information from them that might prove helpful. I might also be able to convince them that it would be in their best interests to assist in this endeavor. But you will have to keep your men in check. We don't need any more roughhousing or killing."

Dmitry thought hard for a moment. Perhaps the fool was right. His men were excellent divers, but they had no knowledge of wreck diving or any expertise in salvage work. He would give the professor an opportunity to work with the captives. If nothing resulted from his efforts, he could always revert to his own means of persuasion.

"Very well, I will allow you to try this your way for a little while. But my men will be watching you. Don't try anything foolish or I will explain to our people that you were washed overboard during a storm."

Stompmeyer glared back. "You wouldn't dare!"

Dmitry shoved the man down into a nearby chair while he held his throat with one hand. "Do not cross me or you will find my wrath unbearable. Now go and accomplish what we were sent here to do."

33

Jack pulled the light closer to the manuscript and continued to read on, translating the French in his mind as he went.

My great-uncle had become a member of these knights by order of our grand leader, Simeon Ben Judah. Ever since the destruction and looting of our Temple, we have vowed as a people to recover our lost treasures and restore our heritage. As watchers, we, the Sons of Zadok, have taken our places amongst the looters of our treasures and sacred possessions, biding our time, waiting until the moment was right to recover our prized possessions. When the knights uncovered the Temple's treasures, buried throughout our ancient homeland, it became my family's duty to watch over this treasure until the time to retrieve it was right. We watched as the knights recovered the ancient maps and, site by site, slowly began to accumulate our lost treasure. We saw the knights grow in strength and wealth as they conquered the Muslim armies and recovered some of our lost treasures.

When Jerusalem fell and the knights retreated to Acre, they took with them the treasure they had accumulated, including our sacred possessions and Solomon's gold. After the fall of Acre, as they retreated from the Holy Land, they took with them most of our lost treasure, including the ancient maps detailing the locations of the remaining hiding places, which had been out of their reach. The treasure was dispersed throughout numerous Templar safe houses, where it was carefully concealed for many years. My uncle, Adam Bonfils, also infiltrated the knight's order and became a trusted emissary for them. When the Templar Grand Master, Jacques de Molay, became suspicious of the plans of King Philip IV and Pope Clement V, he ordered the treasures removed from France. My uncle was among the select few who were chosen to transport the treasure to safety. He escorted the sacred items to Scotland, where he was welcomed by the Sinclair clan and provided refuge for many years. The vast treasure was thought to be safe there while the Church persecuted the Templar Knights in France, England and many of the surrounding kingdoms. Only Henry Sinclair and Robert the Bruce in Scotland ignored the conspiratorial persecution thrust upon the knights by the Pope and King Philip IV. Eventually, the treasure was hidden in the Orkney Islands with the Sinclair clan. When my uncle learned of my birth, he convinced my parents to join him in the Orkney Islands. The secrecy of the Watcher's creed was impressed upon me as I grew up. My father and uncle had both given their vows to watch and protect our sacred treasures.

When it was thought to be no longer safe in Scotland, I was recruited to accompany my father and uncle on a great seafaring voyage with Prince Henry Sinclair. We sailed for many days across the ocean until finally reaching a large landmass we named New Scotland. There, we, along with the contingent of knights sent with us, made preparations for hiding and protecting the Templar treasure we had brought with us, including the sacred treasures of our Holy Land.

Secret tunnels were dug on a small island nearby and, over the course of the next ten years, we resided in harmony with the red men we had encountered, who we knew as Micmacs. Since our voyage to this land had been kept a secret from the other kingdoms and the Church, our Templar leaders were confident that their wealth and treasure had been adequately protected. A small contingent remained in this strange land, consisting of myself, my father and uncle, and one hundred others.

When the Prince returned to Orkney, word was sent to other Watchers of our voyage and location. Preparations were made and two ships were built by our brothers in the Mediterranean to sail to our location and reclaim our holy treasures, stolen from our Holy Land so many centuries ago. We were notified by our brethren in the Mediterranean when the ships made sail and we readied ourselves for their arrival. We impatiently waited for their clandestine arrival. When the day finally came, we retrieved our stolen treasures while the remaining knights were distracted by some of our band.

Once the treasures were safely loaded onto our ships, we sailed in two separate directions, one ship to the east and ours to the south. Care was taken to ensure that, if pursued by the knights, at least one of the ships would safely return to the Holy Land.

We sailed for three days on a southerly route along the coastline of this strange land. On the eve of the third day, we spied the Templar fleet in fast pursuit of our ship. In front of us lay a huge storm. Our captain had no choice but to sail directly into the storm. The Templars continued to pursue us as the storm increased in intensity around us. The Templar fleet had closed in and commenced firing on us until the intensity of the storm required our attackers to concentrate on the elements rather than us.

As soon as we thought ourselves safe from impending harm, the entire wrath of the storm turned upon us. Our ship was battered by massive waves, some nearly as high as our crow's nest. The ship was rocked from side to side. As our crew tried to maintain control of the ship, the rest of us were ordered below to secure our load in an effort to stabilize our vessel. After what seemed like hours, everything suddenly became still and quiet. It appeared as if the storm had suddenly abated. Just as we began to feel a modicum of relief, the sky grew ominous once again. Then, suddenly, tons of ocean came crashing down on us, relentlessly, without reprieve. The ship rocked and we heard the central mast crack, crashing through the deck below. A huge crackle was heard as the hull began to give way. Water began to gush in, uncontrollably, as the ship rocked one last time before the ocean lifted the entire craft up in the air, spinning us around like a top and swallowing us whole, swallowing our vessel, its crew and its entire contents deep into the bowels of the sea.

Many of my comrades were either crushed by the cannons or by the other contents of our ship. Some were thrown from the wreck and must have drowned in the turbulent sea. Others, like myself, gasped for air and attempted to escape the clutches of the sea and our sinking ship. I was lucky and located a pocket of air within the hold, maintaining my capacity to breathe while the ship sank to the bottom of the ocean depths. When we finally came to rest, I tried to escape certain death from being swallowed by the sea. I was able to wrestle myself away from my ocean coffin only to realize we had come to rest many fathoms below the sea. I could not swim up, so I swam straight and miraculously entered this cavern.

Upon entry, I realized that it was large enough to accommodate my needs for both space and air. Initially, I felt alone and abandoned, until I came to realize the Lord had saved me and provided me with this sanctuary. Exhausted, I lay giving praise to my Savior, contemplating why God had chosen this path for my comrades and me. Suddenly, an epiphany struck. Our treasures were not meant to be held by the Templars, or any non-Jews, but the world was not yet ready for the return of our treasure to the Holy Land. God had chosen this place to protect His treasures from the rest of the world. He had led us to this vault to secure and protect our most holy of artifacts. We no longer had a High Priest to wear the Breastplate, and until the world was ready for the return of the High Priest, when the Messiah would finally arrive, the secret of its resting place would be protected from the pilfering of man by the sea and its surroundings. It would be up to me to secure its secret here, in this cavern.

Jack was astonished at what he had just read. Was it possibly some hoax by some insane diver who had discovered the cavern at an earlier date? Could a 15th-century warrior have actually survived a wreck at sea and managed to live in this place, one hundred feet below the surface? He needed to catch his breath and think for a moment. The earlier events of the day were beginning to take a toll on him, and his present revelation had stretched the limits of his senses. He needed to rest.

34

"Where have you been, Professor? You look like shit." Tom watched as the man limped back into their cabin, disheveled, with a worn and serious look on his face.

"Our captors are insane. They think we have some vast treasure that we are hiding from them. They mean to find it by any means necessary, even brute force." Stompmeyer looked directly at Carly, sending a shiver down her back.

Sean suddenly jumped up. "What the hell are you talking about?"

"I told you. They insist that we have located a treasure from the wreck below. They know about the box and the jewel and intend on stealing what they believe amounts to a fortune from our wreck. They are nothing more than common pirates."

Geoff was not so sure. Common pirates did not possess the equipment, technology or training of these men. Still wary of the German and his motives, he questioned the man further.

"What happened to you? Tell us from the beginning what they said to you and what you told them."

As the rest of the crew gathered around, Stompmeyer began to relate his encounter with Dmitry in as much detail as he could muster from his actual conversation with the maniac, as well as what he could fabricate. Of course, he conveniently left out any reference to his prior association with the man, as well as their business relationship and common employer.

"After interrogating me and slapping me around, he warned me that he was not a patient man and would require answers soon. He seemed upset about the loss of his man and intent on exacting revenge."

After Stompmeyer had ended the recital of his partially fabricated encounter with the Russian, the crew apprehensively turned toward Sam.

"What are we going to do? Billy's dead from those creeps and we may be next. We haven't found any treasure, only some old military equipment. If the guy knows about the box and the jewel, he knows everything we do. That means we're expendable."

Sean was right. It seemed their captor possessed most of the knowledge they had acquired and did, in fact, mean business. Their usefulness was fast coming to an end, and he was sure the man meant to leave no witnesses.

"Let's not lose our heads yet," said Sam. "This is our boat and our waters. If we keep calm, we may be able to use this knowledge to our advantage. I don't think they are familiar with these waters or the weather patterns of the region. If only we could get to a radio, we might be able to raise the Coast Guard."

Sam was right. Their captors may have imprisoned them for the time being, but they clearly were not familiar with the area or the peculiarities of the *Scavenger*. If they could only stall long enough to formulate a plan until help arrived.

"Where did you leave that portable radio?" Geoff asked Sean. "I know you didn't put it back in the equipment locker. You never do."

One of Sean's many faults was his lack of organization and sloppiness. He never put things back where they belonged and often misplaced critical pieces of equipment. Perhaps this was one occasion when his fault would turn out to be a blessing in disguise.

"I'm not sure."

It was a typical response, but totally unacceptable under the circumstances.

"Come on man, think! For once in your life step up to the plate and be responsible. Shake the cobwebs out of that liquor-soaked brain of yours and remember where you left the damn radio!"

"Leave him alone. If he hadn't thought of that guy with the camera on the dive expedition, we wouldn't have known about the wreck in the first place. Cut him some slack, will you!" Carly quickly came to Sean's defense as she moved to his side and clung to his arm.

"I think I left it in my cabin under my dive bag. But how are we going to get to it?"

Sam called everyone over, out of sight of the guard at the door.

"Professor, how many men were in the hallway when they brought you back?"

"Only the one guard outside the door, why?"

"If we can distract him long enough for Sean to get into his cabin, perhaps he can radio for help. Anyone got any ideas?"

The crew stood pensively gazing at one another. Suddenly Carly began to move towards the cabin door.

"What are you doing?" Sean asked as she began to unbutton her blouse and partially expose her breasts.

"Don't worry about it. Just keep an eye out for your

opportunity to slip out of here and get to that radio."

Carly continued towards the door and grabbed the handle. It was locked from the outside. She banged on the door with both fists until, finally, the guard opened it.

"What is it?" the man said as he raised his weapon with both hands, aiming the butt at her face.

"I feel sick. I need to get to the head as quickly as possible. Please, let me out of here."

The man took one look at Carly's disheveled appearance, blouse half-hanging out of her shorts, hair tossed to one side, and one breast half-dangling out of her top. He stopped his aggressive action and stared at her with longing eyes.

"Please sir, I beg you. Take me to the head, or let one of my friends here help me. I really don't feel well and need to get out of here now."

Sean grabbed her by the waist and started to guide her out the door, glancing at their captor warily. The man motioned for them to exit, then quickly locked the cabin door behind them. He directed them to continue as he watched Carly walk down the hall in her tight shorts. When they reached the bathroom, the guard gestured for Sean to move to the side. As Sean moved away from Carly, edging towards his cabin, Carly flung herself onto the guard. Startled, the guard reached out to push Carly off. As he did, his hand brushed across her exposed breast. The guard began to caress her as Carly twisted her body, giving the man better access to her private parts. She began to groan, lifting her head up towards her captor's, neck outstretched, her tongue wiggling through her partially open lips, in search of an erogenous target.

Sean looked at the two figures erotically entwined and quietly slipped into his cabin, fighting the jealous urges rousing inside him. He quickly located the portable radio and prayed the battery had enough power to make the urgently needed call. As he powered the radio on, he glanced around the room, ensuring his privacy. After a few moments, he breathed a sigh of relief when he heard the Coast Guard respond to his urgent SOS. He quickly gave his coordinates, along with a brief description of the situation, before the radio went dead. He tossed the dead radio back under his dive bag, then groped under his mattress for the switchblade he kept stored there. As he felt the handle, he heard Carly's raspy voice shriek, "I think I'm going to throw up. Let me go, unless you want me to puke all over you!"

Sean peered out from his cabin door and saw the guard jump away from Carly as she threw herself over the toilet. Her face was over the bowl, body heaving, while she gagged and spit into the toilet. Sean stared at her: both her breasts were now exposed, dangling outside her shirt, nipples stiff and erect.

Damn her, he thought, *why did she have to make such a spectacle of herself?*

After a few minutes, she slowly turned her head towards the hallway. Spying Sean, she started to get up and turned towards her captor. "Do you mind if I have a little privacy to get myself straightened out?"

As the guard took one step back, she quickly shut the door and turned on the faucet. Sean stood in the hallway, fists clenched, holding back the desire to pummel the guard. The man turned and pointed his weapon at Sean as if he were reading his thoughts.

"Get back over by the door," the man barked as he pointed the weapon towards the cabin. "I'm not sure I'm through here yet."

They could hear Dmitry's steps coming down the stairs as Carly opened the bathroom door.

"What's going on here?" Dmitry yelled, as the guard grabbed Carly's arm, groping towards her now covered breast.

"Th-the girl was sick and was escorted to the bathroom. I think she threw up just as we got her here," the startled guard stammered.

"And what is this one doing out in the hallway?"

"I dragged her to the bathroom," said Sean. "She was too weak to walk on her own and Igor here wouldn't take her by himself." He grinned as he pointed towards the guard.

Dmitry yelled something in Russian and the guard quickly released his grip from Carly's breast. He then shoved both prisoners down the hall with the butt of his weapon as Dmitry walked behind. As the cabin door opened, Carly and Sean were pushed inside. Dmitry followed them in and faced Sam.

"You are the leader of these men?"

"I am their employer, if that is what you mean."

"Why are you out here?"

"I think you already know. We found this old wreck and have begun exploration. That happens to be what we do for a living. What is it that you're looking for, anyway? Our ship is old and not worth much, and we have no real treasure that would interest a pirate."

"Ah, but we are not pirates. It is your wreck and its treasure that interests us. What is the secret to the box you have uncovered?"

Sam turned away from his inquisitor, shrugging his shoulders as he glanced in Geoff's direction.

"I will return in ten minutes. I suggest you consider cooperating with me or the consequences will be most unpleasant."

As the Russian left with the guard, Sean glared at Carly. "I hope you enjoyed yourself out there."

"Next time, *you* can get felt up by that goon, asshole!"

"Stop bickering, you two. Sean, were you able to get a message out on the radio?"

Sam knew the situation was grim and was in no mood for Sean and Carly's infantile squabble.

Sean gritted his teeth as his face reddened. "I think the radio had enough juice to get one quick message out. I know the Coast Guard picked up, but I can't be sure if they received the whole thing. I don't think the radio went dead until after I gave them our coordinates. What do we do until the cavalry comes?"

They all huddled together, trying to devise a plan while awaiting their optimistic rescue.

35

"Captain, quick! Come take a look at this!" the young ensign excitedly yelled from behind the radio controls. It was the boy's first assignment and he was unsure if he had heard the frantic message correctly.

The Captain was an eighteen-year veteran, having been on active duty during the heightened security in the days after 9/11. He was a tall man, standing 6'3", sporting a black beard and mustache, more closely resembling the Gloucester fisherman than a Coast Guard officer. Captain Richard Matthews was looking forward to his impending retirement in a little over a year and was hoping his last thirteen months would be incident-free, unlike the bulk of his crew, which consisted mainly of new recruits hungry for excitement, the most eager of whom was the young ensign.

"Calm down, lad. What is it you are ranting about?"

"Look, sir. This message just came through. An urgent SOS."

The ensign replayed Sean's call for the Captain to hear.

"Pull up those coordinates. Let's see how close we are to these supposed poor distressed souls."

The Captain had seen it all during his lengthy service. He was skeptical of an SOS claiming capture by pirates off the coast of Florida. After all, this wasn't Somalia or South America. It was probably some prankster testing out the Coast Guard's response time to a phony SOS, similar to the kid who pulls the fire alarm in school.

"There! It looks like we're about seventy kilometers southwest of their location. What should we do, sir?"

The Captain looked at the screen and then back at the ensign. "Check with radar. Does it show any activity at those coordinates?"

"Looks like two ships, huddled close together. What do you make of it, sir?"

"I'm not sure. Contact headquarters and find out if they have any reports of missing vessels in the area. Oh, I also want any information on this *Scavenger* vessel. Let's find out who we're dealing with before we proceed."

The young ensign quickly went about his assigned tasks. Within minutes he had obtained a brief history of the *Scavenger* and its known crew. As he turned to hand the printout to his commander, an urgent message came over the radio from headquarters. White-faced and visibly shaken, the young recruit removed his headpiece and handed it to the Captain.

"Well, what is it, man? What's wrong?"

"HQ wants to talk to you directly, in private, sir."

With a questioning look on his face, the Captain accepted the headgear from the ensign and saluted the man as he exited the cabin. Once the cabin was secured, the Captain placed the headpiece on his head and began to communicate with his base. As he did so, he briefly perused the printout the young ensign had handed him, which contained the information he had requested about the *Scavenger* and its crew.

"I understand, sir. Yes, right away. I'll put my crew on full alert and have HQ kept fully abreast of all stages of the operation. I figure it will take close to an hour to come into contact with them. Any idea of what we are to expect? How many subjects are we to anticipate? What kind of weapons do they have on board?"

The Captain was uneasy, taking on such a task with such little information, especially with his novice crew. He slowly shook his head as he received the vague responses to his queries. *How the hell do they expect me to carry this off without providing me with the intelligence I need as well as an experienced crew?* he thought to himself.

Resigned to the orders he had just been given, he immediately reviewed all the available information on the *Scavenger* and its crew. Perhaps some of their crew members could be of assistance, if they were still alive and in any condition to help. He then reviewed the known information on the Russian group. While the dive boat was not of any great significance, he was wary of its size. *Why such a large vessel? What might they be carrying on board, and how many men do they have with them?* he thought to himself.

As he began to review the dossiers of the men known to be with the Russian, Matthews's face began to wince. It was clear to him that his men would be outmatched, at least in experience, by the Russian crew. Did headquarters really believe they were sending his boat on a rescue mission or a suicide mission? He would need a lot of luck, hopefully some divine assistance, and maybe some good old Yankee ingenuity in order to pull this off.

As he left the cabin, he directed the ensign to call for a full battle alert. He would address the crew shortly, but he wanted them to all be battle-ready. Eagerly, the young man carried out his commander's orders as Matthews walked down the corridor to his cabin.

36

Jack awoke with a start. How long had he been asleep? He looked at his watch and was relieved that not more than an hour had passed. He rose and began to examine his surroundings more closely. Apparently, the young knight had furnished the cavern with remains from the wreck. In fact, the man had been quite inventive in his decorating style.

Over time, the man had been able to salvage a desk, a cot, and some implements from the ship's galley. He had even managed to figure out a way to cook while he remained in his underwater prison. As he looked around, Jack chuckled to himself, imagining the young knight setting up his "bachelor pad" in the cavern, complete with chairs and a full array of furnishings. He could just imagine the man entertaining the local groupers while he wrote his memoirs.

Jack continued to explore the cavern and was amazed at the fresh water cistern and shelving his host had devised. How long had this man lived here before his death, Jack wondered?

Had he truly resigned himself to his fate, or did he long to breach the surface? These were questions Jack knew he would never know the answers to, but at least these thoughts kept his mind off his own predicament.

He began to more closely examine the treasures the knight had so valiantly rescued and ensconced in the cavern. He saw a box that closely resembled the one they had recovered and opened aboard the *Scavenger*. As he searched for its key among the treasure, he found many Judaic artifacts, including several urns containing ancient-looking coins with an inscription that he could not read on one side and a cornucopia with a pomegranate in the center. He also uncovered bracelets and rings, as well as silver trumpets. The knight had accumulated quite a collection from the sunken ship. How long had he labored in his task?

Jack estimated the value of the treasure in the millions. There appeared to be jewels of all kinds, some even embedded in what looked like a table covered in gold, with two gold poles passing through golden rings located on its legs. He leaned forward for a closer look at the intricate carvings on the table, wondering about its purpose. As he did, he glanced back at the knight's skeleton still seated in its final resting place, the nautical chair behind the captain's desk. Still holding the box in his hand, Jack examined it more closely.

He thought there was something odd about it. The symbol appeared the same as the one he saw on the boat, but only smaller. Could it be too small for another amulet? Perhaps he should have been looking for a coin or a ring that might hold the key. He surveyed the treasure trove then glanced back at his silent host. Shaking his head, he chastised himself for not being more observant initially. Slowly, he walked over to his silent benefactor and gently lifted the skeletal remains of what had once been the man's left hand. As he did, a golden ring slid off its boney resting place, landing on the desk below with a clang.

"Sorry, old friend," Jack whispered as he gently placed the hand back on the desk and lifted the ring for a closer inspection. Jack felt foolish as he examined the ring containing the Star of David, and the hamsa with the eyes strategically placed within the star's angles. Lifting the ring towards the box, Jack took a deep breath, slowly exhaling while he said a silent prayer. He inserted the ring into the indentation on the side of the box, carefully matching the star and each eye with its identical twin. After waiting a moment and observing nothing of significance, he heard a faint snap. As he removed the ring, the box began to open before his eyes.

Inside was another parchment scroll. Jack slowly unrolled the scroll and examined the strange markings. They appeared to resemble the other box's markings, but Jack could not be certain. He had no training in ancient languages and once more wished that Carly, or even the professor, were there with him. At the bottom of the scroll, there appeared to be a map with strange markings. More puzzled than ever, he carefully rolled up the scroll and replaced it in its hiding place. Closing the box, he put the ring on his own finger, and his thoughts turned to his friends aboard the *Scavenger*. It was time he returned to the surface to help his friends.

37

"**Battle stations, everyone!**" the ensign shouted. "Red alert! Red alert! Look lively now!"

The adrenaline was coursing through the young man's body, causing him to feel as if he were walking on air. He kept shouting to the rest of the crew as he ran through the ship, taking two stairs at a time as he descended from the bridge.

The young crew was surprised by the ensign's cries. None had ever considered the possibility that they would engage in any type of combat mission so soon, and so close to their own shores. As the inexperienced crew scrambled to man their battle stations, Captain Matthews emerged from the bridge to address his men. With his Chief Petty Officer beside him, he tried to instill all the confidence he could in his untested, novice crew.

"Men," he began, speaking through a megaphone, in plain view of his crew. "We have a situation. There are two ships less than one hour away. One of them is a treasure-hunting ship, the *Scavenger*, which we believe may have been boarded by pirates. There is another vessel adjacent to the *Scavenger* which we believe contains the hostiles. I want to caution all of you. Intel advises us that there may be some mercenaries aboard the pirate vessel, some of whom may be ex-Russian Navy SEALS. They must be considered extremely armed and dangerous, so I want you all on full alert...AND DON'T TAKE ANY CHANCES."

All at once the young crew turned toward one another, palms sweating and an eerie chill coursed through every man's body. Six months out of basic training didn't match up to the experience these mercenaries appeared to possess.

"Now we've got a state-of-the-art vessel, armed with the latest technological advances," the Captain continued. "Every one of you has had sufficient training to excel in this type of situation. All of you need to remain calm and cautious, and use all the skills and training you learned in the academy." Captain Matthews tried to be as reassuring as possible, hoping that he was not sending these brave young souls to possible doom.

After hearing the Captain's words, the young ensign suddenly began to turn green, the adrenaline rush having run its course as the reality of what they would soon be facing began to sink in. He tried to catch his breath, but was beginning to hyperventilate. These pirates were not the run-of-the-mill drug runners he had expected to encounter. These were cold and hardened combat soldiers! What chance did unseasoned rookies stand against such odds?

"Shouldn't we wait for reinforcements?" the ensign asked the Captain.

"Are you questioning the orders I just gave, ensign?"

"No...no, sir. It would just seem—"

"It would just seem that you are out of line and bordering on insubordination," the Captain interrupted. "You have your orders. Now carry them out!"

Matthews knew the young ensign was right, but he had been directed to intervene immediately. As the crew armed the ship's weapons, Matthews stared ahead at the open sea, thinking about the young crew of the *Sentinel,* wondering how they would face the uncertain adversity which lay ahead.

The *Sentinel* was indeed a state-of-the-art vessel. Commissioned in 2008, it was the latest in the Coast Guard's fleet of Fast Response Cutters, or FRCs, as they were commonly referred to. It was 140 feet long, armed with a remotely operated 25mm machine gun and four .50 caliber machine guns. There was a crew of eighteen raw recruits, two chief petty officers and two officers. Equipped with the most sophisticated radar and navigational systems available, it was designated as a formidable weapon for patrolling the waterways, assisting in search and rescue, drug and illegal immigrant law enforcement, as well as national defense operations. With a top speed of almost 35 miles per hour, it was clearly built for the type of task it was now undertaking. Matthews only hoped his crew could rise to the challenge they would soon be facing.

"Sir! We've got both vessels in sight. We should be in contact within five minutes. What are our orders, sir?"

Matthews's attention now turned to the young ensign who had, at last, seemed to compose himself and restore his false sense of courage.

"Have the men ready to board both vessels, fully armed and fully alert. Make sure no one takes any chances and everyone backs each other up."

"Aye-aye, sir," the ensign responded.

Matthews returned to his command center and had the radioman try to hail personnel on both approaching vessels. After several futile attempts, Matthews grabbed the microphone for the loudspeaker.

"This is your Captain. Men, be on full battle alert! We have not gotten any response from either vessel. Consider all occupants of each vessel hostile, armed and dangerous. But be careful. There may be innocent civilians aboard."

He then switched the microphone from the ship's loudspeaker to its public address system.

"This is Captain Richard Matthews of the United States Coast Guard FRC Sentinel. All occupants are directed to come topside immediately with hands visible. Any weapons must be discarded immediately."

After a few minutes of nonresponsive silence, Matthews repeated the instructions again. It was becoming all too clear that the pirates were not going to comply and an armed encounter would be likely. Matthews turned to his two Chief Petty Officers and directed them to get the men ready to board the *Scavenger*, and to expect armed resistance.

38

Dmitry warily monitored the Coast
Guard ship's transmissions from his vantage point within
his command ship. After taking some time to survey the
situation and his options, he radioed Borya with his latest set
of instructions.

"How many men do you have left on the *Scavenger?*" he
asked.

"Seven," Borya quickly replied.

"I want you to bring the professor and the old man to me
immediately, along with the relics they found, then prepare
your men for some company. I believe the United States Coast
Guard intends to board the *Scavenger.* I want your men to be
ready for them and welcome them properly."

"I understand perfectly. What do you want me to do with
the remainder of the crew?"

"Eliminate them!"

As Dmitry signed off, a devious smile crossed his face. He

was not sure of the significance of the Americans' discovery, but knew that he would have a better chance of exploring further once he escaped from the area with the professor and the evidence from the *Scavenger*. He did not relish the thought of engaging in a prolonged battle with the United States Coast Guard and realized that the *Sentinel* would only be the first of many to come if he lingered too long.

Dmitry turned toward the intercom and told the captain to ready his crew for an immediate launch upon command. After directing the rest of his team to be on continued alert in the event the *Sentinel* directed its attention toward his boat, he slowly climbed the stairs leading to the bridge to watch the drama begin to unfold.

Suddenly Captain Matthews's voice barked through the megaphone laced with a sense of urgency. "This is your final opportunity. You are being directed by the United States Coast Guard to immediately come topside and show yourselves, unarmed, with hands in full view!"

Dmitry knew the man's words were falling on deaf ears. As he reached the bridge, he could see Borya readying his men for the expected onslaught. Six of his men deftly spread out across the deck of the *Scavenger*, secreting themselves from the Coast Guard's view. Borya and one of his men disappeared below to carry out the second part of Dmitry's orders before the Americans began their boarding maneuvers.

Timing was everything in his line of work, and he needed to buy his men some time to complete their mission aboard the *Scavenger* without interference.

"Viktor!" he quickly yelled down toward his man standing at the cabin door. "We need a diversion. Get one of the other men and get down under that Coast Guard cutter. Take it down any way you can before they can board the boat. Do you understand?"

The man nodded his assent. He quickly disappeared below

with one of the other men and began to don his diving gear and gather the necessary equipment. Within minutes he was fully attired and had gathered some ammunition and detonation equipment, including several limpet mines. The two men nodded silently at each other, grabbed the remainder of their gear and quickly disappeared into the ocean, fixing their attention toward their designated target.

39

The crew of the *Scavenger* impatiently listened to the commotion above. Sean's heart was pounding as he heard the commands from the *Sentinel*. "Sounds like the cavalry has arrived," he smugly announced to the rest of the crew.

"Don't get too cocky," Geoff said quickly as he pointed to the two Russians making their way through the halls of the ship. "They look like they mean business, and I don't think they intend to cooperate with the Coast Guard. Get ready. I don't think this will be a friendly visit."

Tom nodded in agreement and motioned to the crew to spread out through the room. Spying the fire extinguisher mounted on the wall, he grabbed it from its resting place and moved into a defensive position by the doorway. Carly slowly moved into the middle of the room intending to act as a decoy, turning any attention away from Tom's hiding spot. As she did so, she called Sean over and threw her arms around him, planting kisses up his neck as she quietly whispered in his ear, "What did you do with that knife of yours?"

"It's in my belt behind my back, under my shirt," he replied.

Hearing his response, she slowly spun him around so his back was facing away from the door. "Let me get it. Maybe we can get close enough for me to shove it in one of those sons of bitches."

"No," he whispered back as he reached behind and stayed her arm. "It's too dangerous. These guys mean business. They're too well-trained for you. Let me take care of it."

Reluctantly, Carly relaxed her grip as she felt Sean furtively remove the knife from his waistband.

As he watched his friends get themselves into position to defend themselves, Jim began to desperately look around the room for his own manner of defense. After several futile attempts, a thought entered his mind. He picked up the aerosol can of Lysol spray with one hand as he placed the other hand in his right pocket, surreptitiously searching for his lighter.

Just then Borya and his lackey, a stocky Ukrainian, entered the room with their guns drawn.

"What's going on?" Geoff demanded.

"Out of my way," growled Borya.

"Look, we've tried to cooperate with you guys. We heard the Coast Guard out there. Just leave us alone and we'll mind our own business," Geoff continued.

"Enough," said Borya as he struck him on the left temple with his gun.

Sam quickly ran to his friend's aid. "What's wrong with you? You could have killed him!" Sam looked up at the Russian as he knelt beside Geoff.

"You, come with me," Borya barked as he pointed the gun towards Sam.

"Wh-what do you want? Where are you taking me?"

"Don't worry. You'll be well taken care of, that I can promise you." Borya laughed as he quickly grabbed Sam by the wrist and began to drag him out of the room yelling for the professor to follow.

Sam tried to struggle, but he was no match for the huge Russian. As he was slowly dragging the older man out of the room, Borya turned towards his companion.

"You know what to do, yes?"

The man nodded and raised his weapon, slowly attaching the silencer to the muzzle's tip as he began walking towards Jim. Quickly closing his eyes, Jim said a quick prayer and turned to face his assailant. Then he opened his eyes, raised the aerosol can while pressing the nozzle with his finger, pulled the lighter from his pocket and held it in front of the spray. As he lit the lighter the spray ignited, sending flames directly into his assailant's eyes, causing the man to drop his weapon to the floor. Jim continued to attack the man with his improvised flamethrower, not allowing his assailant any respite.

Seeing the attack on his companion, Borya threw Sam to the side pushing him and the professor into the nearby wall and pointed his weapon at Jim.

"You fool! What do you think you are doing? I will make you pay for your insolence!"

Borya placed his right foot to his rear and brought his gun up with both hands. As he was taking aim, Tom jumped from out of his hiding spot, firing the extinguisher directly at Borya's eyes. Startled, Borya turned his attention towards this new foe. Seeing his chance, Sean gently pushed Carly away from him and towards the floor, out of harm's way, with one hand. He then quickly turned towards the startled Russian, gripping the knife in his right hand behind his head. Distracted by Tom and the fire extinguisher, Borya failed to see Sean as he threw the knife at the Russian's chest. Before he could get off a shot, Borya suddenly felt a sharp pain as the knife found its mark, puncturing his lung. He slowly fell to his knees before collapsing completely to the ground.

As Carly lay on the floor, watching in awe as Sean felled the Russian, she saw his companion's gun on the ground within arm's reach. Ignoring the screams and confusion surrounding her, she dove for the gun and aimed it at the surviving mercenary. Jim's aerosol can had been completely expended by this time and its flame had begun to die out. Although in obvious pain, the Ukrainian was beginning to get his bearings and was reaching for the small automatic holstered in his boot. Carly pulled the trigger, sending six shots into the man's abdomen.

"You bastard!" escaped from her lips before her legs gave way beneath her and she nauseously crumpled to the floor.

Tom dropped the fire extinguisher and looked around the room. Blood was splattered throughout, and the stench of death and burnt skin permeated the air. Sam lay sprawled on the ground, semi-conscious, with a huge bruise above his right eye. Jim was visibly shaken, surprised at the courage he had exhibited. Groggily, Geoff began to groan as he held his head with his hand, blood seeping down the side of his face.

Sean cautiously walked over and checked the fallen attackers.

"They're both dead," he stated as he turned towards his companions. Seeing Carly on the ground, shaking and in tears, he quickly ran to her side.

"Hey, are you all right? You did damn good back there, you know."

He cupped her face in his hands, wiped the tears from her eyes and brushed stray hairs from her face. Then he pulled her head towards his and kissed her on the lips.

"It's all right. Hush, it'll be okay. Everything will be just fine."

Sean pulled her body close to his and cradled her head against his shoulder as he gently rocked her from side to side.

"Sam, are you okay?" Tom asked.

"I think so. What the hell just happened?"

"I think they meant to kill us and take you with them."

"But what about the Coast Guard?"

"These Russians mean business," said Tom. "They're obviously professionals and I don't think they give a damn about the government."

"Then it's not over yet, and that Coast Guard ship is in danger. If they were able to board us so easily, they might be planning on attacking the cutter. We've got to warn them somehow. Are you guys up to it?"

They all looked around at each other and nodded in agreement. They gathered themselves up and each grabbed a weapon from the dead men. In silent unity, the group slowly began to exit the cabin and ascend to the upper deck.

40

Jack began to rummage around the cave, searching through the vast arsenal collected by the French knight. As he approached the pile of shields, he glanced quickly at the contrast between the shields containing the Templar cross and the gold shields adorned with the Star of David. He laughed at the irony of the two symbols contrasting with each other as they lay buried together in their oceanic tomb. He continued past the spears and javelins before stopping at the assemblage of swords and daggers. He tried to picture himself in his scuba gear and wetsuit with a broadsword strapped to his side. The image brought a chuckle before he quickly discarded the thought and began to examine the various daggers at his feet.

Some of the daggers were quite elaborate, containing emeralds and diamonds carefully placed in the hilt. One bore the Templar symbol engraved in the pommel, with emeralds of escalating sizes embedded in the grip. Carefully implanted in the center of the guard was a larger emerald. The decorative handle extended into the center of the ricasso leading into the blade, starting with a dual-edged sawtooth merging with the flat shaft that trailed to its tip. Jack chose this one as he marveled at its craftsmanship. Oddly enough, it felt comfortable in his hand. The weight was evenly distributed throughout, and the blade had remained remarkably sharp over the centuries.

He continued his search for armament as he rummaged through the false Templar's stash. At the foot of his skeletal companion lay a dagger sheathed in lambskin. Jack bent down to take a closer look. He let out a gasp as his eyes focused on the grip. Inlaid with small precious and semiprecious stones was the symbol which had launched this whole nightmare: the hand set within the Star of David. The blade was slightly curved, and had a minor gray patina to it. At the base of the blade appeared symbols which Jack could not decipher. They resembled the symbols on the parchment that he had discovered earlier as he had examined the box on board the *Scavenger* with Sam and the others. Perhaps it was some Hebrew word or saying; perhaps a name or clue to the mystery that had been unraveling over the past days. Jack did not know, but chose to take the weapon with him.

His armaments nearly complete, Jack continued his inspection of his host's massive cache of arms. Alongside the cavern's wall he spied various types of bows. He was able to discern the long bows and crossbows piled in the corner. Some of the other objects were more puzzling in appearance. There were a few weapons which vaguely resembled the crossbow, appearing to be an ancient and distant relative of the crossbows Jack had any familiarity with. The almost mint condition of all the weapons buried within the lair greatly surprised Jack. He picked up the strange object and began a closer inspection. It felt remarkably light and appeared well-preserved despite its obvious age. The centuries had been kind to it and the mechanism appeared fully functional. It was made of a hard and polished wood, combined with what appeared to be horn and sinew, and tied together with animal tendon. Jack vaguely remembered some of the weaponry training he had received while in the service and concluded that the object was, in fact, some sort of crossbow made from a composite material.

The stock was also of a highly polished wood containing intricate carvings. The tip of the stock resembled the head of a lion, slightly angled, with an open mouth, as if it were roaring ferociously at its enemy. Delicately carved along the side of the stock were small six-pointed stars: Stars of David. The string appeared to be made of some sort of plant material. A quiver lay alongside and contained numerous differently styled bolts, some with feathers and others that were just plain. Jack chose a few of the plain, non-feathered projectiles and tested out the bow. Content that he had armed himself as well as could be expected under the circumstances, he donned his dive gear and readied himself for his ascent to the surface, strategically placing his weapons so they did not interfere with his gear, but were within easy reach if needed quickly. If he could have seen himself in a mirror, he would have laughed at the anachronistic sight about to embark from the cavern.

As Jack slowly slid into the water, he thought of his comrades above and silently said a prayer for the safe return of all those dear to him. He floated through the cavern's opening and kept a wary eye out for the lionfish and jellyfish whose timely arrival hours earlier had saved him from almost certain annihilation. He swam towards the wreck, taking care to keep himself as camouflaged as possible in the event the pirates chose to return. As he swam around the wrecked ship, he spied air bubbles above him fifty feet ahead. He looked up and saw two divers heading towards the *Scavenger*. It looked like they were dragging something with them. Jack tried hard to make out the objects and suddenly realized they were limpets, naval mines. At first Jack thought they were heading towards his friends on the *Scavenger*. As he took a closer look, however, he realized that another ship had arrived in the vicinity while he was in the cavern exploring the ancient mysteries from centuries before. The divers with the limpets were swimming in the new ship's direction.

Stealthily, Jack began to follow the two divers from a safe distance. He was curious to find out what they were up to, and also thought he might have an opportunity to even the odds with the element of surprise on his side. As he closed the gap between himself and his two targets, a feeling of dread quickly overwhelmed him. "These guys mean business and have no fear of anyone or any government," Jack said to himself. Jack quickly recognized the ship being targeted by the pirates as a U.S. Coast Guard cutter. It was obvious that the divers intended to attach the mines to the ship. Jack knew he had to do something quickly or many young men would meet certain death.

Jack lunged forward, kicking with his finned legs with all his might. He knew he had to close the gap quickly and quietly. The medieval crossbow did not have the distance or accuracy he would need and the SPP-1 was really a close range weapon. He needed to get closer, using surprise to his advantage. As he closed the gap, the two saboteurs separated, with one heading towards the bow, and the other towards the stern of the vessel. As Jack caught up to the unwary diver near the stern, Jack unleashed the crossbow and carefully aimed towards the man. The bolt sprung from the ancient weapon and found its mark, lodging itself deep within the man's chest before he could realize he had been attacked. The water immediately surrounding him turned a cloudy shade of crimson as the man grabbed his side, dropping his satchel of destruction towards the ocean floor.

Jack quickly turned his attention towards the surviving diver just as the man had finished attaching the mines to the hull and had set the timers to detonate. As the saboteur swam away from the cutter in search of his comrade, he spied Jack furiously swimming towards him. After glancing around and locating his fallen comrade slowly sinking towards the ocean depths, the man turned his attention to Jack. Having lost the element of surprise, Jack withdrew the underwater pistol from his BC and quickly fired a shot in the other man's direction. The bullet nicked the man's right arm, but did not slow him down. Jack realized he would not have time to get off another shot at the man so, instead, he began defensive maneuvers, trying to gain a better strategic position from which he could launch another attack.

As Jack swam, trying to avoid the man's onslaught, he noticed the glint of steel emanating from the diver's left hand. The man was now aiming a spear gun directly at Jack. Jack knew he had no time to lose. Jack saw the spear shoot from the weapon as he quickly reacted, furiously letting the air out of his BC, which caused him to sink deeper towards the seabed. Jack felt the spear whiz by his mask as it fell harmlessly in the coral below. Before he could recover, Jack saw the attacking diver reach towards his regulator hose, trying to cut his lifeline with the knife in his hand. Instinctively, Jack reached into the quiver attached to his own BC, grabbed one of the remaining crossbow bolts, and blindly shoved the point towards his attacker's throat. Between the momentum produced by the diver's attack on Jack, and the force of Jack's thrust, the man had no chance to escape. As the bolt entered the man's throat, he let out a gurgle while his left hand dropped the knife meant for Jack. The diver fell into Jack, forcing their two bodies down into the sand on the ocean floor. As Jack tried to wrest himself loose from the dead man an explosion rocked the area, sending currents and shock waves in Jack's direction.

Jack looked up from beneath the dead man watching in awe as the Coast Guard cutter split in two and slowly sank in the murky, silt-filled waters surrounding him. Jack stared as the remains of the ship fell silently on top of the cavern he had taken refuge in just a short time earlier. He thanked God he had left the underwater sanctuary, or else he surely would have been buried below with his skeletal companion. Jack's heart was heavy, though. He was cognizant of the senseless loss of life which he had just witnessed, and distinctly aware of the threat the pirates posed to his friends above. The Coast Guard crew, rather than being the saviors of the *Scavenger*, had fallen victim themselves to whatever maniac was in command above. With no time to waste, Jack inflated his BC, beginning his ascent to the surface one more time. He could only hope that he could render better aid to his friends than he had been able to render to the unsuspecting Coast Guard crew.

41

Captain Matthews waited only minutes for a response from the pirate vessel before dispatching the Short Range Prosecutor from the rear of the *Sentinel.*

"Ensign, I want you to select five men and board the SRP with Chief Petty Officer Clark," the commander barked loudly. "I don't trust these pirates and I doubt they intend to surrender without putting up some sort of fight."

"Aye-aye, sir!" the young ensign quickly responded while smartly snapping to attention at his commander's orders. As nervous as he was, the young ensign felt secure in his Captain's leadership and judgment. Hurriedly, he selected the five men and gathered his gear before boarding the small SRP.

While the SRP was built to accommodate ten men, the ensign was glad to have the added room provided by the smaller crew. He checked the machine gun mounted on the front, ensuring there was an ample supply of ammunition. As soon as the Chief Petty Officer arrived, the order was given to launch the Rigid-Hull inflatable craft. As it began to circle into position adjacent to the pirate vessel, the crew heard a loud explosion and turned in horror as they witnessed the *Sentinel* break apart in two. The force of the explosion sent waves rushing at the small craft, almost causing it to capsize. They could feel the heat on their faces from the intensity of the flames as their mother ship slowly broke in two, sinking with amazing speed to the ocean depths below them.

"Wh-what the hell?" the Chief Petty Officer exclaimed while the rest of the small crew remained frozen, expressions of shock and despair creeping over their awestruck faces. "Those goddamn sons of bitches! Ensign! Snap out of it and get your men in ready position! It's payback time. Let's show those creeps who they're dealing with. Get on that machine gun and start blasting away. I want that boat blown in two just like they did to ours!"

The men slowly shook off their shock and got into position. The ensign grabbed the machine gun and started firing at the pirate vessel, strafing the side of the boat, trying to hit the fuel tank. As the Russians scrambled topside, the rest of the Coast Guard survivors began showering the deck with a barrage from their own weapons. One of the Russians fell writhing in pain from the gunshot wound to his abdomen as blood spewed aimlessly out of the man's body.

"Dmitry! Quick! Sergei's been hit. What do you want we should do?"

Dmitry glanced around at his remaining men as they tried to fire back at the Coast Guard inflatable.

"Dmitry, look!" yelled another crew member.

As Dmitry spun around, his eyes widened and his forehead bulged, a sure sign of his anger and frustration, as he saw the white helicopter with orange stripes crest over the horizon. The shape and sound were unmistakable.

"Coast Guard. HH-60," he muttered aloud. "Quick!" he

yelled. "Tell the captain to hoist anchor and take us away from here. In fact, Yuri, I want you to take over operation of this boat now. Take immediate evasive maneuvers and get us to safety."

Dmitry was not pleased at the prospect of giving up, at least temporarily, the quest which he had so recently begun, especially after making the headway he had by learning the secrets uncovered by Stompmeyer and the *Scavenger* crew. He knew that the Coast Guard's intervention was quickly making this part of his mission too dangerous to continue. He also knew he would always be able to locate the German through the GPS he had implanted in the man's cane. As he mulled over his options in his mind, the ship's engines quickly roared to life, causing the boat's hull to jerk in the air as they began to speed away to safety. Yuri was his best pilot and he knew he could trust him to evade the airborne and seafaring pursuers so savagely chasing after him.

Meanwhile, the crew aboard the *Scavenger* watched with a mixture of fear, despair and amazement as the battle between the Coast Guard and their foreign captors waged. The bubble of salvation they thought had been provided to them burst quickly when the *Sentinel* exploded in the midst of the hostile waters, sending their one-time saviors to a watery grave. As the small inflatable struck back at their captors, glimmers of hope began to emerge. When the pirates retreated to the open ocean waters, attempting to evade both the inflatable and the Coast Guard attack helicopter, sighs of relief escaped from those standing on the *Scavenger's* deck. For the first time in days, the crew felt a modicum of security in knowing they had not been forgotten by their government.

"This is *Rescue One*," a solitary voice crackled over the radio. "*Scavenger*, does anyone below read me? Please acknowledge."

Sam quickly ran to the radio receiver and responded to the inquiry. "This is the *Scavenger*. Thank God you guys appeared when you did. What the hell is going on and where did those guys come from?"

"That's what we would like to know. What happened to the *Sentinel*?"

"Those bastards blew it up right before our eyes. I don't think those poor souls knew what was happening until it was too late. Thank God they launched that small inflatable before the explosion. At least there are some survivors," Sam continued.

"Where's Jack?" the voice on the radio asked anxiously.

It was at that point that a tinge of familiarity struck a chord in Sam's mind. "Brian, is that you? How the hell...?"

"Yeah, Sam, it's me. I'll explain later. Let me speak to Jack."

"I don't know where he is. We haven't seen him since the first dive yesterday morning when those goons showed up and took over. They killed one of my men while Jack was exploring the site below. The rest of my dive crew surfaced with those goons, but Jack did not. I think he was alive at some point, because they were asking a lot of questions about him. He must have caused some kind of ruckus below for them to have shown such an interest in him. But I fear the worst, since he never surfaced and there's no way he could survive at that depth for that length of time, even if he had a constant supply of air. There are no landmasses for miles around, so even if he surfaced, I'm sure hypothermia would have set in long ago. I'm not looking forward to telling Alexandra."

Sam began to choke at the thought of imparting the devastating news to Jack's wife. There was a somber air of silence as the two men briefly lost themselves in thought and remembrance of their close friend.

"Look, there. Off the port side. Something just surfaced. Quick, shine a light over that way!" Tom yelled, breaking through the gloom that had engulfed the crew over the loss of their friend. As the object began to get closer, they could tell it was a diver. Unsure of whether he was friend or foe, Sean quickly picked up one of the automatic weapons they had commandeered from their captors. While carefully pointing it in the diver's direction he yelled out, "I've got a gun aimed right at your head! Inflate your BC and keep both hands in the air where I can see them!"

The diver slowly complied and, as he approached the ship, he lifted his mask from his face and removed his regulator from his mouth.

"That's not quite the reception I expected. How long are you going to make me stay like this? I'd really like to come aboard and take a shower and climb into some fresh clothes."

"Jack, is that really you?" Carly cried out, as tears slowly flowed down her cheeks. "We thought you were dead!"

"Sorry to disappoint you, but it looks like I'm going to live to see another day. Can I come aboard now?"

"Put that fool thing down!" Sam barked to Sean as he motioned to Jack to board the vessel. "Someone help him up, quickly."

PART
TWO

42

Rachel Lyons was never a morning person. She dreaded the bothersome ring of her alarm clock and would procrastinate in removing herself from the warmth and security of her bed. Her morning ritual consisted of knocking the alarm off her nightstand and burrowing herself under the covers until she heard the incessant ring of her telephone, reminding her that she was late again for work. This morning would be no different.

"Good morning, sunshine. Get your lazy ass out of bed. You're already an hour late for work and we've got a deadline to make. Remember, you've got that meeting this morning?"

"Damn you, Robert! You know I've got it under control. I was just on my way out."

"Sure you were, sis. If I didn't cover your ass on an almost daily basis, you would be out of a job."

"Yeah, sure. Well, thanks anyway. I'll see you soon."

"Try and get here before noon! The meeting starts at 11:30 and I don't know if I can cover for you this time."

"Anything you say, darling brother."

Rachel Lyons and her brother, Robert, were 32-year-old twins, American transplants from Chicago trying to make their way in the world of journalism by working for the Israeli newspaper *Haaretz*, headquartered in Jerusalem.

Rachel dragged herself out of bed and stumbled into the bathroom with one eye shut and one eyelid fighting to separate itself so she could see where she was going. She grasped the shower handle and screamed as the icy water sprayed out.

"Shit! No hot water again. What else can go wrong today?"

Hungover from the night before, she resigned herself to the icy fate she was about to experience, telling herself it served her right for her debacle last evening. What had she been thinking, mixing a bottle of wine with a six pack of Goldstar? Her head was going to throb for the rest of this day, that she was sure of. She had sure made a fool of herself last night, trying to pick up that Israeli soldier. How was she to know he was married? And just how had she gotten home. anyway? Her thoughts were too muddled to make any sense, so she continued with her frigid shower, rinsing herself off as quickly as possible and throwing on her clothes, hurrying for her appointment at the paper. She really wished she had a cup of coffee, but, as usual, she was out of coffee and her pot was broken, anyway.

After throwing on her cleanest outfit, she quickly brushed her hair (thankfully she kept it fairly short), skipped the makeup, which she rarely used anyway, grabbed her bag and stumbled down the two flights of stairs from her apartment. As she tripped on the last step, she grabbed hold of the wall and bounced out the door to the street. On her way to the paper she quickly stopped for that much-needed cup of hot black coffee, taking large gulps as she rushed to her meeting, willing the sledgehammer in her head to stop pounding.

Rachel glanced at her watch as she rounded the corner and headed towards the building's entrance.

"Damn it! 11:28. I'm going to be late again," she thought to herself.

"Morning Avi! I'm running late again. Can we skip the security shit, just this one time?" Rachel coyly asked the security guard at the entrance.

"You know I can't do that. Why do you ask me the same question every day?"

"Because I'm always late, you idiot."

"You know, for a Goy you can be pretty irritating sometimes. Put your bag down so I can scan it and let's get you to your meeting. I'll call ahead and tell them you're downstairs on your way up."

"Thanks, you're a doll, even if you are an idiot."

Rachel waited at the elevator for what seemed like an eternity until the doors opened and she was finally able to enter and continue on her way to her meeting. She hoped Robert was able to stall them until she arrived. Minutes later, the doors reopened and she scurried down the hall to the meeting room.

"Sorry I'm late, but I got delayed."

All eyes turned as the petite blonde entered the room with an effervescent flair that only she could muster. Rachel knew she was the darling of the editorial staff and had wrapped them around her finger from almost the first day she had arrived. It was about the only thing she still had going for her in this country.

"Gentlemen," she began, "you know I've been working on that human interest piece regarding the educational exchange program being proposed between some of the Arab and Israeli children. I think the proposal has been finalized and is about to be presented to the Israeli and Palestinian governments."

"So we've heard. But where would this educational experience take place, if agreed to?"

"The proponents are talking about building a school in a neutral location, somewhere outside of Jerusalem, but not in Palestinian territory. I don't think they've made any public announcements of the proposed sites, but I think I may know some of the frontrunners."

"I really don't think we should be devoting our resources to such sketchy reporting. I say we pull the plug on this thing now, before it gets out of hand. Besides, it's never going to get off the ground and, even if it does, it won't work anyway," the large, curly-haired man seated at the head of the conference table angrily replied. Zvi "Larry" Wasserman was the CEO of the newspaper and one of the wealthiest men in Israel. He owned several publications, a hotel chain, and a shipping business. He had no use for the Palestinians, and detested the terrorism employed by the Arabs. Joining forces with them was the last thing he wanted his newspaper behind.

Obviously annoyed with the non-journalistic interference from the paper's CEO, Rachel continued on with more fervor than before. "This is a story about education and the hope it can bring to this country. It was education that ended slavery in my country, America, and it was also education that brought an end to most dictatorships. Education took us out of the Dark Ages and brought an end to the feudal system. It has helped in offering an alternative to the poor and decreasing crime. It caused the fall of communism throughout Europe and brought an end to the Cold War."

"And your point, Miss Lyyyyooonns?" Wasserman smugly dragged out her name with obvious intention.

"Wasn't it your great Prime Minister, Golda Meir, who once said 'We will have peace with the Arabs when they love their children more than they hate us?'"

"Golda Meir was a fool and that statement has no relevance today. She said that in the '70s, and things were quite different then!"

"Were they, Mr. Wasserman? Do you mean to tell me that Israel is no longer fighting daily for its freedom and survival? That this is such a peaceful and serene nation without any major outside threats?" Rachel's sarcasm did not go unnoticed.

"That's enough Miss Lyons! May I remind you who pays your salary? I trust this editorial board will tell you what is news and what is trash. We will tell you what we want you to investigate, write about, and how we want you to say it." Wasserman was a man used to getting his own way and did not take kindly to having his authority questioned.

"News? Report the news? That's a joke. As journalists we have always had the power to make the news. We choose which events to report and, once we do so, we begin making the news. After all, does anyone care about a tryst between two lovers? Is that news? In most circles it would be viewed as flat-out porn, or maybe the subject of a steamy romance novel. But when one of those lovers is a politician, we now deem it newsworthy and, by doing so, have the power to change the face of nations."

"What in the world are you rambling on about?"

"In 1987, America's presidential race was thrown into turmoil when the frontrunner, Gary Hart, was discovered having an extramarital affair with a model. As a result, Hart withdrew from the running and the Democrats fielded a weak choice, Michael Dukakis, who lost the election in a landslide to George W. Bush. In 2008, newly elected New York Governor Elliot Spitzer was forced to resign in disgrace, shortly after his landslide electoral victory, after the press divulged his extramarital affair and trysts with high-priced prostitutes. You think we only report the news? Not so, my friends, we choose to report what we want, what we judge newsworthy, and thus we make the news! American President Franklin Roosevelt had a mistress living in the White House, and the American public was clueless because the press did not report such trash. American President John F. Kennedy was a known womanizer, yet the American public was not kept 'informed' of his activities by a sympathetic press corps. How dare you tell me we only report the news." Rachel was nearly out of breath, red-faced and almost yelling at the man who held the fate of her employment in his hands. She was on a roll and would not stop, even after her brother glanced at her and signaled for her to calm down before she had gone too far.

"I don't think Mr. Wasserman is trying to muzzle a free press, Rachel," her brother interjected. "I think he is only trying to obtain the proper balance between our reporting limitations and the financial constraints the current economy is reaping on our paper."

It was a meek attempt to diffuse the issue, but the only effort Robert could muster. He had looked after his sister for as long as he could remember, and knew that this time he might not be able to stop what she had put into motion.

"Are you about finished, Miss Lyons?" Wasserman asked without giving her a chance to respond. "Because, as far as I am concerned, you are finished, not only with this meeting, but with this paper. Please leave while we discuss the terms of your termination. I suggest you not say another word since anything further could very well effect the generosity of your termination package."

Rachel was stunned. She knew the day had not started out on a positive note but, somehow, she had managed to cause a bad day to spiral uncontrollably and disastrously downward. She slowly turned to leave, fighting back tears while glancing at her brother's ashen face. She had brought yet another disappointment to her family, adding to a continuing long list. She had thought that this one time she could make a difference...that her coverage of what had appeared as a minor footnote would jumpstart a revolutionary change in attitude and perspective. Unfortunately, it would appear that she was dreadfully wrong yet once again.

43

"I know you may not believe me and that you mistrust my motives, but please, Mr. Katz, hear me out before you arrive at any conclusions," Professor Stompmeyer began to plead his case to the owner of the *Scavenger.*

"*I* don't know, professor," Sam shot back. "If not for you, we might not be in this mess, and Billy might still be alive." Sam was obviously irritated and upset over the events of the last few days.

"I had nothing to do with that!" Stompmeyer insisted. "As far as I knew, I was to listen and evaluate what you had found and then report back to my superiors. I didn't even know that assassin was trailing me and thought he had orders to wait until I contacted him to determine if his assistance was needed at all. I swear it!"

"How can we trust him? He's lied to us from the beginning. I say we turn him over to the authorities and let them handle this." Carly had begun to interject her opinion with fervor and emotion. "We all could have been killed and those creeps wanted even more from me!"

"I am truly sorry, Miss Edwards, for all that has befallen you, but you must believe me that I had nothing to do with the actions of those men. They were aware of the amulet before I even met you. Why do you think I was in Florida at the exact time that you were docked and preparing for your next excursion? I was sent here fully expecting you to seek me out. I was — how do you say it — planted here?"

"The man makes sense, Sam," Jack interrupted. "He didn't have any opportunity or ability to contact anyone once aboard the ship, did he?"

"Mr. Talbot, I have a slight confession to make," Stompmeyer meekly interjected. "I did send an email to my superiors shortly before your dive, but it only confirmed what they had already suspected, that there was some sort of treasure buried in a sunken ship. I gave them no further information, nor was I able to communicate with them after that. Dmitry must have already been on his way, tracking us somehow, since it was not that long afterwards that they attacked us. And as a further gesture of my good faith, it was I who misled Dmitry as to your existence. I never told him about you, thereby ensuring your survival."

"Maybe the man's got a point," Sam said while slowly stroking his chin. "All right, tell us everything you know about these creeps before we go any further. And by the way, just how the hell did you ever get involved with these characters?"

"It's a long story that started quite some time ago."

"That's all right, we've got lots of time, professor," Sean said with a sarcastic tone.

"All right then. I will tell you. There was once a young archaeology professor who was enamored by one of his students. As time passed, they became closer to each other and, eventually, spoke of marriage. Since neither were close to any family members, plans were made to leave the University at the semester's end and marry before the new semester began. However, before any plans were finalized, tragedy befell this idealistic young professor. The young student (Rebecca was her name) disappeared, without a trace. The young man was consumed with fear, doubt and confusion. He was lost without her and looked for her in all possible locations. It was only with the assistance of a new group of acquaintances that he was ultimately able to discover the fate of his beloved."

"Do we break out the violins now or at the end?" Sean asked.

"Sssh! Let the man speak," said Carly as she glared at Sean and motioned for the professor to continue.

"Yes, thank you Miss Edwards. Speaking of the past does not come easy for me, so I thank you for your indulgence. As I was saying, after Rebecca's sudden disappearance, the man felt lost and alone. It was only with the assistance of his newfound 'friends' that he was able to survive and ultimately discover Rebecca's fate. It was on a cold and rainy day in September when the discovery was made. In a wooded area outside the walls of one of the local aristocratic family's majestic homes, her mutilated and ravaged body was found. Of course, the police were never able to discover her murderer and the case was soon closed and shelved as unsolved. Many said that the police looked the other way because of the murder's proximity to the rich and connected. The official version was that no clues existed. But the young man's associates knew better. They were able to uncover a trail from Rebecca's home straight to the young lord who resided with his family in that majestic home. Protected by his 'nobility,' as well as his wealth and power, the young lord appeared to be untouchable. It was at this point that the young professor began to realize the power that wealth and privilege could bestow. As he turned to his 'friends' for support and guidance, overcome with grief and a feeling of helplessness, he slowly began to change. His 'friends' showed him how he could get even, wreak vengeance, so to speak, upon the murderer of his love. Eventually, with the help of his new 'friends,' he was able to get his revenge. The young lord was found dead, the victim of an 'apparent suicide' at, coincidentally, the same time his family's wealth and position evaporated. With the young lord dead and the lord's family wealth and name in ruination, the young professor became indoctrinated into the lowly ways of the underworld. Overcome by his grief, the man began a relentless search for power and wealth, fueled by the seeds of greed and avarice that had been planted by his associates. He realized what power and recognition meant and what mountains they could move. From that day forward, he used his skills to help those associates (those who would become the Cartel) become more rich and powerful, while seizing some of that power for himself. Yes, I was that man. I'm not proud of what I have become, but without those connections, I would not have been able to uncover some of the treasures I found over the years, treasures that would have been lost to the world forever."

"And how many of those treasures have been kept from the world by your friends, either through black market dealings or transformations?" Sam was obviously not impressed by Stompmeyer's rationalization of his actions.

"You misunderstand me, sir. I do not ask for your acceptance, but only offer this information in an attempt to explain where I have come from. None of my actions over this time period have brought my Rebecca back. There has been no solace to my grief. Power and greed have allowed me to exist, but not to live or enjoy life. Only when I am on an expedition, when I am searching to uncover the ancient mysteries, am I able to forget my own shortcomings and flaws and find some measure of peace of mind."

The crew had listened intently to Stompmeyer's confession. As they mulled his words over, considering what to do with him, he again began to speak.

"I know you have your doubts about me. But you must

believe that you are on the verge of a great discovery. The amulet and mystery box are only the tip of the iceberg. They must be part of a vast treasure or contain the clues to some ancient Hebrew mystery. Not since the legends of Solomon's Treasures has there surfaced any equivalent artifacts pointing to the existence of such treasure in the hands of the Hebrews."

"What can you tell us about Solomon's Treasures, professor?" Jack inquired in a serious and urgent tone.

"Why, most of the tales appear to be the sort that legends are made from. If they are to be believed, King Solomon had amassed an enormous quantity of gold and silver, worth billions by today's standards. From that wealth, he built a grand Temple, inside of which could be found the Ark of the Covenant, which housed the Ten Commandments. Also inside was the Golden Menorah, made from gold the Jews took from the Egyptians during their exodus from the land of Egypt. King Solomon also made two hundred massive shields of pure gold. There were, of course, many other objects made from bronze, copper and other valuable metals and substances. When the Romans conquered Jerusalem, they supposedly transported fifty tons of gold, silver and precious artifacts to Rome. Ancient historians have written accounts containing lists of the precious spoils taken by the Roman conquerors. The Arch of Titus in Rome depicts this great event, commemorating the sack of Jerusalem. Contained upon the arch are depictions of the conquering Romans bringing Jewish slaves and their spoils back to Rome, including the great menorah, as well as other valuables. For nearly three hundred years, historians tell us that many of these valuables were on display for all the public to see in the Templum Pacis — the Temple of Peace — located in the Forum in Rome. After the vandals sacked Rome, it is believed the treasure disappeared with them. Some say the treasure was loaded on a boat by the Vandals and taken to Carthage in Tunisia. During the first Crusade, it is believed the treasure was recaptured and possibly sent to Constantinople. From there, little is known of its whereabouts, or whether it still exists. Some say it was vastly over-exaggerated while others claim it never existed. Some believe it was recovered or discovered by the Templars, and lost again when the Templars fled the Holy Land after their defeat at Acre. There are a few who believe that the Templar treasure, among other things, consisted of at least a portion of Solomon's Treasure, and disappeared to North America."

"What are you talking about? North America? You can't be serious." Carly was almost hysterical as tears of laughter were slowly edging their way out of the corner of her eyes. The other crew members could not contain themselves and were shaking their heads and holding their sides in amusement from the professor's ridiculous assertions.

"Knock it off, all of you. Let the professor continue!" Jack chided the boisterous crew. "Professor, please continue."

"Yes, of course, Mr. Talbot. As you may all know, after their defeat at Acre, the Templars returned to France. But the French king, King Philip IV, wanted to rid himself of the Templars, thereby eliminating the large monetary debt he owed them and, at the same time, acquiring for himself their vast treasure. The Pope, Clement V, was under the king's control and, after moving the papacy from Rome to Avignon, France, began the events which led to the destruction of the Templar order. After an investigation was launched by the Pope, on Friday the thirteenth, 1307, orders were issued to arrest the Templars. More than one hundred knights, including their Grand Master, Jacques de Molay, were arrested and charged with heresy. They were tortured and eventually killed. Their treasure, however, was never found. Some of the knights escaped France and took refuge in other European countries. While the Pope tried to effectuate the arrest of the remaining Templars, many countries resisted. Spain and Portugal continued to receive the Templar order, which was eventually absorbed by other local orders, such as the Order of Montesa in Spain and the Order of Christ in Portugal. Records tell us that there were supposedly three thousand Templars in France at this time, more than fifteen thousand Templar houses throughout Europe, and an entire fleet of ships under Templar control. They all seemed to have just vanished, along with their treasure and archives containing their vast holdings and records of financial transactions. Many rumors and theories have been disseminated concerning their fate. One historian has claimed that a group of knights arrived in Scotland and assisted Robert the Bruce in defeating an English invasion. Eventually, they sailed from Scotland to the Americas through the efforts of a Scottish prince or earl, Henry Sinclair or Saint Clair, the Earl of Roslyn. It is said he landed in North America with a group of Knights Templar and buried their treasure somewhere in Nova Scotia. Just like the search for Noah's Ark and the Holy Grail, many stories abound, but no hard proof exists as to the accuracy of the tales, or even the existence of the artifacts. Many have lost their lives and fortunes in seeking such ghosts."

Jack was clearly uneasy and took Sam aside. "I need to talk to you in private, immediately. Do you think the professor will be safe here if we leave him alone with the crew?"

"I will take care of this." Sam turned away from Jack and motioned to Tom. "Tom, Jack and I have some business to discuss. I want you to watch the good professor and see that no harm comes to him, understood?" Sam glared at the rest of the crew, staring intently at Sean, making sure he received the man's full attention.

"Aye-aye, sir. No one is to touch our good professor here." Tom stood beside the German, patting the man's shoulder with one hand as he, too, glared at Sean.

Convinced that all was under control, Sam led Jack out of the room and into his cabin.

"Now, what was that all about?" he asked.

44

Dmitry hesitantly reached for the video monitor as his connection with headquarters was completed. "There has been a—"

"We are well aware of your failure, Dmitry." The curtness and accusatory nature of the man's tone became more obvious to Dmitry as the conversation continued. "You had but one simple mission, and not only did you fail miserably, but you also managed to bring the entire wrath of the United States government upon us! Your actions not only jeopardized this mission, but also seriously endangered the very existence of this organization! Well, speak up! What do you have to say?"

Dmitry cautiously looked around. Thankfully, he was still alone in his cabin. He quickly locked the cabin door, assuring there would be no intruders or interruptions, then calmly attempted to finesse his way out of the mess he had landed himself in.

"As I was attempting to explain, I believe Stompmeyer

either intentionally or carelessly led us into a trap. We had commandeered the vessel and all was going as planned. I was able to locate the amulet and believe that it will lead us to a wealth of treasure. There was a shipwreck located beneath the vessel and we think it may contain the treasure. However, before we were able to investigate the situation further, we were attacked by a Coast Guard vessel. Rather than endanger our mission and risk certain capture, we initiated defensive tactics and subdued the attackers. However, additional reinforcements arrived before we could continue. Realizing that our situation was hopeless, we immediately took evasive action and vacated the area. We were able to lose our pursuers and have safely concealed ourselves for the present."

"You have never failed us in the past, but I hope you realize that not only are you expendable, but you are on the precipice of extinction. Your explanation is lame, at best, and seems more like an excuse I would expect from an amateur. You had best make sure that there is nothing out there to link this fiasco to us!"

There was an eerie threat in the tone of the man's voice, laced with certainty and finality. Dmitry was well aware of his own limitations if the organization was no longer willing to back him up. Without their support, he would become an open target for the many enemies he had made over the years. As he was considering his predicament, the sound of machine gun fire resonated about.

"What was that?" the man on the other end inquired after the shots had stopped.

"Oh, nothing to worry about," Dmitry quickly answered. "Just cleaning up some loose ends here, making sure nothing is traced back to us. We will be leaving this boat shortly and moving to a new location, where we can better monitor the situation. I can still track Stompmeyer as well as the salvage company's second-in-command, so I think I can safely say that we have not yet lost the treasure. Once we have obtained it, I will personally take care of the double-crossing professor."

"You had best do it quickly. There are some among us who feel you have worn out your welcome. If you don't produce results in short order, I will no longer be able to support you and the order will go out to terminate our alliance. Have I made myself clear?"

"Completely. Do not worry. This has been a slight setback, but I am regaining control of the situation as we speak."

There was a knock on the cabin door just as Dmitry was concluding his conversation. "Yes, what is it?"

"We have eliminated all potential witnesses, as you ordered, sir." It was Yuri, dutifully reporting in.

"You have permanently silenced the ship's crew, yes?"

"As you ordered. We have also removed all traces of our equipment from the boat and have readied the explosive devices. They can be detonated at your command once we have removed ourselves. There will then be no trace of this boat or its crew."

"You have done well, my friend. Tell the others to gather up the remainder of their gear and board our backup vessel, then set the timers to detonate in ten minutes. You are sure the boat will travel far enough out to sea on its own after we have gone?"

"Without a doubt. I personally locked the autopilot in a sea-bound direction. The engines will be set for five knots. That should give enough time and distance between us before the explosion. Since the boat will be heading out to open sea, I don't anticipate any interference from any other ships, but if there are, then the boat will explode upon impact. Either way, there will be no trace of us or the ship's crew. After all, dead men tell no tales."

Both men laughed as they finished gathering up the remainder of their gear and boarded the backup boat. Dmitry lauded himself on his foresight to implement a backup plan, with a reserve boat waiting in a secluded cove, in the event they needed to make a quick getaway if something went wrong with the original plan. Dmitry had not survived all these years by being careless.

"Where do you want I should take us?" Yuri asked Dmitry.

"Chart us a course for Islamorada. I have reserved a group of private cottages where we can regroup and plan our next course of action. In the meantime, I will check on our good professor and try to obtain his location. Then perhaps we can figure out what our 'friends' are up to."

As the boat set sail for the Florida Keys, Dmitry thought about the day's events and the ominous conversation he had just been engaged in less than an hour earlier. He began to seethe from within. *Who was this man who had attacked and killed his divers? How had he eluded his men earlier in the day, and where had he hidden when they had searched the ocean for him? What treasures were really buried in the shipwreck, and how had the Coast Guard been alerted so quickly? What did the professor really know, and how much had he divulged to the authorities?*

There were far too many unanswered questions for Dmitry's liking and he had much too short a time to find the answers. He was fully aware that the Cartel would not be patient much longer. Not only would he now have to look over his shoulder worrying about the authorities, but soon he would have to look over his shoulder worrying about his comrades as well. He knew there were far too many young and eager soldiers out there impatiently waiting their turn to take his place in the organization.

As he tried to get a bearing on Stompmeyer through the GPS tracker he had secretly placed in the man's cane, he was becoming increasingly more paranoid and uncharacteristically worried about his own predicament. With most of his men either dead or wounded, and having lost his most trustworthy men to this phantom diver and ragtag crew of salvagers, the rage began to rise within him and slowly overcome the fear and paranoia he had felt. He was going to enjoy destroying the *Scavenger* and its crew and would take special pleasure in dealing with the phantom diver and traitorous professor. As the signal began to come in with more clarity, he began to develop a plan of his own.

45

Rachel was convinced that this was a story which could be printed somewhere, by someone, in some newspaper. She was becoming increasingly irritated, both at herself for not being more assertive and aggressive, and at *Haaretz* for being so narrow minded and shortsighted. She was more determined than ever to cover this story, with or without her paper's, or rather ex-paper's, help. As she walked briskly away from the entrance to *Haaretz*, her cell phone began to ring. She quickly searched through her purse and soon located the ringing phone.

"Hello," she answered, slightly out of breath.

"Miss Lyons?" the voice on the other end asked timidly.

"Yes it is. How can I help you?"

"Are you still interested in the Israeli-Palestinian Education Project?"

Stunned, Rachel quickly looked around before answering. "Why, yes I am. Why do you ask?"

"Can you meet me at Mount Scopus within the hour?"

Rachel glanced at her watch and answered, "I think I can, but why do you ask?"

"Just meet me there and I will explain everything," the man replied.

As he was about to hang up, Rachel hurriedly inquired, "But how will I know you? Who should I look for? What are you wearing?"

"I will find you."

"Well, at least can you tell me your name?" Rachel tried to finish her sentence before she heard the click of the receiver and the end of the conversation. As she spun around in despair, she wondered who this man was and what he wanted from her. Realizing that this might be her only chance to redeem herself and get her story in print, she decided to throw caution to the wind and calculated the quickest and easiest route to her meeting place at Mount Scopus.

Since her first arrival in Jerusalem, Rachel had always been fascinated by Mount Scopus and its history. Located in the northeast portion of the city, with a captivating view of the entire metropolis, one could truly experience the holiness of the three major faiths intertwined within the Old City walls.

Historically, it had always been a strategic base from which Jerusalem's enemies would launch their attacks on the city. Roman legions had encamped there before conquering Jerusalem, and the Crusaders used it as their base before retaking the city from the Moslems. Standing atop the mountain lookout, Rachel could feel the breeze through her hair as she cast her eyes about, studying the ancient city walls, the Old Temple site with the Dome of the Rock, and the magnificent cemetery connecting the Mount of Olives to the Old City walls. As her mind wandered, imagining herself in the time of King David, she was shaken back into reality and current times by the piercing sound of her cell phone.

"Hey sis, where are you? I've been trying to reach you since you ran out of here."

"Not now, Robert. I need some space. By the way, thanks for that resounding round of support this morning. It really underwhelmed me!"

"Come on, sis. What did you expect me to do? You saunter in late as usual without any regard for the seriousness of the situation, without any preparation for the barrage you had to know was coming, and then you bait the only guy who would ever even consider saving your hide. And you want me to commit hari-kari along with you? Where would we be then, with both of us out of jobs?"

"I guess you're right. Anyway, I can't talk now. I'll give you a call later, okay?"

"What's going on? Are you all right? Where are you anyway?"

"I'm fine. I'm on top of Mount Scopus contemplating my future. I'll talk to you later."

Rachel had no intention of getting into any further argument with her brother, at least not just yet. She realized he was right about this morning. She had somehow managed to mess things up again, and her temper had certainly not helped her in her quest. This time she swore it would be different. She would be better prepared and plan her actions more responsibly. After she met this mysterious caller, perhaps she would have a clearer picture of what this controversial education project was really all about. Perhaps then she could get the full story and present the complete picture to the newspaper. She might even be able to get her job back.

"Miss Lyons, I'm so glad you came."

Rachel turned to face a small man with a long graying beard.

"My name is Saul," the man said as he held out his hand to greet her.

"Saul? Like the first king of Israel?" Rachel asked as she politely shook hands with the man.

"Ah, you are well versed in our ancient history, no?"

"Not really. That's about the extent of my learning. What is it you wished to tell me?"

"My, but aren't we the impatient one? I guess since we've gotten the formalities out of the way, you want to get right to it, eh?"

"Well it's been quite a long day for me and I really don't know what it is you wish to tell me or why you brought me out here."

"You do not like the view?"

"Well, it is magnificent, but I've been here before."

"Very well, what is it that you know about this education project?"

"Only that there had been a proposal brought about by some group called Ir Amim to open up a joint education center where Palestinians and Israelis could study and interact together, in peace."

"That's very good. Very basic, but very good. There have been several prominent groups on both sides who would like to end the hostilities and move forward in the twenty-first century toward a peaceful settlement of the Israeli-Palestinian issue. They believe that the first step is to get the two sides together at a young age and teach them, side by side, about each other's beliefs, traditions and cultures. Come with me and look out there. What do you see?"

The man took Rachel's hand and guided her along a path overlooking the East Jerusalem suburb of French Hill.

"What do you see down there?" he asked her again as he pointed outward.

"A suburban development with people milling about. I think it's called French Hill, isn't it?"

"You seem to know your geography quite well. Yes, you are correct. Now look beyond. See that fence? Do you know what lies beyond?"

"It's a Palestinian refugee camp, I believe. Isn't it?"

"You continue to amaze me. Yes, it is called Shuafat. It has been inhabited for over four thousand years, first by the Canaanites, then later as a Jewish settlement during the Roman occupation, and, for a time, even the Crusaders. It was occupied by Jordan after the creation of Israel in 1948. It was the Jordanians who built the refugee camp in 1964 with the assistance of the UN. It was later annexed by Israel after the Six Day War in 1967."

"I really appreciate the history lesson, but what does this have to do with me?"

"Why is it that you Americans are always so impatient? You need to learn a little restraint. Knowledge of the history of the area can lead to a better understanding of its inhabitants, as well as a better awareness of the issues and tensions facing its population."

"You make me feel like I'm back in school, and I really hated school. It's been nice meeting you and chatting, but I really must be getting along now. I can see this conversation is not going anywhere and you really have nothing to offer me."

Rachel started to turn away when the man grabbed her arm.

"Please, do not go yet. Do you know where it has been proposed that this joint education center be located?"

"I thought that information was not for public dissemination."

"It's not, but I can show you the exact proposal detailing the project and its plans, as well as its proposed location."

"Just how did you get your hands on such a document?"

"I would rather not say at this time. But please, would you accompany me, and I will show you the proposal as well as the planned location?"

Rachel thought for a moment. She was out of a job and had no viable means of support. This story was her one opportunity to shine and prove them all wrong. If this panned out, she would have it made as a freelance journalist, or even as an established writer on staff. She really had nothing to lose and much to gain. The man seemed harmless enough, and he appeared to be interested in striking a deal with her for some unknown reason, perhaps publicity for his cause.

"Okay, but I can only spend about another hour with you. My boyfriend's expecting me back soon," she lied to the man, just to be on the safe side. She then followed him to his car and, as they drove off, she began to hope that it had not been a mistake to trust this stranger.

46

Jack followed Sam into his cabin and quickly locked the door behind them.

"What's this all about, Jack? Why the secrecy?"

Jack removed Bonfil's diary and ring from his BC and showed them to his old friend.

"Did you wonder where I hid for all those hours after the Russians attacked us at the wreck?"

"We all thought you were dead. After the shootout with the Coast Guard and our own narrow escape from those maniacs, I really didn't have much time to think about it. Sorry."

Jack began to recount his journey and discovery of Bonfil's cave. He briefly described the mounds of treasure located within the cavern and then handed the diary to Sam.

"It's all in there, the entire story, from the looting of Jerusalem to the sack of Rome and the recovery by the Templars. Look at this ring! It has the same symbol as the amulet. I'm telling you, there's a wealth of treasure out there, some of it below us and the rest, who knows where. But I think the box, amulet and ring can lead us to it all."

"You may be right. Do you think you can find the cavern again?"

"I'm certain of it. It was only a short distance from the wreck. That's what saved me from those goons. It was unbelievable. It was like a regular caveman apartment. I can't believe that guy lived down there all those years. I wonder what happened to his companions, though. Do you think the second ship ever made it out of the North American seas?"

"I don't know, but let's first see what's below us. Then we can try to unravel the mystery of the box."

Jack reached out for Sam and, with a pensive look on his face, asked, "What about the professor? Do you really think we can trust the man? I mean, we had our doubts before this excursion started, and now that we know how deeply connected he is to the Russians and their masters, I'm kinda worried about keeping him too close to us."

Sam thought for a moment before replying, "But don't you think it's better to keep him close to us where we can keep an eye on him? Besides, we may still need his knowledge of antiquity, as well his knowledge about that Cartel."

Jack shook his head in agreement, "Maybe you're right. After all, what is it that they say, *keep your friends close and your enemies even closer?*"

The two men began to formulate a plan of action. It was agreed that they would begin a search of the seabed after the Coast Guard inquiry was complete. In the meantime, they needed to get the ship cleaned up and organized for another dive, but most important of all, they needed to get their rest and recover from the grueling ordeal they had just endured.

After discussing their plans, the two men separated. Jack returned to his cabin to get some much-needed rest and Sam returned to the crew, giving them instructions so that they would be ready for the dive when the time came.

As Jack was heading towards his cabin he spied Brian leaning against the ship's railing, looking out at the ocean. "Thanks for your timely arrival. You really brought the cavalry in this time."

"What have you gotten yourself into, Jack? I thought this was supposed to be a nice relaxing dive trip for you. You know, she's really worried about you, and she senses that something's up. What are you going to tell her?"

Brian was right. Jack hadn't thought about Alexandra amidst all the turmoil and action. Now that he was catching his breath, his mind drifted back to thoughts of his wife. "The truth. I've always found it works the best, my friend."

"Well, you should tell her now. She overheard some of my conversations before I left and was becoming quite suspicious. Of course, I couldn't tell her anything, even if I wanted to. I really did not know what was going on or how involved this thing had become. Once I began to contact some of my government sources and realized the danger you guys were getting yourselves into, I had been pretty much sworn to secrecy and couldn't tell her, nor did I really want to tell her. I think it only made her more suspicious."

"I guess you're right. But I really can't tell her from way out here. It would be kind of awkward, and besides, these international calls are not the most secret or secure. I'm afraid it will have to wait until we return to shore."

"And when is that going to be?"

It was obvious that Brian knew his friend well. He could tell that Jack had no intention of returning to shore with him at this time.

"I think you better tell me the whole story, Jack," Brian continued. "Just what is it those thugs were after?"

"Why don't you come with me to my cabin? I'll explain everything there."

Jack put his hand on Brian's back as he began to walk the two of them to his cabin. Once inside, he motioned for Brian to sit and began to describe in detail the amulet and box, as well as the parchment discovered within the box's hidden chamber. As Jack recounted his escape from the Russian divers and his discovery of the cave, Brian moved closer with renewed interest.

"You're pulling my leg, now. You mean to tell me that dude lived in that cave, underwater, for months, like four hundred years ago? No way!" A look of disbelief came over Brian as he let out a nervous laugh.

Jack continued to describe the contents of the cavern and showed his friend the Frenchman's diary. As Brian looked on, Jack interpreted some of the pages, which described in detail the knight's journey from France, Scotland and finally Nova Scotia.

"You trying to tell me you've found Solomon's lost treasure? And even if you did, what's all that got to do with this box and what the hell is a stone of fire?"

"I don't know for sure. Maybe it's another lost treasure pilfered or 'recovered' by the Templars. I only know I can't abandon everyone now. We need to explore further, and we need to do it now, before those Russians return. Don't forget, they know where this place is, too."

Brian knew Jack was right. He couldn't just leave his friends in a lurch. He also knew that with a mystery such as this, Jack would be drawn like a moth to a flame, sinking his teeth into the puzzle until he solved it, leaving no unanswered questions. Knowledge was both his friend's strength and weakness. There were few people Brian was acquainted with who had the intelligence and thirst for knowledge, that Jack had. Jack was the type of guy who would go to a museum for the first time and spend hours reading all the information about each of the exhibits. He would scour the travel brochures trying to ingest every ounce of knowledge about his destination. Unfortunately,

Jack rarely knew when to come up for air and call it quits. Brian was worried that this was becoming one of those times.

"I think I'll stay as long as you're staying, Jack. I'm not leaving you alone."

"Brian, thanks for the support, but I really think you should return to the mainland. Besides, I need you to look after Alexandra and Paige till I get back."

"Not this time, buddy. I think you're the one who needs looking after. Besides, you just got my curiosity all revved up with your tales of knights and secret treasures. If you're worried about the girls, I can have some of my buddies keep an eye on them for the next few days until we return. Now, how about at least emailing Alexandra to let her know you're all right?"

Jack thought for a moment and realized his old friend was right. He would feel safer knowing Brian was around watching his back, and that his wife and granddaughter were not in any danger. As far as he knew, the Russians had no idea who he was. But just to be on the safe side, he decided to take Brian up on his offer and have some of his friends keep an eye on them until he returned.

Jack opened up his laptop and signed into his email account. "You win. I'll send Alexandra an email. Now will you leave me alone for a little while? Go talk to Sam and the rest of the crew and bring yourself up to speed on this whole mess, but be careful not to tell our professor anything about the diary just yet. I'm still not sure we can trust him."

Brian agreed and left the cabin as Jack began to peck at the keyboard.

Honey, it's been a little hectic here. Hope to be back in a few days. Miss you and Paige. Give her a kiss for me. See you all soon.
Love, Jack

Jack hit "send" on the screen then began to google all he could about the Templars, the Roman invasion and sack of Jerusalem, Solomon's Treasures and the sack and fall of Rome. His cave-dwelling friend had aroused Jack's own curiosity and he needed to know as much as he could about the events described in the knight's diary. As tired as he was, Jack forced himself to concentrate on the wealth of articles he discovered from his internet search.

Brian found Sam in the main crew area

talking to Carly and Tom. "Hey Sam. Got a minute?"

"What's up, Brian? Where's Jack?"

"He's getting a little shut-eye. I think this whole experience has worn him down. Guess he's getting soft in his old age."

"I wouldn't sell him short. The man saved our necks when those divers tried to mine the boat."

"You know I'm only kidding. He's still one of only a handful of men I'd want watching my back. Did you ever find out who those Russians were working for and how they found out about your treasure hunt?"

"The professor told us they work for this Cartel. We're still not sure how they found out about the amulet. Stompmeyer said they have eyes and ears all over the world in the most inconspicuous places."

"How much information did they seem to have?" Brian was somewhat aware of the Cartel's existence and knew of the

Russians' entry into the states. Beyond that, his intelligence sources had dried up and he was beginning to get concerned about the full extent of the information these thugs possessed.

"Well," Sam began, "they knew about the amulet and were familiar enough with my crew and ship. They may have found out about the box once they boarded us. I don't think they knew about it beforehand, though."

"What about Jack? Did they know anything about him?"

Sam paused for a moment and thought hard about what the Russian had said earlier that day. "I'm not sure. He was trying to find out who had attacked his men while they were below capturing Geoff and the others, and killing Billy." Tears began to well up in the old man's eye's. Billy had been a crew member for some years now, and Sam was the type of employer who treated his crew as family. He recalled nurturing Billy along through some of his rebellious times. The thought that Billy was dead, much less murdered, especially on one of Sam's excursions, was almost too much for the kind-hearted man to bear.

"I know it's hard, Sam. But it wasn't your fault." Brian put his hand on the man's shoulder and looked him straight in the eye. "Look at me, Sam. I think you know I've seen a fair amount of killing in my time and I'm telling you, you had no way of knowing this was going to happen. I only found out about the Russians and their movements long after you guys had left for sea. And I still had no way of knowing what they were up to. They snuck up on you guys, totally undetected, using state-of-the-art underwater technology and expert Russian Navy frogmen. These thugs had all the experience and know-how on their side. Even with that, you and your crew gave them quite a whupping."

"Yeah, but at what price? Billy's dead, my crew's a wreck and a whole Coast Guard ship and most of its crew were destroyed by those creeps. All for what? Some old treasure and a riddle?"

"Get a hold of yourself, Sam. I really need to know if those guys knew any personal information about Jack. Think hard, please," Brian implored.

Geoff had walked by the men as they were talking and overheard Brian's inquiry.

"After those goons brought us topside, their leader began to threaten and interrogate me and Jim. Jim let slip that Jack was still down there, but I don't think he gave those guys any specific information about Jack other than that he was a New York lawyer."

Brian froze as he heard the words. *Damn it,* he thought to himself. *Maybe Jack was right. If anything happened to Alexandra or Paige he would never be able to forgive himself.*

"Thanks for your help. I've got something I've gotta do. Can I go somewhere in private?"

Sam offered Brian the use of his cabin and watched as Brian quickly left the group.

"Is everything all right?" Sam called out as Brian was leaving.

"I sure hope so," Brian responded as he hurried towards Sam's cabin, pulling his satellite phone out as he ran.

It only took Brian two minutes to get through to his friends on the mainland. He quickly explained to them what had taken place and directed them to set up surveillance on Alexandra and Paige in order to ensure they were kept safe.

"I don't know if those goons know about the women, or can even locate them, but I don't want you to take any chances. Use my security clearance if need be, but I want them protected at all costs. Just be careful who you talk to about this. That Cartel has ears all over. If they don't know about the women, I don't want to tip them off, understood?"

Brian was torn. He had an uneasy feeling about this. Should he leave Jack alone having already narrowly escaped death's clutches once, or should he remain with his friend and hope his men on the mainland could contain any danger Jack's family might be facing? Either way, Brian felt he would be on the losing end of the choice he made. He tried to put himself in the Russian's place, knowing the bits of information that the Russian had found out during his short time on the boat. How likely was it that he could identify Jack and track his family to New York or Florida? And even if he did, would he dare chance exposing himself by placing Jack's family in danger?

Brian knew he never was much of a gambler, usually because he never chose the right cards or bets. After weighing all his options and considering all the possible scenarios, he began to eliminate the least likely of the choices.

It was a pretty safe bet that the Russian would not try to attack the boat again while it was out at the treasure site. There was too much military activity around after the destruction of a Coast Guard cutter. There was no way the man would be so foolish or careless as to risk another engagement with the military. Besides, he probably had some kind of bugs or tracking devices planted onboard, which would allow him to keep an eye on the ship without risking his own exposure.

After his escape, the Russian would regroup and find a safe haven where he could monitor the *Scavenger* and plan his next move. That would give the man time to try to find out more about the *Scavenger* and its crew, as well as the treasure it was hunting. It would also give him more time to size up his enemy and try to find out all he could about Jack. Brian thought hard about how the man would do that and where he would start.

All of a sudden, it dawned on him. The thought struck him like a lightning bolt. "The dock! You asshole. Why didn't you think of it sooner?" Brian chastised himself for being so slow and complacent. He needed to get out of there and back to the mainland, now.

As he rushed out of Sam's cabin he began dialing the phone again. He spoke to the man on the other end of the line and demanded a sea plane be readied immediately. Within minutes, a skiff appeared, manned by a Coast Guardsman. Brian gathered his limited gear and told Sam to tell Jack he would see him later, that he had decided to let Jack go it alone on his "Indiana Jones adventure," that he had some things on the mainland that needed looking into.

Brian waved to the crew of the *Scavenger* as the skiff headed out towards the waiting seaplane. A worried look crept over him, replacing the smiling facade he had displayed to Sam and the others as he left their company. He prayed he was not too late as he contacted his friends on the mainland and relayed his concerns, quickly boarding the sea plane as it took off from the choppy surf.

48

Dmitry quickly began searching for information on this mysterious lawyer from New York.

"I want to know his name and everything about him! And get me a photo, too! I want to know what this man looks like," he yelled to his men.

Quickly, two of his men began searching all the databases for possible information. Another began scrutinizing all the surveillance tapes of the *Scavenger* from when it was docked before its initial departure. Hours later, an exasperated Dmitry began throwing around papers (and anything else he could get his hands on) in frustration.

"Am I surrounded by incompetent fools? Can't any of you perform one simple task? Do I need to send you back as failures and replace you all with new recruits? Even a novice would have accomplished more than all of you put together!"

"I-I've got something, sir, I think," Yuri suddenly stammered. "Look at this shot shortly before the *Scavenger* launched.

There's the old man standing on the deck with someone we didn't see on the boat when we boarded. Do you think this is the man you're looking for?"

Dmitry moved closer to the monitor to inspect the photo. "It could be. Blow it up and run it through our computers! Maybe we can identify the face."

Yuri quickly punched some keys on the keyboard and initiated the required search.

"Sergei! Take two men and check out the docks. Circulate that picture and see if anyone recognizes it. But be careful. Don't make a scene and don't draw any unnecessary attention to yourselves. I don't know how they knew we were out there and were able to notify the Coast Guard, but I want no mistakes this time. Do I make myself clear?"

Sergei nodded his head in agreement and quickly selected two men to accompany him to the dock.

"Wait!" Dmitry yelled. "Pick up Alena on your way, and use the Sea Ray. You will look more like some pleasure seekers and less conspicuous with a female aboard. Make sure you all dress the part. Call me if you find out any information."

Hours later, after receiving negative results from his team at the docks, Dmitry's mood again soured. With Yuri also failing to make an identification, Dmitry turned to another route.

"I want you to search into the old man's history. Go back to his birth if necessary. There has to be a connection with this ghost man somewhere. If he was not a regular member of the crew and not regularly seen on the docks, the old man had to know him from his past. Find out NOW!"

It had been nearly twelve hours since they had first arrived in Islamorada and begun their efforts to identify Sam's mysterious savior. The mood aboard the ship was getting more tense as time wore on. Sergei was on his way back after reporting negative results, and none of the Russian's databases contained any information on the photograph. Dmitry was well aware that his superiors were waiting for an update, and he was not willing to face their ire without having something to report. He had already failed them once by losing the professor and the treasure and bringing unwanted attention on their operation from the United States government. Another negative report would surely cost him his position, if not his life.

Dmitry returned to his cabin to retrace the efforts implemented thus far. He knew he was missing something and needed to keep a level head if he expected to make any progress. This ghost had certainly gotten under his skin and Dmitry desperately longed to know who he was. He had not met an adversary such as this one in his entire career.. It was imperative that he identify this man and then eliminate him.

As Dmitry lay in his cabin contemplating his next move, one of his men, Andrei, knocked on the cabin door.

"Sir, we think we may have found something!" Andrei yelled through the closed door.

Dmitry quickly rose and yanked the portal open. "What have you found?"

"There was a lawyer in New York who became friendly with the old man after his wife was murdered. His name was Jack and we think he may have represented the old man in his legal affairs before the old man relocated to Florida."

"Have you compared photos?" Dmitry inquired of the breathless Sergei.

"Not yet, sir. Yuri just located the information and thought you should know immediately. He is attempting to obtain more information, as well as a photo, as we speak."

"Good work! Let's see what Yuri has discovered, shall we?"

A smile crept onto Dmitry's face as the two of them headed back to the main cabin. Once inside, Dmitry observed his men fast at work gathering all the available information on Jack Talbot. Before long, a complete dossier had been compiled for the Russian's careful review.

"Well, this is definitely the man on the deck from the video," Dmitry replied. "But can this be? Is this all there is? He's just a lawyer from New York? Are you sure he is not affiliated with any other agency? No CIA connections, Special Service affiliations, or even specialized law enforcement?" Dmitry was stymied. It appeared as if this ordinary lawyer with scuba diving experience had bested three of his most experienced men and had outwitted his entire team. Was there more to this man, or was it just plain beginner's luck, something that Dmitry had never before believed in or encountered?

"He was a prosecutor in New York before going into private practice," Yuri reported. "But I don't see any reference to any other type of law enforcement connections or training. He had some past military experience with an honorable discharge and some medals and commendations, but no other details."

"Keep looking. I want to know everything there is to know about this Jack Talbot: where he was born, where he grew up, his family, what he eats for breakfast. I will return in one hour for a complete report."

"One hour?" Yuri replied incredulously. "That is not enough time."

"That is all you have. We must take action immediately before they realize who we are and what we already know, if it is not already too late. We must take the initiative now and regain the upper hand. One hour! Do I make myself clear?"

Without waiting for a reply, Dmitry turned and left the main cabin. He returned to his own cabin feeling secure that he could now report to his superiors with some positive information. Once he had detailed his progress, he related that the mission was back on track and he would soon be ready to move. As soon as he obtained the necessary background information about his elusive adversary he would formulate a plan of action that would allow him to retrieve the sought-after treasure, and also allow him to exact his revenge on his newly identified foe.

Dmitry checked on the location of the *Scavenger*, secure in the knowledge that the GPS tracking device he had cleverly implanted in Stompmeyer's cane was still operating as expected. He then activated the Trojan installed in Tom's cell phone. Not surprisingly, there was no activity. After all, the man was in the middle of the ocean. The likelihood that he would be attempting to make any calls was slim, especially since all the man's associates were still aboard with him. Dmitry figured that the man would not carry his cell phone with him until the boat was heading back to dock.

The hour went quickly for Dmitry and he reentered the main cabin. "What additional information do you have for me?"

Yuri reported that they had been unable to access the Department of Defense's records on Jack's military service. They had amassed much of the biographical data on Jack that Dmitry had requested. Yuri described Jack's schooling, his stellar performance in the District Attorney's office, his lucrative law practice, his residences in New York and Florida, and his complete family background, including Paige's unfortunate accident and recuperation with Alexandra in Florida.

Dmitry smiled. "Prepare to cast off. Stage two of our mission is about to begin."

49

Jack was baffled over the Russians' ability to sneak up on the *Scavenger* without anyone noticing. How did they know of the ship's location? How did they find out as much information as they had about the treasure, especially if the professor was being truthful with him? Jack voiced his concerns aloud to the crew and a heated discussion erupted, with Carly and Sean pointing fingers at Stompmeyer, Geoff directing blame at Sean and Carly, and the rest of the crew throwing their hands up in dismay.

"Hold it, everyone," Jack interrupted. "I'm not trying to put blame on anyone. That's not going to resolve the issue. Let's stop looking to place blame and start trying to solve the problem. If we don't, those creeps will always be one step ahead of us and will always know what we're doing. Now, Professor Stompmeyer, I'm only going to ask this one more time, but I'm warning you, if you have not been completely honest with us, and continue to be so, I will personally ensure that you are arrested and incarcerated for a very long time. Oh, and by the way, I will also make sure your Russian friends and their Cartel are fully aware of your cooperation, if you understand where I'm coming from."

"I understand completely, Mr. Talbot, and I assure you I have been completely forthright in my comments to you. I honestly have no idea how Dmitry was able to track me. He seems to have this uncanny ability to locate me at any given moment."

"What do you mean?"

"Back at the hotel in Florida, he knew exactly where I was and, after the murder, threatened me with bodily harm if I did not cooperate completely. I attempted to have the Cartel remove him from this quest, but they overruled me. Even after I left the hotel with Mr. Hunter and Mr. Katz without any notice, he was aware that I had boarded this ship. By the way, do you mind if I sit down? My leg is beginning to bother me and I must take some weight off it." Stompmeyer slowly slipped past Jack and limped over to the nearest chair while tapping his cane on the ground.

Jack suddenly looked up at the German. "Professor Stompmeyer, how long have you had that cane?"

"This? Why, nearly fifteen years. I injured my hip during a dig and never fully recovered. Shortly thereafter, I located this cane in an antique shop and have kept it with me ever since."

"May I see it?"

"Of course, but please be careful. I must warn you, there is a special catch that releases a blade from its base." Stompmeyer carefully handed the cane to Jack, showing him the catch used to release the sword from its staff.

Jack began to examine the cane. After several minutes he moved down from the handle, carefully inspecting the stick until he reached the rubber tip at the bottom. Upon removing the tip, he observed that the bottom was bored out, concealing a hidden compartment within. Stompmeyer and the entire crew moved closer to examine the new discovery.

"Hand me a flashlight," Jack said. "I think there may be something hidden inside."

Carly grabbed a flashlight from one of the shelves and quickly handed it to Jack. "What is it?" she asked.

"I'm not sure, but if I were a betting man, I'd guess a GPS tracking device." Jack shined the light into the compartment and carefully removed the secreted object from within. As he held it up, everyone noticed a small LED light flashing at regular intervals on the object.

"Can I see that?" Geoff asked. As Jack handed the object to him he exclaimed, "That's exactly what it is, a GPS tracking device. That son of a bitch! So that's how he found us. Now what do we do?"

Jack thought a moment. "Let's keep it active. We may be able to use this to our advantage. As long as he thinks he is still tracking us, we may be able to keep him off balance, and maybe even surprise him."

"Like spring our own trap?" Sean asked. "I kind of like that idea. When can we get started?"

"Not so fast. We don't even know where that creep is, and don't forget, the man's a pro and quite dangerous. We got lucky the first time. We may not be so lucky the next go-around. Let's concentrate on the wreck and trying to salvage the treasure first. Once we do that, we can try to formulate a plan against our elusive Russian."

The rest of the crew agreed.

"When can we get the go-ahead from the Coast Guard?" Sean looked at Sam while gesturing with open hands. "They've held us up long enough. Maybe they're searching for the treasure for themselves."

"Don't be silly, Sean. They just lost an entire ship and its crew to some madman. They probably have top secret information on that ship that I'm sure they need to recover along with the remains of their crew. That's going to take some time."

"Perhaps we can help them and also do some treasure seeking while we're at it." Sam stood up and reached for the radio.

"What are you going to do?" Carly asked.

"I'm going to offer the United States Coast Guard the services of the *Scavenger* and its crew, of course."

An hour later, the divers began to don their dive gear and prepared to enter the ocean waters to resume their exploration of the wreck and its surroundings. Jack paired with Geoff and Sean paired with Carly as they gathered their gear and did final pre-dive checks.

"According to the Coast Guard, their ship sank in the same area of our shipwreck," Sam reported. "They saw no evidence of our wreck in their search of the surrounding waters. I want you to give the Coast Guard all the assistance they require while you explore below. But be careful and keep together. I don't want anything happening to you down there."

The four divers entered the water and slowly descended below. As they approached the ocean floor, their eyes opened wide in amazement. They were greeted with more than half of the Coast Guard cutter sitting on the ocean floor where their shipwreck had been.

"What the hell?" Sean exclaimed. "Where's the wreck?"

"Sam said the Coast Guard reported no wreck in the area beyond their ship; now we know why."

"Holy Jesus!"

"What is it, Geoff?"

"Look over there!" The three divers followed Geoff's outstretched hand, which was pointing towards the remnants of the rest of the sunken Coast Guard cutter. Hundreds of jellyfish, lionfish and other deadly species were swarming through and around the wreck.

"That looks like the same area where the cavern was located," Jack exclaimed. "The explosion must have ripped apart the cutter, breaking it in two and sending it on top of the wreck and the cavern, burying both at the same time. There's no way anyone's going to get into the area by the cavern with all those poisonous fish around. Let's take a closer look at the main wreck area. Perhaps we can locate our shipwreck."

The rest of the divers agreed and turned their attention towards the *Sentinel,* or rather what was left of it on the seabed floor. There were already several crews of Navy divers searching the wreckage when Jack and the others arrived to lend a hand. Dead bodies were floating everywhere inside the wreckage, and the three men and Carly carefully aided in the recovery of the deceased sailors. After assisting for nearly half an hour, Geoff signaled the others that it was time to return topside. As they took one last look around the wreckage, it was clear that the cutter had completely covered the remains of the ancient wreck and probably destroyed or buried the remaining treasure under tons of mangled steel.

Once the divers returned to the *Scavenger* they gave the disastrous news to the remaining crew members.

"It was awful," Carly sobbed as tears ran down her cheeks. "There were dead bodies and severed body parts everywhere! I've never seen such a catastrophe before."

Sean moved closer to Carly and put his arms around her, trying to console her.

Sam grabbed one of Carly's hands and nodded his head in sympathy. "There is much cruelty in the world, my dear. When you've lived as long as I have, you will learn to enjoy life and the joy of loved ones around you while you can."

"What are we going to do about the treasure?" Tom asked. "If it's completely buried under the wreckage, for all we know it could be destroyed. All our work and all this death, for nothing."

"We still have the box and amulet," Jack said.

"Big deal," replied Sean. "The bulk of the treasure is still down there. No one will believe us, even if we told them what we thought was down there."

"I think you're wrong. Wait right here and I'll show you why." Jack jumped up and quickly left the room.

"Now where's he going?" Tom asked Sam.

"We'll have to wait and see," Sam said as he shrugged his shoulders.

Within minutes, Jack returned carrying an old leather pouch. "I never got to tell you guys what I found while I was hiding below from those assassins." Jack carefully removed the diary from the pouch and showed it to the startled group.

"What is that?" Carly asked. "It looks like some kind of diary. Is that old quill pen writing in French?"

"That's exactly what it is," Jack replied. "It seems that we almost had some of King Solomon's lost treasure in our hands along with part of the Templar fortune."

Carly turned towards Stompmeyer and smiled in astonishment as the German moved closer to examine the diary. "Isn't that one of the hypotheses you offered when we were first examining the box? How did you know?"

"I didn't, Miss Edwards. I only repeated one of many rumors, or now I should say, 'theories,' about the lost Templar fortune and its relationship to the looted Jewish Temple's treasures. But Mr. Talbot, where exactly did you find this diary? It's amazing, if it is, in fact, authentic."

Jack sat down as the crew gathered around him and recounted his experience in the cavern. As he described the vast treasures he had witnessed hidden in the cavern walls, he recounted the knight's tale as it appeared in the diary.

"What happened to the other ship?" Sean asked with anticipation.

"I don't know," Jack replied. "The only thing the diary tells us is that each ship took off in a different direction. I would assume the other ship traveled east, but whether it ever arrived at its destination or wrecked at sea is something I don't believe we will ever know."

"Can we examine the box and amulet again, please?" Stompmeyer asked Sam. "Now that we have some context to place it in, perhaps we can unravel more of its mystery. The parchment must mean something, or else the box must contain something else we have not yet located."

Sam agreed and retrieved the artifacts from the vault. As he lay the box and amulet on the table, Jack exclaimed, "Oh, I almost forgot! I took this off our knight's finger before I left the cavern." As the group turned towards Jack, he held up the ring he had slipped onto his finger.

"Why, that looks like a smaller version of the amulet!" Sean cried out.

"Indeed it does," Stompmeyer said as he took a closer look at the ring. "May I see it, please, Mr. Talbot?"

Jack handed the ring to the German and watched as the man opened the box with the amulet Sean had recovered. Stompmeyer then removed the parchment from within the box and carefully placed the ring inside, giving it a quarter turn as it set within the smaller engraved symbol. A clicking sound was heard as the box revealed yet a second hidden compartment containing a small map with more words or symbols.

"What is that?" they all cried out in unison. "Not another hieroglyphic clue to unravel?"

"I'm afraid so!" Stompmeyer exclaimed with joy. "It looks like our quest is not yet over, my friends. Perhaps this will lead us to more of the Temple's treasures, or even the innermost secrets of the Templars themselves."

"But we're not archaeologists, we're salvage divers," said Sam. "We can't go traipsing all around the world looking for some unknown treasure. We'd be like fish out of water."

"You're right," Jack said as he rose to his feet. "But we have to check this thing out. We owe it to Billy and those poor Coast Guardsmen. Why don't we let Carly and Professor Stompmeyer make a closer examination and try to decipher what's on this second parchment before we jump to any conclusions. Perhaps it will give us some clue as to the second ship's navigation path, or at least inform us as to what we might be looking for."

"I guess you're right, Jack. But it seems we've gone to a lot of trouble for nothing, here."

"That may be, but let's give it a shot anyway. Now we all have to be extra careful. We can't let any of this slip out. We need to know what this parchment says without letting the whole world know, especially that Russian SOB!"

Everyone agreed as Carly and Stompmeyer retired to continue their research in a more quiet area.

50

As Brian rushed from the seaplane and jumped into the waiting car, he pulled out his cell phone and quickly dialed to one of the men he had sent to keep watch over Alexandra and Paige. "Any suspicious activity?"

"Nothing."

"Keep your eyes peeled. These guys are pros and they could show up anytime."

"Roger that."

Brian felt a little more at ease knowing that he had been able to place two men on watch outside of Jack's apartment. If anything happened to Alexandra or Paige, he would never be able to forgive himself, nor would he ever expect Jack's forgiveness. He had watched Jack's back all through the war. After the war, Jack had used his connections to help Brian get a high security clearance job in the government. When Jack left the District Attorney's Office, Brian had retired and opened his own private investigation and security firm. After a few lucrative years, mostly through referrals from Jack, Brian was able to expand throughout several states. But the relationship he had formed with Jack and his family was special. They treated him like one of their own, and to him, they were the only family he had.

As he headed down Interstate 95, Brian marveled at the beautiful Florida sunset. It was a shame that such beauty was often overlooked and overshadowed by such evil and violence. The radio was on, and reports of renewed violence in the Middle East and Afghanistan obscured the peace and tranquility of the moment. As the driver flicked through the stations, more news came across the air waves: a murder in Miami, a robbery in Fort Lauderdale. It seemed there was no escaping the savagery of the civilized world.

It had been nearly forty minutes. Traffic had been light and they were making good time. Brian thought he would check in once more with his men and alert them of his impending arrival. Brian pressed the redial button on his cell phone. He heard it ring five times before the voice mail message played: "Leave a message at the beep."

Brian felt the hair on his back raise up as his body began to slightly tremble. Something was wrong. He had felt it upon his arrival on the mainland, but had pushed it from his mind after his initial conversation with his man. Now there was no denying it. Danger was in the air and he had to get to Jack's apartment now. There was no time to waste.

"Step on it!" he yelled to the driver. "I think we have a situation. Keep a sharp lookout. There's no answer at the house."

Brian felt helpless as the sedan picked up speed and jetted through the intersection, narrowly missing a turning car. He redialed the number and received the same message. Frantically, he dialed the number to Jack's apartment.

"Hello?"

"Alexandra. Thank God. Is everything all right there?"

"Brian? Is that you? Of course everything is all right. Why would you ask?"

He was not sure if he was overreacting, but he quickly relayed his fears to Jack's wife after briefly describing the events at sea.

"Are you sure Jack is all right?"

"He's fine. Really. He should be home in a few days, as soon as they finish their exploration. Don't worry. Half the local Coast Guard is with him. It's you I'm worried about right now. I want you to make sure all the doors are securely locked and the windows closed. If you see anything unusual, dial 911 immediately. Don't wait! Do you understand? I'm only a few minutes away."

"Don't you think you're overreacting just a bit? What danger could Paige and I possibly be in?"

"Alexandra, don't argue with me! If you're not in any danger, then there's no harm done."

Suddenly there was a loud crash as the door to the oceanfront balcony shattered. Two assailants quickly entered, deftly pushing the shards of glass aside with gloved hands. One was a man, thin and gaunt, with sandy blond hair and a pencil mustache. The other was a tall female with long black hair. As Alexandra yelled, Brian felt his body tense.

"What's happening, Alexandra? Speak to me!"

Then the line went dead. Brian quickly dialed 911 and gave the location of the condo. As they turned down the drive, Brian saw one of his lookouts lying in the bushes. Only the tips of his shoes were visible. As the car screeched to a halt, Brian jumped out and stood over the man's body. His throat had been slashed and his body had been tossed into the bushes in an attempt to hide the corpse from any passersby.

"Quickly!" Brian yelled to the driver. "Circle around and

head them off. I don't know how many there are, but they can't have gotten out yet."

The driver sped off, leaving Brian alone on foot. Brian pulled out his Glock 9mm and headed towards the condo, carefully surveying the area as he ran to the building, keeping an eye out for any intruders. As he approached the front of the building, he felt a bullet whiz by his head and saw it hit and splinter the doorway in front of him. He quickly turned, crouched on one knee and fired a round at his attacker, striking the man squarely in the chest. After taking a moment to ensure there were no other assailants nearby, he continued up the steps and entered the main condo building.

Dozens of hysterical residents were running about, contributing to the chaos and mayhem caused by the shooting and violence. Brian pushed his way past the crowd just as he spied Alexandra and Paige being led towards the dock area by their two captors. Seeing no other way to reach them, Brian covered his face with both hands and lunged toward the plate glass window overlooking the Intracoastal Waterway.

As he crashed through the glass and hit the ground, he ducked and rolled, landing back on his feet, gun pointed towards the two abductors. As the woman turned and fired at Brian, he squeezed off two carefully aimed shots. The first struck her in the abdomen while the second entered her heart, killing her instantaneously. The force of the two shots pushed her into her partner, causing him to lose his grip on Alexandra. As the man released his grip, Alexandra tumbled to the ground. The man continued towards the dock, grabbing Paige by the waist and swinging her into the boat waiting in the water. The boat took off just as Paige landed inside of it with a thud.

Brian jumped up and continued running after the boat. As he did, Paige's captor stood up and fired three rounds at him, causing him to duck for cover. As the man turned to jump into the speeding boat, Brian's driver appeared at the dock and tackled the man. The two men struggled as Brian raced towards them. By the time he could reach the dock, the boat carrying Paige had left the canal and had safely jettisoned away.

Brian turned towards the captured intruder, striking him squarely across the jaw with the barrel of his gun. "Who the hell are you and where is he taking the girl?"

The man looked up at Brian and with a smirk on his face, shrugged his shoulders and replied, "I believe I have the right to remain silent. I would also like to call my lawyer."

Brian glared back at the man, and was about to strike him again when the police arrived. As they took the man into custody, Brian approached a sobbing Alexandra. "Are you all right?" he asked her.

"Paige! Where is she? Where have they taken her? What is going on, Brian?"

Alexandra collapsed in Brian's arms as he tried to console her. "I don't know. But I won't rest until I find out.

"Hold up a minute!" he yelled to the policeman. With Alexandra alongside him, he stood inches from the cuffed man's bleeding face. "If any harm comes to her, no jail will keep you safe from me. Rest assured of that!"

The man looked Brian square in the eye and just smirked before he was led away in handcuffs to a waiting squad car.

51

Rachel began to get nervous as the sedan descended the mountainous trail from Mount Scopus and headed towards the refugee camp. "Surely we're not entering the Palestinian area, are we?" Rachel asked Saul nervously. "I mean, you don't intend to cross the barrier, do you?"

"But of course we must, if I am to show you what you came here for, Miss Lyons. Do not be afraid. It will be but a simple matter to cross over, and no harm will come to you, I assure you."

Rachel was becoming more anxious as the sedan continued its course towards the barrier. She had always been rash and impetuous, but this time she may have outdone herself. *What an end to a banner day,* she thought to herself. Perhaps she was getting just what she deserved after all. Sweat began to form on her brow as she leaned over towards Saul. "Is it getting hot in here?" she asked. "Can you please turn on the AC?"

"I'm afraid it is on, Miss Lyons. Are you not yet accustomed to our climate?"

"Maybe we should turn around and go back. I might be coming down with something," Rachel groped for a neutral reason to terminate the excursion before they reached the barrier.

"We're almost there. Please bear with me but a few more moments. I assure you, it will be well worth your while, and we can stop to get you something cold to drink and cool yourself off once we cross the barrier."

Rachel could see that the man was not going to allow her to graciously withdraw. She hoped she was not making a mistake, but figured she had nothing more to lose at this point other than her good sense and personal well-being.

"Very well, but I hope we get there soon. I don't know how much more of this heat I can stand."

The driver quickly brought the car to halt just before the barrier checkpoint. As the guards checked the vehicle over, the driver flashed some credentials and said something unintelligible in Arabic. After a cursory glance at Rachel and Saul, the guard motioned the driver to continue on.

The sedan slowly rolled through the checkpoint and continued on its way. Soon they reached a dirt path that was all but camouflaged by some olive trees and a rock wall. The car turned up the dirt path and continued towards some old ruins.

"Where are we?" Rachel asked. "Is that a cross?" she remarked, pointing to an object on top of the rubble.

"Yes it is, Miss Lyons. We are passing the site of the old Crusader Church built around 1169 AD. It is said that the pilgrims would pass this way on their trek to Jerusalem. Upon their first sight of the city, they would place crosses as they removed their shoes at this spot."

"Why remove their shoes?"

"They believed that by doing so they would be closer to Jesus, humbling themselves as he did, and making themselves more worthy for his blessings."

"But it's just a heap of stone and rubble now."

"Alas, that is true. But at this location, besides the chapel, there also existed the ancient Roman villas of the Jews, erected after 70 AD."

"70 AD? Why does that date ring a bell?"

"That was the year the Romans destroyed the ancient Jewish Temple in Jerusalem, sacked the city and basically destroyed most of the Jewish identity there. The Temple's treasures and holy artifacts were looted, sacked and sent to Rome along with thousands of Jewish slaves."

"Is that what those coverings are over there to the right, archaeological digs of the villas?"

"Yes, very observant. That is where the archaeologists have been excavating. Thus far, they have located a number of houses containing stone vessels, as well as the remains of two public bathhouses. They say they have even discovered stone basins that were used to hold ashes recovered from the Temple site, which had been destroyed by the Romans during the Jewish revolt."

"That is all very interesting, but you said you would show me some plans and get me a cold drink in a place where I could cool down. Is it very far from here?"

The man began to laugh. "Far? Hardly so. We have but a few meters to walk and we shall have arrived."

Rachel looked around as signs of confusion crept across over her face. "But I don't see anything other than rubble and archaeological digging. Are you trying to play with my head?"

Saul grabbed Rachel's hand and led her down a pathway between the rubble. As they descended the steps cut in the stone, a small hut came into view. Several Arab children were running about kicking a ball while two small dogs ran after them, barking and nipping at the children's heels. An old woman was beating a rug with a stick, hopelessly trying to get some of the dirt from the fabric. The smell of fresh baked pita-bread mingled with the aroma of cooked meats and vegetables permeated the air. It was as if someone had opened a door and allowed them to walk into a whole new city. From the steps of the rubble and demolished buildings, a Palestinian city had arisen.

"Where do these people live?" Rachel asked Saul.

"You are looking at their homes, Miss Lyons. This is where they eat, sleep and occupy the majority of their time."

"But are there no schools? No businesses? Where do they work? How can they afford to live?"

"Unfortunately, until we have arrived at a peaceful coexistence and can treat all our brethren with civility and respect, outrages such as this refugee camp will continue to exist. As long as the extremists continue their reign of terror, the simple villagers and general population they claim to so zealously represent and fight for will continue to suffer and remain ill-fed, ill-cared for and illiterate."

"But why does no one try to do something?"

"It is not such a simple task, my dear. Israel believes that, in order to ensure its own security, it must isolate the Palestinians and keep them separate from the Israeli citizens. The barrier, and numerous checkpoints, have prevented most bombings and other forms of large-scale terrorist attack. Until the Palestinian Authority shows itself capable of governing its people in a civilized manner and of controlling its more extremist factions from committing further acts of violence, the schism between the two nations will continue to expand and drive an ever-widening wedge between the two societies."

"Welcome, Saul, my brother. And who is this charming young lady you have brought to our humble village?" An old man had walked over the small mound of rubble and approached the two visitors.

"This is the young reporter I told you about, Rachel Lyons. Miss Lyons, meet my good friend Nasim Khatib."

As the two shook hands in greeting, Saul continued, "It was Nasim's idea to promote the joint education program. He is one of the leaders in this camp and suggested this location for the first test site."

"Yes, I thought it was a fitting location to mingle the cultures together. Its proximity to Jerusalem, the most holy site in the world to the three major religions, was the first factor which intrigued me about this location. The discovery of the Crusader church and ancient Roman Jewish village historically made this an appropriate site. We as Palestinians, as well as Jewish and Christian Israelis alike, all have deep connections to this area. It seemed only natural to try to get the Israelis to sit down with us in this joint endeavor."

"That is correct. It was a smart political move, since the Christian factor with its missionary leanings fully endorsed the proposal. It was more difficult to convince the rest of the Israeli population, as well as the Palestinian authorities."

"I'm not so sure you have succeeded in convincing both sides," said Rachel. "There have been many articles written against this proposal from both sides, and both the Israeli Parliament and the Palestinian Authority are still debating its worth."

"That is why we have asked you to come, Miss Lyons," Nasim continued. "Saul and I feel very strongly about this endeavor and believe we can plant the seeds for a lasting peace amongst our nations. After all, we are all brothers, descending from the same ancestor, Abraham."

"And it's from the argument that Isaac stole Ishmael's birthright that the Arab hatred for the Jews evolved," Rachel solemnly reminded the two men. "What makes you think that both sides can put away their distrust and maybe even hatred for each other?"

"Because they must," said Nasim. "The Israelis are obviously here to stay. They have made great strides in developing this land, both agriculturally and industrially. For a small nation, they have developed into a substantial power in the Middle East. Other Arab nations have recognized Israel's right to exist, perhaps more out of economic necessity than a sense of morality, but regardless of the reasons, they have spoken out against the increasing and senseless violence and terroristic acts committed by the extremists. Look at Egypt and how it has attempted to moderate a lasting peace. We believe that if our two peoples can sit down and learn together, they will eventually overcome the prejudice and mistrust of generations and will forge the foundation for a peaceful coexistence."

"Quite a noble thought," Rachel replied. "But I highly doubt your plan has a snowball's chance in hell of succeeding."

"Does that mean you will not help us?" Saul asked dejectedly.

"To the contrary. This might be quite interesting and could generate much interest as the story develops. When can we get started?"

The two men led Rachel to a small house where they showed her the construction plans for their lofty project. They explained that progress had already been made in removing much of the rubble from the targeted area, and the workers would soon be ready to begin excavation of some of the old villas and the church itself. Rachel promised to return the following day with camera equipment. As she rose to leave with Saul, Nasim handed her a small object.

"What is this?" she asked him.

"It is a coin one of the workers found while removing the debris from the area. I give it to you to bind our agreement and also as a gesture of good will and luck. The symbol on the face is an ancient good luck charm, 'The Hand of Fatima.' Keep it with you to ward off evil. It was just discovered this morning before you arrived, so I think it was a sign from Allah of the righteousness and validity of our venture."

"Why, thank you, Mr. Khatib. I think it's lovely. I will see you tomorrow, then."

As Rachel and the old man left, the Arab smiled, content in the knowledge that this young woman would help him publicize his valiant efforts.

52

The crew of the *Scavenger* were busy running down leads as quickly as Stompmeyer and Carly handed them out. Stompmeyer used the internet to research all possible meanings of the strange writings they had uncovered in the second secret compartment, contained within the inner sanctum of the box. Tom and Geoff took turns examining the box and its mechanism, searching for a clue as to its composition and history.

"Hey Geoff, what if we took a picture of the trap and forwarded it to Eli? He used to be pretty good at opening those secret latches when he dove for Sam."

"That might not be a bad idea, Tom, but first we should run it by everyone, and then we need to try to locate him."

"That's not a problem. Last I heard, he was working for some shipwreck museum in Delaware. I'll get my cell phone. I think I had a contact number for him in my address book."

As Tom went to his cabin to retrieve his phone, Geoff discussed the idea with Sam and the others. Tom had just returned when Jack reminded them of the need for secrecy. "We don't know how the Russians found out about the amulet in the first place. The more people we let into our circle of knowledge, the stronger the likelihood that those goons will find out we've discovered more of the treasure. I'm not so sure I want to meet up with those guys again. Do you?"

The rest of the crew agreed with Jack. Reluctantly, Tom returned to his examination of the box while the attempts to decipher the code on the parchment continued. Tom was secretly seething inside, upset that the crew rejected his suggestion to bring his friend, Eli, on board to help in unraveling the code. With his attention split between his sulking and the code, he was unaware that Dmitry had activated the Trojan hidden in Tom's phone. Dmitry was now able to monitor the conversations of the *Scavenger* crew, as well as any progress they were making on their discovery.

Carly and Professor Stompmeyer were feverishly working on translating the parchment. The writing was faded and difficult to decipher, even under the best of conditions. The makeshift lab on the ship did not present the optimum environment for such a daring task. However, under the circumstances, it would have to do. For the most part, the box had kept the parchment safe and watertight, but some seawater had seeped through and caused some of the fragile letters to smudge and even completely disappear. The ancient Hebrew text made the translation even more difficult.

After several hours of intense study and comparison, Stompmeyer screamed, "Carly! Quickly, bring that laptop over here, now!"

"What is it, professor?"

"Pull up our notes on the original parchment you first found in the box. Do you still have that book on ancient languages? Bring that, too. I need to do some comparisons. I think I may have figured out part of the writing."

Carly unplugged the laptop and brought it to the professor. "I'll be right back with the book."

Carly quickly left the cabin while the professor scrolled through his notes on the laptop. As he did so, he jotted some words and letters down on the notepad, darting quickly between the parchment and the laptop. Within minutes, Carly returned with the book the German had requested.

"Did you find anything?"

"I think so. Look at these markings. Doesn't that look like the word 'stones' from the first parchment you uncovered?"

Carly moved closer to examine the two. "I think you're right, professor. Can you make out anything else?"

"It looks like the words 'Judah' and 'Messiah,' but I'm not positive. I think the phrase has something to do with the Stones overlooking Judah until the coming of the Messiah."

"Stones?" Sean questioned. "What stones?"

"I'm not sure, but it must be referring to the Stones of Fire from the first parchment."

"You mean the High Priest's breastplate with all the precious stones from ancient Israel?"

"Yes, Mr. Knight, I believe so."

"But what is the rest of it all about? Jesus came and no one has uncovered these so-called Stones of Fire."

"Quite correct, Mr. Knight. But you see, the Jews do not believe that Jesus was the Messiah. And besides, Jesus was crucified before the destruction of Herod's Temple. The Romans invaded Jerusalem and destroyed the Second Temple, or Herod's Temple, in 70 AD, while scholars place the crucifixion between 26 and 36 AD. In any event, the High Priesthood was still in existence at the time of Jesus's death, and so the Stones of Fire would still have been worn by the High Priest for many years after the crucifixion."

"Then what is the parchment trying to tell us?"

As Stompmeyer was explaining, the rest of the crew

gathered around to hear. "I believe the breastplate may be hidden in a place where it is near Jerusalem, waiting for the Jewish Messiah to arrive."

"That's very interesting, professor, but just where can it be that it has remained undiscovered all for nearly 2,000 years?" Jack asked.

"I'm not sure, Mr. Talbot, but if I can decipher the rest of the parchment, I believe I may be able to uncover the clue."

Stompmeyer returned to the parchment while the rest of the crew anxiously shuffled about the cabin. Tom got up from his chair and began to leave.

"Where are you going?" Sam asked.

"I've had enough for one day. It's not like we're ever going to find those gems, anyway. They're surely not in the ocean below us."

As Tom turned to leave, Geoff cried out to him, "Don't forget your phone!"

Tom quickly turned around, grabbed his phone, then stormed out the door.

"What's got into him?" Geoff asked.

"Not sure, but he's sure got some bug up him."

"Leave him be," Sam said. "He's just upset over Billy and blames Stompmeyer and his gang. He's not happy that Stompmeyer's helping us and trying to decipher the text without the help of his friend Eli. He'll get over it. Just give him some time."

After another two hours of fruitless examination, the rest of the crew decided to call it a day and retired to their cabins for the night.

Jack spent a restless night in his cabin. The last few days' events were starting to wear on him and he could not shake the feeling that the Russian was somehow still spying on them. He had known their every move from the time they had first decided to enlist Stompmeyer's aid down to their wreck dive.

He knew their exact location at sea and knew about their discovery of the box and amulet. Two innocent civilians were dead, as was a Coast Guard crew, and now the scum had disappeared without a trace. He was far too dangerous to simply ignore. Where and when would he strike next?

As dawn broke, Jack decided he had laid awake and tossed enough. He slowly arose from his bed, threw on a bathing suit and went topside. The ocean waves were lapping against the ship's bow just as the sun was beginning to peek out from the horizon. Jack could see the orange glow of the sunrise beaming in perfect symmetry with the glimmer of the waning full moon from the night before. He felt the warm ocean breeze caressing his cheeks as he leaned against the ship's railing. He heard the waves striking the bow as the salty ocean spray struck his forehead. He looked around at the orange horizon and took a deep breath before he dove into the water. *Nothing like a brisk dip first thing in the morning to get the blood flowing and shake the cobwebs out,* he thought to himself. He missed his wife and granddaughter and longed to solve the mystery so he could return to them in Palm Springs. He promised himself that he would call them after breakfast.

53

The crew was finishing their hearty breakfast when Stompmeyer came running in.

"We did it!" he exclaimed.

"Did what?" Geoff asked.

"We finally figured out the interpretation."

"Well, are you going to tell us what's on the parchment?"

"But of course. Now you must realize that much is missing, and we had to infer some of the meanings."

"Come on, get on with it," Sam said.

"It would appear that we were right. The best interpretation we could make of the most prominent line which survived is that the stones are overlooking or watching Judah, waiting for the arrival of the Messiah. We think the writer was referring to the hiding place of the Stones of Fire, keeping the breastplate safe and hidden until the kingdom of Israel rises again during the coming of the Messiah, as prophesied by the ancient Israelites."

"Okay. So where is this hiding place?"

"Alas, I don't know."

"What do you mean you don't know?" Sam asked.

"It's not clear. The only clues are that it is overlooking Judah. That could be anywhere in Israel or its borders."

"I doubt that," Jack said.

"What do you mean?" asked the professor.

"I couldn't sleep last night, so I googled the Messiah and learned that Jewish tradition holds that the Messiah is to enter through the Golden Gate located on the eastern side of the Temple Mount. If the breastplate is hidden watching for the Messiah's arrival, it has to be in some proximity to Jerusalem. Could the writer have been referring to Jerusalem as Judah?"

"Well," mused Stompmeyer, "it is possible. But where could it be hidden? When the Romans defeated the Jews they destroyed most of the city. According to the Jewish-Roman historian Josephus, the Temple walls were destroyed, as were most of the city walls and fortifications. The towers were left standing to demonstrate to the world the magnificence of the city and how well fortified it was before the Romans had subdued it. Many of the buildings were destroyed as well, down to the very foundations. To quote Josephus, 'there was left nothing to make those that came thither believe it had ever been inhabited.'"

"So where does that leave us?"

"I don't know, Mr. Katz, but I don't believe we'll find our treasure in Jerusalem."

"What about the outskirts?" asked Jack. "Are there any ancient villages or dwellings within close proximity?"

"There are many ancient cities," answered the professor. "The caves at Qumran, where the Dead Sea scrolls were found, are not more than forty kilometers from Jerusalem."

"No, that's too far. Anything closer?"

Carly pulled up an ancient map of Jerusalem and the surrounding area online. As she began to encircle the old city,

Stompmeyer slammed his hand on the table. "But of course!"

"What?" the crew yelled in unison.

"There was an excavation a few years ago in the northeastern section of Jerusalem, about three kilometers from the city. If I recall correctly, the Israelis were planning to expand their railway out along the Ramallah Road. During the excavation they uncovered what appeared to be an old Crusader-era church, as well as the remains of an ancient Jewish settlement dating to Second Temple times."

"Where was this found?" Jack asked as he moved closer to the computer screen.

"Over in this area," Stompmeyer responded while pointing to a small area on the map appearing on the screen. "It's a suburb of Jerusalem called Shuafat. There's a Palestinian refugee camp located there, I think. It's located on the ancient road from Nablus to Jerusalem. It could meet your specifications of being within close proximity to Jerusalem. If the zealots were looking for a place to hide the breastplate, it would only be a short distance for them to travel, assuming they could get past the Roman guards during the siege."

"Even assuming that this Shuafat is the place, how do we find this so-called hiding spot, especially in the midst of a Palestinian refugee camp?"

As the crew pondered Jack's question, Sam's satellite phone rang.

"Hello?" Sam said, speaking into the receiver.

"May I please speak to Jack Talbot?" the voice on the other end responded.

Sam handed Jack the phone with a puzzled look on his face. "It's for you," he said.

"Listen carefully, Mr. Talbot. I will only say this once," the voice on the other end ominously echoed with a heavy Russian accent. "If you value your granddaughter's life, you will do as I say."

"What the hell are you talking about?" Jack yelled back into the phone.

"Oh, you have not yet heard? Well, then, let me be the first to advise you. Your darling granddaughter has graciously decided to continue her recuperation in our care, for the time being. I'm sure she will make a full and complete recovery, provided you follow my instructions completely."

Jack was beginning to sweat with nervous fear. What was this maniac talking about? Was it possible that his beautiful, sweet, innocent Paige had fallen into the clutches of this maniac? What had happened to his wife, Alexandra? Was she all right? Thoughts were racing through his head at lightning speed.

"You bastard!" he yelled. "If any harm comes to her, I will personally kill you! What have you done with my wife?"

"Temper, temper, Mr. Talbot. As far as I'm aware, your wife is in perfect health, as is your granddaughter. Now, enough of this chatter! We must get down to the business at hand. You have such precious little time, and you surely don't want to waste it on this trivial nonsense, now do you?"

Jack caught the sarcastic tone immediately and realized that the Russian was interested in something extremely important. "Okay. What is it you want?"

"That's better," Dmitry said with authority. "I want those precious gems, as well as the amulet."

"What gems are you talking about?" Jack asked innocently.

"Don't play games with me, Mr. Talbot. I already have a score to settle with you. You have killed some of my most trusted men and caused the death of several close and loyal comrades. I want those gems. Those…what did you call them? Oh yes, those Stones of Fire. And I want them delivered to me within seventy two hours. Do you understand?"

Dmitry had become agitated and was now yelling through the phone. His voice had escalated and now resonated through the speaker, loud enough for the rest of the crew to hear the gist of the conversation.

"What the heck are Stones of Fire?" Jack asked the man while still trying to play dumb.

"Seventy-two hours, Mr. Talbot. I will be in touch with you and provide further instructions."

Jack realized the man was serious and had somehow obtained access to the information the *Scavenger* crew had uncovered.

"Wait!" Jack exclaimed. "All right, but if you know about the Stones of Fire, you also know we don't have them."

"Then get them!"

"We don't know where they are," Jack began to plead.

"You know they are in Israel. I'm sure you can locate them with your extraordinary powers of deduction. Besides, that beautiful young girl's life depends on it."

"But seventy-two hours is not enough time. I will need to fly to Israel and attempt to locate the area we believe the Stones may have been hidden. Even if I can locate the area, there is no guarantee that I will be able to find the Stones. Israel's a big country, and we're not one hundred percent sure where to look."

"Try Shuafat, and stop playing games with me. You now have seventy-one hours and forty-five minutes. The clock continues to count down, and you have not even left the ship yet."

Jack realized the Russian was looking for an excuse to goad him and would relish in bringing harm to his innocent and unsuspecting granddaughter. Jack decided to acquiesce to the Russian's demands. He meekly responded to the Russian's last comment, "All right, I'll get to Israel as quickly as possible, but please, I need more time. It's got to be at least an eighteen-hour flight and it will take me at least two to three hours to get to the Miami airport from here. I need more time if I'm going to succeed and deliver the Stones to you. And you never mentioned, how will I get in touch with you?"

"You will take Mr. Reed's telephone with you and I will contact you accordingly through his line. And you are correct: the flight time is between eighteen and twenty-three hours, so I suggest you get moving and not waste any more time."

As Jack was about to protest, the line suddenly went dead. "What the.... That bastard!" Jack screamed.

The crew gathered around Jack in an attempt to console him.

"How did he know about the Stones?" Sam asked while turning towards Stompmeyer with an accusing glare.

"I told you he has eyes everywhere. I surely did not tell him," the German replied nervously. "You've got to believe me."

"We'll worry about how he knew later," Jack interrupted. "Somebody please get me my wife on the phone, and Sam, do you think you can reach Brian for me?"

"Of course," Sam replied.

As the crew began to scurry, about they suddenly heard the roar of a helicopter engine.

"What the hell now?" Jack exclaimed.

"Look, I think it's your wife and Brian," Carly cried out over the racing sound of the engine.

The crew all ran topside as Jack led the way. Within minutes, Alexandra and Brian had boarded the ship and were describing to Jack the events that had occurred on the mainland hours earlier. As Jack was attempting to console his hysterical wife, Brian filled Jack in on the information he had been able to gather on Dmitry and his gang. When Brian had finished, Jack described the conversation he had with Dmitry minutes earlier.

"Then it's true," Jack moaned aloud. "The bastard really does have her. I think he would like to kill her to get back at me for interfering with his scheme. This is all my fault."

"Stop it now," Sam said. "You did not cause any of this,

and how were you to know how evil this creep was? Besides, if it weren't for you, we would all be dead now, and that scum would have the entire treasure for his cartel, or whatever his gang is called."

"Sam's right," Brian said. "Stop feeling sorry for yourself and let's start planning how to get Paige back. I've got my top men working with the police, Interpol, and homeland security on this. In the meantime, we need to get you to Tel Aviv, and quickly."

"Do you have a plan?" Jack asked.

"I think I can pull some strings and we can charter a private jet to get you directly to Tel Aviv, rather than wasting time routing you through New York or some European city, but we'd better get moving. We have no time to waste."

"Wait a minute. I need to get Tom's phone first."

"Why?" Brian asked.

"That creep required I bring it with me so he could contact me."

"But why Tom's phone?" Alexandra had suddenly perked up.

"That's what I was trying to figure out, only we don't have the time."

"I wonder," Brian began. "Was Tom present when you guys were talking about these Stones and interpreting the parchment clue?"

"Sure he was. He was examining the box while we were discussing the clues, why?"

"Where was his phone?"

"Right there beside him on the table. He wanted to get a friend of his involved in the deciphering, but we decided it wasn't a good idea. We didn't want the information leaked out to the wrong people," Jack replied sarcastically. "I guess we just weren't careful enough after all."

"Was Tom around when you obtained the other information that was ultimately leaked out?" Brian continued.

"Now that you mention it, I think he was," chimed Sam, who had joined the group as Brian initiated his questions. "Where are you heading with this, Brian?"

"I think the bastard somehow planted a Trojan inside Tom's phone."

"A Trojan? What's that?" Alexandra asked.

"There's this program you can use, kind of like a virus, which you can send to a cell phone. It allows the sender to monitor all phone calls, text messages and, even better, allows the sender to turn the phone into a bug, an eavesdropping device, at whim."

"Are you serious?" Sam asked.

"Damn it. I bet you he's right," Jack said as he pounded his fist against the cabin door. "I should have picked that up sooner. There was no other way he could have known. I remember reading an article in one of *Trial Lawyer*'s magazines about that Trojan thing. I don't know what made me think that after locating the GPS in Stompmeyer's cane, there would not be other toys in that Russian bastard's arsenal."

Brian asked Sam to bring Tom up without his cell phone. After the two arrived, Brian questioned Tom about his cell phone use before leaving the dock. After several minutes, they realized that Tom had unknowingly released the Trojan, thinking it was one of the regular updates to his phone service.

"I'm really sorry guys, but I didn't know. I'll throw that damn thing overboard."

"No, you can't. I'm supposed to take it with me to Israel."

"You can't do that," both Sam and Tom cried out together. "That SOB will be able to track you and keep an eye on you the entire time."

"I know, but we'll just have to figure something else out. Got anything in mind, Brian?"

"I might have a trick or two up my sleeve. But we'd better

get going. We don't have much time. Grab whatever you need for this trip and let's get moving. We have a plane to catch."

Jack quickly grabbed a few things from his cabin, then took the ring and amulet from below. "We might need these," he said as he turned to say good-bye to the Sam and the crew.

"I'm coming along, and I think we should bring the professor with us. He speaks the language and knows more about the land and the archaeology than we can cram on the flight there." Sam already had a bag packed and was putting his hat on as he held one hand out.

"No, it's too dangerous."

"Not another word," Sam interrupted. "This was my expedition and I need to follow this through to the end. Besides, Billy was a good friend of mine and I owe it to him to finish this thing."

"We're coming along, too." Sean and Carly had just joined the two men arguing. "I found the amulet that started this whole thing, and between Carly and the professor, we should hopefully be able to track down the Stones' hiding place."

Jack threw up his arms in surrender. "I can't argue anymore. We need to get going. Come on, Alexandra. Brian can have one of his men pick you up when we land in Miami. They'll put you up in a safe spot till we get Paige back."

"Fuck you, Jack Talbot!" Alexandra thrust both hands forward with full force into Jack's chest, pushing him against the railing and almost causing him to tumble overboard. "I'm not letting you out of my sight! Those bastards almost killed me. They took my granddaughter right from my arms, and now they mean to kill her, and maybe you, too. I'm coming along and there's no use trying to argue."

Jack could see the fire in her eyes as her cheeks reddened and tears rolled down the sides of her face. The anger that had welled up inside her had suddenly brought clarity to Jack about the current situation.

"All right then, let's get moving. Tom, get me your cell phone, now."

As they boarded the helicopter, Jack removed the battery from the cell phone. "If there's no juice, it can't send a signal, right?" he pointed out to the group. "Maybe that will give us time to formulate a plan without being stepped on."

Jack's actions, while valiant, were unnecessary, since the flight back to the mainland was conducted in complete silence. The five men and two women were too deeply entrenched in their own private thoughts to speak, and modern technology has not yet progressed to the point where a person's thoughts can be intercepted. As the helicopter approached the landing field, Brian began barking instructions on his own phone to his men waiting below.

54

The wind had begun to blow more furiously around the ruins on the hilltop village adjacent to the refugee camp. Clumps of sand floated in the thick, humid air as Rachel returned to Shuafat for her second meeting with her two newly found benefactors.

"Saul. Mr. Khatib," she cried out as she waved at the two men standing by the church ruins. "I did some research on my own and think this project may indeed be newsworthy. Has there been any progress in clearing the work site for construction of the new facility?"

"Unfortunately, there has not been any progress, Miss Lyons," Khatib answered dejectedly. "As is usual in our country, especially when it comes to Palestinian affairs, there has been some unexpected red tape thrown in our path."

"What do you mean?" she asked.

"Apparently a dispute has arisen over the old church structure and the ancient village buildings. The government now believes that they should be restored as tourist attractions rather than for the originally planned educational purposes."

"Why, that's preposterous!" she exclaimed. "Why can't it serve a dual function?"

"What do you mean?" Saul asked.

"Couldn't it be restored as a joint project between both the Israelis and Palestinians? They could open the area as a joint educational experience and still allow the general public access to view the historic site. Then the public could observe both nations educating their populace side by side in peace and harmony."

"I don't know if either government would agree, but it sounds like a fantastic idea, Miss Lyons," Khatib responded excitedly. "Perhaps if you wrote an article about such plans, we could sway popular opinion towards such a project."

"I'd be glad to. Could you show me around some more? I would like to explore the site more fully and also take some pictures for publication with the article."

Excited at the prospect that progress was imminent, the two men began to show Rachel the recently uncovered sites. The church was not much to look at, having weathered centuries of destruction and neglect. What remains there were consisted mainly of a mud brick foundation, with what once must have been a vaulted ceiling, and the remnants of an arched window. Beyond that, not much else remained to distinguish the structure from any other ruin.

As they walked around the crumbling remains, Rachel turned to Khatib and asked, "How can they tell this was once a church?"

"When it was first excavated, there was part of a mosaic floor uncovered with a depiction of a fleur-de-lis superimposed upon a cross. The Israel Antiquities Authority quickly claimed the find had historical and religious significance as a Crusader-era church. Others have disagreed, but the label has remained."

Rachel snapped several pictures of the structure as she strained to find any evidence of the mosaic floor. "What happened to the floor?"

"Unfortunately it was destroyed during one of the many missile strikes. As you can see around you, there are still many highrise buildings scarred by bombs and missile strikes, which give the impression that this is still a battle zone."

After leaving the church, the men led Rachel to the ancient village site. As she spun around, she marveled at the remains of the spacious dwellings and neatly laid walkways and roads. "Whew!" she whistled. "This must have been some settlement. Were these buildings all villas? Look how large they were. When did you say these were built?"

"It is believed they were built sometime around the fall of the Second Temple in 70 AD. Look at the exterior facades, how detailed the stonework was. If you look closely you can also see the remains of the frescoes on the interior walls. It is believed that this was a wealthy section of Roman Jews who were somehow allowed to remain after the Roman destruction of Jerusalem."

"How do they know this was a Jewish settlement?" Rachel asked as she quickly snapped photos of the neat row of houses set along the lane.

"Mostly from the artifacts uncovered during the excavation. They found stone vessels, which were only used by Jews for storing and serving food. It was believed that the composition of the vessels would prevent the transmission of any impurities. Amphoras found on the site containing wine imported from Italy and Greece also spoke of the wealth of the inhabitants."

"Look! There's that Fatima sign again." Rachel pointed towards the entranceway to one of the villas on the right. "I thought you told me that was an Arab symbol."

"No, no, my child. I did not mean to mislead you. The sign has been used by many peoples over time to ward off evil. In fact, I'm sure if you search the shops in Jerusalem, you will find many such signs with the Star of David engraved within the palm." Khatib shook his head as the crook of his mouth smirked in jest.

"Perhaps your school could be located within one of the old villas. Could I include that thought in my article?"

"As you wish, my dear. When might we expect to see the finished product?" Saul asked impatiently.

"Just as soon as I finish examining the site here. Let me get a few more photos of the settlement. I think the centerpiece will be this villa here with the hand. Perhaps the two of you would like to stand in the doorway while I capture the magic of the area? What better photo to launch the series than the two founders of this education project standing in the doorway of such an exquisite ruin?"

The two men looked at each other for a moment, then moved into position, allowing Rachel to take her photographs. After several more hours at the site, photographing the various ruins and the village population, Rachel packed her notes and camera equipment and left the hilltop village for her tiny Jerusalem apartment. As her driver navigated the winding roadway back to the city center, she removed her cell phone from her purse and dialed.

"Hello, Robert. It's me. I need a favor," she blurted out.

"Hey Sis, I'm doing well, how are you?"

"What did you say?" she asked, completely missing the sarcasm in Robert's remarks.

"Never mind. It's just that I haven't heard from you for days, and now all you want is a favor from me."

"Aw, don't sulk, Robert. It's just that I left that refugee camp I told you about and I think I've got a great human interest piece. If I can knock it out before tonight's deadline, do you think you could get it into print in time for tomorrow's edition?"

"I don't know. You know you've burned most of your bridges here."

"Please," she begged. "It's really important to me, and I think it will generate a lot of reader response. Besides, I've got some great photos to go with the piece. What do you say?"

"I'll see what I can do, but you need to get everything to me before nine."

Rachel looked at her watch and realized she had less than three hours to put something together. "You're the best, bro. I won't let you down. Should I meet you at your office?"

"If you want it published, that would be the best place."

Rachel quickly hung up as the taxi pulled up alongside her apartment. Hurriedly, she gave the driver some shekels and headed towards her apartment entrance.

"Shalom!" she yelled to the driver as she ran inside to compile her article.

55

Brian was just finishing explaining his plan as the helicopter landed in Miami. He quickly made arrangements for the equipment he would need as the rest of the group gathered their belongings and readied themselves for the transatlantic flight to Tel Aviv. Before long, Jack was leading Alexandra up the stairs to the chartered jet.

"Are you sure you want to come along? You realize this could be dangerous?"

Alexandra just glared at Jack, darts springing from her charcoal eyes. "We're not going to get into this again. We've discussed this enough and I'm through talking. I want my baby back, now! So let's get moving."

Jack was astounded at her resilience and determination. He realized there was no sense in arguing with her, so he continued up the steps and entered the airliner's cabin. After making himself comfortable, he began poring over the intel that Brian had provided about the Russian and his operation.

If he was going to rescue Paige, he would have to familiarize himself with every facet of the goon's operation. He would also have to figure out a way to discover the secret location of the breastplate, for without it they would have no hope of rescuing Paige.

Sam was the next to enter the plane, chomping on his half-smoked cigar, carrying a pile of guidebooks of Israel.

"We're not going on a tour, you know," Jack chided his old friend.

"I'm not planning to, but we should know as much as we can about the area so we can navigate the territory with as little difficulty as possible, don't you think?"

"Whatever you say, old man. I've got my own studying to do," Jack said with a wave of his hand as he returned to his papers.

Carly and Sean entered, arm in arm, and found a secluded area in the rear of the cabin. With romance still in the air around them, they settled into their seats as Carly rested her head on Sean's chest. They were doubly excited since they were about to embark on such a dangerous adventure, together, while engulfed in a mood of sensuality. Jack took one look back at them and immediately questioned whether he could rely on their ability to remain focused on the task at hand, rather than their obvious desire for each other.

Professor Stompmeyer slowly navigated the last step into the cabin, using his new cane to stable his unsteady legs. This entire experience had taken a lot out of him. He no longer carried himself with the aristocratic swagger that he had been accustomed to. Humility and remorse had taken their toll on the man, and he was now concerned for the safety of this young child whom he had never met. He had provided Jack with all the information he could muster about the Cartel, as well as Dmitry and his background. Hopefully he had provided significant information which would enable his new companions to successfully defeat the cold-hearted maniac he had once been associated with. As he took his seat, he removed a notebook from his briefcase and began reviewing the notes he had made regarding the inscription and translation. He periodically jotted down a note in the margin as he reexamined the photographs of the medallion and other artifacts uncovered at sea.

As Brian walked toward the jet, a man stepped out from the shadows and approached him from behind. Sensing the intruder, Brian spun around in one fluid motion while withdrawing his automatic from its holster.

"Who are you?" he demanded. "What do you want and how the hell did you get in here, anyway? This area is off-limits to the general public."

"Please put your weapon down, Mr. Laird. I mean you no harm. I have come to offer you my assistance in this time of need." The man stood still with his hands in the air, palms outstretched, stating his case with sincerity.

"How — how do you know my name, and what do you mean, this time of need?" Brian was clearly surprised at the man's appearance and apparent awareness of their desperate situation.

"You are wasting precious time, Mr. Laird. Suffice it to say that we are on the same side and would like to rescue both the little girl as well as the Stones of Fire. May I put my hands down? This position is getting rather uncomfortable."

"Who the hell are you? I'm not going to ask you again!" Brian shouted, unnerved by the man's knowledge of Paige's predicament as well as the existence of the treasure.

"Let me board the plane with you and I can explain on the flight. You will be needing me to aid you in your quest," the stranger continued in an even voice, showing no sign of fear or discomfort.

"Man, I don't think you understood what I asked you!" Brian

shouted, clearly upset and on the verge of losing control. "This past week has been hell on earth without you showing up. If you don't want to join your ancestors in the great beyond, I suggest you start answering my questions. I'm beginning to lose my patience and I don't have much time, as you obviously know. Now cough it up. Who the hell are you and where did you come from?"

Sam and Jack had heard the commotion created by Brian's encounter with the stranger and both peeked out of the jet's doorway as Brian continued with his tirade.

"Who's the stranger?" Jack yelled down.

"That's what I'm trying to find out. If he doesn't respond in five seconds, I'm going to leave him here on the tarmac as a corpse, then we can find out when we return."

Jack took a second look at the man and a surge of recognition struck him. "Wait a minute. I think I've seen this guy before, but where? Do I know you?"

"Ah, Mr. Talbot. I was sorry to hear about your loss. As I was telling your associate, I would like to lend my assistance to your cause. We are, in essence, allies, you see. Could you please tell Mr. Laird to lower his weapon?"

"See what I mean, Jack? The dude won't give us a straight answer. I think he's a spy. Let me at least call security to have him locked up so we can get on our way."

"No, we don't have time for that. Search him and bring him aboard. We can question him during the flight. After all, we'll surely have enough time to get better acquainted."

Jack gestured to Brian to bring the man on board the plane. As the two men slowly climbed the stairs, Jack faced the stranger and stated in a blunt tone, "I expect you will answer all our questions once we have taken off or I may accede to Mr. Laird's wishes and turn you over to him. As you can see, he is not in the best of moods."

"You need not worry, Mr. Talbot. As I previously stated, I

am not your enemy. I think you will be intrigued by what I am about to tell you, and yes, I will answer any and all of your questions once we are airborne. But please, let's not waste any more precious time quibbling over minutia."

As the newly increased group settled in for their long flight, the jet engines fired up and spewed out a tremendous roar. The wheels unlocked and the plane began to jettison off the ground, beginning its rapid ascent into the blue abyss above. Before long, the plane leveled out on its skyward trek to the Holy Land.

Jack warily eyed the stranger as the plane continued on its course. Midway through takeoff Alexandra turned to her husband and asked, "Who is he, Jack? Do you really think we can trust him? I'm not so sure it was wise bringing him along. Suppose he reports back to those Russians? What chance will we have then?"

Jack could see the fear and concern spread over his wife's face. Part of him agreed with her assessment, but deep inside there was a feeling, sort of a gut feeling, which had pushed him to let the man come on board. Somehow, Jack sensed that the man was telling the truth and was, in fact, an ally, one who might turn out to be helpful in this perilous undertaking.

"I know how you feel, honey," he said as he turned to face her, placing his hands on her cheeks and pulling her closer towards him. "I initially thought the same way, but I've got this gut feeling that we're gonna need him, and I think he's telling the truth."

"I hope you're right, because we really have no room for error. One mistake and we'll never see her again." Tears began to well up in Alexandra's eyes as she pleaded with her spouse for some sign of hope.

Jack knew that unless they located the Russian quickly, and before he could realize what they were up to, they would never see Paige alive again. Even if they located the Stones and turned them over to the man, Jack knew there was basically no chance that he would release Paige alive, and a slim chance that he would allow the rest of them to survive.

As the captain turned the "seat belt" sign off, Jack gave his wife a quick kiss on the cheek as he told her that now was the time to speak to the stranger. "I'm going with you," she said to him. "I need to hear what he has to say."

Alexandra followed Jack to where the stranger was seated. As they approached the man, he turned to greet them. "I see you are now ready to listen to what I have to say," he said with a smile.

"We're interested in anything you can tell us, but first, tell us who you are and how you became so well-informed."

"Very well, Mr. Talbot. My name is insignificant, but I will tell you anyway. I am called Ari and I am a watcher."

Jack turned to his wife with a shrug, then looked back at the man with a serious glare. "What the hell is a watcher?" he asked with obvious disbelief.

"Perhaps I should start from the beginning," the man continued. "While there are few of us surviving today, more than two thousand years ago we numbered in the hundreds. We were a secret band of Temple priests, entrusted with the safety of the sacred treasures of my people."

"What people?" Alexandra interrupted.

"Why, the Jewish people, Mrs. Talbot. It was our duty to ensure the safety of such important treasures and religious articles. When the Babylonians razed Jerusalem and destroyed Solomon's Temple, we were there to rescue the Ark of the Covenant and deliver it to hidden safety, where it rests today, waiting for the return of the Messiah and the rebuilding of the Temple. After Herod rebuilt the Temple, there were some of us who felt the treasures should be restored. In fact, some of the buried items were returned to the Temple, such as the Golden Menorah, the golden Table of Shewbread, the Stones of Fire, as well as many of the vessels of gold and silver. Others felt that these treasures should remain safe and hidden until the coming of the Messiah. Thus a rift developed between brethren. It was decided we would split up, with some of us watching over the concealed treasures, and the rest of us remaining to ensure the safety of those treasures that were returned to the new Temple."

"You can't seriously believe the rubbish this imposter is spouting," Professor Stompmeyer warned as he sat down across the aisle from Jack. "I couldn't help but overhear the nonsense coming from this man's mouth. This tale that he is spinning is nothing but a diversion, meant to focus your attention away from the task at hand."

"Not so," the stranger insisted. "Throughout the centuries we have infiltrated many groups who have sought our ancient treasures. For example, we were hidden among the Knights Templar when they pilfered the treasure from Jerusalem and hid it across the Atlantic. It was our ship you found sunken off the coast of Florida, carrying part of the stolen treasure that we had liberated from the Templars."

"This is all poppycock!" Stompmeyer exclaimed. "What do you know about the shipwreck?"

The stranger held out his hand and displayed a ring on his right hand. As the group examined the man's outstretched hand, they noticed a hand imprinted on the ring's face, set within the Star of David. Jack studied the ring and then removed an object from his own pocket. He brought the object alongside the stranger's ring and compared the markings between the two.

"Where did you find that?" the stranger asked in astonishment.

"So it appears you don't know everything after all, Mr. Watcher," Jack replied with a grin. "Continue with your story and perhaps I will then tell you mine."

By this time, the rest of the group had listened to various parts of the man's saga and had become intrigued by it. They had all moved closer and surrounded him, nearly smothering him with their curiosity. "Yes, please continue," they all insisted.

"Very well," Ari said. "When it was discovered that part of the Templar treasure contained a portion of the Temple treasure, it was decided that some of our group would infiltrate the society and remain close to the treasure, watching over it until we could return it to safety at a later date. We knew the Templars transported the treasure to Scotland when the Pope had the Grand Master arrested for heresy. We later received word that the treasure was again moved to North America, where it was to be secreted until the Templars found the need to publicize their bounty. We developed a plan to retrieve the treasure and return it to the Holy Land. Two ships set out from North America in different directions loaded with the stolen treasures we were able to retrieve. One ship sailed south along the eastern coast of North America. It was never seen or heard from again. That was the ship you located before the Russians attacked you."

"Do you know what was being carried on that ship?" Jack asked.

The man looked up and wrinkled his brow as he replied, "It carried most of the treasures recovered, such as the golden shields of Solomon, the Golden Table of Shewbread, many gems and other items of value."

As the man spoke, Jack thought back to his time in the cave and recalled the many artifacts and treasures he had seen neatly stored inside. "So that was the Table of Shewbread," he muttered just above a whisper.

"What was that you said?" Ari asked him. "Did you actually see the Table?"

"What's he talking about?" the rest of the group began to ask.

Jack reached into his briefcase and withdrew the journal he had recovered from the cave. As he offered it to the stranger, he began to explain. "During my escape from the Russians, I found an underwater cavern not too far from the ship. I hid inside while they were searching for me. It would appear that one of your 'Templar watchers' had found the cave centuries ago. He must have been the sole survivor and removed most of the treasure from the sunken ship into the cave, where he waited with it in hopes of a rescue, or perhaps the coming of your messiah."

"Please, Mr. Talbot, do not make light of our beliefs," the stranger interrupted, obviously upset by Jack's remark.

"I'm sorry. I didn't mean to jest. The man must have stayed inside the cave for years, living on fish and nourishment from the ocean. He even set himself up a little room inside the cave, furnished with items retrieved from the ship: the captain's writing desk, some chairs, and a bed, among other things. Stacked along the walls were the treasures he had been able to remove from the ship. I saw this magnificent golden table inside the cave. It must have been the Table of Shewbread."

"What the heck is a Table of Shewbread?" Brian asked.

"In the Books of Exodus and Leviticus there is mention of the table," Professor Stompmeyer relayed with enthusiasm. Having heard the stranger's story and then Jack's verification of the existence of the ancient treasures, he was having a hard time containing his excitement.

"According to scripture it was made of acacia wood overlaid with pure gold. It had poles that could be set inside it to allow it to be carried from place to place as the Jews wandered through the desert. In Leviticus, God directs that twelve round cakes, which we believe were unleavened bread used to symbolize the twelve tribes of Jacob, were to be placed on the table every Sabbath. I always thought it was just another symbol or myth, like Noah's Ark. Did you really see it, Mr. Talbot?"

"Yes, professor, I did. It was an amazing sight, even though I did not know the significance," Jack replied before turning to the stranger and continuing his tale. "As I waited inside the cavern, I found that journal on the desk and became intrigued by its contents. As I read through it, the writer detailed the same saga you just told us. Unfortunately, the ship was unable to weather a ferocious storm and sank along with its precious cargo. The poor man must have died while writing the last entry in the diary. His skeleton was still in the chair when I discovered it. On his finger was this ring. It seems it held the answer to our mystery box. Once I returned to the ship, I used it to open the box and discovered the parchment hidden inside. But you already knew about the secret of the ring, didn't you?" Jack asked as he faced Ari.

"Yes, Mr. Talbot, I am aware of many uses for these rings. When we have completed our rescue of your granddaughter, I trust you will lead me back to this cave?"

"Unfortunately, both the shipwreck and the cave were destroyed, or at least buried by the explosion when those bastards blew up the Coast Guard cutter. At the very least, they're buried beneath tons of steel from the broken pieces of the destroyed cutter."

"What can you tell us about the Stones of Fire?" Sam asked the stranger.

"As you may know, in the Book of Exodus, God tells Moses to make certain garments, including a breastplate for Aaron, his brother, to wear. Aaron was to be the High Priest of the Jews and his descendants would follow in his footsteps. They would wear special garments made of specified materials and colors. The breastplate would contain twelve precious stones, each one symbolizing one of the twelve tribes. It was to be held together with pure gold and worn by the High Priest on all religious and other special occasions. The breastplate was also called the Stones of Fire, a reference to the twelve stones which it held."

The crew gasped collectively as the stranger answered Sam's inquiry.

"But where is it now?" Carly asked.

"We are not completely sure. We believe it was hidden by one of our clan somewhere in the hills surrounding Jerusalem. We know it has to be in that vicinity, because it was one of the last objects removed from the Temple as it was burning. There would not have been much time to remove it too far, and the Romans were everywhere, so it would have been nearly impossible to transport it over a great distance," Ari answered with much assurance in his voice.

"So how are we going to find it in time to rescue Paige?" Alexandra asked.

"We don't need to find it," Jack said.

"What do you mean?" Alexandra asked with a confused look on her face.

"We don't need to actually find it," Jack continued. "We only need to make those goons believe we did."

"But if we don't find it, we won't have anything to trade with," Alexandra replied.

"Not exactly," Jack responded. "If we can make them believe we have the Stones, then we may be able to buy some time to formulate a rescue plan."

"Just how are we going to do that?" Sam asked.

"Ari, I'm sure you have enough connections in Israel to allow us to pull this charade off, don't you?"

"I might be able to persuade some members of the press to cover this 'unique' find, but I will need some time to orchestrate this."

During this entire exchange, Brian had remained silent while sitting in his seat, fiddling with a contraption he had removed from his suitcase. "I think I've got it!" he suddenly exclaimed.

"Got what?" Jack asked his friend.

"The way to track that bastard," Brian replied with a smirk. "All we need now is to wait for his call, and I think I can pinpoint his location."

"But you told me to leave the phone back in the States and you would have your people take care of everything. You know I don't have the phone with me."

Brian smiled and held up a cell phone with his free hand. "This is state-of-the-art, my friend," he began to explain. "It's kinda like a clone of Tom's phone. I had it worked on before we boarded the plane. When the Russian calls Tom's phone, the call will be patched through to this phone. He'll be tracking Tom's phone and whoever is carrying it, thinking it's you, but you'll be able to communicate with him through this phone. Oh, and this phone has one other addition not found on Tom's phone."

"What's that?" Jack asked.

"A reverse GPS tracker. Once we connect with the Russian, I'll be able to track his location and we should be able to find Paige."

Alexandra looked at Brian, then turned toward Jack with a hopeful gleam in her eye. "Do you really think this could work, Jack?"

"It's got to work, honey. I'm sure Brian knows what he's doing. I think we should all try to get some sleep. I expect it's going to be a long day ahead of us."

56

Dmitry was beginning to get nervous. He had been ringing Tom's phone for over an hour without receiving a response. "That fool must have turned the phone off," he thought to himself. "If the Cartel did not want those Stones so badly, I would have terminated the girl an hour ago."

"Get hold of our man at the marina, now!" he ordered. "I want to know where that boat is and when it is expected to dock."

"Yes, sir," Yuri quickly responded as he hurried out of the room.

Dmitry threw the phone on the desk and looked out the window from his hotel suite. He could see the ocean mist floating towards the shoreline. There were people milling around on the beach watching the waves. It was still too chilly for any serious swimming, but there were a few diehards who insisted on braving the cold for a quick dip. His thoughts wandered back to his homeland while he watched the fools below attempting to enjoy themselves.

Suddenly his thoughts were interrupted as Yuri reentered the room, allowing the door to slam shut behind him. "The boat just sent word to the docks, sir. They expect to arrive within the hour. Apparently they had some engine trouble, which caused them to delay."

Dmitry studied his man for a moment, then turned back towards the desk. As he picked up the cell phone once more and began to dial he asked, "Are you sure there was engine trouble? Did there seem to be anything said out of the ordinary?"

"Not at all, sir. No one else seemed to question the report, and the ship is apparently on its way to dock. Why? Don't you believe there was engine trouble?"

"I believe nothing I do not see or cannot confirm with my own eyes."

Dmitry returned to the cell phone as it began to ring. After the fifth ring a voice answered, "Hello. Is that you? I want to talk to Paige, now."

"Ah, Mr. Talbot. I'm glad you finally decided to turn the phone back on and join us. You are trying my patience, and I warn you, that is not a good thing to do. Another futile attempt and I would have rid myself of the problem without hesitating. Do I make myself clear?"

"Perfectly, but I still want to talk to my granddaughter. I need some assurance that she is safe and unharmed."

"I will only remind you this once. You are not in charge. You do not call the shots. Your wants and desires are meaningless to me. You are to follow my instructions to the letter. I will tell you what to do and when to do it. Do I make myself clear?"

Jack hesitated for a moment, bit his lip, then grunted out a response, "You're calling the shots, but I warn you, no harm better come to her."

"Don't threaten me, Mr. Talbot. It will not advance your chances any, and will not do you any good. Oh, and another thing: I don't want you turning off that phone again, do you understand? I've been trying to reach you for over an hour now and my patience is wearing thin, just as your time is quickly running out."

"I'm sorry, but I was in the water with some of the other divers. We had some engine problem and they needed help clearing the props. It slowed us down quite a bit. I didn't like it any more than you do, so I figured if I lent them a hand, we could get under way that much quicker. I understand there's a plane leaving Miami for Israel in about four hours. Once we dock, I'll be able to throw a few things together and get on that plane, but it's still going to take more than twenty-four hours to get there. I'm really going to need more time. Especially now that we were delayed this long at sea."

"I will decide if there will be any extension of time. But first, I want you to stand at the bow and wave towards the dock as you enter."

"Why would you want me to do that, and just who will I be waving at?"

"That is of no concern of yours. Just do as I say and I will give you further instructions at a later time."

As Dmitry ended the call, Jack turned to Brian with a smile. "That was good work. He didn't even have a clue we're about one hour from landing in Tel Aviv. That bastard sure is distrustful, though. I assume he wants to make sure I'm still on the boat. How are we going to handle that one?"

"Don't worry about a thing," Brian told Jack. "I've got everything covered. My man on the boat could pass as a dead ringer for you, at least from a distance of a hundred yards or so. Just keep alert, though. This guy's no dope. He'll probably have you talking to him again on the cell phone once the ship docks. He may even try it while you're waving at his men at the pier."

Jack realized his friend was right and began to prepare

himself mentally for the next ruse. He was amazed at how quickly Brian had devised this scheme and put the pieces into motion. With the little time he had, Brian had carried off this phase nearly flawlessly.

"How did you make out tracking our friend?" Jack asked excitedly. "Any luck getting a fix on him?"

"Nothing specific. It appears he is somewhere in Florida, but I'm not quite sure where yet. Hopefully I can pinpoint his location during his next call."

The plane was just beginning its final approach towards Tel Aviv when the cell phone rang again. "I see you can follow instructions when given the proper incentive," Dmitry said.

Jack quickly responded, "I told you I would, now when can I speak to my granddaughter? It's been a long journey and I'm tired. I need to get off this boat and throw my things together so I can get to the airport and head to Israel. Are you going to let me talk to her or not?"

Jack continued looking at the monitor as he spoke to the Russian, intent on keeping him on the line as long as possible so Brian could hopefully get a fix on the man's location. As he watched the screen in front of him, he was awed at the sight he saw. It was like watching himself in the mirror or, better yet, watching a movie, and he was the star. There he was, or at least it looked like him, standing on the deck of the *Scavenger*, cell phone in one ear mumbling something and waving to the people on the dock with the other hand.

"I told you before, do not antagonize me, Mr. Talbot!" Dmitry barked into the receiver. "Now listen closely to me. Once the ship docks, you are to take the first cab you see and head directly to your residence. Do not make any stops along the way, and no phone calls. Do you understand?"

Jack acknowledged that he understood the man as Dmitry continued to deliver his instructions.

"Once you have reached your residence, get your

belongings and immediately go to the airport. A reservation has been made for you on El Al flight 8033. You can pick up your ticket and further instructions will await you at the El Al reservation desk. Have I made myself clear?"

A worried look appeared on Jack's face as he realized that the ruse might backfire once his decoy entered the cab. Even if the man was able to pass himself off as Jack, how was he going to get through airport security without being discovered as an imposter?

"Mr. Talbot, why are you hesitating? Do you understand my instructions? I told you before, I am not a patient man."

"Sorry," Jack mumbled back. "I told you, it's been a long and trying day and your demands are beginning to stress me out. I'm worried about the safety of my granddaughter, and I'm not even sure I'll be able to find the stones once I get to Israel. I really need you to give me more time, and I beg of you, please let my little girl go. She's got nothing to do with this, and I know you know where I live and are watching me, so I also realize you can reach me at any time. You don't need her to force me to deliver the stones to you. You've made your point, so why don't you release her now?"

"You really astonish me, Mr. Talbot. Do you take me for a fool like that German? You know quite well that I will not release your granddaughter until you have delivered to me what I want. For such a well-established attorney, you really are being quite naive. Now, enough of this babble. I understand from my man that your ship has completed the docking process. I need you to follow my instructions now or you will have no chance of being reunited with your granddaughter."

As Dmitry disconnected the call, Jack looked at the smile on Brian's face and realized that he had been able to trace the Russian's exact location. Brian was already speaking into his own phone, barking instructions to his men on the ground.

"What are you doing?" Jack asked, the fear and concern

obvious in his tone and in his facial expression. "You can't do anything that will put Paige at risk."

"I know. I'm only positioning my men so they can watch our friends without being noticed and get a better idea of where he is, how many men are with him, and hopefully where he has Paige."

"But what about my double? What's going to happen when he gets in the cab? Won't the guy realize it's not me?"

Brian shook his head and laughed, "I told you I had it covered. Between the man's natural features and the makeup we put on him, not even your wife would realize the difference."

As he said that, Alexandra glared at the two men and with increasing rage in her voice responded, "I don't know what you two think you are doing. This is no game! A little girl's life is at stake! Our little girl!"

"Easy, Alexandra," Brian replied. "I know this is no joke. I'm doing everything I can to gain control of the situation. You must know that this man has no intention of releasing Paige, even if Jack gives him what he wants. In fact, he will probably use Paige to lure Jack to him and then kill them both. Paige's only hope is that we find out where he is holding her and either break her out of there or come up with a plan where Jack can rescue her when he delivers the stones."

"You're not intending on giving this monster what he wants, are you?" Alexandra shrieked incredulously.

"Take it easy, honey," Jack said as he tried to soothe his frantic wife. "Brian was just providing some options. We'll develop our plans better once we land and get a better idea of where these stones may be hidden. Don't forget, as long as Dmitry thinks we're still in the States, we've got at least a one-day head start on him."

Jack's comments brought some relief to Alexandra and she began to settle down.

"What's going to happen at the airport when our guy shows

up without a proper passport?" Jack continued to ask his friend.

"Already taken care of," Brian replied. "One of my men will be waiting for him at your condo with full instructions and a bona fide U.S. government-issued passport with your name and his picture on it. He'll breeze through customs just as if he were you. But don't worry, I'm making sure he takes no chances. We have no idea who is already in on the Russian's little conspiracy or who the Russian has on his payroll, so I've already advised my men to be careful on who they contact and what information they provide."

Jack was just beginning to relax when the chief flight attendant announced that they were starting their final approach to Tel Aviv and all passengers were required to take their seats and buckle up. Jack looked out the window as they dropped from above the clouds. Dawn was just beginning to appear on the horizon. The sun was floating along the sky like a red beach ball, its rays piercing through the clouds, sending javelins of light down to the people who were just starting to stir in the city below. Jack wondered how there could be such beauty and majesty in the world God created, coexisting with such inhumanity and evil. As his thoughts wandered, evaluating all the philosophical arguments on the subject, the plane suddenly jolted as the jet's wheels touched the ground and skipped along the runway. Alexandra firmly gripped his wrist as the plane was landing and snapped him out of the philosophical trance he had slipped into.

"We're here," she said. "Now what do we do?"

57

Rachel was in awe of the ruins that lay in front of her. Many of the mosaic tiles were still completely intact. It was a miracle that they had survived this long and remained in such pristine condition. She had insisted on returning to reexamine the ruins after she had finished her article and sent it to her brother along with the pictures she had taken.

As the workmen slowly began to clear away the rubble and better expose the villa and its contents, Rachel continued to snap photographs as she felt amazement at what she observed.

"How is it that this was never discovered earlier?" she questioned Khatib.

"I told you," he replied, "this area was originally occupied by Arab refugees after the creation of the State of Israel in 1948. Jordan annexed the area and the surrounding villages when it annexed the West Bank and East Jerusalem. Once Jerusalem was reunited by the Israelis after the Six Day War, Israel reclaimed this entire area, ultimately setting a portion of the land aside as a Palestinian Refugee Camp. Between all the poverty and fighting conducted over the years, this area lay undiscovered, a vast rubble field of debris and dirt. It was not until Israel recently decided to expand its rail system that this archaeological site was discovered."

Rachel stood pensively as her Arab associate explained the history of the area. As she looked around at the ruins of the ancient village, she heard the roar of fighter jets flying overhead. The rest of the villagers continued on with their work, slowly excavating the site and meticulously removing the rubble and debris from the main sections of the dwellings.

A worried look came upon her as the jets continued circling above. Saul was the first to notice her anxiety and quickly spoke in an attempt to assuage her fears.

"Don't be alarmed," he said as he moved closer to her and put his arm around her shoulders. "It is merely an Israeli Air Force training exercise. They periodically fly over this area as a show of force and to indoctrinate new pilots. As you can see, they are barely noticed by the villagers."

Rachel breathed a sigh of relief and continued examining the dwelling before her. The building was built in a perfect rectangle. The stonework on the exterior was wellworn, but bore evidence of the care and skill that had gone into its original construction. She looked up and gazed at the extent of the rubble and debris which rose nearly twenty feet above her.

"This is like a city underground," she said. "How many years did this site go unnoticed?"

"No one knows for sure, but it seems to have been left this way, undisturbed, for centuries," Saul replied. "You should not really be so surprised, Miss Lyons. After all, I'm sure you are familiar with the Cardo in Jerusalem, are you not?"

"Of course I am. Some of the best shopping lies along its path," she replied. "Why do you mention that?"

"Because it is not much different from what lies before you. It, too, lay undiscovered for centuries, until modern excavation uncovered its ruins. The modern-day city rests many feet above the old Roman Street. Do you see the similarity now, my dear?"

Rachel thought for a moment, then slowly nodded her head, realizing that the old man was correct. Centuries of sand and debris would eventually cover these homes after they had been abandoned and left discarded by their occupants in the mid second century. Over time, the small village would lay, buried and forgotten, with nature guarding the treasures stored within the crumbling walls of the villas below.

As Rachel continued to explore the villa's ruins, she marveled at the intricate mosaic tiles which lay almost intact before her.

"I can't get over the colors and designs. The Star of David appears nearly everywhere. And look at that, what was it you called it yesterday? Oh yes, that's the Hand of Fatima, is it not?"

"Quite right, Miss Lyons," Khatib replied.

As Rachel continued to examine the ancient village, she kept looking up the street. Not only was there tile work inside the remains of the dwellings, but there also appeared to be mosaics where the sidewalk would normally be found.

"Is this a sidewalk?" she asked incredulously.

"It would appear to be so, yes," her companion replied.

Rachel knelt down and examined the mosaic sidewalk more closely. There appeared to be Hebrew writings or letters placed adjacent to Jewish symbols. There were Stars of David, seven-branched candelabras, and even the lion of Judah. As she continued to walk up and down the Cardo, she began to realize that the symbols were carefully placed near the entranceway of each dwelling. It appeared that the symbols were both decorative and served some sort of function, such as a means of identifying the resident's tribe or affiliation, or even his trade.

Rachel continued to snap photos of the sidewalk mosaics as she walked the length of the Cardo, then returned to her companion, who had waited for her at her starting point.

"This is really extraordinary!" she exclaimed to the old Arab.

"Why so?"

She explained her observations to the old man, then suddenly stopped mid-sentence. "There's that hand again," she said, "but it's not only a decoration. It would appear to also be a symbol identifying the occupant of this dwelling. How can that be? I thought you said it was an Arabic symbol."

"I did, but it is also known as the 'hamsa' or 'Hand of Miriam.' We told you that it was used by many cultures over the years."

"But if it was meant to ward off evil spirits and bring good luck, why is it also used for identifying the occupant's trade or association?"

"That we cannot answer. Perhaps your theory is misplaced, after all."

Rachel was insistent that she had correctly analyzed the function of the mosaic decorations meticulously placed outside each dwelling. Her mind refused to concede any error or mistake. Instead, she decided to take more photographs of the interior and exterior of this particular dwelling, choosing to write her next article on the mystery behind its occupants.

Hours later, weary and exhausted from examining the ruins and mosaics, she bid her benefactors farewell and returned to her apartment in Jerusalem. After taking a quick shower to revive herself, she examined the numerous photographs she had taken and chose the best ones for her article. She decided to grab a quick bite to eat and, after ordering a falafel, she returned to her room to begin writing before the night's deadline passed. Two hours and four Goldstars later, she had the first draft completed.

As the night wore on, Rachel made the necessary changes to her article, then called her brother.

"Robert, I've got the next installment in my series. Can I email it to you? I really want to get it out in the morning's edition. I think there's some real fascinating stuff inside."

"All right, sis, but you're really starting to push it, you know. I've stuck my neck out quite far for you this time. We better start getting some responses to your series or it's my ass on the line. Then there will be two unemployed Lyons in Israel."

"You're the best, bro. You know I love you. It's on its way now. Make sure they don't change a thing, especially the photos I've included."

"Photos? You never said anything about pictures. I'm not sure they'll give me that much page position."

"I trust you. You'll be able to swing it. Gotta go. I'm beat. I've been up for nearly twenty four hours. Gotta get my beauty rest, you know. Good night."

58

Jack turned towards Alexandra as the plane taxied to the terminal. He was about to speak when his cell phone began to ring. The exuberant and spiritual feelings Jack had been experiencing would have to wait. As he reached for the phone, Alexandra gently touched his hand and cast a worried look at her husband.

"Don't worry, honey," he said. "It's all going to turn out okay. We'll get her back soon, safe and sound, then I'm going to kill that son of a bitch.

"Yeah, I'm here," Jack curtly replied into the receiver.

"Ah, Mr. Talbot. I'm glad you are keeping alert. Excellent. Now that we have the correct rapport established between us, I will provide you with your next set of instructions."

"I'm listening," Jack replied impatiently.

"Do I detect a sense of agitation in your voice, Mr. Talbot? That will not do. Now listen closely, because I will only say this one time. I am not in the habit of explaining or repeating myself. Once you arrive at the airport, you will proceed expeditiously to the terminal and board the plane as we had discussed. Once you have been seated, further instructions will await you in the seat pouch. Oh, and do have a pleasant flight."

Dmitry barely held back a chuckle as he ended the call.

Jack turned to his wife and friends and relayed the latest set of instructions. He was still worried that his double would be discovered and all of the efforts exerted thus far would have been wasted.

Brian sensed his friend's apprehension and placed a hand on Jack's shoulder. "Don't worry. Everything's under control. My men have discovered the bastard's location. They're trying to formulate a rescue plan as we speak. I've got men at the airport and contacts on the plane for Israel. The passenger in the adjacent seat and some of the flight crew are also with us. We're being extremely cautious. Nothing's going to go wrong."

"Sure, nothing except Murphy's law." Jack glanced at his friend.

Brian shot back a reassuring look and smiled. "Got that covered, too."

Jack and his companions quickly cleared customs, thanks to Brian's contacts, and were immediately met by members of Israel's secret service, the Mossad. As Brian exchanged greetings with the group's leader, Sam turned to Jack and shook his head. "Is there anybody that guy doesn't know?"

"The man's got some interesting and extensive contacts, Sam. He's a good and resourceful friend, I can tell you that much," Jack replied.

They were quickly escorted out of the airport and led to a group of waiting black SUVs, fully equipped with all the amenities and a driver.

"They're going to take us to Jerusalem along the fastest route possible," Brian informed the rest of the group. "Just sit back and enjoy the ride. Once we get to the city, they will help us try to locate any possible sites for further exploration.

They're just as interested in recovering such an artifact as we are. I think the search will go much quicker and easier with their help."

Before long, Jack and Alexandra had settled themselves in the rear compartment of one of the SUVs. Sam and the professor made themselves comfortable in the third row seat while Brian sat up front with the driver. Sean and Carly cuddled together in the rear seat of the second SUV while the stranger, Ari, rode shotgun up front.

"What if we can't find the Stones?" Alexandra asked her husband as she valiantly fought back tears.

"Don't worry. I'm sure we'll find them. If not, we'll go to Plan B."

"Plan B?"

"Yeah: we lie. Either way, we need to convince this creep that we have what he wants. Once we do that, we can negotiate an exchange. Besides, I've got a few ideas of my own, depending on how things pan out."

Alexandra was not fully convinced, but she had faith in her husband. He had never let her down before and he had always proved himself to be resourceful and resilient in the past. She gave Jack a quick peck on the cheek before resting her head on his shoulder. She was exhausted and needed to relax. The stress of the last few days, as well as the jet lag, was beginning to take its toll, even as she fought to stay awake and alert.

Jack looked at his wife with admiration as Alexandra slowly closed her eyes and began to drift off. He loved his wife immensely and refused to disappoint her. He only hoped that he had enough time and luck to carry out the ruse that had been set into motion. He knew his Russian adversary would not be fooled for long. Dmitry was cunning and had apparently escaped detection for a long time. Jack knew they would need to move quickly if there was any chance in rescuing his beloved granddaughter.

As Jack watched the countryside flash by through the window, he pulled open the morning edition of *Haaretz*. The weather prediction promised a hot and humid day, clear, with no rain forecast. The rest of the news consisted of the normal reports of Hamas terrorists captured by Israeli soldiers as a civilian bombing was thwarted, political fallout over the government's attempt to displace recent Jewish settlers in an effort to maintain the fragile peace hanging by a thread between the Israelis and Palestinians, as well as local news regarding recent and upcoming visits of various heads of state and religious icons. Jack continued to browse through the paper until he reached a human interest article buried towards the rear. His body stiffened as he turned towards Stompmeyer.

"Professor, look at this!" he exclaimed.

The German leaned forward as he tried to examine the article and its photo. The title read: *From the Ruins of the Ancient Past, Hope Springs from the Ashes.*

"This appears to be an interesting article, Mr. Talbot. If I were not engaged in the search for the Stones, perhaps, intellectually, I would be intrigued by this new discovery and explore it further. However, the building of a Jewish-Palestinian institution of higher education on the grounds of an ancient village hardly interests me at this time."

"Read the description of the mosaics found. It's our sign, the hand with the eyes inside the Jewish Star. Do you think it is merely a coincidence?"

"Let me see that article," Stompmeyer retorted. As he adjusted his spectacles on the bridge of his nose, he let out a grunt. "I wish there were a better photo provided. All I can discern are the remains of a Roman-era village rising from the rubble of a Palestinian refugee camp."

"But look at the description. All along the main street are Jewish signs. The writer takes great pains to describe the many common signs before focusing on the strangest of all, our sign. Its location would also fit the general area Ari believed we should be searching, on a hilltop within the vicinity of Jerusalem."

"I think you may be on to something, Mr. Talbot. Perhaps we should try to locate this newspaperwoman, Rachel Lyons."

Jack showed the article to Brian as he asked him to ask their hosts to help them locate Rachel Lyons. He then asked if arrangements could be made to contact the rest of the group, including the Watcher, so that they could be apprised of this newest development. Almost instantaneously, a Bluetooth connection was made with the other SUV as Jack eagerly related the contents of Rachel's article.

"Good work, Mr. Talbot!" Ari declared. "I will have my people meet us at Shuafat. I trust that is where we are now heading?"

"Let's not jump the gun," Jack cautioned. "We only have limited time. First, I think we need to locate this Rachel Lyons and find out more information. If it pans out, then we can proceed to the site and hopefully locate the Stones."

Unaware of the interest she had aroused by her article, Rachel was sipping her morning coffee as she reached for her edition of *Haaretz*. After finding her article buried towards the rear of the paper somewhere between the classifieds and the obituaries, she jumped up and knocked her cup over as she muttered a curse at the editorial board and her brother.

"Those sons of bitches!" she exclaimed. "What the hell did they do to my article and photos? I'm going to wring his neck when I get a hold of him!"

Rachel reached for her phone and dialed her brother's private number. "Thanks for stabbing me in the back, bro. Did you guys intend on destroying my article or did your incompetence get the best of you?" she screamed into the phone, barely giving her brother time to register her disdain and contempt.

"Whoa, sis," Robert responded, trying to calm her down. "What the hell are you screaming about, anyway?"

"Did you read today's edition?"

"Not yet, why?"

"How could you let them cut my article? And what happened to the photos I gave you? You printed the worst and least exciting of the bunch."

"Sis, you know I had nothing to do with that. Once I submitted it to the board, they made the decision on what to print. I had all I could do to convince them to run the article in the first place."

As the words began to sink in, Rachel realized her brother was right. Even though her anger towards her brother was subsiding, she was still seething deep inside, incensed at the ignorance and short-sightedness of the editorial board.

"It's just that I really thought this article could make a difference. The photos were just spectacular and unique, and the project itself was so worthwhile."

"I know, sis, but at least it got published. Maybe I can get them to authorize a follow-up article, or maybe a miniseries on the project's progress.... What? Oh, okay.... Hey, sis, let me get right back to you. I've got another call I need to take."

As Rachel heard the phone disconnect she began to compose herself and started searching for her notes and photos. She knew her brother would go to bat for her, but she also knew there was no way the ultraconservative board would allow her to do any follow-up series. Instead, she decided to rewrite her article and submit it to one of the local magazines for review. Rachel was deep in her revision when the doorbell to her apartment disturbed her thoughts, its buzzer shrieking irritably through the silence.

"Go away, I'm busy!" she yelled across the room into the intercom. "I'm not interested in anything you're selling."

"Rachel Lyons," a stern voice responded through the

speaker. "This is Mossad. It is imperative that we speak with you immediately. Open the door and let us in, NOW!"

Rachel began to sweat profusely. What did Mossad want with her? What could she possibly have done? Her mind began to race at lightning speed, recapping her recent movements. Had she reported something inappropriate in the past? Perhaps she had been observed meeting with some suspected Palestinian terrorist? Fear shot through her spine as she realized she was no longer an employee of the newspaper, and once that relationship had been dissolved, so had the paper's protective shield. She was now on her own. Nervously, she managed to move her nearly paralyzed body towards the intercom. Her voice shook as she replied, "What is it you want?"

"We need to speak with you immediately. Please open the door and let us up now."

Rachel fidgeted as she allowed the strangers entry into her apartment. She carefully examined the man's credentials as he walked in, with Jack and the others following closely behind.

"What the hell is going on, and who are all these people?"

"All will be explained shortly. Mr. Talbot, I believe you wish to question this woman?"

Jack stepped forward and tried to calm Rachel down. "I apologize for the intrusion, but this is an emergency and we don't have much time. Miss Lyons, please sit down. My name is Jack Talbot. I'm interested in the article you wrote in today's *Haaretz*."

So that was it. She should have guessed the government would try to put a muzzle on her reporting this joint cooperative effort between Arabs and Jews. As her back abruptly stiffened, Jack noticed the immediate change in her body language.

"Miss Lyons, you misunderstand our intentions. Do you have any other photos of the village other than the one published in the paper?"

"Why, so you can attempt to circumvent the seeds of a peaceful generation from germinating?"

"Miss Lyons, I already told you, you misunderstand our intentions. I don't have the time to fully explain, but let me assure you that it is a matter of life and death. I'm sure you took other photos. May we see them please?"

Unsure of what she should do, Rachel began to look around at the group of people who had entered her abode. As her eyes moved from Stompmeyer across the rest of the crowd, she suddenly stopped and gazed at the tall and slender woman who had just entered the room.

"Jack, I just awoke. Brian told me about the article. Is it really the place? Can this woman help us? Will we be in time to save Paige?"

A flood of emotions quickly swept over Alexandra. She had been holding everything in for so long, but it seemed her brief rest had energized the fears and trepidation she had tried to contain all this time.

Something about this woman and her demeanor made Rachel decide to cooperate with her uninvited guests. She motioned for Jack and Alexandra to follow her towards her laptop.

"All the photos I took are here on my computer. There are quite a few. Help yourself." Rachel motioned with her hand as she pointed to the screen.

After only a few minutes, Jack called his friends over. "Look at this. It's the same sign! What do you think, professor? How about you, Carly?"

The group quickly reached the general consensus that they were on the right track. As they thanked Rachel and turned to leave, she asked if she could accompany them. Jack agreed, provided she swore not to report or divulge anything until authorized to do so. Though puzzled by the demand, she quickly agreed as she grabbed her things.

Brian took her by the shoulder and directed her towards their waiting vehicle.

"Miss Lyons, this is truly a matter of life and death. A young girl's life hangs in the balance. I trust you would not do anything to jeopardize this child's safety."

The group quickly entered their respective vehicles and the SUVs sped off towards Shuafat. As Jack gazed out the window at the walls of the city, he briefly explained the need for secrecy and urgency to Rachel.

The small caravan soon left the city walls and wound its way around the outskirts of the city towards the hills of Shuafat. With the skyline of the Dome of the Rock and the Church of the Holy Sepulchre rising behind them, a feeling of hope and promise surged through the small group.

59

Dmitry turned to Yuri, his trusted lieutenant. "It is time. Ready the jet and make sure our guest is comfortable. We may need her before long."

The man nodded and briskly exited the room. As he did so, he reached for his cell phone and dialed, providing detailed instructions to his men waiting at the airstrip. In less than five minutes he had finalized takeoff arrangements with his men at the airport and directed that Paige be surreptitiously transported to the waiting jet. After assuring that everything was in order, he returned to his commander to report his progress with confidence and pride.

As Yuri reentered the cabin, Dmitry was finishing his conversation with his superiors in the Cartel. Dmitry's hand was upraised, signaling Yuri to remain silent at the entryway.

"Everything is in order. The American is preparing to take off for Palestine. He has been provided with all the incentive he needs to complete our mission without hesitation. I will be departing as well. I intend to land before him so that final arrangements can be in place upon his successful location of the treasure.... No, we have not yet located the German, but I am sure my men will find him soon. He has no place to go.... Yes, of course. He will be silenced as soon as he is located."

Once he was finished with his conversation, he motioned for Yuri to enter the cabin. Yuri dutifully reported to Dmitry and then followed his leader out to the limousine waiting by the dock to take them to the airport. Seated in the rear, sandwiched between two burly Ukrainian mercenaries, was a frightened five-year-old girl who stared blankly ahead.

The last twenty-four hours had been a nightmare for Paige. She had never before experienced such fear. She desperately longed for this nightmare to end. Where was her grandmother? What had happened to her during that craziness from the other day? Would she ever see either of her grandparents, or parents, again? What did these strange men want with her?

She was a bright and precocious child, independent and mature beyond her years. She had realized near the beginning of this ordeal that it was necessary for her to keep her composure. While it was hard in the beginning, as frightened as she was, she had managed to think of the time she spent with her grandmother, rocking on the porch swing or swimming in the pool. She would picture her grandmother's gentle and reassuring smile whenever it became difficult to contain the fear she kept buried deep within her. Other times, she would imagine her grandfather's strong arms, lifting her into the air and swinging her about, as he would often do, while she would laugh and cry out, "More, Poppy! More!"

As the limousine pulled away from the dock, she wondered to herself where they were taking her next. She cautiously glanced around at her surroundings as the marina receded out of sight. The two men alongside her remained motionless, as if they were statues set as decorative bookends. She tried to study each one without drawing any attention to herself.

"Ah, my little one. You are a brave little girl," the guard on her right side said in a gentle voice.

Paige was startled at the man's words and tone. This was the first time anyone had really spoken to her since her abduction, other than to bark orders at her.

"Let us play a game," the man continued. "Imagine we are going on a great adventure. Would you like that?"

Paige hesitated. She did not want to upset this man, since he surely frightened her, and could obviously cause her great harm. She also was apprehensive. After all, she had been violently kidnapped while her grandmother was assaulted. She had been separated from her family and loved ones and kept a prisoner in a small, dark room for what seemed like an eternity. This man was a stranger to her, one of a group of strangers who were keeping her prisoner. And hadn't she always been taught not to associate with strangers?

Instinctively, Paige slowly nodded her head in agreement to her captor's question.

"Good," he replied. "Let us imagine that your ship has been attacked by pirates and you alone have escaped. You must remain perfectly quiet to avoid capture from them. Do you think you can do that?"

Paige nodded her head again while she wondered why this man was interacting with her.

"Let us see how still and silent you can be. Try to remain so for the entire car ride."

The man's companion quickly glanced at them before turning back towards the road. As he did so, Paige swore she caught the beginnings of a smirk crossing the man's face. She continued to remain silent and looked at the scenery whisk by as the car continued on its path. It was not long before they approached an airfield. As the car entered the main area, the guard again turned to her.

"We are here. Now for the next leg of our adventure. You have reached a safe place but must continue on before the pirates catch up to you. We are going to sneak you aboard an airplane and fly you to a place where those nasty pirates can never touch you. Do you understand?"

Paige hesitantly acknowledged the man's question and began to feel herself lose control. Did these people intend to take her away from here? Did they intend to take her out of the country? She could barely feel herself breathe. She feared she would never see her family again. Panic swept over her and she could contain herself no longer. She braced herself and tried to climb over her captors towards the door.

"Let me out of here!" she yelled, kicking and screaming at the top of her lungs. She tried to claw her way past the goon on her left, but he was too big and quick for her. It only took seconds before the man had wrapped her in his huge arms across his lap.

"Enough of these foolish games," he snapped at her. "If you do not calm down immediately, I will tie you up and gag you. Do you want that? I am not as soft as my comrade over there. Do you understand?"

Paige could barely breathe as she was wrapped tightly in the man's embrace. She was on the verge of passing out when she suddenly began to relax, and her body went limp. Sobbing, she tried to contain her tears and slowly brought herself back into control. As she did so, she could feel the man slowly release her and place her back onto the seat.

"Am I going to have any more trouble out of you?" the man asked.

Paige shook her head and softly whispered, "No."

The car approached the hangar just as Dmitry began to board the plane. Paige was escorted to the jet by the two men.

As she nervously glanced around, she noticed that there were no other people in the area. She felt just as alone now as she had before when she was locked up in that little room by the dock. She slowly walked up the steps to the plane. As she did so, she could swear she heard her grandfather's voice coming from the cell phone Dmitry had placed by his ear.

"What do you want? The plane is just beginning to board. Unless you want me to miss it, you had better make it quick."

Paige's eyes lit up. It was her grandfather. Was he coming to save her? Where was he? She looked around, but saw no one other than her captors.

"Poppy!" she exclaimed as she started running toward the phone.

Suddenly, she felt her waist tighten as she was lifted in the air, her legs dangling in space.

"Let me go!" she yelled as she flung her arms wildly at the giant holding her.

"Paige, is that you?" Jack's voice bellowed through the earpiece. "If you or any of your men lay a hand on her, I swear—"

"I suggest you immediately calm yourself, Mr. Talbot, or we can end this relationship here and now and the fate of this child will be on your head. Do you understand me?"

Jack bit his lip and fought to control his rage. He knew the Russian would always have the upper hand if Jack acted on his emotions. He needed to somehow gain control of the situation, and in order to do that, he needed to make the man believe he was continuing to acquiesce to his commands.

Jack drew a deep breath, exhaled, then meekly replied, "What is it you want of me?"

"That's better. I want you to remember what's at stake here. I am fully aware that your plane will be taking off shortly. Make sure you have a relaxing flight and speak to no one. My men will be watching your every move and if you do anything to arouse their suspicion, I will revise my plans, understood?"

"Yes, I do. Can I at least speak to my granddaughter for a moment?"

Dmitry thought for a moment. As he did, Paige yelled out, "Poppy, are you flying with us?"

Suddenly the line went dead. Jack's body began to tremble as his face started to sweat. He turned and yelled out, "Brian! They're moving her. They must be on a plane or boarding a plane. Do you think they could be heading here?"

Brian was on his phone before Jack could finish his sentence. He had thought his men were closing in on Dmitry's hideout. Now he had to increase his efforts to locate the madman. If he was on the move and Paige was with him, the danger level had now been cranked up a few notches.

"I think we've got him," Brian said. "We think he's in the process of taking off on a private jet. It's a Gulfstream G550 luxury jet. It has a range of almost seven thousand miles and is touted as the longest-range business jet in the world. Even though his flight plan calls for Brazil, I would bet the bank he's on his way here. That jet could easily make it from Florida to Tel Aviv with miles to spare, and he probably wants to beat you here so he can monitor your progress and continue to call the shots."

"I think you're right. Ari, do you think your friends can keep an eye out for our elusive Russian? But make sure they are very careful. I don't want any harm to come to my granddaughter."

The watcher nodded his assent.

"I will make the request now. Do not fear. They are as silent and undetectable as air. They will not be seen by your foe."

60

After the cell phone conversation between Dmitry and Jack, Rachel began to realize the urgency of their quest as well as the intense danger involved. Although a veteran reporter, she had never before been so closely connected to espionage or the clandestine movements of the underworld. She was excited and frightened simultaneously. Did these people actually believe that violence could erupt at any moment? After that thought cleared her mind, she gave a silent chuckle. Here she was in Israel, heading toward a Palestinian refugee camp, and she actually harbored reservations about the possibility of sudden violence erupting? She had been a reporter here for several years now and had witnessed firsthand the violence of the extreme Islam jihad. After all, this was Israel and violence was beginning to seem a way of life here, a constant reminder of the frail balance reached between two opposite, yet very similar cultures.

As their jeep came to an abrupt stop, Rachel poked her head out the window and yelled up ahead, "What is it?"

"We have just received word. We cannot proceed any further. Riots have broken out in Shuafat. We have been instructed to turn around. It is no longer safe."

Just as Rachel had been consumed by her private thoughts, Jack too had been lost in deep reflection. He was concerned about how his granddaughter would adjust after her rescue, and he was also planning all the contingencies to ensure that she be rescued unharmed. His train of thought was interrupted by this sudden, unexpected obstacle.

"What's going on?" he asked. "What riots? We have to go on. We only have a limited amount of time before those bastards arrive and I want to make sure we're completely ready for them."

Ari approached Jack's vehicle and informed him of the situation.

"They claim it is too dangerous to proceed on until the demonstrators have been immobilized."

"But we can't wait. Isn't there any way we can continue?"

Ari thought a moment, then spoke to one of his contacts from his cell phone. The next five minutes seemed to take forever. As Jack grew impatient, he glanced around at Alexandra. How he wished she had not come! Not only did he have to worry about Paige's safety, but now he was concerned for the safety of his wife, as well. He knew Dmitry and his men were all professionals. They would not go down without a fight, and he would need to utilize his only weapon, surprise, to its maximum efficacy.

"All right," Ari reported. "The military has succeeded in cordoning off the excavation site. They have strategically placed themselves between the crowd and the site. How long they will be able to hold that position is uncertain, but if you wish to tempt the devil, we can proceed with caution, but we must do so quickly."

Without hesitating Jack replied, "Let's go! Now! And be careful."

Jack and his friends continued on towards the dig. Brian and Ari took point and kept their eyes peeled for any sign of trouble ahead. Sean and Carly brought up the rear as they kept watch behind. Within the hour, they saw the ruins rising atop the hill before them. After traveling as far as their vehicles would take them, they continued the rest of the way on foot. The sun was beginning to scorch the earth and burn its path in front of these foreign invaders. It was barely ten o'clock in the morning and the temperatures had already soared into the high nineties. It seemed that man and God were throwing every conceivable obstacle in these crusaders' path. Undaunted, the group stoically continued onward, finally reaching the peak where the village ruins lay spread before them in all their ancient glory.

"It's amazing," gasped Carly as she struggled to catch her breath after the rugged climb.

Professor Stompmeyer could barely contain himself as he hobbled towards the first villa, moving as quickly as his maimed legs would take him. "Yes, my dear. You are correct. This is truly a magnificent find. Such a unique village. Nearly intact after practically two thousand years. This is almost as amazing as the discovery of Pompeii and Herculaneum."

After quickly looking around, Jack turned to Rachel and took her by her arm. "Where is the villa with the sign you mentioned? Quickly, please. Can you take me to it?"

Rachel nodded as she pointed towards the center of the row of houses. As she led Jack towards the home, the rest of the group cautiously followed, with Brian and Ari bringing up the rear this time.

"What happens if the mob breaks through the soldiers' barricade?" Brian asked Ari.

"Then we better hope we've retrieved what we came for and are long gone by then," Ari replied.

"I was afraid that's what you were going to say."

"Look, there it is, just like I told you," Rachel exclaimed as she pointed to the star and hand chiseled into the ground in front of them.

"Amazing!" exclaimed Sam. "It's just like our sign!"

The small group continued into the entranceway of the villa. As they looked around, they clearly saw the tiled signs and engravings throughout the home.

"Now what? How do we know that anything of value is still here?" asked Sean.

"We don't. But we must have faith," replied Sam.

"It does not look like anything in here has been ransacked, unlike many sites I have seen."

"That's good news, professor. Where do you suggest we look first?" Jack asked as he moved in closer to examine the etchings on the walls.

"Perhaps we may find a loose tile or brick in the floor or wall," Stompmeyer suggested.

The entire group began to search the villa thoroughly, looking for any kind of hiding spot or area where their treasure might be buried. But after nearly an hour of fruitless labor, they began to feel discouraged.

"We're not getting anywhere." Carly turned to Sean while she threw her arms out in disgust. "I think we're at a dead end. If there had been anything here centuries ago, don't you think someone would have already found it?"

"Not necessarily," Stompmeyer said. "After all, the Dead Sea scrolls were not found for nearly two thousand years, and then only by pure accident."

While the crew began to bicker amongst themselves, Jack continued to scour the villa for any type of clue. As he walked from one room to another, he kept getting the feeling that something just wasn't right. It wasn't until he made his fourth pass through the doorway that it suddenly hit him.

"Say, Brian, come over here a minute," Jack called out.

As Brian walked over he shouted back at Ari, "Keep a lookout outside! It's been fairly quiet out there for quite a while. I don't like it."

"Brian, doesn't something seem odd or out of place in here?"

"Yeah, us," he replied.

"No, seriously. Look at these walls. Don't they appear unusually wide to you?"

Brian began to examine the walls and started to tap against them.

"They appear solid enough, but then again, for their thickness, I would expect them to be. I think you're just being overly imaginative. They may be wide, but so what?"

Jack ignored his friend's skepticism and examined both sides of the central wall more closely. As he did, he noticed the engraving of the star and hand in the center of the wall. While the design was a larger reproduction of the one they had observed at sea, it somehow appeared different. Jack kept staring at the design until it finally hit him. The design consisted of one large Star of David with a Hamsa located in the center, just like the amulet found at sea. But in place of the eyes that usually made up the outer boundaries of the star, there were exact miniature versions of the amulet.

As Jack moved towards the wall engraving for a closer inspection, Carly suddenly yelled out, "I think the crowd has broken through the police barricade! I heard gunshots, and it looks like there is a lot of movement coming from the village area. I think we had better come back to examine this place another day."

"No, wait," Jack said as he ran his hands along the central engraving. "We don't have time to return. Dmitry will have landed by then and will start calling the shots again. Come here! Look at this indentation. Doesn't it appear deeper than the rest of the engraving?"

Ari made his way through the group and began to examine the spot.

"You may be right. I think this is a keyhole of some sort."

Ari then took his ring and began to insert it into the depression in the wall.

"Look!" he exclaimed. "It's a perfect fit!"

As he finished his sentence, he heard a click come from within the wall.

"Jack, I think it's time you came up with a miracle." Brian was now making his way towards them as he pointed at the crowd assembling on the hill at the end of the Cardo. "It looks like Carly was right. There's a crowd breaking through the barricade and heading this way. Somebody better think of something real fast, because we've got no place to go or hide."

"Shhhh," Jack whispered as he held his finger up to his lips.

Suddenly, there was a loud metallic sound emanating from the central wall as Ari began to swing the wall inward.

"What the hell?" Brian exclaimed. "That looks like stairs leading down into the ground. Anybody got a light?"

Stompmeyer stepped up and produced a pocket flashlight. "It's small, but it will have to do. Everybody listen closely. You must all stay close together and walk carefully. These stairs are old and could crumble at any time. There also may be booby traps set for intruders."

Stompmeyer entered through the opening in the wall as Jack and the others followed close behind. Sean was the last to enter. As he did, he quickly returned the wall to its original location just as he heard more gunshots and voices enter the villa from the street.

"Keep quiet, everybody," he whispered. "I think the crowd

found its way into the villa. Don't make a sound or we'll be discovered, and then they'll start tearing this place apart."

The group slowly made their way down the stairs, descending deeper until they discovered a small room at the bottom. Torches were affixed to the wall, but they appeared to have reached a dead end. Stompmeyer ran his fingers along the corners of the wall several times, then began to shake his head.

"What are you looking for?" Jack asked.

"There has to be some sort of release or keyhole. This room is too small to justify such an elaborate secret entrance above. There has to be something more beyond that wall. We just need to find a way in."

Ari squeezed past the rest of the group and appeared alongside the professor. He reached forward and began to brush away the dust and dirt from centuries of neglect. After ten minutes of cleaning, they could see faint writing on the wall. Much of it had faded and was difficult to make out. Some of the characters and lines appeared to be missing. Ari carefully ran his hand across the markings, then took a step back as he examined them again.

"I think it's a message in Hebrew," he finally said with a tremor in his voice. "It looks like it may be ancient Hebrew, but some of the markings are too worn to read."

Stompmeyer moved closer to shine his light directly on the message.

"I think you are correct. It does indeed appear to be ancient Hebrew, but I can't quite make out what it says."

Jack grabbed one of the torches from the wall and lit it using Sean's lighter.

"Here, does this help any?" he asked.

The professor and the watcher both edged closer to the writing in an attempt to decipher its message. Slowly, together, they began to translate the etchings on the wall. As they gradually sounded out the words, they each looked at the other as if in disbelief.

"It appears to be part of the prophesies of the Hebrew prophet, Ezekiel, does it not?" Stompmeyer asked the watcher.

"I think you are right. That's exactly what it is. Portions of Ezekiel Chapters 11 and 36. But why would those words be here, on this wall, far below the main village and out of sight? It doesn't make any sense, does it?"

"Are you two going to keep the translation a secret while you bicker over why it's been placed on the wall?" Carly chastised the two scholars.

"Sorry. I guess we got carried away," Ari replied. "Well, it's a little rough, but I think you'll be able to get the gist of the meaning. Professor Stompmeyer, please correct me if you think I've misinterpreted anything."

Ari began to translate the message:

Although I have removed them far off among the nations, and although I have scattered them among the countries, yet have I been to them as a little sanctuary in the countries where they are come;

I will even gather you from the peoples, and assemble you out of the countries where ye have been scattered, and I will give you the land of Israel.

Be it known unto you; be ashamed and confounded for your ways, O house of Israel.

In the day that I cleanse you from all your iniquities, I will cause the cities to be inhabited, and the waste places shall be built.

And the land that was desolate shall be tilled, whereas it was a desolation in the sight of all that passed by.

And they shall say: This land that was desolate is become like the Garden of Eden; and the waste and desolate and ruined cities are fortified and inhabited.

"That's it?" Carly asked. "What does it all mean?"

"It's relating the fall of Jerusalem and the displacement of the Jews from Jerusalem and Israel after the Roman conquest in 70 AD," Stompmeyer started to explain to the group.

"Wasn't that when the Second Temple was destroyed?" Jack asked.

"Exactly. It's also around the time that the authorities believe this village was built. That's what makes this place so unique and interesting. It was long believed that most of the Jews were dispersed throughout the Roman Empire as slaves after the conquest of Jerusalem. For a Jewish village, especially one of apparent wealth and stature such as this one, to be erected here is an oddity, indeed."

"Yes, and the prophesy relates the return of the Jews to Israel after God's exile has ended," Ari added.

"Perhaps the occupants were counting on the return of the Jews and the resurrection of a Jewish state and the Temple when they wrote those words on the wall?" Jack surmised. "After all, Ari, you told us that you and the rest of the watchers were entrusted with the responsibility of safeguarding the ancient relics and sacred items from the Temple, right?"

"Yes, we were. But I have never been told of a place such as this."

"There has to be a way to get behind that wall," Jack said. "I can't imagine this little area being built for any particular purpose. It's too small and narrow down here. Why would someone go to all that trouble to create this secret passageway leading to this small cubicle? It makes no sense, unless there was a way to get beyond that wall."

Jack continued to examine the wall while holding the torch in one hand. As he did, he noticed that the same symbol of the Hamsa inside the Star of David was etched around the handle of the torch. Although he couldn't locate any hinges or traps along the wall, he continued to examine the corners and edges until he finally noticed it.

"Of course, I should have seen it sooner. Look." Jack pointed toward the torch holder on the wall. "Look underneath the brace. There's the symbol again."

Jack took the torch with his left hand as he raised his right hand and stuck the ring into the opening below the torch brace.

"A perfect fit!" he exclaimed as he turned his wrist slightly to the right. Suddenly, the wall began to creak as it slowly opened.

"Well, I'll be damned!" shouted Sam. "Another secret hiding place. Jack, you're a genius."

The wall opened just wide enough for the group to enter the next chamber two abreast. As they eagerly entered the room, their eyes began to adjust to the darkness amplified by the two lit torches and Stompmeyer's small flashlight. The chamber had opened into a large anteroom with hallways splitting off in multiple directions. They split into three groups, each with one of the light sources leading the way. After several minutes of exploration, it soon became clear that the entire area beneath the village had been created to store the Jews' ancient treasures and sacred items not already pilfered by the conquering Romans. There were chests of gold and gold items such as candelabras stored in one chamber. Another chamber held priestly clothing and other attire.

As Stompmeyer entered a third chamber, he could not believe his eyes. He was in awe as he approached the huge, seven-armed Menorah completely encased in gold. "It's unbelievable!" he exclaimed. "Come quick! You all must see this. I can't believe my eyes! I think I've discovered the Menorah from the Temple."

Everybody entered the chamber to see what the professor

had gotten so excited over. As each one entered, they would stop and gaze up in amazement at the lost treasure. Ari was the last to enter. As he did, tears rolled down his face. He looked up at the ceiling and suddenly began to pray. He had spent his whole life studying and learning about the many Temple artifacts. His entire adult life had been dedicated to searching for the treasures stolen from his people centuries earlier. Yet some of the most important treasures had been here, hidden in his homeland, all along.

"I don't understand, professor. I thought the Menorah had been captured by the Romans and sent to Rome after the destruction of the Temple. Isn't that what's depicted on the frieze on the Arch of Titus?" Carly asked, obviously confused.

"You are quite correct, my dear. However, some have theorized that the Menorah stolen by the Romans was a clever replica. You see, some believe that the Jews were aware that they would not be able to survive a Roman siege, so preparations were made to salvage many of their sacred religious artifacts. After the destruction of the First Temple, the Babylonians had pilfered or destroyed many of the significant items used by the Jews during the First Temple period. Some were ultimately returned when the Jews returned from their exile, but many were lost forever. Those with foresight did not want a recurrence of that tragedy, so they made plans in the waning days of the Second Temple to replicate, in secret, as many of the items as they could, and then they replaced the originals with the copies, unbeknownst to the general populace. Apparently they were successful. They must have somehow hidden these items from the Romans until they could be moved here."

Ari had overheard the professor's explanation and moved closer. "You are correct, professor, in all respects but one. There was an old legend I had almost forgotten. It seemed so implausible. Supposedly there was a tunnel leading from the Temple out of Jerusalem to a secret hiding place, the same hiding place where the First Temple artifacts were buried. Remember the Copper Scroll found as part of the Dead Sea Scrolls?"

Stompmeyer stroked his chin and thought for a moment. "Indeed. Now that you mention it, I do believe you are correct. Isn't there a passage in the scroll claiming that the Temple's treasures, as well as a chest with the vestments of the High Priest, are hidden in a mountain?"

"Yes, exactly. 'In the Valley of Achor, under the hill that must be climbed, hidden, lies a silver chest, and with it, the vestments of the High Priest, all the gold and silver of the Great Temple and all its treasures.' Now I truly understand what it means. I think it also means that this entire complex, this village, was built to ensure the treasures would be safeguarded over time. These chambers must somehow lead back into the center of Old Jerusalem, directly to the site of the Second Temple."

"I hate to break up this archaeology seminar, guys, but we need to get back to Jerusalem," said Brian. "It's getting late and our Russian friend should be touching down shortly."

Brian turned to lead the others towards the exit when Sean suddenly stopped.

"Shouldn't some of us stay here to watch the treasure?"

"I think it should be safe for the time being. We're the only ones who know about this, and I think we can all be trusted. Can't we?" Sam looked at Sean with a smile.

"Besides, the only ones with a 'key' are Ari and myself," Jack said, continuing Sam's thought. "Once we leave the chamber, I'll make sure the wall is locked shut again. I'll do the same for the stairway entrance once we are all topside."

Reluctantly, Sean followed the rest of the group outside, turning once to get a final look at the treasure that was slipping through his fingers.

61

Dmitry's plane was making its final approach to land just as Paige felt the need to go to the bathroom. As she started to get up, one of the guards turned and asked her where she thought she was going.

"I-I've got to pee," she stammered. "Re-eally bad."

"All right. But make it quick. The plane's going to be landing."

Paige got out of her seat and made her way to the lavatory. As she was seated on the toilet, she recalled her grandfather's voice from the conversation earlier. He seemed so confident, so sure of himself. She really wished he were there now. She knew in her mind that if he were there, he would take her away from these horrible men. It was at that moment that a thought struck her. Perhaps he was on his way right now to rescue her. All she had to do was find a way to hide from these terrible men until he arrived.

Paige looked around in the lavatory. It was so small, but

maybe she could find a hiding place. She kept looking around, knowing that she did not have much time. The ceiling seemed so high to her, but she noticed the air conditioner vent and recalled something from a movie she had watched with her grandfather. She carefully climbed onto the sink and stretched as far as she dared. After several tries, she was able to pull the grate down, almost falling to the ground as she did. She knew she would not be able to climb up to the ceiling, but that was not her objective. Silently, she climbed off the sink and carefully eased her way into the storage cabinet below the sink. As she took a deep breath, she closed the latch on the storage cabinet's door and sat in silence and darkness, waiting for her grandfather to rescue her.

The jet was beginning its final approach to land just as Dmitry started looking around for Paige.

"Where's the girl?" he yelled to Yuri.

As he did, the rest of his men started looking around the plane.

"She went to the head," responded Leonid, the burly Ukrainian. "I'll go get her." The man arose from his seat and knocked on the lavatory door. Upon hearing no response, he yelled in, "Hey, little one! Are you all right in there? You need to hurry up, the plane is getting ready to land and you need to be back in your seat. Hey, can you hear me?"

Yuri watched with amusement as his man kept banging and yelling through the closed lavatory door.

"What's the matter, your little pet slip its leash?"

Leonid glared back at Yuri with a burning look in his eyes.

"Watch what you say to me. I don't take any insults from anyone. Do you understand me?"

"Calm down, Leonid. Come back to your seat. If she wants to experience a landing on the toilet, let her. We'll get her after we land."

The Ukrainian shook his head and returned to his seat.

Within minutes the plane dropped altitude and landed. As the jet slowly made its way to its designated hangar, two sets of eyes watched from a distance while describing in detail through small transmitters the jet's progress.

As the jet taxied down the runway, Yuri and Leonid unbuckled their seat belts and approached the lavatory door.

"Okay, we are on the ground now. It is time for you to open the door, little one," Leonid softly spoke through the closed door.

The two men tried to listen but heard no noise. Yuri motioned to the burly Ukrainian and stepped back as Leonid started to kick at the door. Realizing that the door opened out, rather than in, he stopped for a moment and look at Yuri.

"It's not going to open this way," the Ukrainian said as he pulled his PSS silent pistol from his side. The weapon was developed for the KGB and Spetsnaz, the Russian special forces. It contains six rounds of special SP-4 "silenced" ammunition and makes no more sound than an airgun. It is the assassin's weapon of choice and fires shots that can penetrate a steel helmet. Leonid fired three perfectly placed shots into the lock and the door was quickly opened. As he looked around the empty space, his face began to turn red.

"That little bitch! She's trying to escape through the air vents. Look!"

Yuri poked his head around the man's large frame and saw the grate hanging from the ceiling. Dmitry's men spread out to look for her.

"We don't have time for this nonsense now!" Dmitry barked as he watched the jet approach the private hangar, which had been especially prepared for their arrival. He observed the ground crew surround the jet, readying the aircraft for the passengers to deplane. "Yuri, you come with me," he ordered. "Leonid, you take four men and find the little brat. The rest of you, follow Yuri."

As the plane slowed to a stop, Dmitry led his men toward the exit. Leonid directed the remainder of the group to disperse throughout the jet and search for Paige. Outside the plane, men were converging in small groups of three as Dmitry's men began to exit the jet.

Yuri led his men down the ramp just as Brian came around the rear of the plane with two Mossad agents. Yuri recognized Brian from Paige's kidnapping and immediately drew his firearm. Brian fired two quick shots in succession. The first struck Yuri mid-chest and the second went straight through the assassin's heart.

The two men immediately behind Yuri jumped off opposite sides of the ramp and attempted to take cover underneath the jet. Each of the Mossad agents aimed their Uzi's at the two escaping Russians and fired several shots, striking their targets with deadly accuracy. Dmitry realized that his men were under attack and retreated into the safety of the plane with his two remaining comrades.

"Take cover!" he yelled as he fired several shots towards the two Mossad agents. His men quickly closed the door of the plane as the pilot attempted to restart the engine. While the battle had been raging on the ramp, Jack and Ari had silently cut the fuel lines leading to each of the jet's two engines located in the rear of the plane. With three of his best men already down, Dmitry attempted to quickly assess the situation before deploying his seven remaining confederates. He realized the plane was out of commission and would be of little use to them in an escape. As he looked out one of the seven right side windows, he recognized Stompmeyer huddling inside the hangar. It was at that moment that he realized he had been outsmarted by Jack and his friends.

Dmitry's face began to turn red as he spun around and faced Leonid. "Where's the girl? Haven't you found her yet?"

Leonid shamefully shrugged his shoulders and acknowledged that his men had failed to locate Paige.

"We've looked everywhere, but have not been able to find her. Short of physically tearing the aircraft apart, we cannot figure where she went."

Dmitry glared at his subordinate. "If the situation weren't so dire, I would shoot you myself for your incompetency! Deploy one of your men at each of the exits and wait for further instructions."

Jack was not happy at how events had unfolded. He knew there was a strong likelihood that Paige was aboard the jet. By converging on the jet as it landed before ensuring that all of its occupants had deplaned, Paige's safety had been jeopardized. He had wanted to wait until all the passengers had left the cabin area before approaching, but the Mossad had insisted on surrounding the plane and attempting to capture the men as they disembarked. Jack was about to attempt to enter the plane when he noticed his wife running out of the hangar.

"Alexandra, stop! It's too dangerous. Get back under cover," he yelled to her as he left the undercarriage of the plane and ran towards her. As the two met, she began to scream at him, "Where's Paige? Is she all right? How could you let them shoot while she was still on the plane?"

Jack attempted to calm his wife down. "You know I had no control over this. I tried to handle this differently, but the Mossad insisted."

"We never should have gotten them involved in the first place!" she screamed back at him.

"Then we would not have been able to enter the country and get this far. Think about what you're saying. I'm worried about her, too, but your going off half-cocked isn't helping matters any. Please, get back in the hangar where you are safe, and let me try to get to Paige."

"What are you going to do?" she asked.

"Don't worry. I've got a plan. Just get under cover and stay there until this is over. I promise you, I will do everything in my power to get our little girl back safe."

Jack looked into his wife's eyes, put each of her hands in his and squeezed them tightly. "I swear." He then gently turned Alexandra around and walked her towards the hangar. After ensuring that she was safely under cover, he returned to the plane's undercarriage. As he reached the wheel area, the cell phone began to ring.

"Mr. Talbot, you disappoint me."

"Why is that?" Jack replied.

"I would have thought that you valued the safety of your granddaughter more than this. Tell your friends to back away or you will never see her again."

"Don't be a fool, Dmitry. You're not going to harm her. She's your only protection. Without her as a living hostage you know you and your men are as good as dead. Besides, I have no control over the Israelis. Your best chance is to surrender now, while you and your men are still alive."

Jack knew he had to keep the Russian talking and occupied while he attempted to locate a way to enter the plane and rescue his granddaughter.

"Let me speak to my granddaughter now."

"Not yet," Dmitry replied. "First I will provide you with a list of my demands. Once they are met, then we shall see about you speaking to your granddaughter."

Jack thought he could detect a hint of uncertainty in his enemy's voice. Years of training in the courtroom gave Jack a sort of sixth sense in detecting when his adversary was bluffing. Jack had that same sort of feeling now. Had the man already harmed Paige? Had something happened to her? Perhaps she was not even aboard the plane? Thoughts raced through Jack's head at mach speed as he tried to analyze the situation and his options. He knew it made no sense. Paige was definitely boarding the plane when he had last spoken to Dmitry, prior to the Russian's departure from the United States. There would be no logical reason to leave Paige in the States. But it was becoming obvious to Jack that Dmitry did not have control of his granddaughter. The thought made him even more concerned, because he could not imagine what had happened to her.

"I'll tell you what, Dmitry. I'll turn the phone over to the Mossad agent in charge and you can negotiate with him."

Jack turned to Ari and handed him the phone. "Keep him busy for as long as you can. I'm going to try to get into the plane."

Ari nodded his assent and continued speaking to the Russian while Jack examined the area around the jet's landing gear. With the help of a few mechanics, he was soon able to remove the outer casing and slowly made his way into the underbelly of the plane. Ari had done a good job of keeping Dmitry distracted, and by doing so provided Jack with sufficient time to enter the plane undetected. Once Ari realized that Jack had accessed the undercarriage unseen, he proceeded to demand that Dmitry and his men surrender immediately or the assault would commence.

For the first time in his life, Dmitry had met a group who played hardball as mercilessly as he did. Without the girl, he knew it would be difficult to bluff his way out.

"Where the hell is the brat?" he yelled to Leonid in desperation.

"I have no idea, sir. What are we going to do?"

Dmitry knew that his only means of escape would be to sacrifice his men, using them as decoys while he tried to slip away unseen.

"We're going to have to blast our way out of here," he said to his remaining men. "You men, grab the rocket launchers and automatic weapons now. I want one man by the main exit and the other by the emergency exit. Upon my signal, both

of you fire simultaneously into the hangar. Keep firing the
rockets until the rest of us slip out of the emergency exit on
the other side. Then you follow us out. Understand?"

Dmitry assigned Leonid to one of the rocket launchers. It
was Dmitry's expectation that his attackers would be distracted
by the assault on the civilians he knew were in the hangar,
thereby buying his group some time to effectuate their escape.

Upon Dmitry's signal, his men simultaneously opened the
exit doors and began firing into the hangar. As the rockets
exploded, the Mossad agents were taken by surprise. Some of
the shells struck flammable liquids and started a chain reaction
of explosions. The civilians in the hangar were also caught off
guard and tried to escape the raining hail of shells. One of
the shells exploded twenty feet from Hermann Stompmeyer,
scattering debris onto the German's body, knocking him
unconscious. Carly screamed as the shells began to explode.
Sean quickly reacted, throwing her to the ground, protecting
her body with his.

One of the shells punctured a hole through the side of the
hangar near Alexandra. As the smoke cleared, she saw some
of Dmitry's men slipping from the plane. "They're trying to
escape on the other end!" she shouted as loudly as she could.
Brian and Ari turned and watched as three of Dmitry's men
jumped to the ground and ran towards one of the waiting
jeeps. As the three reached the jeep with the expectation of
impending freedom, three short blasts from snipers perched
atop one of the adjacent hangars quickly brought them to the
ground.

Two more of Dmitry's men slipped quietly from the plane
and attempted to maneuver to safety. Ari and Brian quickly
gave chase and captured the two before they could make their
getaway. After restraining the two, they turned them over to
the police, who were just starting to arrive. Realizing that Jack
was somewhere in the plane with Dmitry and whatever was left

of his gang of assassins, they ran towards the stranded jet in hopes of aiding their friend.

While the fireworks were exploding outside, Jack was slowly making his way through the maze of equipment and control lines located in the underbelly of the plane. Eventually he surfaced inside the cabin area, spotting Leonid firing a rocket launcher towards the hangar where he had left Alexandra. Instinctively, he lunged at the behemoth from behind, knocking him off balance and to the ground. The man deftly rolled to his side and returned to his feet to face Jack. As he moved closer, Jack's SEAL training and experience returned to aid him in his defense. Thrusting his legs forward, he aimed both feet into Leonid's knee, cracking the kneecap and causing the huge man to collapse in pain. Without giving his foe a chance to recover, Jack sent his foot into the man's throat, silencing him for good.

Jack turned just as Leonid's comrade lunged from his perch towards Jack. As the man shoved his right arm towards Jack's chest, Jack realized the man had a knife aimed at him. Jack leaned backwards as far as he could, allowing the man's own energy and momentum to carry him past Jack and into the interior wall of the jet. Before the man could recover, Jack followed with a merciless volley of punches to his enemy's solar plexus. Satisfied that the man was no longer a threat, Jack finished with a punch to the head, forcing him into unconsciousness.

As Jack landed his final blow, he slipped and fell on top of his foe. At exactly that moment, a bullet whizzed past his ear, missing him by centimeters. Jack dove for cover behind one of the luxury seats just as several more bullets struck the empty space his body had left. Jack pulled out the 9mm Glock he had been provided and began firing back at his assailant.

"You have certainly been a surprise, Mr. Talbot!" Dmitry yelled to Jack.

"That was the general idea. Where's my granddaughter, you bastard?"

"That's a good question. Unfortunately, you will not live to learn the answer."

Dmitry again rapidly sent a rain of bullets towards Jack's hiding place. Jack knew the seat would not be able to withstand the high-caliber bullets much longer. As he searched for a way out, he noticed that the overhead area above Dmitry had come loose from the battle being waged between the two sides. Taking a gamble, Jack aimed and fired into the overhead area. A large chunk separated from the roof and came crashing down into Dmitry's side, causing him to lose his balance and drop his weapon.

Jack decided to take advantage of Dmitry's momentary state of confusion. He jumped up and raced down the aisle, mustering all the energy and speed he could to tackle the madman before he had a chance to regain his bearings. Jack reached Dmitry just as he started to get up. Dmitry looked up as Jack threw his body into the Russian, slamming him back to the ground. They immediately began to wrestle as Dmitry tried to wrap his arm around Jack's neck. Jack twisted and escaped from Dmitry's grasp, sticking his elbow into the man's jaw. Dmitry's head snapped back and struck the edge of the galley wall. Semi-conscious, Dmitry collapsed to the floor, unable to move.

Jack took a deep breath and stood over the groggy Russian. As he glared at his adversary, he heard a whimpering sound coming from the lavatory. Cautiously, he made his way towards the source of the sounds. Jack peered through the doorway and noticed the closet storage door slightly ajar. As he got closer, he recognized Paige's small fingers wrapped around the edge of the door. Softly, Jack called out, "Paige. It's me, Papa. It's all right baby, come here. Come to Papa, honey."

Jack held out his arms as his frightened five-year-old granddaughter slipped out of her hiding place.

"Poppy!" she exclaimed. "It really is you. I thought you would never get here."

As Jack wrapped Paige in his arms, they both began to cry. Elated that his granddaughter was safe, Jack thanked God, then looked into his granddaughter's azure eyes.

"Don't worry, I'm here now. Everything's gonna be all right. Let's get you out of here and to your grandmother."

Jack held Paige tightly in his arms and started to rise. As he did, he noticed a blurred movement out of the corner of his left eye. He turned just as Dmitry's fist lashed out against his cheekbone. Reeling from the surprise attack, Jack attempted to protect his granddaughter from any injury. He rolled to his side, cradling Paige in his arms as he kept her safe from harm. Gently, he set her in the corner before he sprang to his feet to face Dmitry.

"You have interfered with my plans for the last time. It is time to say good-bye to your granddaughter."

As Dmitry attempted to make good on his final threat, a switchblade appeared in the Russian's right hand. He slashed at Jack's chest just as Jack jumped back, narrowly avoiding the blade's deadly path. Dmitry attempted to catch Jack unaware as he backhanded the blade towards Jack's face. Jack raised his right arm, blocking the attack as he swept his leg around, hooking Dmitry's right leg and pulling it out from under him, causing him to lose his balance and fall to the floor. Dmitry released his hold of the blade as he struck the ground. Jack quickly kicked the knife out of the Russian's hand as Dmitry rolled to his left, deftly returning to his feet to face Jack once again.

The two men squared off against each other, wildly swinging their fists and kicking at one another while each man attempted to get the upper hand. Finally, Dmitry landed a blow to Jack's abdomen, causing him to double over in pain and collapse to the floor. Seeing his opportunity, Dmitry retrieved his knife and approached Jack, who was now laying helplessly on the floor. With his arm raised, Dmitry scowled at Jack and taunted him one last time.

"It's time to say your prayers."

As Dmitry knelt down to finish off his enemy, two shots rang out, causing Dmitry to keel over, blood gushing down his back. Jack struggled to push the man off him and saw his wife standing a few feet away, a gun in one hand and Paige tightly held with the other.

"He won't bother anyone anymore," she said as she let the gun drop to the floor. "Are you all right?"

"I am now," Jack smiled back, "thanks to you."

62

The sun shone brightly in the late morning sky as Jack walked through the streets of the old city. Alexandra walked alongside him, leaning her head against his shoulder, with Paige skipping happily in front of them. The shops and alleys were just beginning to get crowded as the smell of hummus, tahini, falafels and other Mediterranean fare permeated the air. From a distance, they could hear the Muslim call to prayer as they passed a group of Israeli soldiers and some Chassidic Jews heading towards the Western Wall, the last visibly remaining evidence of Herod's great Temple. As Jack passed the Church of the Holy Sepulchre, a Coptic monk pushed past two Roman Catholic priests as they were exiting the cathedral.

Jack turned to Alexandra and shook his head. "Why can't they all just get along together? There's so much history and religion here, yet it seems nobody wants to turn the other cheek or live by the golden rule."

"They're just human beings, honey," Alexandra said as she hooked her arm in Jack's.

"When are we going to get to go to the old village, Papa?" Paige looked up at her two grandparents as she tugged on Jack's arm.

"We're on our way to meet the others now. Then Rachel will take us there. Why are you so anxious?"

"I want to see the secret tunnel. Brian said there was all kinds of jewels and shiny stuff hidden there. Is that true?"

"You'll just have to wait and see. Look, there's the others now. Hurry up, let's get going."

They joined the rest of their group and piled into the van Rachel had commandeered from the newspaper.

"And how's my pretty little 'Rainbow Brite' this fine morning?" she asked as Paige stepped up into the van.

"Is it as pretty as they said it was?" Paige asked Rachel.

"Is what as pretty as who said it was?" Rachel replied laughingly.

"Oh, never mind. I'll just have to find out for myself." Paige scowled as she stomped down the aisle and dropped into her seat.

Jack and Alexandra shook their heads as Rachel laughed, closing the door behind them.

In the rear of the bus sat Carly and Sean, oblivious to Paige's pouting. Carly was staring intently into Sean's eyes, relaxing in his strong arms and relishing the peace she had recently found. She was now at peace with herself and the world, envisioning a future with someone who truly cared for her. Sean nibbled on her ear as he wondered what lay in store for the two of them.

Before long, the group had arrived at the top of the hill and entered the archaeological site abuzz with workers, scientists and clergy from around the world. Armed Israeli soldiers guarded the perimeter of the old village as the workers carefully sifted through the earth and debris, searching for artifacts and other items of interest. As the group left the confines of their vehicle, Ari exited the "Watcher House," as it had come to be called.

"I've been expecting you for some time now!" he called out. "I thought you would have been here earlier this morning."

"We would have been," Sam replied, "but a certain trio took their time getting to the meeting point and decided to sightsee through the old city." Sam motioned towards Jack's family as he smiled.

Paige ran towards the entrance of the main villa, and everybody followed her. Ari welcomed them all in and led them to the secret chamber, which had been kept sealed and guarded since they had left to intercept Dmitry earlier in the week.

"Would the young lady like to do the honors?" Ari asked as he handed the ring to Paige.

Paige looked up at Jack with longing eyes, and he just nodded and lifted her up to the keyhole.

"Put the ring on your finger and insert it into the star." Jack took hold of her hand and gently guided it into the small indentation. The wall began to move and the door opened as Paige gasped in disbelief.

"It's like magic!" she exclaimed.

"Now it's going to be a little dark down there. Do you still want to go?"

Paige nodded her head as she began to pull herself through the opening in anticipation.

"Slow down, little one. I'm coming," her grandfather replied.

Carefully, they all descended the stairs leading to the antechamber. Saul and Nasim followed behind them with their own archaeological crew. Jack and Alexandra allowed Paige to accompany Ari in further exploration of the many chambers located in the secret tunnels below. Jack looked on as the Israeli Antiquities Authority directed the work of Arabs and Israelis; Jews, Christians and Muslims; all working side by side in harmony, all with a common goal: to find the truth and preserve the ancient past.

In the corner Jack spied the professor, carefully brushing debris away from some artifact, with a bandage wrapped around the wound to his head and his leg encased in a cast. Maybe there really was magic in this land after all and redemption was truly just around the corner.

"Perhaps this is the true meaning of the Hamsa," Jack wondered aloud. "Not keeping the evil eye away, but rather being the all-seeing eye, uniting the nation with the Hand of God. Maybe it's not too late to find peace and harmony in the comfort of our neighbors."

Alexandra smiled and embraced Jack as she looked into his eyes and parted her lips.

"I love you," she whispered to him as they kissed.

ACKNOWLEDGEMENTS

IT TOOK SEVERAL years for me to complete the research and find the words to put into this, my first novel. Without the unwavering support of my wife, Terry, who initially lit the spark to start this journey and gave me her support and insight along the way, this book would have never been. She gave me her love, her patience, and stood beside me through the many hours it took to write this, including while we were away on our many vacations. During the times I questioned myself or lost my way, she was always there to prod me along and find the right path.

I also need to acknowledge my children who gave me their editorial help and ideas before I submitted my manuscript to the folks at Vantage Press. Finally, I need to thank all the staff at Vantage Press, including my fabulous editor, Molly Black, who turned my dream, *Stones of Fire,* into reality.

CPSIA information can be obtained
at www.ICGtesting.com
Printed in the USA
LVHW041023120520
655430LV00002B/62